UNNATURAL DISASTER

UNNATURAL DISASTER

THE FAITHWALKER SERIES BOOK FIVE

THE LEGACY OF THE TREE OF LIFE
AS PASSED DOWN THROUGH THE GENERATIONS
TO THE UNKNOWN

DARRYL MARKOWITZ

FaithWalker Publishing

The Faithwalker Series
Book V: Unnatural Disaster

Copyright © 2021 by Darryl Markowitz

Published by:

Faithwalker Publishing
An imprint of Darryl Markowitz

Cover and Interior Design: Creative Publishing Book Design
Cover Art: Bogdan Maksimovic

ISBN Paperback: 978-0-9818469-4-1
ISBN eBook: 978-0-9818469-5-8

Printed in the United States of America

Author's Note

This is one of the most painfully pro-life books you will ever read! The pain an expectant mother and father, a whole country will suffer to protect the life of the unborn. Though the characters are fictitious, the pain is real! So is the love from whence the pain cometh.

Acknowledgment

My deepest appreciation to my editor, my artist, my book designer.

My deepest thanks to those of Lincoln County Hospital, Kansas for putting up with me as I wrote this book in between patients and Barb and Jayne and Michelle put up with me asking if they wanted to hear a scene. Sorry Jayne for scaring you.

My special thanks to all the unknown *faithwalkers*. Their hearts and minds aren't afraid to ask the toughest questions because they know they'll get answers. They know how to walk by and with *meaning*.

My very deepest appreciation to Lana, my wife, for being an integral part of my life.

CHAPTER 1

Freedom in the Eye
the Beholder

Marta tossed her three braids of gleaming medium brown hair behind her as she stood under the Tree of Life wearing a simple brown peasant dress. She even had a blue ribbon with gold trim tied to her middle braid just like Lady Stephanie. She had become one of her most devout fans because over the break, that's all she wanted to do, was watch *her.*

Eve, with very long reddish-brown hair befitting our first mother, smiled at Marta. "You look lovely. Are you ready to teach your fist official lesson?"

Marta cleared her throat and looked out at her class sitting on the soft Heavenly grass. "I am. Besides watching Lady Stephanie, Oh God, I don't know how she can bear it all, I have also researched and thought very deeply about where we left off last season. I have come to the conclusion that you, dear Mother Eve, did *not* do as most of us believe! But first, my dear students, what *do* you believe about why our Mother disobeyed God?"

A new addition, Sarah, of Earth age nine, beautiful green eyes, dark blond hair, raised her hand and got an Eve-like Marta nod. "She ate the forbidden fruit because she wanted to be wise as wise as God. That's what it says." Everyone else agreed.

Marta smiled. "Those are the printed words in the Holy Bible, but what do they mean? Just like *that,* you think our dear Mother, here, would just decide to disobey God?"

Everyone looked over to Eve and began shaking their heads.

Marta smiled. "As we watch Lady Stephanie down *there,* we see her always striving for the clear, true *meaning* of things. And her difficulties, as with many of us girls, is that she always seems to have many different emotions all at once. What do you say about trying to identify how our first Mother really *felt* before her seeming *betrayal?*"

All the children's eyes widened. How could they know? They could just ask her, but Marta doesn't seem to want that. *She wants us to think for ourselves.*

Marta's face lit up with a glow. "That is *exactly* what I want. I don't want you to merely *have* thoughts and feelings. I want you to *own* them. And to *own* them, you need to appreciate their full meaning first. Let's leave this lesson right here so you have time to think and feel."

Marta then brought her middle braid forward, grabbed hold of the ribbon, smiled, and disappeared. All her student's mouths dropped open with the common thought, *Just like Lady Stephanie!*

Freedom. It suddenly took on a whole new meaning after Colonel Asa turned his brother's funeral, by Captain

Joshua's last wishes, into a surprise outdoor wedding ceremony right up there on the outdoor stage! Colonel Asa, *himself,* proudly performed the service for sixteen-year-old Lady Stephanie and seventeen-year-old *King* Vaughn, who still hated that title.

For Stephanie, she was prime marrying age, but for Vaughn, he was considered young but only because most young men hadn't achieved enough success to be responsible for a wife. Vaughn had been quite able even back up North when he was only sixteen. But his young age was another reason Vaughn had labored to keep that *King* title a secret, along with much, much more that needed to be hidden. That royal office had been given to him by his thankful long-forgotten people that he rescued from destruction from the rule of the brutal North. A people that made the whole world uneasy.

However, for the good of all, Asa had exposed them both to the whole country with *national* news coverage. Asa, being in charge of military intelligence was privy to much of Vaughn and Stephanie's mysterious lives from both up North and now in the South and there was no way he would let the United for Christ lose such important assets. The weight of secrecy would have been too great a burden for them to bear, and it made them far too vulnerable.

After hours of celebration between the rows and rows of tables that had been suddenly carried over, as the good Colonel had also thrown a perfectly coordinated surprise super-feast, and after swarms of media interviews with *both* Lady Stephanie and their new *Captain* Vaughn, Stephanie had looked at her God-given husband, and said, "Let's go home." And *that's* when Vaughn understood that *freedom* took on a whole new meaning.

Vaughn took his Queen's hand and started to head to his military barracks, but Stephanie headed to her lavish apartment in the judge's compound. They ended up tugging each other back together in a sort of elastic rebound because neither would let the other go. There was a moment when they looked into each other's loving eyes and then Vaughn headed to Stephanie's apartment. Later, he managed to sneak away back to the barracks, and he started to pack up all his worldly treasures- three changes of uniform, some toiletries, and underclothes. His *comrades* came out from between the beds and began slapping him on the back, laughing, and saying things like, "Well, now you *know!*" "Say goodbye to your *freedom!*" "Who's the boss *now*, huh?" "Don't forget about us *Captain* Vaughn." But he took it all with good humor, though it did cause him to reflect.

He looked them all in the eye. "Ever since I met Stephanie, I wanted to marry her. And through all the suffering we've gone through not being able to be together, we never felt free. Now we are!"

They all now knew *some* of that suffering, as their Colonel had born the whole truth to the nation, but that being past, they laughed so hard some of them collapsed onto their bunks. "He doesn't know." "Wait on it, *you'll* see!" "Once you say, *I do,* you *don't!*" And they howled in laughter some more, many of them being married for some time. When

Vaughn said Stephanie is different, they mocked him even more. "Different? We *know* there's *no one* like our dear Lady Stephanie, but she's *still* a *woman!* You'll see."

Now, months later, still residing in the Judge's quarters kindly supplied by the United for Christ's government, one could say they had a life together, finally. Well, all the furniture was standard issue, but it was very comfortable just like all the cream-colored walls comfortable. Though Vaughn and Stephanie did really like all the dark stained wide oak trim between the walls and ceilings with matching base boards. They both loved wood, and if it was ever possible to have their *own* home, that's one feature they would surely insist on. But the best part of the furnishings was the luxurious deep-matressed bed surrounded by mahogany bedposts rising to support a frilly, white lacey canopy special for Lady Stephanie.

Sinking into Stephanie's plush, red living room couch while sitting across from each other, Stephanie, dressed in her humble brown peasant dress, emphatically stated, "I can't believe this! This is . . . ridiculous!" Stephanie tossed her single red braid behind her, as her rich brown eyes made sure she held Vaughn's attention. "Do you see all these requests from . . ." She struggled to describe it as she shoved the pile of disorganized letters into Vaughn's face, which caused him to reflexively jerk his head back. He decided it would be best to just let her finish her feelings, which had been rather intense, lately. Even before they got confirmation that Stephanie was indeed pregnant, now a good three months pregnant, she'd already exhibited . . . natural behavioral changes.

One by one, Stephanie described the main point of each letter as she slapped each down upon the cushion. "*This* is from the Prophets for Christ." She glared at him, making sure he understood her anger. "*This* from the *Resurrected* for Christ!" Again, that same glare, but Vaughn knew she wasn't angry at him, though any onlooker would certainly think so. He unbuttoned his black military uniform trying to get a bit more comfortable as his wife continued. "*This* is from the *Undivided* for Christ. Vaughn this is *absurd.* There are at least ten more just like this, all different groups, all wanting me to endorse them as the *true* way, and all claiming their particular judge is . . . I don't know . . . something special. I had no idea Christianity was so fractionated. When we came here, I thought, 'OK, it's a Christian country,' but I had no idea that word *Christian* didn't mean *one* Christian, and I thought that after we became national with our meaning, our purpose, our life stories, that . . ." Finally, she became lost for words. The discovery that the *type* of Christianity in their little town where they've settled for the last year isn't the *same* Christianity across the whole country became shocking, to say the least.

Vaughn sighed slowly, carefully, so his wife wouldn't think he sighed at her. He ran his fingers through his thick, dark brown, almost black, wavy hair. "I love you so much." He found himself saying that more frequently lately, but he always meant it, always had that same intense feeling in his words. And every time he said it, Stephanie paused in self-reflection and then readjusted her emotions, becoming calmer. Yet, with far deeper and serious implications in what she now addressed, her self-diagnosis brought a tear into her eyes. "Darn it! I *hate* getting so overly emotional and all watery over everything. I thought I'd grown out of all that."

Staring helplessly into Vaughn's dark brown piercing eyes, she pleaded. "What are we going to do? This country is so divided, and time is shorter than ever. We *need* unity if we're even to have *any* chance at all, and Jargono's spies are sure to exploit every division we have, just like they did before and had everyone *hating* me."

With more tears, Stephanie reflected upon their history, that she and Jargono were the very last Appendaho, and that her dearly departed best friend, Arlupo, had told her that Stephanie and Jargono were both *faithwalkers,* but that Jargono far surpassed her abilities. It was hard to grasp how Jargono could have that much power and be so evil, and yet, he wasn't evil in any sense of the cliché. He was far more complex than that, which meant Jargono was exceedingly dangerous, not to mention that he always left a glimmer of possibility open. Enough to allow Stephanie to entertain hope that he might understand eventually, in spite of him killing all the rest of her people.

Vaugh ran his fingers through his hair, again, nodding in disgust, and he continued their mutual thoughts. "Not that he needs to exploit anything. I really think he has the power to take us over any time he wants, but I think he enjoys all this—he enjoys proving how inferior everyone is to him. I think he enjoys watching *us* squirm the most!"

True. They never doubted for a moment that both Jargono and his *queen* kept tabs on them. It was just a fact of reality. Stephanie knew it was never far from Vaughn's mind, but she felt compelled to ask—actually she'd felt compelled to a lot of things lately. "How are we going to handle those damned demon offspring? We're no closer to any solution." And then the unthinkable. "Do you think Jargono knows? I mean, if he watches us and all, maybe he heard us and plans to gain control of them."

He took her hands and squeezed them. "I don't think so. If he knew about those vile spawn, I'm sure he'd destroy them, but he hasn't. I just took a little trip and checked-up on things. No change. You know my love, since we both can travel, well, anywhere, why don't we take a little ethereal vacation? Go to some remote island." This 'travel' he referred to was ethereal travel, the ability to enter the Ethereal Corridor and pop out anywhere on Earth, or *down below,* or even Paradise.

Her eyes melted and she squeezed his hands, too. "Oh God, a sunny beach. I love the sun." But her responsibility had no such word like vacation in its vocabulary. "Vaughn, that's so sweet, but . . . you're sure if Jargono knows about them, he won't plan to use them somehow?"

Suggesting a vacation failed to distract Stephanie, so Vaughn just shrugged, saying, "Nah, he hates the demons as much as we do. Look, even though Jargono turned him into it, he was glad when you killed your demon-father."

Ooops . . . wrong choice of words—demon-father. Her voice rose several octaves. "*Vaughn!* I can't *believe* you just said that!" But this time she caught herself, "Oh my, there I go again. I never knew being pregnant could . . ."

Vaughn just continued as if she wasn't upset. "I'm actually even considering popping in on the good King Jargono and telling him about them!"

Jargono had usurped the former corrupt Northern dictatorship and it was actually questionable whether that was an improvement. Either way, the result would have been the same. Vaughn and Stephanie had to flee what used to be the northern half of the former United States for the southern half that was created after the second civil war now almost one-hundred years prior. That civil war resulted from the Great Religious War fifteen years prior to that where terrorists had spread a horrible plague that wiped out all of the major cities of the *heathen*, and in response, those *heathens* turned all the Muslim countries into a nuclear wasteland. Even a hundred years later, the *heathen* world still struggled to recover, but at least they could.

As Stephanie responded, she didn't seem all that surprised that Vaughn would tell Jargono about the Earth demons, and it became clear to Vaughn that she'd entertained that very same possibility. "The only thing is, Jargono always does what we don't anticipate. Telling him about the demon offspring might . . . I don't know. And once we do, the Ethereal is sure to react . . . some way . . . I don't know."

Vaughn slowly sighed again, lifted her hand to his lips, and kissed it. "Well...I don't want to wait until we're up against the deadline. Fifteen months is all we have at the most before we're looking at a lot of baby demons, and I don't think they'll be cute, but I *really* think that within a year from now . . . we *have* to act . . . whatever that'll be. We may have no choice but to go to Jargono. He's the lesser of the evils we face."

Stephanie's eyes went distant. "Oh God!" She peered into Vaughn's eyes waiting for him to respond, but when he didn't, she realized she was expecting him to simply read her mind, which was her ability, not his. "Vaughn, what if . . . what if he already knows, and *knows* that we'll have to act! All he has to do is wait on us to show up! Then *trap* us! Not to mention *Karen*. She'll *definitely* be expecting us." Stephanie was unconsciously rubbing her tummy.

The nature of natural disasters, as terrible as they can be, is that recovery always follows close behind. Lava cools and plants and animals return. Washed away beaches and towns are quickly rebuilt. Lost lives are grieved over but then life returns. Everything has a nature, and amongst the natural world they ebb and flow together in what some might call a balancing act.

But Earth human-demon hybrids, well, that's in a whole other class of its own, though biblically, they actually can be found if you look close enough! And unlike Jargono, those demons *will* destroy humankind without any reservation at all. They were a main reason God brought the Great Flood and only the occupants of the ark survived. The demons are an unnatural disaster, the kind which destroys any balance or hope of natural recovery.

But the Ethereal isn't natural to the Earth, either, and *faithwalkers* have one foot in both worlds. And then there's

Vaughn, not a faithwalker, but of a long forgotten ancient biblical people that the atheistic North knows *nothing* about, and the South, where they now reside, only knows of from Holy Bible stories. And yet, many things the Lord has given Vaughn to do, wouldn't exactly fall under the normality of the mere physical world, either.

Vaughn reflected upon Colonel Asa who three months ago exposed all of Stephanie and Vaughn's intimate secrets to the whole country, what Judge Matthew had done to her and how she sacrificed herself, how Vaughn killed him, and much, much more. At first, they were both terribly embarrassed and fretful, but Colonel Asa finished by explaining that he wanted the whole country to know their impeccable character and how much the country needed them, and he chided the country for how badly they had treated their now undoubtedly rare heroes. But more than that, he explained to all that he wanted the full, blatant truth out so that Jargono and their other enemies couldn't use the truth to hinder the defense of the United for Christ. So much had happened in just the last year.

Vaughn stared into his beloved wife's eyes. "Unfortunately, you're absolutely correct about all the dangers. Fortunately, Colonel Asa made it far more difficult for Jargono to leverage us. But one thing, Stephanie, you have a *lot* of help now that we *never* had before. I think of everything you're doing now, baptizing more and more souls who *all* have actually been receiving the Holy Ghost, gaining a *new* heart, *this* is going to make the difference we need in the war. In fact, *that* may be the reason Jargono hasn't attacked us yet."

Stephanie grabbed his hands, "You think so? Why would he even care? He thinks that's all just delusion."

Vaughn shook his head. "*He* might think it's phony, but his spies are going to tell him about all the miracles they're doing, and how, in spite of all his attempts to divide us, our holy people keep bringing the country back together. And you keep adding to our numbers every week! *And,* regardless of whether he thinks it's all delusion, miracles still mean power to him, and that power he doesn't understand well. *That* will give him pause."

Stephanie broke down balling again and Vaughn took a slow, deep breath then let it out gently. She asked, "You really think I'm making a difference? I don't know. Ten here, ten there. I don't know. And how long before all these," she picked up the letters again and pushed them in Vaughn's face, "*factions,* decide *we're* a greater threat than some enemy up north? They're pressing me Vaughn, they want an answer, but I *can't* endorse *any* of them. Maybe I should . . ." Stephanie's eyes went wide. Her eyebrows went up as she stared past her husband. Then she flinched. Then she grabbed his hand and pressed it against her tummy.

After a bit, Vaughn's eyebrows raised, too. "It's got to be a boy! Powerful little kick for that age. Although, I do recall, like ten minutes after we made love, you told me you were pregnant!" He had that glint in his eye.

She pushed his hand away, and as he leaned over to kiss her, she pushed him away, too. "Well, I was *right,* wasn't *I?*"

Vaughn wisely answered, "You are *always* right," and he smiled at himself for his perfect answer. It turned out that the Book of Wisdom that King Mafferan and Queen Yenagoa had left for him thousands of years ago in the Sacred Cave was *excellent* at marriage counseling, though Vaughn never told Stephanie he was consulting it for such things.

She eyed him, thought for a second, then apologized for yet *another* emotional swing, and Vaughn consoled her. "It's OK Stephanie." He leaned over and kissed her tummy, then looked into her rich brown eyes. "You need to pray to understand the changes you're going through."

"You don't think I have? *Vaughn,* how could you say . . ."

He leaned over and kissed her on the lips. "I have to take care of some business. I love you so much." And he vanished.

CHAPTER 2

Treachery and
the Truce Violation

Marta was there early under the Tree of Life and she was glowing a beautiful, comforting shade of gold. Every student who arrived experienced it before anything else. Once everyone was there, she asked, "What was your first experience, *ever?* In your mind or heart?

All the students knowingly blurted out, "Our feelings. As mortal babies we loved before anything else."

Marta smiled, "Being up here has certain advantages of clear memory and understanding, to a *degree!* Has everyone thought of your answer to yesterday's question? What do you say about trying to identify how our first Mother really felt before her seeming *betrayal?"*

Robert, fourteen Earth years old with brown hair and bright blue eyes, got the nod first. "Well, I'm not a girl," and the girls started giggling and the boys rolled their eyes, "but I would have to say maybe she felt overwhelmed? I mean, all of the sudden, there you are, there's this man saying this is now bone of my bones, she shall be called WOMAN." And he tried to echo his voice which didn't quite work, and everyone laughed again, but Robert laughed at himself, too.

However, Marta jumped in with another question, "First, how do you think that made Eve feel being named like that? And could there have been a better way for Adam to act that would have produced a *different* feeling! And *what* would that feeling *be?*"

Robert couldn't help himself and interjected, "I so love your questions."

Marta tried not to blush and continued. "Do you see how sensitive Vaughn is to Stephanie? He seems to have learned something about the nature of a woman that Adam, frankly, didn't possess at that time. But how could he know?" Then Marta paused, smiled, then said, "Well, that's it! That's our lessons for today because there is so much meaning in it already! Till next time." And she grabbed her braid and her ribbon and vanished.

Having been such a short class, many of the children stayed to discuss the questions for next lesson. Sherry, a girl of ten Earth years, dark brown eyes and black hair, quickly shared, "I don't think I would have liked to just be named like that! I mean, it's true what Adam said, but . . ."

But Stephan, Earth years 11, black hair, blurted out, "Yea, but Adam was *in charge!*"

And Carrie, Earth age 5, with bouncy, red, curly hair and soft brown eyes, countered, "Well, you're *stupid!*"

And Marta faded back in! The students were shocked. Had she been *listening* to them? "Now children, you *know* we have no secrets up here. We can even walk into anyone's abode without knocking. There is nothing to be ashamed of here. *But* you all just demonstrated great understanding! Carrie there, was right!" she looked over to Stephan and stuck out her tongue, "but so was Stephan," he smirked back, "But so was Sherry!"

But Carrie called out, "How can we all be right?"

Marta smiled, "*That* is the *perfect* question! You see, all Lucifer had to work with to bring Adam and Eve down, was only what was right in them! Now children, I want *you* to figure out how he brought our dear beloved first Mother and Father down, using *only* what was right! This is also the nature of attack the demons are launching against our poor Lady Stephanie. They also are trying to trap her with what's right!" And this time she vanished and didn't return.

Highest Councilor ScrabaGag peered through his dirty blue orb with his faithful underling Grinchback floating beside him. The orb, having been created from the Beginning, floated in the center of a large Ethereal room and it was the *only* accoutrement within the four dark gray ethereal walls, but the very ether, itself, was a transparent grayness. Grinchback, with his tail scratching his large bulbus head, met his Master's Great Eye with his own. "Master, I don't think Vaughn considered the full extent of the danger to himself that his cleverness in saving us, saving everyone, has produced."

Highest Councilor squinted at him and placed his very long tail into his massively muscular arm which protruded from the center of his serpentine body. His tail tip tapped at the end of his arm showing irritation. "Are you *worried* for your new *friend,* Grinchback?" His Master had turned several shades darker.

Grinchback met him Great Eye to Great Eye. "Master, you misunderstand. I told you, if I could, I would consume him in an ethereal second. More than even his wife, I would choose *him* to consume, but we know we can't lose him. If Vaughn dies, in less than a year we would lose all orb functions. I dare say that would destroy us. We would turn on each other, and eventually, only . . ." he whispered the next part, "only the Father would be left!"

Highest Councilor eased off bearing down his Great Eye upon his trusted underling. The Great Eye occupied most of the Alpha's huge bulbous head and they used it to see, but also to *consume!* "True. That young man should be given credit. He boxed *everyone* in, both above and below. And I have to say, if you hadn't gone behind my back and *befriended* Vaughn as you did, we would both be on the wrong side of the Eye right now." He looked back over at Grinchback, who became shocked to see his Master's color change. Highest Councilor's shimmering had added the same dirty brown color that Grinchback had developed from his friendship with Vaughn when suddenly his dark grayness had incomprehensibly changed!

Seeing *that* upon his Master, with no little surprise, Grinchback considered, *Maybe Master will hear what I need to tell him, now.* "Master, I know that ever since *Queen* Karen jilted you . . ."

Highest Councilor didn't even bother touching his underling, his wrath had so increased that he used his ethereal power to freeze Grinchback and raise him above his Great Eye so he could drop him in and consume him just like they saw the Father consume HrorrarrAggrang. But his underling put up absolutely no resistance at all! It gave the Councilor pause. Then he set him back to mid float. "You were right about her Grinchback. All along, I was thinking about my tail up her skirt and *not* what I should have been considering. And *now,* she has all that power we gave her, but we have *no* return on our investment."

"Master, I *know* we now have a special bond, you and I, unlike *ever* in demon history, except maybe HrorrarrAggrang had something like that with the Father, but they had been together from the very beginning. The point is, we *are* stronger together like *this,* more so than if you consumed me. And . . ." He peered at his Master closely to make sure. The dirty brown had come back. "And I think we *still* need Vaughn's friendship in the same way!"

Highest Councilor ScrabaGag crossed his very long tail in his arm but *didn't* tap! He simply waited on his underling to speak his eye. Grinchback continued, "We are in great conflict of demon interest *because* of the great investment made into our Earth demons. *But* that was your *former* Master GrrraGagag's plan, *not* yours. As sly and intelligent as I've heard you describe him, he couldn't have foreseen what solution Vaughn created. None of us could."

Grinchback paused and his Master gave him the continue eye. "The Earth demons have no feeling for you, for *any* of us in spite of the reality that *you* in fact raised them through your ever-careful ever-watchful Great Eye. They also seek to kill Vaughn, and your former *lover* Queen Karen wants him dead, to say the *least!*"

Now Highest Councilor began to tap his tail in his arm, which made it more difficult for Grinchback to continue, but Grinchback's dirty brown changed shade again, into a new definitely clear brown color with a reddish overtone. His Master noted it, and Grinchback replied, "Master, again I say, if you want to consume me that is your right, but I *have to* speak my eye to you, for *our* own good. Instead of *Queen Karen* protecting our earth demons from Jargono, she *now* also will protect them from *us.* She feels only *she* has the power and the respect to control them."

Highest Councilor ScrabaGag sighed, a sort of slowing of his ripples and a gurgling sound. "She *does* have the power. No doubt about it. And *together,* when the Earth demons mature, *together* they will be more powerful, I believe, than even Jargono. You were right, my faithful underling. I *should have* listened to *you!*"

Grinchback bowed low to his Master, saying, "No flattery Master, but there has *never* been a Alpha like you *ever.* We need to destroy all the Earth demons!"

Highest Councilor ScrabaGag blinked twice then sighed again, "You know I *hate* waste, but I am afraid you are right. The only problem is, and I confide in you Grinchback, knowing it is *our* secret, we no longer have the power to do that! Not only does Jargono have those infernal blue bolts that kept my Great Eye from consuming him, his wife has them, too." The Master then studied Grinchback wondering if he should confide in him further.

This was all new to the Alpha. Such a serious question would *never* have been considered except as a ruse, part of a greater plan. But the Highest Councilor had changed ever since Grinchback and Vaughn accomplished his salvation. The Highest Councilor pulled up Stephanie's tree within the orb. "*Master!*" Grinchback shouted, turning away quickly from the extreme brightness, but the Highest Councilor dimmed the orb to its maximum setting.

When Grinchback turned back around, his eye gawked and his tail pointed. "What's *that?*" Stephanie's tree, though completely filled with powerful glow, nonetheless had, as it were, a bright star bursting with intense glow within the center of her trunk.

ScrabaGag merely said, "Her unborn child. *Vaughn's* unborn child." And the Master left the rest unsaid.

Grinchback folded his tail over his shoulders and let the tail tip hang down limply behind him and he whispered, "We have to destroy it!" Then he asked, "Why is it so *bright*? We've *never* seen that before in our Forest. It's not even mentioned in the manual!" Every time a human being is born, they get a directly connected spiritual tree in the Dead Forest which manifests the human's condition. The Alpha 'tend' the Forest so that their *crop* of humans has maximal taste.

ScrabaGag nodded, blinked twice, then spoke. "Remember I told you my former Master had asked me to research

Vaughn's lineage? Well, I finally got around to doing it after I witnessed *this.*" His tail thrust into the orb and its tip vibrated at the bright star. "Sadly, for your friend . . . for *our* friend, he really does come from the Jews! He's not simply one of those wannabes which is what we assumed they all were. In fact, all his current people are real Jews!"

Grinchback was amazed. "Master, I thought we had long ago destroyed all those people."

"Apparently not. They dropped out of our sight because for so long they had lost knowledge of who they were. But as I did my research, it turns out that we Alpha all simply ignored their little special extra glow, not realizing it came from the Blessing of their Generations. Even we, who studied Vaughn so closely for his whole life just didn't draw the connection."

"But Master, why would that now produce *that?*" And his tail did like his Master's.

"Because Stephanie is descended from the Appendaho, keepers of the Tree of Life, and that Tree *is* the *meaning* of their *glow.* Vaughn's people, the *Jews,* are the people of what they call *True Words.* And together . . ."

"The child possesses *both* sides" And Grinchback floated backwards in amazement not *just* realizing the threat of such children. Grinchback whispered, "Master, they *love* that child. More than *anything.* More than *themselves.* I know they do. I actually have come to understand them, believe it or not."

There was silence in the Highest Councilor's room for quite a while, until he whispered, "Regardless, we can't let that child be born, but . . ."

"Yes Master?"

"We *can* let it be born if we convert him to *us!*"

Grinchback floated in amazement. "How? How could that be possible?"

Highest Councilor ScrabaGag pulled up his former Master's secret files on Jargono and Karen and simply let them play for his underling. When it was done, Grinchback exclaimed, "So that's how they came to be like they are. But you really think we can successfully taint her child?" And *then* Grinchback realized the consequences and settled all the way to the floor. "Master," he whispered, "It would be better for Vaughn and Stephanie if we simply destroyed it!"

Just then they felt a familiar presence enter their ethereal room and the Master quickly shifted the orb's contents. Vaughn gave a bow to the demons and they actually bowed back. Grinchback, if it was possible for a demon to look guilty, just stared at his friend.

Vaughn smiled, "Grinchback," he quipped. "Aren't you happy to see me?"

In the next instant Grinchback raced up to Vaughn and wrapped his tail around Vaughn's neck and Vaughn threw his arm around the demon's sort-of-neck embracing him. Highest Councilor looked on with still some amazement, but not like it used to be. "To what do we owe the honor of your visit King Vaughn."

Vaughn noted that there was no sarcasm at all, no animosity at all in the Highest Councilor's words. So Vaughn went to the orb, brought up the demon's and Karen, and then proceeded to make the *exact* same case that Grinchback just did to his Master about the Earth demons!

Grinchback and his Master simply eyed one another, and Vaughn said, "I see you've both already discussed the same thing!"

ScrabaGag gave a nod to Grinchback who explained to Vaughn why they didn't have the power to destroy the Earth demons. Vaughn said, "Come on you guys," and Vaughn tried to reach up to put his arm around the Highest Councilor, but he was too large for it. So the Highest Councilor actually lowered himself so Vaughn could reach. Vaughn said cheerily, "So we have a little problem to solve. We've done that before. Right?"

Throughout their conversations the demons seemed odd, lackluster would actually fit the description. But Vaughn felt that if he and Stephanie could keep Karen occupied, then that would leave it open for the Highest Councilor to destroy the Earth demons. Grinchback replied, "But Jargono will defend his wife."

Vaughn quickly pointed out that if he showed up that would be fine because then Jargono himself would realize the threat and destroy them himself. "No, Karen has kept all this under wraps for herself. She knows she couldn't summon her husband."

"Master," was all Grinchback said, but the Highest Councilor knew what his underling wanted him to do.

The Master went back to the orb and pulled up a file he had proudly marked DEMON CONQUEST. A naked Karen floated in this very ethereal hall and was in the throes of pleasure with the Highest Councilor's tail between her legs, and at the moment of her orgasm, a ball seemed to float within the Highest

Councilor's tail and into Karen and she turned deep gray. After *that*, the gray moved within her and became invisible!

Vaughn stood in stunned silence until the Holy Spirit made known unto him, and he whispered, "She's one of you, now!"

The Highest Councilor slammed the orb vision shut and buried the file. "Jargono hasn't an arrogant clue!"

Vaughn turned to Grinchback, "Have you investigated where the rest of her powers came from, what they are?"

Grinchback looked at his Master and hung his bulbous head. "I never thought to do that and neither did Master."

"Would you please do that and let me know? We have to know fully what we're up against." Vaughn nodded to them both and disappeared.

The demons looked at each other waiting for one to speak. Finally, being Master, the Highest Master, ScrabaGag said, "If we follow his plan, even *exactly* the way he laid it out, it won't work. Though the Earth demons aren't mature yet, together, they still have enough power along with Karen to beat us all."

Grinchback said, "He's trying to protect his wife and unborn child, but Stephanie *must* join in the fight. *That* would be more than enough power to win."

"True, but that would *also* give us the opportunity we need to taint the child! Even a single drop of Earth demon blood in her mouth or mixed into a wound would be enough to do it. She probably doesn't have a clue."

"Then neither of them would know we were responsible. They would think it happened in the heat of battle *if* they would even understand that much. They won't even realize till *after* the child is born, and like Jargono, the Appendaho never realized it until it was too late."

But his Master shook his bulbous head. "No, my underling, they *did* know! They just didn't want to believe it! It was the only time they had *ever* violated their chief rule, Reality is what Reality is, no matter the pain."

Grinchback nodded. "I'll do the research on Karen he requested. He's right, you know. We should have already known this."

"I'll tell the Earth demons the child is a great threat to them. Karen has already told them but coming from me might make the necessary extra difference in their ferociousness. I'm also going to lodge a formal complaint about the child as a Truce Violation."

Grinchback's eye widened. "Master, I don't see how you can legitimately make such a claim. There's nothing . . ."

"Not in *that* truce!"

Grinchback floated in amazement. "There's *another one?* How come I was never . . ."

"Because no one likes to talk about it. *Before* the Great Flood, when Earth demons roamed the Earth, the *Cursed One* who would later become their *Christ* told us his Father was going to destroy the Earth. Of course we protested, but we knew we would lose that fight. So what we *did* do was bargain for the future." He paused to see if his underling might even be smart enough to figure the rest out.

After a while Grinchback said, "Oh my Great Eye. You made them promise not to allow such children after the flood was over." Then more realization floated into his eye. "*That's why the Tree of Life ended up on one side of the Earth and the Jews on the other.* They were *never* supposed to come together!"

"Not exactly. We knew their Christ was to come, but we *argued* for the position you just took. The *compromise* was that we all would allow for their Christ, if we could also at a future time have *our* Christ, but also, *only* their Christ could enter the Earth with that kind of power and specialness beyond what their normal holy people had!"

Grinchback nodded, thinking aloud, "*Beyond* what normal holy people have." He pulled up Stephanie again in the orb and grayed the image completely down. Then Grinchback threw on a special filter that removed Stephanie so that *only* the unborn child floated in mid orb.

The Highest Councilor was again impressed with Grinchback's orb manipulations. "Look closely at the child as you did when I showed you his mother when she was an infant but *already* born."

Grinchback peered deeply into the child and it immediately squirmed, then a bright flash of light surged through the orb and the Highest Councilor grabbed his faithful underling and pulled him away just as the ball of bright light whizzed by his Great Eye! "*Master,* the mother knew! She protected the child against even this!"

But ScrabaGag shook his bulbous head. "She *still* doesn't understand her feelings yet. And because the child is even so much holier than she is, she feels somewhat inadequate! But she's not consciously understanding this, which is why she's so upset all the time and can't seem to control it. She couldn't have sent that light ball!"

"Master," Grinchback whispered. "The child? Even *this* young?"

"Which is why I prepared to pull you from the orb before you were damaged!"

Grinchback uttered in ethereal amazement, "You *do* have a case of a truce violation!"

Highest Councilor ScrabaGag said, "I'll draw up the violation charges myself, this time. I don't want you to have *anything* to do with it because I don't want *your* friendship with Vaughn disturbed. Not only *that,* for this, I will seek the Father's stamp of approval which means . . ."

"That he takes all the credit for it."

"*We* don't want to provoke Vaughn, well, as little as possible. And I have to tell you Grinchback, friend or no friend, there's *still* something special going on with him we don't understand, besides just being a *Jew*! I feel he will have *much more* power than even his wife!"

Grinchback had always felt that, but to hear the way his Master said it, sent quivering through his ripples. "More?"

"Yes, but I fear he will have *less* control over his emotions than her when he's tested!"

CHAPTER 3

Trapped Between
Right and Right

Marta came late, which was the first time. But the students wondered if it was on purpose. At first, they tried avoiding talking about the lesson because they figured Marta would be listening. But as Heavenly time went on, they couldn't help it. How could they all be right from last lesson?

Sean, twelve Earth years old, with red hair, had been thinking ever since the question came up. "Well, Adam *was* in charge, *but* God was in charge of Adam and he didn't treat Adam the way Adam treated Eve!"

Carrie said, "God isn't *stupid!*" and she shook her head making her red curls bounce while staring at Stephan because of what he said last lesson.

But Stephan began nodding with no one in particular in focus. "You *are* right, Carrie! I *was* stupid, just like Adam! God asked *Adam* to name everything, but *God* created them!" he paused a moment because the picture of understanding came before all the words. "And those were just *animals!*"

All the students nodded. It made so much sense, but what did?

Marta's soft voice sounded all around them, "How did Adam feel when God allowed him to name everything?"

Sean immediately said, "Like he owned everything?" then he thought a moment, "Ahh, well, at least in charge of everything. I think it made him feel . . . *important!*" And everyone hearkened back to last year's lessons on importance.

Then Carrie said, "I *told* you it was stupid!"

Marta's soft voice was barely audible, it was so still in its sound, but they all heard it, anyway. This reminded them, too, of last year's lesson on the Stillness. "Why?"

Carrie's eyes went up, looking into the beyond, trying to put words to the immediate picture that had flashed in her heart. "Becaaaause . . . Eve didn't feel important!"

"Why?"

Robert quickly answered. "Because all Adam did was tell her everything. This is called this, that is called that. I think day after day of that, I'd hate it, too!?"

"Why?

Sarah, dark blond hair, Earth age nine, said, "Because all she did was just listen. Why couldn't *she* name something?" But then she wasn't sure because Adam had named everything even before Eve was created.

Marta appeared sitting under the Tree of Life and all the children whirled around. Smiling, she said, "You've learned so much and we're about to learn so much more. Let's see what happens next lesson!"

But Ralph, Earth age twelve, dark eyes with black hair, spoke up. "But you didn't teach us anything, today. You weren't here, ahhh, except for only one question and a few *why's!*"

"Why should *I* teach you when you do a better job of it, *yourselves!*"

Eve popped in all of the sudden and promptly hugged Marta! "That's it!" she handed her a glowing paper and Marta looked at it with tears. Eve turned to the class. "Marta has passed her test. I've observed her these three lessons and she has been superb, with the kind of innovation better than I have ever done! Everyone has their gifts. Marta's is *surely* being a teacher! And now it's official. From now on, you are all her students for eternity!"

Yinauqua stood in the middle of their perfectly round heavenly living room, at the very center of a perfectly round Appendaho royal blue rug with special gold Appendaho design, wearing a matching Appendaho dress, everything in their home had *perfect* meaning, which made what her husband just brought to her completely inconceivable, so much so, her heavenly heart pounded. She said for her husband to read it *again.* That would make it the *tenth* time. Mafferan, garbed in his usual simple soft brown tunic, and tan shirt and pants, and an always neatly trimmed gray and brown square beard, tugged on it a few more times then obliged her.

IT IS WITH THE DEEPEST REGRET AFTER
ALL WE HAVE SUFFERED TO RESTORE THE

*BALANCE THAT WE MUST FILE THIS VIOLA-
TION OF TRUCE 6B. APPEARANCE OF UNBORN
UNJUSTIFIED CHILD ON EARTH. RESITUTION
REQUIRED: CHILD MUST BE DESTROYED
BEFORE BIRTH.*

SEALED BY THE FATHER OF ALL,

LUCIFER

His Queen stood speechless, staring at the orb image they had included of Stephanie's unborn child! "The *nerve* of those *demons*. How did they even get this image? And after showing *this* to us, then they *demand* we have our daughter's child *destroyed?*" She looked into Mafferan's heavenly rich brown eyes through her tears and his face turned hard, saying, "They left something out!"

"Left something out?" she whispered. "What could be left *out?*"

"The other logical *balance.*"

Yinauqua shook her head, unable to think any more.

"That the child could be born tainted, like Jargono."

Yinauqua clutched at her heavenly stomach. "But . . . but . . . that would be *worse.*"

"Precisely. And they left it out on purpose."

"Why?"

"Because it's the obvious *unspoken* threat that's always most powerful. It *means* that they know we don't have a choice in this!"

"No choice?" Yinauqua rasped, she could barely get the words out. "What are you going to do?" Then his Queen thought for a second then grabbed him by his heavenly tunic and *yanked* him toward her! With eyes blazing, she softly said, "And *don't* leave me out of this, *at all!*" The understatement of her tone meant to imply far more, and Mafferan had to take the threat seriously.

"Alright. You *know* I love you as much as I love the Lord."

"I asked you, *what* are you going to do?"

Mafferan didn't even bother considering a clever answer. His wife had been to her utmost limit the last time, so he gave her the unbridled truth that she wanted. "I am required to report the violation to her, ahh, to both of them."

Yinauqua turned dark, something Mafferan *never* saw her do, not even during their horrific time when they were mortal. She always had a certain acceptance and faith for the future. "You're going to tell our daughter, the *faithwalker, Queen* Stephanie, *Lady* Stephanie, the *faithwalker* who of *all* people on Earth understands the *Oneness* of all life *better* than *anyone* maybe even *ever . . .*" Yinauqua could hardly speak the words. They barely came out as a whisper. "You're going to tell her she has to abort their child?"

Mafferan ran his hand through his heavenly hair, something he hadn't done quite like that since he was mortal. "In essence, that is what the violation requires. Come with me and we can tell them together!"

Yinauqua stood as if frozen. "I foresaw none of this. Oh Lord God. How can *any* of this work out?" She looked at her husband then looked down. "I can't come. I just can't."

And Mafferan disappeared.

Vaughn and his beloved wife were rolling on the luxurious bed in a tickle fight with their five-year-old adopted daughter, Lynnara, her flowing bouncy brown curls scattering in all directions as she strategically took her Mom's side. Obviously beaten, and all overjoyed, Vaughn cried out, "Mercy, *mercy*, I give!"

Lynnara looked up with her joyful dark brown eyes seeking her Mommy's wisdom, "Give what?"

Just then Mafferan popped in, pulled up a simple wooden chair he'd just created, and sat down. This was *not* behavior they'd seen before nor understood, because he clearly looked defeated. Even little Lynnara calmed and sat quietly.

Vaughn broke the silence, "What, the Earth demons are ahead of schedule? I'm working on a solution."

It didn't make sense to Stephanie, but she asked, "Is Mother alright?"

Mafferan knew she spoke about Yinauqua, her ancient ancestor. "No. No, she's not, and neither am I."

Vaughn turned dark and shimmering and Stephanie began to blaze. Even little Lynnara had fire in her little eyes. Mafferan handed the notice of violation to Vaughn.

He sat silent for a bit, then whispered, "After *all* I've done? You bring me *this?*" And waves of blackness swung out from him so violently that the whole judge's compound began to shake. Everyone thought it was an earthquake.

Stephanie grabbed the notice from her husband and read it, then calmed and her fire disappeared. She merely laughed and shrugged it off. *That* reaction actually scared Mafferan.

He hung his head and spoke softly. "I know I don't have to say anything further. I know you all understand perfectly all the ramifications." And he began to fade out, but Vaughn grabbed him by the arm!

Surprised that Vaughn could even successfully do that, Mafferan just helplessly looked on. "You want us to *kill* our unborn child?" Vaughn disappeared!

And reappeared up in Heaven at the very place where Mafferan had taken him before. He stood upon a multicolored jeweled walkway that went far into the distance and was simply suspended in mid Heaven. "Lord God, *my* Father, who has delivered me from all my tribulations," Vaughn held out his hand and the violation notice appeared in it! He shouldn't have been able to do that, but his faith *only* conceived of *that* result. He gave it no second thought. "Please Father, tell me what this is." And he held up the notice. God had spoken directly to him from right there, before!

There was silence. Abraham materialized beside him, along with another man with a broad white beard whom Vaughn didn't know. Vaughn looked at them and merely nodded, saying, "I'm sorry, but I'm just not here to talk to you." And he went down on his knees and pleaded with all his heart, all his soul, all his mind, and all his might, "What is this? What would you have us do?"

There was no answer. Only silence. Abraham took the notice and read it. Shocked, he gave it to his partner. He read it, then crumpled it up, threw it in the heavenly air and it burst into flames and disappeared. Vaughn looked up at him with pleading eyes. "Why hasn't the Lord answered me? The Holy Ghost inside me has no answer. Why?" Then Vaughn thought about his rudeness, and said, "I'm sorry. My name is Vaughn, and I know I shouldn't have barged in . . ."

The man spoke, and as he did Vaughn saw a familiar blackness radiate from him in an intensity he'd never seen nor felt before. "My name is Moses, and what you've read about me is only a tiny portion of my life. The Lord isn't answering you, neither is the Holy Ghost, because you *and* your wife, already know the answer! And you also know we can't tell you because?"

He wanted Vaughn to finish the thought. "Because the answer must come from the inside out."

Abraham spoke. "We know you didn't need all this in the midst of all you have to do." He looked over at Moses questioningly, and Moses nodded. "If your enemy is slowly gathering forces against you, when is the best time to attack?"

Vaughn looked up. "Now!" and he tried to leave but couldn't.

Moses spoke. "Yes, now. But that doesn't mean without planning and without the help you know you need."

Vaughn said, "We have many holy people now. I'm sure they can help."

They both shook their heads. Moses said, "They'll all die. They would go with you without question, but their calling isn't to that kind of battle."

"Then what," Vaughn asked. "Please father Moses, tell me what you have in mind." Moses waved his hand and the small orb that held Vaughn's truce program between Heaven and the Ethereal and him appeared. Moses brought up himself in the past and the orb showed Vaughn some of Moses life, how that the children of Israel rebelled so often, how he erred when he struck the rock the second time, and how he did so many miracles with his staff. Everywhere Moses went, his staff went. Everywhere. And then Vaughn saw when the Lord sent him up into the mountain to die. His staff was no longer with him then, and the Lord took him. Then the vision ended.

Vaughn looked up at them not understanding. Abraham put his hand on Vaughn's shoulder. "Go home to your wife now. She needs you. Remember the blessing we gave you. They are there even now. And you two will *always* be together."

Vaughn disappeared, but there was something he had to do first.

For the second time in a week Vaughn appeared in their square ethereal room, but this time he radiated blackness they had never seen before. He held out his hand and the violation notice appeared! Highest Councilor ScrabaGag and Grinchback floated in mid ether and looked at each other *knowing* he shouldn't have been able to do that, and Grinchback recalled his Masters words about Vaughn. "Master, leave us now, please!" And his Master bowed to Vaughn and disappeared.

Grinchback hung his demon head. His colors turned all shades of brown, not a black shade in him. When Vaughn saw it, he took control of the power he was emanating, and drew it back into himself. Vaughn held out the notice and Grinchback waved his arm and took Vaughn into his Master's blackest secret room. Quite small by comparison and almost a full ethereal black, it also was triply protected against any spying.

Grinchback had been pondering a solution but he hadn't told his Master because he was sure his Master would not approve. "Offer a trade," Grinchback said flatly.

There was only one thing of value Vaughn had to trade. "You want me to undue my orb destruction program in exchange for the life of my child?"

Grinchback nodded. "It *might* be a worthy trade to the Father."

After Grinchback let him think a while, he said, "Think about it. You would no longer be the target you are from *Karen,* Jargono, and the Earth demons. They all want you dead so we're cut off. No Vaughn, the orbs stop working."

Vaughn waved his hand again and the little orb from up in Heaven appeared in the ethereal room where it used to reside. Grinchback was amazed, knowing *definitely* that Vaughn should not be able to do *this.* But again, Vaughn gave it no thought. He pulled up Stephanie's tree, then made orb adjustments that Grinchback didn't understand and couldn't clearly follow. Instead of Stephanie and the unborn child simply glowing, they displayed with an infinite varied color display! Grinchback was amazed as he immediately understood what Vaughn did. He substituted various colors for intensity and variation of glow, thereby making it easy to read.

Vaughn allowed Grinchback to actually study Stephanie and the unborn child. Then Vaughn asked him point blank,

"If I made that offer, and I *do* have a right to make it since *I* made this truce. If I make this offer to trade my orb destruction program for the life of our child, will that offer be accepted?" Vaughn already knew the answer because he understood what he was looking at in the orb, and he knew Grinchback did, too.

The way Vaughn looked at Grinchback, the demon knew he had to tell the straight truth. "No. No, they can't. That child, to us as demons, has to be either tainted or destroyed!"

"You mean tainted like this?" And Vaughn pulled up the hidden files on Jargono and Karen, which shocked Grinchback. Realizing that Vaughn was ahead of them all, he bowed to Vaughn out of utter respect. "You knew all along. Well, of course you did, I mean, look at the solution you created to save us all."

At hearing *that,* Vaughn grabbed the demon by his throat, which uncovered Stephanie's handprint, then spoke ominously, "I want a solution, Grinchback. A solution that doesn't entail *killing* my child, nor *tainting* him. And if *any* harm comes to our child, or my wife, I will come down here and make what my wife did to you look inconsequential. I will tear your ethereal essence apart *piece by ethereal piece,* then I'll *plaster it* on top of the stone of the Black River for all to see for ethereal infinity. Do you understand?"

Grinchback placed his tail gently on Vaughn, "Yes Master!" Vaughn let him go. "But not only that. I really understand. May I speak freely?"

Vaughn nodded.

"There's too much for you and your wife, ahh, who hasn't quite been herself lately, to deal with. Stall your response to this . . ." Grinchback squinted at the notice, "necessary but *difficult* situation. Focus first on what you have a chance to win. Then you'll be stronger."

It made sense. Vaughn turned back to the orb, and pulled up Moses, his infinite color program still functioning. Grinchback didn't even approach the orb but asked Vaughn's permission. "May I?"

Vaughn nodded, and Grinchback replied, "Thank you Master!" It was odd calling Vaughn that, but Grinchback felt it flow from his demon lips naturally and Vaughn understood it. Vaughn played back the last time he saw Moses with the staff. He froze the frame. Then went to the next frame. The staff was gone! "Master?" Grinchback asked. "Do you want me to try and find it?" It was obvious what Vaughn was searching for.

"No. Because you won't find it. This secrecy isn't from anyone down here, nor anyone up there! This is from the Creator Himself!"

Grinchback tried hard not to say what was pushing at him, but he couldn't help himself. It made him wonder whether he was terminally ill! "Master Vaughn, what I have to tell you isn't going to be pleasant at *all*. It's on the level, in a way, of when I showed you Matthew together with your wife."

Vaughn turned to face him but remained silent, so Grinchback spoke. "My other Master, Highest Councilor ScrabaGag feels that even with all our help with you, we won't be able to destroy the Earth demons. He also feels you are intentionally keeping your wife from the battle because you want to protect her. But he also told me that without her, we will lose miserably. There is simply no replacing her power."

Vaughn nodded, saying, "I suspected that but kept trying to ignore it."

"Master, denying reality won't benefit you. But . . . there's more."

Grinchback's color changed to a purplish haze. They were both surprised at it. "If your wife helps as needed, we don't feel there is any way for her to escape being tainted. One single drop of demon blood in her mouth, one single scratch upon her body from a demon, and your child will be damned, according to your vernacular."

"Which is what I clearly explained to my wife!"

Grinchback was amazed again, and he bowed to Vaughn, "Forgive me, Master. You have exceeded all of us!" Then Grinchback thought of something that Vaughn couldn't know. "Master, if I may." And he floated in front of the orb and brought up his session with the Highest Councilor and replayed when they were examining the unborn child. When Vaughn saw how his child fought back, it did surprise him.

"Grinchback, is that supposed to happen?"

"Never in demon history has *that* been known to be!"

Vaughn looked him squarely in the eye and smiled. "Grinchback, you are beginning to use the correct language!"

Grinchback had to think about that, but he was glad for Vaughn's smile. He could still imagine his new Master tearing him into little ethereal pieces, and somehow, because Vaughn gave his word, he knew it wasn't a bluff, even if Vaughn, himself, wasn't fully aware that he wasn't supposed to have *any* of the extra powers he had been demonstrating.

Grinchback put his tail tip on Vaughn's shoulder again. "I'm going to draw up a stay of judgment appeal for the maximum duration of three months! They'll have to honor it, but any longer risks the child actually being born, and the Ethereal simply won't tolerate that. They won't Vaughn. I don't have an answer for you on this now, but three months will give us time."

Vaughn's wedding ring began to glow. "Grinchback, watch over this orb for me!" And Vaughn disappeared!

Grinchback couldn't believe Vaughn left the orb in the room. But then again, it really didn't matter. He wouldn't dare mess with Vaughn's self-destruct program which, from here, would jeopardize *all* ethereal orbs. But another odd thing was that Vaughn had left functioning his infinite color-coding program! Grinchback couldn't believe it was by accident. He slowly floated to the orb and tentatively tried to use it. It seemed safe.

Delighted, Grinchback proceeded to use it to investigate *Karen.* He felt that it would help him to understand her better. As he flipped through her history, he discovered that she had been given powers from HrorrarrAggrang, powers of levitation, ethereal powers to project energies, and a special defensive shield that lay hidden just under her skin

From his Master, she had been given ethereal travel, but also, when he mated with her, she had been transformed into a demon, herself. Not obvious, but her blood now ran black, not red. And she *wasn't* an Earth demon. No. She was blessed to be an *actual* Ethereal Demon, while *still* remaining as a human. The difference between her and the Earth demons was how they came to *be* demons. The Earth demons were a result of demon seed fertilizing a human egg. But *Karen* was a full-fledged human who freely gave herself and freely accepted with all the utmost pleasure she could muster, a full demon presence. Grinchback pondered it. "It's like, in a way, when the humans receive that Holy Ghost!" *Master, what have you done?*

CHAPTER 4

A *Very* Special Child, an Old Prophet, and a Rabbit

Marta appeared right in the midst of everyone. Another first! The students were beginning to enjoy the surprises every lesson. "So Eve didn't feel important. Do you think Adam wanted her to feel that way?

Craig, short black hair, Earth age thirteen, said, "No. Not at all. I think he really meant well. I mean, he was probably just so excited with and in love with Eve that all he wanted to do was give to her everything he knew."

Marta turned a full circle catching everyone's eye. "Does everyone agree with that?" and they all nodded. "So Adam was doing the *right* thing?"

Now there was a pause, and all the students kept looking at each other and whispering, until Sarah pushed her blond hair out of her face, and said, "He didn't *mean* to hurt Eve. I mean, make her feel bad, unimportant. But that's what he did!"

Marta narrowed her eyes at everyone and turned full circle, again. "So when the serpent said to Eve that the fruit of knowledge of good and evil would be *good* for her, what was she thinking?"

Running his hand through his curly red hair, Ralph said, "I think that this made her feel like she had the chance to be important!"

But Sarah said, "Not like *that.* I mean, I don't think she was wanting a *bad* importance. She wanted to have *meaning* . . . ahh, *purpose,* instead of just looking pretty and him doting over her, and her just *listening* all the time."

Carolyne's green eye's flashed, "But not like that, either! I mean, it's true what they both said, but she *loved* Adam, I'm sure. Even though he made her feel bad, it wasn't on purpose. She probably blamed herself for her bad feelings! I think she wanted Adam to have something important from *her,* because he was giving her so much all the time."

Marta smiled. "See how much knowledge is right there for discovering? "So what you are all saying is, that neither Adam nor Eve were intending to do evil? They both thought they were doing right?"

This time there was a long pause, so Marta said, "Do you all think this question should be tomorrow's lesson?" And they all nodded.

V aughn popped into their bedroom ready for battle, glowing with deep blackness, but when he looked around all he saw was his wife and Lynnara sitting on the bed in prayer. As he calmed himself, he asked, "Stephanie, my ring glowed. I was afraid you were in trouble."

She picked up her head. "I'm sorry Vaughn, you were gone so long, and I had no idea where you were. At one point I lost all sense of you *completely*!"

He studied her, not realizing she was ever able to sense him like that! What's more, it didn't seem to occur to her that this was new! Stephanie jumped a bit then smiled. "Your son wants you to put your hand on my tummy. He says he likes that!"

"My *son?*"

"Yes, of course, you said it yourself." When she realized he was only half joking, she said, "I just know it's a boy. Just like I knew ten minutes after we made love that I was pregnant."

Vaughn nodded with understanding and sat down on the bed and placed his hand on his wife's tummy. Lynnara liked that and came around to the other side and did the same thing.

Stephanie put her hand to her husband's cheek. "Vaughn, you've been utterly perfect this whole time. I'm so sorry I've been so emotional. I really can't get a handle on it."

Vaughn smiled, then turned to Lynnara. Her hand was still on her third Mommy's tummy. "What do you feel, Lynnara?"

She smiled, knowing *exactly* what King Vaughn was asking her. "I feel little Michael, of course!"

Stephanie's and Vaughn's eyebrows went up, both saying, "Michael?"

And with an, *Of Course,* look, she replied, "Yeaaaa. Didn't you know?" When she saw King Vaughn still waiting for her answer, she concentrated further on what she felt. "Michael says to tell Mommy to stop worrying so much. And that he loves her so much, that she's the best Mommy in the whole world . . ."

Stephanie couldn't help her amusement and asked her daughter, "So, little Michael *told you* all that?"

Lynnara scrunched her eyebrows together understanding her third Mommy's meaning *exactly.* "Mommy, you're a *faith-walker.* You *know* Michael doesn't know words yet." She shook her head at her Mommy.

Vaugh couldn't help but follow up. "So, Lynnara, how did you know Michael said all that if there were no words?"

The little girl sighed. Sometimes it could be so very hard raising your parents. "Daddy, I can understand little Michael *perfectly.* I *know* what he means."

And Stephanie raised her eyebrows, again, holding back laughter because of Lynnara's straight-forwardness. "Oh, I see. You know what he means."

But Lynnara knew Mommy's meaning here, also, that in fact, she *didn't* believe her, and her little feelings were hurt. But Lynnara was *never* a child to give up. That's why when her third Mommy, the bestest Mommy she ever had, told her to leave Mommy in the Dead Forest to die but to save herself, that's why she didn't listen. *That's* why Mommy is here right now. Because *Lynnara* doesn't give up! She got a very deter-mined look then said slowly to them both. "Michael speaks in MEANING! *Very clearly!*" She enunciated to make her point. Then she put her hand back on Mommy's tummy to finish.

Lynnara continued, "Oh, and that he's so happy to be made from both Mommy and Daddy together and that makes him feel so very special to have such special parents. Oh, he loves you, too, Daddy, as much as Mommy. And he chased the demon away!"

"*What?*" His Mother said, turning *very* black. In the next instant Stephanie disappeared! Vaughn was immediately aware he lost all sense of her and was about to pop back to the Ethereal when Lynnara, his new daughter, took his hand. "Don't worry Daddy. Mommy just went downstairs to straighten them out!" When Vaughn became even more determined to join her, Lynnara said, "You're not supposed to go. She has to do this herself!" She was looking Vaughn straight in the eye with the utmost honesty and little girl knowledge, and for some reason, Vaughn didn't exactly know why, he listened!

Lady Stephanie appeared in the Highest Councilor's ethereal room! Her first time there. She was clothed in her holy royal blue dress with the gold and red embroidery of Appendaho design down the front, along the neck and hem. Her traditional Appendaho three braids were back with the holy blue and gold ribbon tied onto the middle braid at the center. Highest Councilor recognized her presence immediately and began to welcome her, but Lady Stephanie held out her hand and a blazing ball of concentrated blue light with a golden center sped forth faster than anyone had ever seen! The blue ball hit Scraback dead center, sunk into him and then the gold *exploded,* creating a gaping wound and *slamming* him up against his own ethereal wall!

She turned to Grinchback who coiled up into a defensive ball and peered through the slimmest slit between tail loops.

Stephanie warned him, "*Don't move!*" He blinked his assent, then the *faithwalker* strode over to the Highest Councilor, grabbed him by the neck, and pulled his great massive eye to within inches of her. In a deadly steady voice, she informed him, "If *any* of you mess with *my* child *one more time,* just even once, even a little graze, there will be much more left upon *you* than a *matching* handprint to go with your *underling!*" She waited for the Highest Councilor to realize his neck was smoking, then she asked, "Do you understand?" The Highest Councilor bowed as well as he could under the circumstance and Stephanie disappeared.

Grinchback slowly uncoiled, retrieved their unholy Black Oil from the cubbyhole next to the orb and began daubing gently upon his Master's wounds. Highest Councilor Scraback spoke calmly, "I told you, Underling, she's *much* more controlled than her husband!"

"Master, we now have matching *faithwalker* neck handprints. Maybe we can start a new Alpha fashion. Wear it as a badge of honor!"

His Master began a demon chuckle, then broke out into a full demon laugh, a sort of chortle accompanied by vibrant shimmering and dramatic rippling. He put his tail around his faithful underling. "Grinchback, we have them *exactly* where we want them! No way out!"

"Good Master. Here!" Grinchback handed him the stay of judgment appeal.

ScrabaGag nodded. "Excellent. Go file it with the Father and as soon as you give it to him, don't linger."

Grinchback disappeared and reappeared in the farthest corner of the Father's deepest, darkest, blackest room. He wasn't just going to pop right in front of *Him* blind. Ever since Master Vaughn bested the Father, Grinchback felt the Father had determined to eat him. But upon appearing, Grinchback's eye practically popped out. There, a good ways off, with the Father's tail wrapped around HrorrarrAggrang in friendly repose, they discussed everything that had just been transpiring, and they had a blue orb with them, one that Grinchback had never seen before! Which meant that it also wasn't infected with Vaughn's destructive orb virus. . . . which meant that if his virus triggered, all the orbs would be destroyed except *that* one! Which meant . . .

Grinchback had to think fast. He got away with popping in unnoticed, but he strongly doubted being able to pop out without being discovered, unless . . . he began fading out very slowly. After a few minutes, he was totally gone and reappeared outside the Father's front door. He knocked! There was some scrambling going on inside then the Father opened the door using his infinite ethereal power. "Oh, Grinchback, come in. You know, for some reason, I was just thinking about you!"

It was the way he invited Grinchback inside. It was *too* accommodating. He laid the appeal on the ethereal floor and vanished as fast as he could. As he left, he could hear the Father bellowing out his laughter.

When Grinchback popped back to his Master, without even thinking, he put his arm on him and popped his Master into their secret room. Highest Councilor ScrabaGag considered this provocation, but when he saw Grinchback looking as if he had seen the apparition of *Christ,* he knew something was terribly wrong.

After Grinchback told his Master all that he saw, the Highest Councilor spoke. "Well, well, the Father forced himself to vomit out HrorrarrAggrang!" And then ScrabaGag bellowed out his joy. "Describe to me the orb *exactly* as it appeared."

"I don't know, Master, it . . . it was like all the other orbs, except . . . well, I guess the blue wasn't *quite* the normal blue."

"Pull up our good Queen Karen and research *everything* from just after our friend redid the truce."

After a while Grinchback squinted at the small orb. "There's something not right, here." And he went into a different program, pulled it up, went to the orb clock, dumped that into the new program, *then* pulled Karen's file into it as well. The orbed blinked twice, then went black.

Highest Councilor shook his bulbous head at Grinchback. "We *just* got that orb back and you've destroyed it."

"Patience, Master." The orb flickered to life again, and when it came fully back, Karen's whole file was clearly marked frame by frame with a time stamp. After that, Grinchback punched in some code, the orb went dark again, but moments later it sputtered back to life with several pairs of slides. Between each pair, it became clear there was missing information. Grinchback then pulled up a different program, fed in the missing time slots, and waited.

"This is my special recovery program Master. It will take a while."

જી

Yinauqua studied her husband as he peered into the golden vision from the orb floating in the middle of their living room. "Are they *supposed* to have all those new powers? They don't even realize what they're doing." She stared deeply at him again.

This time Mafferan looked honestly at her and shrugged!

"OK, you want to play that game? I told you, *don't* leave me in the dark anymore. How did they get those new powers?"

"I honestly don't know! Just like the staff of Moses disappeared, I think the same is happening with them!"

"You mean the Lord is *directly* doing this and not using any of us?"

Mafferan nodded.

Yinauqua had to ask, though it was embarrassing for an Appendaho Queen, a former keeper of the Tree of Life. "But what does all this mean?"

Equally embarrassing for Mafferan. "I don't know!"

જી

When Stephanie popped back to their bedroom, Vaughn and little Lynnara, sitting on the bed, couldn't take their eyes from her. She hadn't been this well dressed or put together in a while. They both spoke together, "You look beauuuutiful."

Stephanie paused, then realized it had been quite a while since she fully took care of herself. Embarrassed, she apologized, "I don't know what's been going on with me." And she sighed.

Little Lynnara pulled her Mommy back down to the bed like before and placed her hand back on her tummy. She

51

smiled up at Stephanie, "We weren't done when you left. We were right in the middle!" She bowed her little head, waited for a bit, then she said, "I asked Michael why Mommy is acting so strange. He said because *both* Mommy and Daddy made him. I don't understand because isn't that the way it's done? That's what you told me Mommy and what we saw when we went underground!"

Vaughn looked up at Stephanie. Apparently, she'd left out this part of her little story. "I'll tell you the rest later." Stephanie pinched Lynnara's cheek. "I can't get away with *anything* around you, can I?" Lynnara emphatically shook her head, but then began telling the *whole* story to Vaughn. While that was happening, Stephanie thought about Michael's answer. She also noted that Michael did seem like the right name! He *felt* like a Michael.

Mommy and Daddy both *inside me. But Michael, ha, is already his own person!* Which means . . . he has goodness from both of us . . . Stephanie tried to imagine what that would be like, to have the special goodness of both Vaughn and her all wrapped up perfectly in a single person. Perfectly, because both of them were holy when the child was conceived. "My God!" And she bowed her head, but that wasn't low enough for her, so she slid to the floor and bowed very low.

Vaughn and Lynnara watched her then. *Lord God, what have you blessed us with for a child? We gave it no thought, but you took from us the very best of us to make little Michael. And now I understand why I've felt the way I have been. I'm utterly dwarfed by Michael's goodness! Help us Lord, to raise him according to Your will. Guide us how to raise such a special child.* And right there, hardly even possible, her love for her unborn child increased tenfold.

Stephanie didn't realize it, but she shined in the most beautiful colors they'd ever seem. Pastel blues. Greens, golds, reds and silvers. Vaughn didn't even realize Lynnara and him were holding hands because of the sight. When Stephanie picked herself up off the floor and saw them holding hands like that, it melted her heart and she brushed away a tear. But they noticed something had changed in her. Her posture seemed straighter than ever before and the stress they'd grown used to from her was gone.

Stephanie kissed Vaughn on the cheek and sat next to him then threw her arms around him and laid her head on his shoulder. "I understand now. Michael is a *very* special child. I wish you could feel it. He's so special I was feeling so small without realizing it."

Little Michael pushed his little hand out against Mommy inside. His hand was so tiny, he wondered if Daddy would sense it. Lynnara looked up at Vaughn and told him for Michael, "Put your hand right there!" And she smiled broadly. So Vaughn listened.

It became like a mini Appendaho bonding! As Vaughn, for the first time, felt the person that Michael is! After a few minutes and the special communication finished, he brushed tears from his eyes and lifted Stephanie off from his shoulder. Vaughn opened his eyes wide and his wife understood she was to enter into his heart and mind.

After a few minutes, Stephanie softly whispered, "You understand now. I love you all so *very* much." Then, after a few minutes Stephanie sat up straight, looked Vaughn in the eye and swore a holy oath, "There is absolutely no way, not in *hell,* nor even in *Heaven,* nor upon this *Earth,* nor *anywhere,* am I going to *murder,* or *abort,* or even allow *any harm* to this child. I swear it by the Tree of Life that surely *is* my life, and by all that we have suffered. *This child will be born and born holy!"*

And both Vaughn and Lynnara said, "*Amen."*

Just then Stephanie squinted above Vaughn's head. A dark grey arm quivered and struggled to reach him. When Vaughn noticed his wife's concentration, he said, "It's alright. I think it's a message for me!" After a bit, when Vaughn allowed the gray arm to make contact, it lingered there a few moments, then vanished. Vaughn looked up into Stephanie's eyes. "We have three months."

Lynnara kept waiting for more. She studied her third mommy, the best Mommy she ever had, and saw a terrible strain on her down deep. She couldn't tell how deep 'cause she was far too young. She looked at her Daddy and couldn't tell anything there, either, but she knew she needed to know. "For what? For what three months?"

Vaughn and Stephanie looked at her and told her the truth. "We don't know, dear. We only know what we are *not* going to do."

Vaughn reached and picked up the King James old ragged Holy Bible from their nightstand. It's black cover with gold letters seemed to have weathered from much use. Vaughn absently thumbed through the pages. Stephanie touched his arm, "Holy Bible and not the Book of Wisdom?" She knew why he had picked it up, even if he hadn't fully realized why. Vaughn thought for a moment then nodded.

He continued to thumb through from the Old testament then to the New and back to the Old, but then he felt strongly the answer he sought was in the Old. He closed his eyes and thumbed through again. And Vaughn came upon First Kings Chapter 13 which he read aloud.

And behold, there came a man of God out of Judah by the word of the Lord unto Bethel . . . 8 And the man of God said unto the king, If thou wilt give me half of thine house, I will not go in with thee, neither will I eat bread nor drink water in this place. 9 For so was it charged to me by the word of the Lord, saying, Eat no bread, nor drink water, nor turn again by the same way that thou camest . . .14 And the old prophet, who was told by his sons all the deeds of the young man of God, went after the man of God, and found him sitting under an oak . . . 15 Then he said unto him, Come home with me and eat bread. 16 And he said, I may not return with thee . . . 18 The old prophet said unto him, I am a prophet also as thou art, and an angel spake unto me by the word of the Lord, saying, Bring him back with thee into thine house, that he may eat and drink water. But he lied unto him. 19 So he went back with him and did eat . . . drink . . .20 And it came to pass, as they sat at the table, that the word of the Lord came unto the prophet that brought him back: 21 Thus saith the Lord, Forasmuch as thou hast disobeyed the mouth of the Lord . . . 23 . . . a lion met the man of God and slew him. . .

Stephanie began to weep. Little Lynnara buried her head into her Mommies bosom and Stephanie hugged her. "Vaughn, why that? What does it mean for *us*?

Vaughn turned black. "It means, we can't be like that man of God who listened to someone other than the Lord, *whoever* they may be!"

Stephanie shook her head. "Oh Vaughn . . . we are *alone*."

But Lynnara picked up her head, her little eyes blazing. "No we're not Mommy. Don't cry. We're all together right *here!*" And she patted her Mommy, her Daddy, and her brother Michael inside Mommy, and Stephanie's tummy glowed!

Just then a dark portal opened above their heads. A scroll dropped through and landed on the bed, then the portal closed up.

> *YOUR APPEAL IS GRANTED. THREE MONTHS FROM THIS DATE YOU MUST PROVIDE A SOLUTION TO THE INFRACTION OF THE FORBIDDEN CHILD.*
>
> *LUCIFER.*

Moments after that, a golden portal opened up and a glowing scroll dropped onto the bed.

> *YOUR APPEAL HAS BEEN GRANTED. THREE MONTHS FROM NOW YOU MUST HAVE*

A SOLUTION TO THE PROBLEM OF THE FORBIDDEN CHILD.

King Mafferan

Stephanie smiled, politely took both notices, opened her mouth and breathed fire upon them! And they were no more. They laid down, all three together in the soft, luxurious bed that all judges in the quarter were provided, and they fell deeply asleep.

All three were standing facing each other and the day was neither light nor dark. A ball of fire descended down from above and hovered between Lynnara, Stephanie, and Vaughn. And when the fire dissipated, a comely little boy of about five years old smiled at them all at once. His eyes were as the stars above, and his heart pulsed a golden light and he kissed each one in turn, and as he kissed each one, they knew his sweet goodness, his utter kindness, and his tender, bright, and uplifting love. Then he vanished and all three woke up from their common dream.

"Mommy, that was Michael. I'd know him anywhere,"

Stephanie looked at Vaughn, her husband, the man whose face she saw in the window that dreadful night so long ago when her gang was about to brutalize her, and afterwards, after he rescued her, she held his face in both her hands, saying, This is the face I saw that saved my life, that returned my soul to me. And Vaughn knew her thoughts.

He kissed his wife and his daughter and disappeared. And he reappeared at the top of the holy mountain they had reclaimed and Vaughn knelt before the Tree of Life, which had previously sprouted right after they had made love there, but was now a sapling, with full, large, fuzzy leaves, about five feet tall! Its tender branches spread out, and Vaughn bowed to the ground weeping. The Tree began to glow, and all the inhabitants below, who were forbidden to come up because they had grossly offended the Lord God, they could see the bright glow atop the holy mountain, even though the full moon shone brightly. One young lady spoke, "We are all doomed for what we did. Even for how we are now."

And the Tree of Life glowed brighter until it outshined the sun at noon day, then it became a vision. And when it became a vision, Vaughn raised his head and beheld Moses in a tent with a young lad. "Take this, young man. Go to the next village, and if anyone asks you what have you, Say to them, The prophet told me this is the Lord's Staff of Indignation. Do you want it?"

So the boy left, and on his way, a stranger here, a stranger there asked about the staff and the boy answered *exactly* as the Prophet told him. And they all fled in terror. Until the boy came to another young man of about ten years old, and he asked, "What have you there?" And the boy said, "The prophet told me this is the Lord's Staff of Indignation. Do you want it?" And the young man said, "Yes. I shall take it. And so the boy handed it over. And the boy that had it went home to his father and roused him from a nap. "Father, you must come with me." And his father asked him, "What do you have there, my son?' And the boy answered, "The prophet

said this is the Lord's Staff of Indignation. Do you want it?"
And his father shrank away from him. But his son came closer
and took his father's hand, saying, "Then you must take me
to where I show you. The journey is far, but we must put this
away against the Day of Judgment." And his father rose up
and accompanied the lad until they reached a mountain, and
a cave, and the boy climbed in. After a while the boy climbed
out, without the staff, and said, "Break down the stones
above the cave's opening father and bury the staff." But his
father asked, "Then how will they find it when it's needed?
But the boy answered, "The Lord shall give this to whom *He*
chooses, and *no one else.*" So his father broke down the stones
and buried the cave.

And then the vision began to speed through time, and
the mountain saw many wars, many were slain there, many
dead bodies laid atop the mountain and were not buried until
the bodies went back naturally to the dust of the Earth. And
then a great drought came upon the land, and the whole land
changed, and much desert arose. The streams had dried, the
life had left, and the mountain became as a dead mountain.
And time moved on for a thousand more years until a young
man and a young woman came alone to the mountain, and
the young woman stretched her arms wide and turned in a
circle, and the young man prayed, and the mountain lived
again. And the young man and lady, looking like a King and
Queen prayed, and the Lord placed a protection around the
mountain. And the young couple, deeply in love, planted the
sacred seed she had sworn to protect, and then made love, and

awoke to the Tree of Life sprouting anew. And they rejoiced, then departed.

Vaughn fell over onto his back, looking heavenward. "Ahh Lord God, what have you done with this wretched boy, who isn't even a full-grown man?" And a great thunder rolled down from heaven, and within that thunder, *causing* the thunder, was the voice of Being speaking softly. "Making him a King before the entire world! Take up my Staff. Meditate upon it. Turn not to the right, nor the left, but serve Me, I AM the Lord God of your Fathers, of Abraham, Isaac, and Jacob. And I AM *your* Lord God. I have placed within your souls, You and your Queen, *My* knowledge of Life. Do not forsake it . . ." And the thunder diminished, and all was silent and calm.

Vaughn lay a long time not moving, until a large brown rabbit hopped upon him. Flinching, Vaughn sat up, and the rabbit moved but then sat up like he was begging like a doggy, his little paws reaching out to Vaughn then withdrawing, then reaching out again. Vaughn smiled, "What are you doin' little fella?"

The rabbit hopped a bit away then turned around and looked at Vaughn. "Alright, I'll play." Vaughn laughed at this oddity, but after what he just experienced, he felt he needed something mundane before he went home to tell Stephanie what happened. Maybe she could help him find the Staff, which, if Vaughn understood the vision correctly, was somewhere inside this very large mountain. He laughed at the thought of him trying to find it,

The rabbit hopped away, and Vaughn followed it, until it disappeared. "Where'd you go little fella?" And as Vaughn scanned the ground in a broad sweep of his vision, his foot caught in a hole and he fell. When he turned back to see it, the rabbit poked his head out of that hole, then turned around and started digging, spraying dirt right into Vaughn's face, causing him to spit it out.

"Well, you got me. You remind me of *Spot*, my faithful dog." It suddenly pained Vaughn, he missed his companion and hoped he was safe up north and being a good hero dog. "Well, goodbye little rabbit." And Vaughn was about to disappear when the rabbit emerged with something shiny in its mouth. And he brought it to Vaughn and dropped it at his feet. Vaughn shook his head, knelt down and picked it up. It looked like an ancient gold coin. Vaughn laughed, "I'm *rich*, little rabbit. Thank you so much."

The rabbit seemed to frown at him then darted back down the hole. More dirt flew out, but this time Vaughn made sure it wasn't in his face. This time the rabbit struggled to bring something up. Vaughn knelt beside it. It didn't seem afraid of him at all but turned and looked at him as if to ask for help to move whatever it was from the rabbit's new home. "OK. Let's see." Vaugh stuck his hand into the hole, felt a stick and pulled it out. But it wasn't a stick. It was an arrow! When Vaughn inspected it more, he realized it must also be an ancient arrow, still very straight, and its fletching still proper. That was kind of amazing to see such a delicate structure so well preserved. It *seemed* to be made from white feather.

Vaughn looked at the rabbit. "Hmm, I used to love to shoot arrows on the farm. One of my farmer friends trained me. I was, in fact, a pretty good shot." Remembering the battles the Tree of Life showed him in his vision that were fought all over this holy mountain, Vaughn knelt down to dig. "I wonder if I can find an ancient bow, and more of these arrows."

So Vaughn began to dig, and the rabbit moved a good bit away. When Vaughn had moved the soft earth enough to squeeze his body in further, he felt around, found two more arrows, tossed them behind him, then his hand touched upon a different kind of wood, and judging from its curve, Vaughn knew this had to be the bow. He knew he couldn't dig deep enough to pull that out, but perhaps if he just grabbed the end, he could yank the whole bow out cleanly, because, after all, it was a relatively thin piece of wood. But when Vaughn yanked, suddenly the earth opened up underneath him and he fell, for what seemed like quite a ways.

But he landed on the soft earth that had fallen first. Vaughn stood up, brushed himself off, but he could hardly see. He was about to pop himself out from there because it was impossible to climb his way out, but something scurried at his feet which caused him to reflexively jump back out of the way, whereupon he tripped in the dark and fell backwards over onto *something* with a clang, sparks flew, and the next thing Vaughn knew there was light! A torch on the ground had been set ablaze from one of the sparks.

Vaughn shook his head at the oddity then picked it up and began to explore. It was an ancient burial cave like the ones he studied about from school. As Vaughn wandered away from the cave in, he noticed the floor was made of large stone inlay. There were other torches at an entryway into another room and he lit those as well. The room he fell into, had standing coats of armor up against the right wall, with coats of arms in between each armor set.

Vaughn turned around to the opposite wall and it had been carved out into recessed shelves filled with skeletons still clothed in their burial clothes, arms folded across their chests. It looked to be medieval occupants from the knights in shining armor days. The back wall behind him was totally caved in, and opposite to that was a barren wall with the entrance into another room. Vaughn walked up to the sets of armor.

One was holding a sword which Vaughn eased out of an armored glove. "Wow!" The handle was jeweled. Vaughn touched the blade and found it still to have a keen edge. He put both hands upon the hilt and raised it above his head. It had excellent balance. Then he began to swing it around. It occurred to him that this very sword may have killed many people. At that thought, the glitter of the experience waned quickly and for some reason Vaughn replaced it exactly as it had been, with a feeling of respect that came over him.

Giant stone blocks framed the doorway into the next room and immediately on the other side were another pair of torches which he lit. It was another room identical to the first, but this room had doorways to the right and left. Vaughn went to the right and lit the torches on the other side of the wall. Junk had been thrown into this room in a massive pile. The appearance of old crates that had once been stacked upon each other now lay in a desiccated heap, their contents long since degraded and chewed away probably by rats that were now long gone as well.

Vaughn went over to the junk pile which stood taller than him and he pulled out several arrows like the ones he found above. The frills of white feathers at their draw end were still quite functional as well, and the wood the arrows were made from felt like steel. "How did they make these to last so long? What kind of wood would be so hard like this?" Vaughn held the ends of one arrow and tried bending it. It had a slight give then went immediately back to being straight. He eyeballed it end to end like the farmer had taught him. Still straight as an arrow! The arrows were light but had incredible tensile strength.

Vaughn started throwing junk off to each side. Old broken weapons, bricks, bowls, pieces of loose armor. For some reason he wanted more of these arrows. And then something shiny caught his eye, the end of a bow buried in more junk. As he uncovered more, he found it to still be strung! "What kind of material could last this long?" He worked carefully to uncover the whole weapon and pulled out an ornately carved, multi layered instrument with what looked to be inlaid with gold and silver. The bow string shined! "What material is *this*?" Vaughn gave a quick tug to it and it twanged like a sweet musical note. He shook his head, came out of the room, looked at one of the coats of armor against the wall, knocked an arrow, drew, and fired! The arrow sang through the air and hit the chest armor true center where Vaughn had aimed. But what was more surprising was that it went completely through it all!

Vaughn went and examined the arrow. He pulled the armor down off the wall and found the arrow had even gone through the back side and made a hole in the stone! He grabbed the arrow just above its point and pulled the whole shaft through the armor. The arrowhead shined golden. The point didn't even have a single nick in it! "What on Earth are *you* made from?" But not only that, the feathers on the other end showed no sign of damage.

Perhaps it was foolish, but Vaughn suddenly had an urge to find as many of these as he could. It was almost as if the Spirit of God, Himself, was urging him, but he couldn't fathom why, at all. This was like a childhood fantasy of knights in shining armor. Vaughn went back to the junk pile. Eventually, he pulled out a good two dozen arrows. He had moved the entire junk pile except for a pile of armor leaning against the wall. "Well, I might as well move you, too, since, well, I moved all the other junk."

So Vaughn lifted up whole suits of armor that had been stacked upon each other, but then, hanging upon a spike in the wall was what Vaughn had hoped to find, a quiver. He hurriedly climbed over armor suits yet to be moved and lifted it off the wall. Bringing it back close to the torch light, Vaughn turned his head and banged it against the doorway. Dust billowed into the air, but he rapped it a couple more times.

The material was finely woven with a kind of golden thread. The body of the quiver had inlaid crosses, and the bottom was a single piece of . . . something. It felt like cloth, but it also felt metallic. Inside the quiver was not at all what he expected. There was a mesh created, designed to hold the arrows in place! Vaughn took the arrow he had stuck in his belt and dropped it in, point first. The fletching came to just the right height. "How is this going to work?" The arrow points weren't smooth but narrow triangles. But when Vaughn grabbed the hen and pulled the arrow out, it came forth smoothly! Upon further inspection, it wasn't a mesh at all that held the arrows, but full sleeves the length of the quiver! Vaughn held it up to the torch light to try and peer inside. It all looked to be made out of that mysterious fine metallic thread! Vaughn also noted the complete suppleness to the whole thing as he went back and filled the entire quiver with arrows.

Coming out of that room, he went across to the other and as soon as he lit the torches, he was agape. It appeared to be an ancient church! On a pedestal rested a book. As soon as he had entered this room, he felt a presence, a good presence! "All this time! All this time and the Holy Spirit still occupies this place?"

He walked up to the stone pedestal and gently brushed off the book. Inlaid gold and silver crosses adorned it. The book seemed to be made out of the very same material as his quiver! He gently opened it and was surprised to feel the strength to the book. He was expecting it to fall apart in his hand. Far from it. The black letters seemed to be woven into the page, each page made from the same supple quiver material. Vaughn turned to the very first page. The language didn't make sense, though some words seemed familiar.

Vaughn looked around the room, noting it was relatively empty, otherwise. No seats, no other adornments to the walls. "Perhaps that was all taken away, or they just stood or knelt on the floor." Vaughn was about to leave when the corner of his eye picked up on a carved indentation in the back of the pedestal. He knelt down to peer inside, but it was too dark. Not wanting to blindly stick his hand in, only a fool does that, he took a torch from the doorway and held it to the pedestal. There was a small dusty narrow metal bottle. Vaughn reached in and as soon as he touched it, he let go! "This is blessed! *Really blessed!* Lord Jesus, what *is* this?"

Vaughn reached in again, took the bottle and felt *something* from the Holy Spirit move all through him. "It reminds me of something like the Heavenly Light Oil Mafferan gave me and that Stephanie had made. Yet different."

The metal bottle wasn't large, fitting easily into his hand, and ornately ribbed with geometric patterns. The top of the bottle flared a bit just above a narrowed neck. No obvious way to open it. "Should I open it?"

First Vaughn took his sleeve and did his best to clean it up. Again, it was gold and silver, but also with a blue inlay between the ribs. "This is so beautiful." Vaughn placed his fingers on the top and gently twisted. It opened slightly! Looking closer, he saw that a space formed between an obvious cork and the bottle, but you'd never know it was a cork until you tried opening it. Vaughn twisted more and found it was designed with an inlaid spiral groove.

He held the bottle to his nose. "Smells like . . ." he sniffed again, "Olive oil! It's not even rancid!" He put his finger to the top of the bottle and covered it completely. "I don't want to spill any of it, just to wet my finger." He tipped the bottle and as soon as the oil touched him, Vaughn began to pass out. He had just enough semblance to cork the bottle before he sprawled onto his back.

He was in this place but not at this time. There were people running in and out in a commotion while prayers were being prayed. Devout, holy prayers. An older man smiled at the congregants and said, "When we leave, we must seal this place. The Muslims must not find it. This shall be for the time of the end." And he held up the very bottle Vaughn had opened. "As was before Noah, so shall it be again. Take from this place as you must to fight the war but leave this here." And he placed it into the pedestal.

"Have you finished master builder?"

"All is in order, Father,"

"I told you not to call me that. I've never ascribed to titles. It's *what* we are that makes the difference."

Then Vaughn seemed to be in the rooms where he had been. He saw people throwing junk into the one room, but the holy man came out and said, "Give me your quiver and your bow." And a knight said, "Your holiness, this be the demon killers ye blessed." But the man of God said, "There are no more demons to fight. Today you fight men, misguided by demon thought, but mortal men nonetheless."

The knight handed over his bow and quiver full of arrows, and the man of God went to the junk room, hung the quiver where Vaughn had found it, then took the bow and the arrows and threw them one by one into the growing junk pile! A man came up to him and took him by the arm and led him back out into the main room and they turned to face a barren wall. "How does it look?" the man asked the man of God. "Perfect, master builder. Just perfect. And only the perfect will understand."

And then Vaughn came out of his trance. "Dear God. Dear Lord God. Dear Jesus. What does it mean? Why am I here?" Then Vaughn thought, *Demon killers? But I thought there were only Earth demons before Noah.* Vaughn stood up and looked around the main room, again. For the first time he noticed long javelins with large, wicked arrow tips leaned up against one wall. He went over and tried to pick one up but was surprised to feel its heft. He also felt these were blessed as well. *What, in God's Name, could* this *be used for? They certainly can't be thrown by a man.* Vaughn looked around the room again but the only thing that caught his eye was a rope wound up and hanging on the wall next to the giant spears.

He went to inspect the rope, but it didn't feel like a rope. *It's like . . . a giant bow string. My God!* He went back to the javelins and managed to heft one enough to look at its base. *It's nocked! My God!* Vaughn stepped back estimating the length of the cord hanging on the wall, then he stretched out his arms and realized the length to be about three times that width, then he looked back at the javelins. *My God! What were they shooting at?* And the old stories of knights in shining armor came back to him along with . . . dragons! *They were real! Why build all* this *if they weren't? The demons he was referring to were dragons! Fire breathing dragons! Stephanie can shoot fire, even from her mouth! Where did they* really *come from? The holy man of God called them demons!*

A presence descended upon Vaughn, a *very* holy presence, yet distinct from anything he'd experienced before, and he fell to the floor again in a trance.

He was standing on the parapet of a castle. Men were gathered at a large crossbow contraption and two burly men took one of the javelins and loaded it, and three men pulled back the bowstring. A large creature roared past them, breathed fire down into the heart of the castle and the men swung the bow around and fired. They missed! They reloaded. Someone screamed, "They're *coming! Climbing right up the walls!*" Vaughn leaned over the parapet and looked down. Creatures, like the humanoid gargoyles on buildings were climbing right up the stone walls! Archers leaned over and fired their arrows, and every single shot found its mark, and each one slew a creature.

Vaughn came to himself again. *Demon killers!* He sat up, reached behind him and drew an arrow from the quiver and looked more closely at it. He pulled the bow from off his shoulder. *They're the same from my vision!* Vaughn put his head in his hands then rubbed his face fiercely. *Are we going* to have to deal with *fire breathing dragons and . . . and . . . what* were *those things? Gargoyles. Part creature part demon. Oh* Faithwalker, *do you* know *why you are here?* It became increasingly obvious to Vaughn that Stephanie had a far greater role to play than he understood. He also realized that Grinchback was right, Stephanie had to help him fight. *But . . . Michael.* Vaughn's gut turned over at the thought of his unborn child being tainted. *We all swore an oath.*

Vaughn picked himself off the floor again. *Why was the man of God so insistent to bury all this? He was so wise.* Vaughn thought about the way the man of God tossed the arrows on the junk pile and then how more junk was piled high over it. Vaughn looked at his hands, then he pulled out his bottle of Light Oil from his vest pocket and he pulled out the ornate bottle from his other pocket and held them. He went down to his knees but not from another trance. Staring at the bottles, he realized, *Ancient King Mafferan thought of us both so long ago. The man of God placed this oil here for* me! *He threw the arrows like he did so they would appear to be junk but someone like me would have a sense that would draw them to it because they're blessed instruments of war.* He paused and realized the enormity of what he'd just said. *Blessed instruments of war! My wife is helping bring forth* real *holy people! We are in a* Christian *country. No matter their divisions, they could understand the importance of* this! *I have to get back. So much to do and so very little time to do it.*

Vaughn was about to pop back home, but another vision slammed into him and he fell over *again.*

A boy was crawling under the earth. He had the Staff in his hand. After he fell into a larger room, he took a stone from his pocket, felt along the wall, found a torch up against it, and the boy slammed the stone against the wall over and over as sparks flew until the torch finally lit. He took the torch and looked over the room. It was the room Vaughn was in now! But with none of the armor and other things, *except* for the inset ledges where the dead were laid. The boy went over to one of the ledges. The corpses, long dead even for this vision, were wrapped in strips of cloth. The boy seemed to be looking for something, and he put voice to what he'd obviously been told. "Go deep into the Earth, to the Room of the Dead. Touch *none* of them." The boy instantly backed away from the wall. "Go to the oil room." The boy held up his torch, saw the doorway where the pedestal was, and walked in. The pedestal was still there! But no book upon it. Instead, there was a jug. "Take the jug of olive oil and pour it over the Staff."

The boy laid the Staff across the pedestal then took the jug and poured out oil that glowed with a golden light. Then the boy reached for the Staff that was now glowing from the oil, but he was afraid to pick it up again. "Fear not to take up the glowing Staff. You are worthy." The boy took it to himself, got dizzy, then straightened. Hugging the Staff to himself, he left the room. "Go to the room of Life and place the Staff in the hand of the Guardian."

The boy went to a narrow doorway in the back, lit a torch and went inside. It was a circular, small room. The ceiling was dome-shaped and right below the ceiling the whole way around the wall were ancient letters engraved. Upon his entering, the letters glowed. Directly across from the doorway was an image of a robed bearded man carved right into the stone wall with his hand extended as if to hold something. The boy rushed forward, placed the Staff in his hand, and then began to run out but stopped at the doorway. "I forgot." He turned back around, knelt before the Staff and placed his little hand upon it, and prayed. "May you bring joy to the righteous, Justice to the ungodly, and life to the fallen." And the Staff lit up the room like daytime.

The boy bowed his face to the floor then took hold of the Staff again. "Be at Peace until the Day of your Return. The Lord's chosen shall come for you." And the Staff's glow subsided. The boy ran out of the room. The vision ended.

Vaughn sat up from the ground again, looking around for that room, but it no longer existed. He stood up facing the wall where should be a doorway. *The master builder!* Vaughn went over to the wall and placed his hand upon the stone where the doorway should have been. Then he placed his hand upon the wall beside. *They look exactly the same, but they don't feel the same! Something is different.*

Vaughn placed his hands upon the stone where the doorway should be, and the stone began to glow with a golden light. "Lord God, Light from the beginning, and Justice for all, grant that I move these stones even as you gave me strength at the Sacred Cave." And Vaughn leaned into the wall and the large stone moved out of place and crashed into another room!

Vaughn extended the torch inside, leaned in, and lit the torch inside beside the entrance. He then hoisted himself up and through the wall and climbed over the fallen stone. When he stood up, he was in the Sacred Room. The ceiling was glowing from the ancient letters above, and before him, the Staff of Indignation and the Staff of Life, the *same* Staff, glowed before him just as in the vision. And Vaughn fell on his face and wept. "What am *I*, Oh Lord Jesus, that I should behold such things?" And he wept sore because of the meaning that was inundating him. In his heart he had always wanted to bring justice to a corrupt world, but the utter scale and depth of Justice this Staff meant was dwarfing. And yet, it wasn't just justice for justice sake, it was also Justice for Mercy's sake, for a deep love for goodness, for people, and Vaughn wept with all those feelings flooding, swirling, tossing his heart and mind where they willed, and all he could do was weep, not knowing where or when he would settle in his heart and mind. His soul was being rent and its contents spilled *somewhere* and he felt himself pour out in many directions.

And then the visions came again, this time of Moses standing before Pharaoh, King of Egypt, of the ten plagues, of the parting of the Red Sea when Moses lifted up his Staff, visions of *war* where Moses held up the Staff that gave power to the children of Israel to defeat their enemies. It brought forth water from a rock. All these things Vaughn had read about. But then the vision opened up further, to things *not* written in the Holy Scripture. A woman wept over her child who had been wrongfully murdered, and Moses laid his staff across him and he lived again. Out of the desert large beasts crawled up out of the sand like giant fiery scorpions. Moses stood upon a hill and shouted to the fearful people, "Behold the Lord God's wrath against abominations." And He raised his Staff high, and lightning arced from the Staff and blew apart the abominations with great roaring angry thunder.

And the Lord spoke to Vaughn. This was *not* a vision. "All that you see now, *that* shall ye do. Greater works than I have done, shall ye do also! Take the Staff now, my son, and depart, for your people shall shortly need you."

And Vaughn stood up, bow across his shoulder, quiver loaded with holy arrows on his back, and he took the staff in his hand, and as he did so, the statue holding it crumbled to dust! And Vaughn disappeared from the room and materialized back in the bedroom where he had last been with Stephanie, but the room was empty.

CHAPTER 5
A New Judge

Marta was back under the Tree of Life before everyone arrived, and she began right away. "So what you are all saying is, that neither Adam nor Eve were intending to do evil? They both thought they were doing right?"

Aaron, dark brown hair, Earth age thirteen, said, "This is complicated. You had asked what was our first experience, *ever*. We all agreed it was from our hearts, that it was love. Because as infants our minds hadn't formed yet. I think . . . that in their hearts they meant no evil. I think . . . that when Eve was offered the forbidden fruit, her heart felt so alive with love and being able to do something meaningful for Adam! I think . . . feeling alive like that, compared to how miserable she had become, feeling so meaningless, well, I think that made more sense to her than believing the fruit was forbidden."

Elaina, another Earth twelve-year-old, with sandy brown hair, said, "Not exactly. I think when the serpent lied, saying that you won't surely die, Eve's *feelings* were so strong *wanting* it to be true that she could bring something so *important* to the man she loved, that she *confused* the truth of that feeling with what the serpent was saying!"

Marta started clapping, truly excited, and said, "In other words, if her *feelings* were sooo true, then what the serpent was saying had to be true?"

Everyone nodded their heads, and Robert said, "She couldn't bear it *not* to be true! The good feelings she had were like the answer to an unspoken prayer! And besides, what was worse? Eating the fruit because God just didn't want them to grow up too fast or continuing to feel horrible? She didn't understand the meaning of disobeying the Lord."

And Marta looked over everyone, and said, "Consider: Eve's pain wasn't caused by any evil Adam did to her. Her pain wasn't evil either. Neither was her need to be meaningfully fulfilled. Nor her need to be lovingly meaningful to her husband. All these good forces pressed upon her until she felt she would tear apart! And then a seeming solution was offered, and *wanting* an end to her pain, *wanting* to be meaningfully important, feeling the truth of that, allowed her to explain away any infraction against God as the lesser of the troubles she was experiencing, because she *wanted* it to be true! Most people are foolish on Earth, religious or not, when they think that Paradise is or was a place without pain."

Marta grabbed a low hanging branch from the Tree of Life again, and bent it forward then nodded her head for all her students to come close. "You see the buds that are just breaking through?" They all nodded. "You see how at first the new life is scraping and twisting against the dry husk that held the bud back?" They all nodded. "That effort against that which is restricting life's growth is like pain! Yet, the husk was never evil!"

All their eyes widened, until little Carrie chirped up in an a-matter-of-fact tone, "Pain is part of Life!"

It had been a whole Ethereal day until Grinchback's recovery program concluded. As soon as the orb had sent him a signal, he popped back into their secret very dark room. Floating before the orb, Grinchback first pulled up how the recovery proceeded. Amazed, he said to himself, "Who encrypted *this?* Never have I seen such levels of deception."

Grinchback summoned his Master who immediately popped in and silently joined his faithful underling. "Highest Councilor, we look upon this new together."

Surprised Grinchback didn't first look for himself, he gave Grinchback a questioning eye.

Grinchback bowed low, then spoke. "Because I feel that we have entered a time only of Ethereal Legend! Where happenings are moved by power and circumstances far beyond us mere lowly demons. These things only the Father has witnessed, but we know of those things only from legend. This is *not* the time to compete against each other."

The Highest Councilor felt his colors change again. They matched his underling in browns, purples and reds, and their ripples had some strange extra motion to them, and their shimmering began to spark with a different kind of blackness.

They turned to the orb and they began with the earliest of the recovered files.

Karen *demanded* that GrrraGagag meet with her! So a portal opened up right in her bedroom right in front of her and a voice said to step in. And she did! GrrraGagag immediately wrapped her up in his coil but instead of screaming in fear, Karen laughed in disgust. "Fool Demon, I'm worth a thousand of you pathetic worms *alive!*"

Shocked, Master GrrraGagag asked, "And how might that be?"

"Because," she said sweetly, though how she managed *that* under these circumstances, GrrraGagag couldn't figure out. "when you give me all of the power I deserve, we will make *excellent* partners right *here* on Earth!"

GrrraGagag released her and she straightened herself out, her hair and her dress. GrrraGagag explained to her that she was in the Corridor. Karen spoke to him as if they were equals. "Let's start with a list of powers you have to offer!"

"Let's start with what *you,* puny human female, have to offer."

Karen hiked up her skirt a bit to check whether her thigh was bruised. Master GrrraGagag couldn't believe his eye.

Grinchback had to interrupt. "Master, you weren't her first!"

But the Highest Councilor became alarmed over something far more significant. "How is it, GrrraGagag, that you were able to withhold this knowledge from me?" And try as ScrabaGag might, he couldn't force that from the demon he'd consumed! "Grinchback, continue."

GrrraGagag said, "I need you to do things on Earth for me. Your red-headed friend needs *adjusted.*"

"Power first!" Karen chirped.

"The power to read minds, is a good start!"

And that file ended. Grinchback and his Master eyed each other in disbelief. "Master, that means, in all her dealings with us, she *already* knew what manipulations we would be employing!" Grinchback pulled up the next file.

"Next power, *please.*"

"The power to cloud the heart and mind with a mental fog."

"What do you take me for? A push over? I can *see* what you're thinking. More *please.*"

"The power to predict a *bit* of the future. And that's *enough* for now."

Both demons were shaking their bulbous heads. Grinchback pulled up another file.

"Why aren't *you* Highest Councilor. The other one is an *idiot!*"

Highest Councilor ScrabaGag paused the orb. "Are you *sure* you didn't look at this first?"

"Master, I swear on my Eye . . ."

HrorrarrAggrang laughed. "Well, you *are* correct in your assessment. It took a great deal of preparation and planning and patience to get him installed so I had the freedom to do what needed to be done. Are you ready for your next upgrade? You are proceeding exactly according to plan."

Karen nodded and a portal opened, and she walked through. HrorrarrAggrang took his arm and touched her forehead with black oil. Then a drop in each palm. Then he opened his Great Eye wide and Karen stuck her hands in! She turned *black.* Then went back to normal.

HrorrarrAggrang spoke. "The power to travel through the Ethereal and all around. And one more *very* special power." Karen tapped her foot, waiting. "With this, you can create an army of very powerful beings, but unless you have more power than they, they will overcome you."

"I'm not worried about that. What's the power?"

"The power to defile. Any creature or human carrying child, all you have to do is merely hold onto them long enough to concentrate so that our Blackness enters into them in some even infinitesimal way. This leaves no marks, no bruises, and is self-guided with demon intelligence. It's what the Sacred Oil did for you."

Grinchback floated in silence and went sickly but his Master became exuberant. "She might be the solution to our unwanted child Grinchback."

But his underling was poised in mid float thought. Seeing it, his Master waited on him.

Seeing that his Master took the time for him, Grinch-back said, "There has *never* been a demon like you Master. They think you are an idiot because they have absolutely *no* appreciation for advanced, *original,* demon intelligence!" And Grinchback turned his darkest black ever. Seeing this, ScrabaGag knew he wasn't flattering but serious, and waited on his underling to continue.

"Highest Most Deserved Councilor, Karen is a far greater threat to us than even the unwanted child! She is determined to lock us out from the Earth by killing Vaughn and Stephanie. And now that *you've* so graciously bestowed upon her *our* kinship, *she* can consume them! Which means, she no longer needs *us*. We are *her* competition now."

Highest Councilor mulled it over. "Let's look at the last file left."

Karen was in the darkest room of the Father! "Welcome to my humble abode, Queen Karen. I see that you have attained quite a little bit of our power. It suits you."

"And what are *you* going to offer? It appears you have a bit of an orb problem."

"You show me yours and I'll show you mine."

Karen waved her hand and an orb materialized. Her smile was so very sweet.

"May I? And the Father began many different orb manipulations. "It's been a while. I'm a little rusty." He split his tail into innumerable pieces and shoved it into the orb. "How were you ever able to construct this?"

"Well, my husband had obtained quite a bit of your *worthless* orb remnants, but with my superior intelligence and new powers and his powers, it wasn't difficult at all. *This,* however, is the only orb that functions as an orb. The rest of what we do are all weapons. And don't even think about simply taking it! There are, shall I say, safeguards."

"What would you like in exchange?"

"A way to control my flock better,"

The Father laughed. "Earth demons aren't like true Ethereal Alpha with full intellect control. However, I can give you mental power that can make them suffer excruciatingly. You *may* be able to train them, for a while."

They floated in silence a long time. The Father having his *own* orb again changed *everything*. The Highest Councilor whispered. "To our Father, he won't care any longer if our orb system completely crashes. In fact, he very well might desire it."

Grinchback wrapped his tail around his ethereal ears. "Master, speak no more blasphemy, *please.*"

The Highest Councilor patted his underling on the back with his tail. "Under normal circumstances that *would* be quite an error, but not under these. If the Father is the *only* orb possessor, that increases his power to unthinkable levels. And from that one orb, he should be able to grow as many others as he needs. Also, he very much wants Vaughn dead, preferably consumed by him. You were correct in your feelings earlier. We are in the time of Legend."

"Yes Master. Legend."

"Is there any possibility you could infect the Father's orb?"

"We have the files of her orb that we just saw. I can learn a bit from them. I don't know."

"We need to take time to assess everything. This is all extremely complex."

And his Master vanished. No sooner than he did, then Grinchback stuck his arm deep into the orb but he couldn't contact his friend and other Master."

ფ

Vaughn's wedding ring began to glow just as he popped back home. He placed his staff in the corner of the bedroom and the bow and arrow set under the bed then went into the Ethereal Corridor. He was about to soar to where his wife was summoning him when Grinchback materialized and his tail grabbed Vaughn and pulled him back from where he was going. If Vaughn hadn't recognized his touch immediately, it would not have gone well for the demon.

"Master," Grinchback called. "I have some very disturbing news. Please summon the orb here."

Vaughn's ring was glowing brightly, and he looked at it. He waved his hand and summoned the orb, again not realizing that he shouldn't be able to do such a thing. But instead of allowing Grinchback to use the orb, Vaughn pulled up his wife to check on her.

Stephanie and Lynnara were standing in the middle of newly appointed Judge John's office. And he, in his righteous black robe with his white shirt collars neatly protruding, coldly stared at her with his dark eyes. He was flanked by three officers of the court who also looked particularly neat, all with perfectly combed black hair just like the judge! Vaughn wanted to review this from the beginning but was fearful to leave real time. The good Judge leaned forward across his desk, "I don't care what the good Colonel said. He's military, not Judicial. And there are rumors he will be *demoted*, even *court-martialed!*"

Vaughn and Grinchback watched in utter amazement. "What *exactly* are you charging *me* with?"

The good Judge pulled a bunch of letters from his drawer and slammed them down on his desk. "These are from many judges across the land accusing you of interfering in their ministries. They say the supposed *holy* people you've sent to them border on *blasphemy!* But *you* are responsible for their *doctrine.* They've all been taught by *you.*"

"And what would you like me to do?"

"Right now, these gentlemen will escort *you* to the judicial *jail* until we sort this out. Your *adopted* daughter, whom you've been dragging *everywhere,* will be placed in some good home."

Vaughn muttered, "This is Jargono's doing." He turned to Grinchback. "Sorry my friend, I have to go."

But Grinchback restrained him again. "Karen has the power to defile, which means, if she takes hold of your wife for probably no more than a few seconds, your child will be tainted."

Vaughn burst out in full blackness but Grinchback smacked him hard on the back with his tail. "You do that up *here,* you'll have every demon in the Ethereal trying to eat you right now! There's more. Karen has supplied the Father with a brand-new orb *not* on our system."

It took a lot to exceed Vaughn's capacities to multitask, but he was overcome, now. Grinchback continued. "The *Father* has given her at least short-term power to control the Earth demons. For now, I think that's the basics, but you need to come down and spend time reviewing *everything.* Neither I nor the Highest Councilor have any idea how to deal with all this, yet. He *unfortunately* wants your unborn child tainted or destroyed. I tell you this, not because I don't think your child would be a tremendous threat to us, but because he is the *least* of the tremendous threats now facing us *all!* Now go, Master, and do what you think is best."

Vaughn stood there in stunned silence, his mind zipping in many directions at once, unable to follow any of them especially since having the visions he just had. "My friend, I'm not sure yet, either. I'm going to have to play this by ear."

Grinchback's eye rolled upwards trying to decipher the meaning of the phrase as Vaughn disappeared and materialized before the good Judge John, grabbed the man holding Lynnara and threw him across the room into the wall. He then glared at the other two holding his wife's arms and they let go. Little Lynnara looked up at her Daddy, and asked, "What took you so long?"

Vaughn pinched her cheek and smiled.

The Judge glared at him. "Corporal Vaughn . . ."

"That would be *Captain.*"

"That is now under review, *Corporal.*"

Vaughn turned very, very dark. Lynnara shook her head. "Oh, oh, you shouldna made my Daddy angry like that."

Vaughn glanced at her then turned back to the good judge. "I'm going to make this very clear to you. I don't care anymore about my rank, your judges, or your laws!"

Stephanie's eyes widened. "Vaughn, calm down please. You . . ."

Vaughn turned to his wife and glared at her! It was a look and a feeling she'd *never* seen him use before to her, but it *wasn't* anger at her, not exactly. She remembered long ago when he first was angry at her when she had told him she was *nothing,* and that she wasn't worth his trouble saving her. He scolded her then, for her own good, and it very much seemed that is *exactly* what he's doing now. And it did something to Lady Stephanie she'd never experienced quite like this before. She hushed and waited on her husband's decisions! *He seems like . . . such a man now! A very* good *man!*

Vaughn leaned over the desk and hauled the good Judge John up from his seat, over the desk and stood him before him. The judge began to protest, and Vaughn slapped him across the face! The court officers flinched, and Vaughn threw down his left arm, a dagger came into his hand then he threw it and it stuck into the wall between the officers. He then reached out his hand and the same dagger materialled within it! All in a mere second or two.

Stephanie's eyes went wide, Vaughn should *not* have been able to do that, and she peered deeply into him. Little Lynnara began clapping and jumping up and down. She turned to her Mommy triumphantly, and declared, "I've been asking *God Jesus,* if Daddy could be like you, too! Cause it just seemed right, ya know?"

Vaughn didn't hear what his daughter was saying. He pulled the judge close, eye to eye. "Do you see how I just appeared in here out of nowhere?" The judge was being obstinate, and Vaughn saw he needed encouragement. He held out his hand and the Staff of Indignation appeared within it!

Stephanie straightened, immediately realizing its tremendous power from God. Her vision went distant as Father Abraham's blessing zipped through history, found the Staff, and presented it to her heart and mind. Lady Stephanie stared at her husband again and tears overwhelmed her. Not tears of sorrow, but of blessings so powerful all one could do was be overwhelmed by their meaning. Stephanie went down on her knees. "Dear Lord Jesus, what have you made my husband to be?"

A still, small voice caused a terrible thunder in the room. "A *judge!*" And *all* in the room heard it. The court officers all went down upon their knees at hearing God's voice and anointment of Vaughn. Except for John who stood defiantly. Vaughn tossed him back against the desk which caused the man to sit on it.

"Do you recognize this?" he asked John. When he sneered at Vaughn, Vaughn said, "You will." And Vaughn cast it down upon the floor and it became a serpent, a large cobra, actually, that immediately raised itself up to stare into Judge John's eyes that, for some reason, kept widening.

"This Staff is the Lord's indignation against corruption. It was reserved for the end of days and given to *me* by Almighty God. Now, do you understand why I no longer care what you say, what you do?"

The judge slowly nodded, unable to take his eyes from where he didn't want to look. The cobra twitched in his direction and a puddle appeared at the judges feet. Lynna said to the other men, "Oh, he's *really* scared." And she walked up to the cobra and began petting its back! "Oh, he's really very soft, Mommy!" Even Stephanie's eyes were wide, not used to spiritual things exceeding her grasp.

Vaughn took the serpent by the tail and it became his staff again. "Now. How long do you think it would take me to visit the thousand or so judges you have in the country at your level? How long to cast this Staff and have it judge each and every one *today!* I think a single minute for each would do. And *that* would mean that in about sixteen hours *most* of you would be *dead!* The understudies who would witness all this would quickly all approve of me to be *Supreme Judge!* In other words, how long do you think it would take me to even be in charge of *you? Your family. Everything you have!*"

Good Judge John's eyes went wide again, for he knew the truth of it. But he just had to rebel. "Is *that* how you would rule us, through *intimidation?*"

And when Lady Stephanie heard *that,* having just been intimidated, well, she kind of lost control. Turning darker than ever before, she held out her hand toward the good judge and then they both disappeared! Little Lynnara threw her hands to her mouth, her eyes widened. "Oh, oh!"

Stephanie appeared between two rows of trees in the Dead Forest, and called, "Grinchback! And moments later he appeared. When he saw Lady Stephanie holding another judge, his eye immediately began to drool. He bounced up and down, saying, "Oh, and you're working as a team now. And you play with my food so well!"

Stephanie smiled at the very demon who had tried to eat her and her daughter before and steal the Seed to the Tree of Life. "Grinchback, give voice to the good old Judge Matthew so *he,*" she shook him, "can hear the truth."

Grinchback bowed to her, "As you wish, Lady Stephanie." Grinchback pulled back a flap from his belly and Judge Matthew's disheveled head of black hair poked out. Judge John went to his knees. Grinchback merely said, "Confess." And Judge Matthew began to spew forth all he had done to Lady Stephanie.

She grabbed John by his righteous black robe and hauled him to stand before her. "You have the *audacity* to accuse *my husband* of intimidation? You, Sir, confuse evil force, which you seem accustomed to, with very righteous God-given *anger*. Grinchback, lick his soul!"

And she threw the good judge to the gray dead Forest ground before the demon.

"Oh, with pleasurrrrre." And Grinchback's Great Eye grazed over him and he howled in torment. "Is there anything else you need from me Lady Stephanie?"

"I think that will do for now." She held out her hand to return the judge and her back home but Grinchback asked her, "Have you spoken with your husband yet?" The question struck her as odd, and Grinchback perceived that she hadn't. "Speak to him right away. The fate of *everything* depends upon it!" And he vanished. Astounded, Lady Stephanie returned.

And tossed the good judge at her husband's feet. "Judge him, Judge Vaughn!"

Vaughn's eyebrows rose, then looked at John. "Do you have a better understanding, now, good judge? Our whole country is being set up. *King* Jargono has maneuvered all of this to destroy our defenses." Vaughn knelt down eye to eye and spoke softly. "I need to know if you sincerely understand what's at stake here. I'll know, we *all* will, *especially* her," and he pointed to Lynnara who clapped her hands again, and said, "If you're telling the *truth*!"

Judge John nodded. "Forgive me," and he sprawled himself on the floor.

Little Lynnara knelt down by his head and put her little hand on it. "You're forgiven Judge John. Now you have to help us beat all the bad men."

In one way, he felt strange that the little girl he was about to send to an orphanage just pronounced forgiveness over him. But then again, he knew what he felt, truly repentant, and he knew what her touch carried with it, God's forgiveness. He lifted his eyes up into hers, and said, "Forgive me, little angel. I have been worse than a fool."

She sat down so that his head was even with hers and threw her little arms around him. "Oh, I've seen *far* worse than *you!* I forgive you."

John stood up and brushed a few tears from his eyes. "What would you have us to do?"

Vaughn instructed him. "Take the surveillance you have of this whole encounter and put it on national news in one hour!"

Stephanie, again, was amazed. *My God, he's become even wiser!*

John bowed his head to Vaughn, "It shall be done, Judge Vaughn."

Stephanie and Vaughn both turned to each other, saying, "We need to talk, *now!*"

CHAPTER 6

We Are *Men*

Marta, standing under the Tree of Life, nevertheless leveled her eyes into all her students. "Now we have to consider what Adam felt when Eve brought the forbidden fruit to him. As we discovered about Eve, that she really wasn't this horrible person that we were naively taught back on Earth, might that *also* be true of Adam?"

The question stunned the children. Even up in Heaven they had carried up the belief that their very first father was a complete disgraceful failure, though they had no right to condemn him. They all sat in dumb silence unable to consider further.

"How did Adam feel towards his wife?"

They all shouted out, "He loved her."

"How much?'

It was an odd question, especially to children, they all thought. *How much? There is a 'much' to it?*

"How did Adam feel *before* the Lord made Eve?"

The children whispered amongst themselves, again. They knew it was written that God said it was not good that man should be alone but that didn't really tell them what they wanted to know. How did Adam feel being alone? It must have been a *really* long time because he named everything *before* Eve was made. They tried to imagine naming *everything,* and seeing every animal having a mate. And they imagined how wonderful everything must have felt, all being so new and perfect.

Marta asked, "When you first came up here, and saw how everything was, what was the *first* thing you wanted to do?"

Carrie said, "Oh, I kept saying, 'Look at *that.* Do you see *that?"*

"To someone else?"

"Well, yea. My guide."

"Now imagine feeling like that for a *very* long time but with *no one* to share your joy, your *meaning!"*

Jane, with black very curly hair, and Earth age of ten, said, "Oh, I would feel *terrible.* I can't imagine it."

After a bit more imagining, all the children agreed. Marta asked, "Now children, how much did Adam love Eve?"

This time they all shouted out various answers on the same theme, "Oh, *really* a lot, So *very* much."

And Marta said, "Now, for our next lesson, What did Adam *feel* when his beloved wife brought him the forbidden fruit?"

In a mere two hours, Vaughn had managed to set the whole country back on track. Judge Asa sent him a message thanking Vaughn for proving that Asa's faith in him was entirely justified. The Supreme Judge of the land dually gave Vaughn an official Judge's title of, believe it or not, *Senior Judge*- a select group second only to the Supreme! This wasn't honorary. It was the real thing. So he was *Captain* Judge

Vaughn, or *Judge* Captain Vaughn. He wasn't sure which, but now wasn't the time to think on it.

Back home, when Vaughn had finished explaining everything to his wife, she first grabbed him and kissed him passionately. Then she said she'd gather all the holy people together with only a request for two tasks for now. Baptize and make blessed weapons! But she also sent a message that she *demanded* that all the judges appear before her at six this evening, outside where she had her wedding. Many said that was *impossible,* but Stephanie retorted that with God, *all* good things are possible, *especially* for a *faithwalker.* It bordered on a threat that they scoffed at within themselves.

Still sitting on their posh living room couch provided to them by the judge's quarters which Vaughn, now, was even more entitled to than Honorary Judge Stephanie, she told her husband, "I am going to straighten them *all* out this evening. You showed me what to do!"

"*I* did?"

"Yes. I've been so gentle with them, careful not to step on their free will, meanwhile Jargono laughs and uses all kinds of force and manipulation. No wonder we can't seem to win. But righteous anger, though forceful, isn't the same thing as using evil force. Righteous anger stated with the truth, 'You've *messed up,* and here are the consequences, and here are the righteous judgments. Reality is, what Reality is. The Day of Judgement is at hand!' That will have quite an affect."

"I couldn't have put it into better words. I was afraid you were going to feed the good judge to Grinchback."

Stephanie burst out laughing. Wiping tears away, she said, "I really considered it, but I remembered the consequences of our actions when we took justice into our own hands. Grinchback was certainly *hoping* . . ." And she burst into laughing with tears again. "You should have seen his Great Eye drool . . ." She was doubled over now. "But under such *encouragement* of righteous anger, he repented, *sincerely* repented."

"I *have to* go to Jargono this evening, while you're speaking to the nation. I don't know that Karen has brought about the beasts I described, but my gut tells me she has, because I wasn't shown all that vision for nothing. It may even be too much for all of us to handle."

"But what are you going to say to him?"

"The truth, and that, maybe, no promises, maybe we can save his wife from the terrible destruction she's wrought upon herself. But I sincerely doubt it possible. The thing is, it won't be us that destroys her, it will be by her own hand, or by Jargono."

Stephanie sat a while just repeatedly shaking her head but decided to focus on the immediate tactical implications. "It's strange to say, but in a way, Karen grounded him. Without her, he's alone. And he really doesn't know how to handle that! But I guess that's the best we can do."

Vaughn took out the ornate bottle of blessed holy oil and handed it to his wife. "What do you think of that?"

"So this is what you told me of, waiting just for you, but from even a different time period than Moses staff." Stephanie held it a while, meditating on it. "My God." She uncorked it and took the tiniest bit onto her finger and began to pass out. Vaughn grabbed the bottle before it spilt.

"*Wheh!*" she said a moment later. "Vaughn, this was produced by *very holy* people. It's surprising because look at all the ancient holy people we've been around. Why should this exceed them?"

Vaughn nodded slowly, corking the bottle again and putting it back into his other vest pocket. "I asked myself the same question. But when I had the visions of all those ungodly creatures, and fire-breathing dragons, and all the folklore suddenly became real, well, I realized that during that time good people were being severely assaulted by evil on a grand scale even we haven't encountered! It really is the stuff of legends. And so, I feel that God responded with increasing power and blessing, which that oil is only a small part of!"

Lady Stephanie nodded in agreement. "Vaughn, something we haven't done in a while, and I don't know when we'll get a chance again." She held out her hand, glowing softly.

"My Queen," Vaughn said, bowed to her, then scooped her up out of the couch and into his arms and she purred while she kissed him. His increased righteousness and holiness made her desire him all the more.

Arm in arm they lay together, their eyes lost in each other's hearts, feeling the oneness of life on every level. "Vaughn, every day I feel little Michael become more and more, well, not more of a person because he's already been a full person for a while, but his little goodness keeps on growing and I love it so." Then Stephanie began to laugh as she pulled away and looked under the covers. "Vaughn, look!"

He ducked under the covers, kissed her tummy, and said, "Yea, you're definitely showing now."

She hit him on the back, hard! "Vaughn, I mean my tummy is *glowing*. You don't really notice with clothes covering it. Can't you see the glow?"

He popped back up and kissed her deeply. "Of course I can see it, and feel it. And, believe it or not, because *you're* carrying the child and not me, but in a way, I can actually feel Michael in my gut!"

"Stupid, you don't know your biology. The child isn't in the *gut.*" She laughed at him. "But I know what you mean. You know, my tummy glow, that's actually Michael."

"I know, my love. I know. That oil that made you pass out. I think it's special for war!"

"My God! I hadn't thought of it like that."

"My question to you is this, Do you think you can reproduce it?"

Stephanie studied Vaughn. He still hadn't realized what new gifts he had. "Did you hear what our daughter said about you when we were, ahh, helping the good judge?" He shook his head. "She said she prayed for you to be like me because it just seemed right."

Vaughn laughed. "Well, that really sounds like our daughter."

But Stephanie saw he still wasn't realizing, so she listed off all the things they saw him do. "The main quality that

Lynnara and I saw was that when a thing just seems necessary to do, you simply do it in perfect faith. You, my darling husband are becoming a *faithwalker,* too! Because of your new daughter's simple but true prayer! And I think, I can't reproduce that oil, because I'm not really a warrior of that kind. But *you* are. You can reproduce it and that's why it was handed down to *you.* That much I *am* sure about with all my being."

Vaughn laid there staring up at the ceiling as his wife's words flooded him. "Wow! And I just did all that without even giving it a second thought. And you're right. That's *exactly* how I feel when I do what I do. And I also think you're very right about the oil and the difference between us. Look at the holy mountain of life God brought forth through you. It's so beautiful. Even though God did bring some of His vengeance through you at the Appendaho village, it was really me that did most of the killing. I think your center is Life and Love, and mine is Justice."

Stephanie laughed at him, grabbed the back of his head and kissed him passionately. "Oh my dear, you so underestimate yourself. You are Justice for sure, God made that clear. But you're Love is even stronger than mine! And so is Wisdom with you. God has blessed me with Peace and Understanding. But He's blessed you with another part of Understanding that I have much less of."

Vaughn smiled his special smile, and it melted her heart. "Are you trying to say, Lady Stephanie, that we're simply perfect for each other."

"I am indeed. And we are raising the perfect family. Can you *believe* that Vaughn? After *all* we grew up with, all the horribleness. Look at us now! Dear Lord God, what have you done for us?" And the babe leapt for joy in Stephanie's womb. "Ohh," she blurted out when she felt it.

The alarm clock rang, and Vaughn slammed his hand down on it and crushed it. Stephanie scolded him, "*Vaughn, How many times do I have to tell you to be gentle?* She waved her hand *again* and the clock was restored. "I think you do that on purpose. Just so you can see me *fix* it."

He hopped out of bed and went to the shower. Sticking his head back through the doorway, he said, "I do." And she through a pillow at him but he closed the door and it bounced off.

☙

From the Ethereal Corridor, Vaughn studied the new palace Jargono now lived in. It was a mixture of Appendaho simplicity and a touch of just about every culture on Earth and in history. But far from looking maniacal or chaotic, he blended it all into wonderful, balanced beauty. Vaughn was completely impressed. He looked at his regular brown ranger uniform with lots of pockets that he loved to wear even more than his black officer's garb and felt he should be wearing at least his officer's garments before he entered Jargono's palace, but he dare not try to use his new faith-walking abilities to change. *Well, the ranger's uniform has more* meaning, *and, after all, Jargono is a faithwalker where meaning is* everything.

Vaughn continued to explore. There was some marble work, but wood trims and engravings were spread through each room, of which were many. The bathrooms were all marble and pure gold. The kitchens had old fashioned grills in their centers, but modern appliances and stoves in the corners. The bedrooms were simply royal with purple velvets and lots of other soft stuff. Karen's wing was heavily protected against intruders via various spiritual alarms and traps, all of which Vaughn discovered and was sure there were other more slyly placed devices that he really didn't care to search out.

Vaughn found Jargono in a reclining room softly playing the piano of what Vaughn believed to be a melody of his own creation. King Jargono sat in utter concentration but only dressed in his usual Appendaho brown tunic, tan shirt, and pants. His medium length straight black hair was also, as usual, combed straight back. His jawline seemed even more accentuated from his emotional involvement in his music. Vaughn doublechecked to make sure it was safe to pop in right here but Jargono had zero defensive devices anywhere because Vaughn was sure he didn't need any.

He materialized beside him, leaning on the piano, just listening and truly enjoying the melody. When Jargono finally stopped, Vaughn couldn't help saying, "Bravo, bravo, truly inspiring." And he wiped a tear from his eye!

Jargono saw his truthfulness and nodded to him. And Vaughn said, "Your palace is also impressive, I really love the way you've melded the artistry of so many styles."

Jargono stared at Vaughn. *He's grown up! And he's got much more power than I ever thought he would have, and even more than I can wrap my mind around.* "You've become quite impressive yourself, Vaughn. Would you like some wine or food?"

"Don't mind if I do."

Jargono sent a telepathic message to his servants. "About an hour. Is that OK?"

Vaughn leveled his eyes into Jargono's, who had the same rich brown color as Stephanie, and Jargono met his stare and grew concerned. "Will we have an appetite after you're done speaking?"

"I don't know. But I think we've reached a certain maturity that would have us enjoy the basics in life in spite of the heartbreak!"

"Heartbreak." Jargono repeated, because being Appendaho, he knew Vaughn wasn't just speaking about himself.

Vaughn waved his hand and the blue orb appeared before them. *That* Jargono didn't expect *at all*. He motioned Vaughn to come over to two black leather easy chairs and Vaughn took the other and positioned the orb where they both could see. Vaughn waved his hand and showed Jargono files on the earth demons, then paused and waited for his response.

Jargono sighed, as many odd things came to his mind. "Those *have to* be destroyed."

But Vaughn replied, "I agree, but I wouldn't go rushing off quite yet." Vaughn handed him Trevor's paper with the coordinates. Jargono nodded, committed it to memory then handed the paper back. "Jargono, there's much more than this. Much more. You need prepare yourself. This is going to hurt badly."

Jargono stared into Vaughn's eyes and sighed. He had detected things about his wife that he just didn't want to believe. "This is ingenious, you bringing this orb to show me. Just you telling me would allow me room to deny reality. *This,* I can't deny. And I thank you for your compassion. Get on with it."

Vaughn showed him first the non-secret files of Karen which included the Highest Councilor *mating* with his wife. At those scenes the whole palace shook. Then Vaughn showed him the secret files including the Father below giving her power to control the Earth demons in exchange for the orb.

"Is *that* it? All of it?"

Dinner arrived and was laid out on a table over against a bay window overlooking a peaceful pond. Vaughn raised his eyebrows and Jargono waived him over to the table.

They ate in silence, then ordered exotic dessert, and while they waited, Jargono said, "You're right. I hate to admit it, but my wife has taken enough advantage over everyone that she has amassed more power than even I can deal with! And it has to be dealt with soon."

But Vaughn still wasn't done. "I'm going to tell you some things that are true, but you'll find it hard to believe. But I need to tell you everything, because it's the *context* that perhaps will convince you that the threat is even ten times *worse* than you perceive now!"

"Now I think you may be spoiling dessert. Let's eat that first."

Jargono had a multilayered pastry with various fillings in every third or so layer, while Vaughn was straight up with the strawberry-rhubarb pie with ice cream. Jargono tried to convince him of something more worthy of his chiefs but Vaughn said there was something important about appreciating simplicity, too. So they swapped tastes of each other's desserts and both savored the new experience.

Then Vaughn explained to Jargono all about his visions and the holy mountain. For some reason, Vaughn worried over none of this because he knew even Jargono would be denied entry into *that* mountain. After he explained his visions, he looked up and met Jargono's eyes to see if he had any inkling of what would be said next.

Jargono said, "I see how you and Stephanie are perfect for each other. You *both* make me think very deeply. But I can't help but feel you haven't made your point even yet. Your point making has become quite famous to me. Proceed."

It was a very Kingly order, Vaughn noticed, from authority, but Vaughn had no trouble respecting it. "I think your wife has also created those kinds of creatures from my visions. I have no evidence of that. But I believe she conceals them from everyone."

Jargono laughed. "Fire-breathing dragons? Gargoyles?"

Vaughn leaned across the table, looked him dead in the eyes, and said, "Yes."

It unsettled Jargono and he let it show. He *never* purposefully let anything like that show, but more and more Jargono began to see Vaughn as close to being equal, and Vaughn had no trouble at all bearing *his* heart and *his* vulnerability. And it took a lot of courage even just to come here.

"Alright. I'm going to do something I've *never* done before. I believe you just because you told me! You're very different from your wife, though I have to confess there was time where I have to admit I loved her, too."

"I know it. It was obvious to us. And actually, Stephanie never meant to hurt your feelings so! She did her level best to reach you with the best that she had. So much so, that I had been convinced that she had actually fallen for you! Think about it!"

And he did. He remembered Stephanie's conversation with him about power while coming into the Appendaho valley. He had poo pooed it in favor of grander things. And then he realized that the deep connection Vaughn had with her even then, would have had him perceive Stephanie's attempts to influence Jargono for the realness they actually were. They *were* loving, truly loving.

Jargono nodded, and a part of him actually seemed to heal! "I want to thank you for that. You *have* brought me understanding. I see that your wife *didn't* betray me at all. She gave it her best shot, even convinced you, I remember that, but it just wasn't for me. I'm sorry now, for how I treated her. It was immature to say the least. Unnecessarily cruel. I'm glad you brought me to this, because we're all going to have to fight together against this evil. And even then, I have to say, we may not win!"

Vaughn knew Jargono was being sincere. "There's one more thing I want you to consider." And Vaughn told him how Stephanie had actually healed Karen before and he told him why, that they were scared of what he would do if she died. He nodded to the truth of it. But then Vaughn told him that they would also do their level best to save his wife! No guarantees, and Vaughn wanted to know if Jargono had any thoughts of how he might contribute to the effort!

Jargono was truly overcome, and he got up and walked away. He even brushed a few tears from his eyes. Vaughn got up, too, and followed him and put his hand on Jargono's shoulder, and said, "No matter how angry you are at her, but you have to admit, though, if respect is going after power, she did that perfectly. But as my wife tried to challenge your understanding before, power is only as good as the desires that drive it!"

He turned to Vaughn, then, with a faraway look, recalling what Stephanie had said and how he got flustered and just ended the conversation. She had bested him there, and he now saw that it was for good reason. "Had I listened more closely to your wife back then, I probably could have helped prevent my own wife from being trapped the way she is now."

Vaughn said, "No matter how angry you are at her now, and for *very* good reason, she is still your true wife. Jargono," Vaugh took his shoulder again, "We are *men!* We are responsible to do our level best for the women we love *even* when they hurt us and screw themselves up! Forgive her!"

Jargono laughed. "Now *that* I'll really have to think about. And I'm telling you now. She's headstrong beyond anyone here, down below, or up there. She won't want any of our help."

Vaughn simply said, "I won't be asking!"

Jargono was truly surprised now. Had Vaughn become like him? "Forcing her against her will? I thought that was against your ethics, Stephanie, too"

"As far as I'm concerned, it's not against my values if the help I give her is a *consequence* of the actions I have to take to prevent her from destroying everything including herself. A very real solution to that is simply finding a way to redeem her! I *will* attack her against her will because she is my enemy, my wife's mortal enemy, but even my wife would agree with what I'm saying and would help! It would be extremely difficult for Stephanie, but I know her!"

Jargono sat down in amazement but was even more surprised that he let it show. Jargono sighed. "For now, our little war is on hold. It's inevitable that I *will* rule the world. You understand that. But first, we have to *have* a world to rule. If Karen succeeds, we won't." Then Jargono took a long pause before resuming. His demeanor clearly strained, he asked, "How would you ever, could you ever figure a way to reverse what the Ethereal demons have done to her? Her blood is black now. I dare not even mate with her anymore, though I'm sure that's why she's been avoiding it, afraid I would discover her *secret*, and that her taint wouldn't work on me."

Vaughn replied honestly, "That's far more Lady Stephanie's department than mine. But if *anyone* could create a solution for this where there is none, it's her! Did you know she's the one majorly responsible for turning the Black River into stone?"

Jargono said he'd heard rumors, so Vaughn told him the story. Afterward he sat in amazement, again. "She totally altered reality? I mean *basic* reality."

"Yes."

"Because it didn't make sense."

"Yes."

"To *her.*"

"Not just to her, but to True Meaning, to God, if you will. Otherwise, it wouldn't have worked."

"I think I understand." Jargono rubbed his smooth chin. "We need to spy out my wife and truly find out what we're up against. Normally I would say let's divide up the task. But this time, I don't think it wise. You obviously can travel. Are up to it?" Vaughn nodded. "Go home and explain *everything* to Stephanie so she understands clearly that I will *not* harm any of you through *all* this ordeal, and I'll even give you a month afterward so you won't feel that the moment we win, *if* we win, that I would immediately attack you."

Vaughn nodded and disappeared.

CHAPTER 7

Out of The Many, One True Christianity

This time Marta was *behind* the Tree of Life where they could barely see just a bit of her. "What did Adam *feel* when his beloved wife brought him the forbidden fruit?"

Ralph spoke up right away. "I would have been really scared."

Marta asked, "Had Adam ever had such a feeling before?"

It dawned on them all that he didn't, and then how difficult it must have been to experience fear for the very first time! They tried to imagine it and shivered and squirmed. "Teacher Marta," Samuel, a twelve-year-old with dark brown hair, said, "I think I speak for everyone when I say we're all overwhelmed with this!"

Marta suddenly stepped out from behind the Tree and rushed right up close to the class. "In the very back of their minds, when the Lord had told them *not* to touch nor eat the forbidden fruit lest they die, way back in their heats they felt fear just from the thought of it, and from a meaning they had yet to understand or even consider, because the *meaning* was real. But when Eve brought the forbidden fruit right up to Adam, just like I rushed out from behind the Tree right up close to you and confronted you with this issue, the secret dread that had been silently growing in Adam, *begging* him to pay attention and understand, well, it smacked him across the head and heart, so to speak, so hard the pain numbed him, actually froze him! What did he see in Eve at that very *first* moment?"

No one wanted to imagine it, but Marta knew they needed to, so she said, "You see how you all feel now? Well, multiply that feeling infinitely but this *is* something you *must* look past. I require a clear, understanding answer from you at the next lesson!" And she vanished! They had never been put on the spot like that since they arrived, and they all began to fidget, none leaving, though class had been dismissed.

At five minutes to six in the evening Lady Stephanie climbed onto the stage which was about seven feet up off the ground and twenty feet wide and fourteen feet deep with steps at each end. A plain podium set eight feet back from the front and dead center. Before it, lay a wide-open area with neatly mowed grass, now filled with rows upon rows of folding chairs. Not the most comfortable seats for any long ordeals, but being *uncomfortable* was part of Lady Stephanie's message. Actually, a lot of discomfort!

Lady Stephanie had asked her people to sit in the back because she wanted all the judges to be as close as possible. What she planned to do had been in the works for a long time. She'd spent many an hour in the Ethereal Corridor spying on Judges all across the land. She was privy to many of their secrets, their various doctrines that gave them distinction, their lusts and greed, but also their true desires to help. In fact, most sincerely wanted to be good judges, but most simply walked in the rut already dug by those before them.

For this occasion, she left her holy dress at home because Vaughn had taught her something by what he did earlier. At first her mouth dropped open when he popped into Judge John's office and threw the man holding Lynnara across the room. She'd thought he'd relapsed to his old ways. *I need to watch that. I have to have unwavering faith in him. I just have to or there's no way we make it out of all this alive. I really have no idea how we escape what's coming.*

Yes, she left her holy dress at home and even her holy ribbon, and her red hair wasn't in braids but hanging free in all its luxurious luster, fullness, and vitality. Brushed to perfection, its shiny, slightly wavey, deep red screamed *power!* A fitting look this evening for the *faithwalker.*

At Six PM sharp, there were only a few judges present, those that are very local, and they kept their heads down and tried very hard to hide their thoughts. The national news media and every other news source panned the rows upon rows of empty seats. Stephanie knew many who were supposed to be there were watching this on the TV.

It's not that they didn't respect her, she knew that. They just didn't want her to interfere in what they were safely used to. In fact, she made good sense to many of them when she'd taken the time to personally discuss many issues, popping in on them unannounced and turning a routine, dull hour into something downright inspiring. Still, routine *must* rule the day. It's just the way things are done. But Stephanie knew the demons *loved* routine. In fact, Vaughn had shared with her just how the Ethereal demons tainted both Jargono and Karen before they were even born using their mother's routines for opportunity. It almost made her paranoid.

Yes, no holy dress this evening. For this occasion, black seemed proper. Black with white embroidery. *Black and white. It's that clear, because gray belongs to the demons. I have to make them understand that.*

At Six O'clock and One Minute Past Stephanie picked up her head and the camera's all focused narrowly upon her. There was fire in her eyes mingled with a deep blackness that radiated outward. The fire did *not* radiate. It stayed within her. The feeling *that* generated made the cameramen fidgety. They were used to her love, not . . . whatever that black energy was.

In fact, the country had begun to get used to her various energy displays. There were even a lot of kids' clubs sprouting up listing and categorizing everything they knew about their beloved heroes and trying their best to explain the different energies and their meanings. It's rumored there's even a card game in the works.

Lady Stephanie briefly stared silently into the cameras. Her other major concern was just how fast with extreme cruelty everything almost fell apart. And *that's* also why she was going to approach this in a new way for her. It's what she learned from Vaughn. She bowed her head and the skies immediately darkened. Great dark clouds roiled above and thunder rolled down and shook everything and everyone to their core. That sound even permeated through the television. A lot of folks thanked God they weren't *there.*

Lady Stephanie lifted up her voice and stretched out her arms wide, as she looked up into Heaven. "Holy Father, Supreme Judge of all. You alone know what we face, the evil in so many forms and fashion that seeks to destroy us and our beloved country. Oh Lord God, I come before you knowing I am but a very small person. To many, they think that I have power, but You know that *I know* that the only True power is in pure goodness. Without Goodness, all of our efforts, whether they be from the simple farmer, the shop keeper, the street vendor, a plumber, a doctor, a lawyer, a *judge,* or even a *faithwalker,* all our efforts will die the death of corruption and come to shame and naught."

All the people across the country said, "Amen," before they even thought about it.

"Holy Father, these are *troubled* times. Just earlier today I, even I, whom You have proven *multiple* times before this country," she paused as lightning suddenly erupted, streaking across the sky with earsplitting thunder that couldn't help but cause fright in all, "Just earlier today I, even I, whom You have proven *multiple* times before the country, was arrested by the local judge here, and they were going to *steal my daughter.*" The lightning crashed into trees and blew them apart. It struck the ground around the meeting area with explosions that created deep holes. When the cameras panned it, everyone watching their TV's shifted uncomfortably and swallowed. *This is new for her,* was the common thought.

"*Almighty God,* our Father Ancient Abraham came and blessed me with knowledge of his children." Everyone looked at each other when they heard *that.* It added to Lady Stephanie the kind of authority coming from the *Old Testament!* "When Moses saved his people from bondage, instead of being grateful, they were *stiff-necked,*" A tornado began to form above. "They were *hardhearted,*" Several more tornados began to form and the wind picked up. "And they were *rebellious.*" Suddenly everything went dead silent! The kind of stillness that is difficult for many to tolerate. The kind of stoppage of time that proceeds before great judgements from above. Many people suddenly found themselves kneeling before their televisions without even thinking about it. It was true the country had just turned *again* against the heroes God had sent them.

"Therefore, *Lord God,* who *is* the Lord Jesus Christ, who has been given by the Father Almighty God *Judgement* over all, and to bring *again* upon the Earth your mighty signs and wonders with plagues and all forms of Judgement, I beg you to answer my prayer *now,* so that this country *not* walk in the ways of those you forbade to enter the Promised Land, grant me *now* my prayer!" And she paused and looked again into the camera, the blackness coming out from around her in waves.

What's she going to ask? was the common fear. "Bring all the Judges I have requested, *here. Now!*" A dark cloud descended upon the podium, the whole venue, and over all the media. All TV's saw only dark black sets and their prayers became fervent. Then a gentle wind came and blew the cloud away and the whole courtyard was filled with judges! Some with food in their hands, many in just their standard white shirt and black pants, some even naked, and many still in their righteous black robes and it looked like they had been deposited just above the seats they were supposed to occupy but then fell over them!

The camera's panned the confusion, the sound of a great commotion filled the television sets as everyone shook and tried to right their seats and sit in them. Some of the judges pulled off their robes to cover the naked.

And Lady Stephanie came out from behind the podium and stood at the edge of the stage with her hands folded behind her back, the wind gently blowing through her hair, staring at them all. Then she motioned with her hands down the length of her new dress. "Do you like it?" she asked the crowd? Everyone looked at each other. Many nodded in fear without thinking, while others seriously appraised it, saying, "It's very cute, fashionable." But others, who understood the *faithwalker,* knew the question had a much deeper meaning.

"It's black and white. *Mostly black.*" And it thundered again out of the stillness. "Like your righteous black robes, the deep black signifies *Justice.*" Lightning erupted again blowing more trees apart and gouging great holes in the earth in the field that surrounded them. Children wrote down in their notepads: *Black is for Justice.*

"The white embroidery is the structure of goodness we are supposed to weave into our lives. See how beautiful it is?" And she acted like a fashion model slowly motioning toward her dress with her hands again. "Did you know that white light contains the colors of the rainbow and everything in between? So much goodness!" Many people felt they were beginning to understand this wonderful analogy. Children wrote in their notepads: *White is for Goodness: contains all her other powers. Gold for Love, Blue for Truth . . . but Red is another kind of Love . . .* They thought about the difference.

"But the white embroidery is fully surrounded by *Justice.*" Everyone expected it to thunder again and they braced for the impact but no thunder came. "The divisions in our country within Christianity have to *end!*" Again, when she emphasized her last word, they expected thunder, they flinched, but no thunder came. They all heard the word, *END,* echo in their hearts and minds.

She held out her hand and a pile of letters appeared in them, and now the thunder roared. When the rumbling drifted away, a calm came again. One by one, Stephanie described the main point of each letter as she crumpled each up, through it in the air, and it burst into flames! "*This* is from the *Prophets* for Christ." She glared at the crowd, making sure they understood her anger. "*This* from the *Resurrected* for Christ!" Again, that same glare, and everyone began shifting in their chairs almost as if they were looking for a place to hide. Even all the followers of all these different churches felt the unease which grew as another crumpled letter was tossed in the air and burst into flames.

"*This* is from the *Undivided* for Christ." Then Lady Stephanie, *Honorary Judge* Stephanie, held out her hands and a large box appeared in them. She then tossed the box way up into the air, it turned over, spilled out innumerable letters, and they all burst into flames. "This is *absurd.*"

"All wanting me to endorse them as the *true* way, and all claiming their *particular* judge is . . . I don't know . . . something *special.* I had no idea Christianity was so fraction-ated. When we came here, I thought, 'OK, it's a Christian country,' but I had no idea that word *Christian* didn't mean *one* Christian, and I thought that after we became national with our meaning, our purpose, our life stories, that . . ."

Lady Stephanie began to weep when she said 'our life stories! All her and her husband's suffering to try to bring goodness to people flooded her, along with how hard the people made it. She hid her face in her hands. Then with her eyes blazing with golden glow, she stretched forth her arms wide, and said, "Why don't you just crucify me now, and get it over with?" And she waved her hand and a great cross appeared on stage. And she waved her arm bruskly and everything around went dark, a blackness that could be seen, a blackness that could be felt, and it made everyone feel like they were being suffocated. And then the cross lit up with glow and Lady Stephanie appeared on that cross, crucified, brutalized, and dying!

Everyone was aghast. *Is that* really *her?* Guilt slammed into them as all across the country their sins claimed them. *They* didn't actually crucify her but it *felt like they did!* Prayers began to be prayed, and people began to wail, "Forgive us. Lord Jesus, forgive us. Don't let her die. Forgive us, Lady Stephanie."

After a while, even Lady Stephanie's hardcore enemies began to be convicted as they beheld her suffering on the cross. It wasn't that all the people merely beheld this sight. They actually felt it. They felt her pain, her torment, her infinite suffering for *them* not just the crucifixion itself. And no one was sure this wasn't actually real! And they all knelt, and prayed, because they realized that whether this vision was real or not, they all felt the conviction, the *meaning,* that was all real. And when *that* word, *meaning,* rested upon their souls, they all knew, *that* was Lady Stephanie.

And everything went dark, again, an horror of great darkness descended upon the people and they cried in earnest. And then the vision was gone and the darkness lifted, and Lady Stephanie stood again on the edge of the stage with her hands folded behind her.

Grinchback silently looked over to his Master, and the Highest Councilor shook his bulbous aching head, saying, "There has never been a *faithwalker* like her before!"

"Did she really crucify herself Master?"

The Highest Councilor employed a few orb manipulations then looked seriously at his underling, "I don't know!" After a long pause, he said, "It appears so!"

"Master, everyone is taking bets on who will ultimately win?"

The Highest Councilor eyed his underling. "What are the odds?"

"Even for them all! Jargono, *Karen,* The Earth Demons, You and I, the Father is even on even odds because of how he was beaten by the humans!"

"So no one thinks the *faithwalker* and King Vaughn can win?"

"Those odds are ninety-nine to one. And so is their child surviving without damage and being born."

The Highest Councilor narrowed his Great Eye at his underling. "Who is the *one?*"

"Master, you know voting is confidential."

Lady Stephanie stood again on the edge of the stage with her hands folded behind her. "You know, I've studied you all so deeply. What am I to do with you? My husband has been given Ultimate Judgment over you by the Lord God, as you well witnessed today. I *cannot* interfere with him.

"You all love the *same* core Goodness. And think about this. Your faith that Jesus is indeed Lord, the only begotten Son of God, that faith didn't come from a *book or religion!* Indeed, your faith that God is *real* didn't come from a book nor from judges, nor from anyone or *anything* except the goodness you know is real in *you!*"

People began looking to each other, asking, "Is that true? It is true, isn't it?"

"Think about it. *Why* is God real to you? Because each individual sees within themselves love, and justice, and truth, and other goodness, and when they look just a little bit deeper into any of those, they realize through that goodness there is a much Greater Goodness, and that in fact, they didn't even create the goodness in themselves, but were created by it, the *qualities* of Being. We never *chose* to be created but the goodness we are made from ever lived in God before we were made. Our personal *choice* began *after* we were given independence. But even the tiny bit of goodness we're made from is infinite to behold and can surprise us every day! We learn from it every day.

"Only a *fool* would think he creates his *own* thoughts! And feelings. Because the *being* from whence they spring was *not* our choice, its simply the goodness that has always been! Our being is our own now because it was *gifted* to us, but it's not our own by our *choice*. But, while we may not be sure all thoughts and feelings are our own, we are *sure* when we own them! And *that's* what makes us more of what we are, growing into an even *greater* goodness! And if it's true goodness, what sense does it make to *disown* them, as if that kind of freedom makes sense! It makes you *dead!* And the demons have *plenty* of thoughts and feelings of *their* own to share with you! Again, while we may not be sure all thoughts and feelings are our own, we are *sure* when we *own* them! Choose life, not death! Our faith in God is because life is real to us, and God *is* Life with a capital L, and His Life is Goodness and we *know* it."

Queen Yinauqua brushed tears from her eyes and looked at her husband. "Did you tell her about that, when you spoke to our son with those *exact* words?"

"No, my Queen, I did not. There is something greater going on here. She even added wonderful words of her own which made the goodness even so much more powerful!"

"The demons have very poor odds for them. They're usually pretty accurate!" His wife said with a certain tone that implied so much more.

"I admit, that in times past, I might have helped just a bit. But I can't any longer."

"You *can't* let little Michael be destroyed." She grabbed her husband by the tunic. "You'll have to lock me up and throw away the key, Mafferan, do you hear me?"

A deep heavenly sigh was felt through the Kingdom of God. Within Almighty God, the Seven are in perfect balance. Love, Justice, Wisdom, Understanding, Life, Truth, and Peace are each a facet on a single seven-sided gem. But in human beings, those mortal and immortal, and even in angels above, one facet sometimes seems to outweigh the other. Only a *faithwalker* has the most complete sense of it, but it's *only* a sense, needing to be translated into a working knowledge within the mind and heart.

The *faithwalker* continued her plea to the people. "In the beginning, in the first year of the Judges for the United for Christ, on the *first* day, there were *no* divisions amongst you! That's because, having separated yourselves from the atheistic North, you were all singular in your sense of faith and justice.

"Where did your faith in Jesus come from? As I said, not from *any* book or person, nor even angel and *especially* not from a *religion!* It *came* from you knowing what love is inside your own heart and mind. And while we all have miserably failed at times, that never robs us of what love truly is and *should* be in us! Knowing that this love *is* real, and that it belongs to a greater *perfect* Love, well, we all know what that Greater Love is capable of, and that it would do the greatest good that it could do. And we all know, by true word and true love, that Jesus *is* the fulfilment of the *greatest* possible love of Almighty God!" And the faithwalker paused, not shining with anything, which, in a way made her seem naked, just like any other ordinary soul. And the people understood the *meaning*.

"Unfortunately, many of you have real faith in our Lord Jesus up to that point I just described but you are unaware how much further your faith can carry you! The Tree of Life, which *is* our Lord Jesus, wasn't just meant to be believed in, its fruit is meant to be eaten. And we can ask through our faith in real Love, with a capital L, what that fruit would be when the greatest Goodness is used to form it. The *main* reason our Lord became mortal was to make for us a far better fruit than the original Tree of Life had! Jesus did that through *experiencing* our mortality, our weakness, our very flesh, and also experiencing a constant onslaught from evil in all forms and fashions. Everything he encountered caused our Lord Jesus to have a natural reaction from his Goodness against our weakness and against all evil, including experiencing death itself. That natural reaction our Lord had was to create a deeper goodness, a wiser, more understanding, more loving, and more determined *mortal* will that would not fail when challenged! A truly new heart and spirit. It's *that* kind of new fruit on the Tree of Life."

Lady Stephanie paused to let the newness of this love and knowledge settle. Her colors radiated like a rainbow and it touched everyone there and people across the nation were putting their hands upon their TV screens. All their hearts kept saying, *This really makes sense. How come we never knew it before? This is so obvious.*

Stephanie continued. "Our faith in the greatest possible Love tells us that when our Lord Jesus rose from the grave, he carried with him all that extra goodness in Spirit and from that newness, he makes for us a new heart and a new spirit laden with all that extra goodness he created and lived *here* by. Our faith in the Lord God performing this extra goodness for us tells us that we can live a far better, more holy life with that new heart and new spirit than before the Lord Jesus made it for us."

And Stephanie paused to let that all sink in, then continued. "In other words, think about what it would actually be like to receive all that extra goodness Jesus made for us while *mortal,* and he sinned not! In these troubled times we now face and *much worse* to come, we need all the extra strength and goodness possible, but we also know that if that *is* possible, then the love of Jesus has done it for us already!"

Lady Stephanie spread her arms wide. "We *can* now defeat evil in ways we never could before Jesus came and died for us, and all we have to do is ask Jesus how to receive his Holy Ghost which carries with it that new fruit. That's how we eat from the Tree of Life. The holy people you now see across the country have eaten this new fruit, and are able to pray for you and offer help. But remember this: Your answers will come directly from the Lord from your inside *then* outward. And also, no one has a right to come between you and the Lord, so be sure not to put anything *less* between the Lord and you, and that would include *any* religion! The *process* of religion is from the outside in! But inside out is the *only* way serving God can be true for every individual. The Holy Ghost has conscious *Being*. Religion is . . . what is it? It's not conscious. It has no conscious spirit to share. So which is greater for you, religion or the Holy Ghost?"

And Stephanie paused again with absolutely no energy display, no specialness at all. She had no idea she would be able to convey so much goodness, so much of her whole purpose for *being*, but little Michael was glowing so brightly. Stephanie looked up into the eyes of everyone around, and said, "It's *that* kind of love and faith that binds us all together, the *greatest* possible love." But having delivered such a deep and moving message of hope, and feeling Michael respond so strongly, Lady Stephanie unexpectedly broke down crying. It came quite suddenly, quite forcefully. At first the people thought it was for them, but then women began saying that this was something that *she* was going through right *now* but they didn't know about it. And then more and more people began to see, indeed, that was the meaning of her grief, now.

She dried her eyes, looked steadfastly into the cameras, and said, "I'm sorry, I shouldn't have . . ." And she couldn't help herself again. And she turned away, trying to get hold of herself. But the threats against Michael, both from below and above, and from Karen, and the Earth demons all kept playing in her heart and mind. *Lord Jesus, help me, I have to finish this, what I began here, no matter what.*

She turned back to the crowd unaware that her unborn child glowed inside her so very brightly. The crowd had hushed when they saw it. Some men said, "Look how strange she's glowing from her tummy." But the women rebuked them, "*Idiots!* She's *pregnant.*" The men swallowed and held their peace.

And when the crowd felt how deep her grief is, their hands began to go to their mouths in understanding, well, the women. The men began to pick up on it a bit, and began to say, "Oh, there must be something wrong with her child." But again, the women scolded them, "You *really* have no brains, do you? Don't you see that tummy glow? *That* child is *perfect.*" And the men were confused, until the women had to explain *again,* "The child is *perfect,* but that child is in great danger!" The men asked, "How do you know?" And the women just replied, "You men are *hopeless.*"

Lady Stephanie tried again, but broke down again, and bruskly turned around. At that point the people began to go onto bended knee. And when the men *finally* began to realize that the *only* explanation for her uncontrolled grief was a dire threat to her unborn child, *then* they realized that threat had to do with Lady Stephanie defending *them!* Because with her power, certainly she could find somewhere safe to stay, but she chooses to stay *here!* Trying to straighten out all *their* hard hearts! Because she had said much worse evil was coming. That kind of love hit them pretty hard. And the men got up from all over the venue, to gather just below the stage, and they went down on one knee, chanting, "Our lives for you! Our lives for you! Our . . ."

Women who had gathered around the seated area came over and started mounting the stage, and one by one, they hugged her, and kissed her. And everyone at their TV sets wanted to be there to do the same. But Stephanie was angry with herself. *It wasn't supposed to go this way. It's not about me. I was going to explain to them about all their individual differences, and how each difference doesn't work, it's the kind of difference not on the Tree of Life. Their differences are like diseased little twigs that will kill the whole Tree if they don't stop. The Lord Jesus said, A house divided cannot stand.*

And all across the country the people prayed for Lady Stephanie and her unborn child. And the prayers ascended to Heaven! A golden light slowly drifted heavenward from across the United for Christ, and all the occupants took note of it. Many discussions evolved, but no one had a solution to a truce they'd all forgotten about. Then the search went up for who was in charge of such a thing, and former King Mafferan stepped forward. Everyone wanted an explanation.

Mafferan stood before the Heavenly Host, and said, "We do what we must for the greater good and to protect the *balance.*" And that was it and he disappeared. No one wanted war on Earth again. When they began to ask each other whether they could even possibly stay out of interfering on Earth if Stephanie's child was about to be destroyed, no one could give a definite answer. When other Heavenly folk began to say that if they interfered, not only would there be open war on Earth between the Ethereal and Heaven but also open war up here, everyone shook their angelic heads.

And then the Lord appeared before them all, covered in clouds of magnificent colors. "What is in heaven stays in heaven. No one shall interfere! It is the *Lord* who chooses whether to answer prayers, and how, and when. The Lord is moved by one the same as many." And the Lord's last word trailed off and He was gone.

There was stunned silence in Heaven. And there was both relief and sorrow in one. "Never has there been a time like this," they all kept repeating. Many turned their glowing trees or golden orbs off because they couldn't watch any longer. That was increasingly the reaction. And on Earth, that resulted in a growing sense of isolation, especially for the faithwalker.

And yet, of their own accord, judges began meeting with each other, discussing their differences. And then, when each group worked things out to be one together, they sent representatives to an impromptu meeting, and these discussed their differences until they hashed it all out. And then, they went back to their original little groups to check if they all agreed.

They brought a chair for Lady Stephanie to sit upon, and food and drink, and bade her to stay with them on stage because they were working on something. Well into the night they worked, and when they finally all agreed, they came before their beloved hero, and asked, "Lady Stephanie, we wish to present to you our new code to serve the Lord, and we would like your approval."

Stephanie no longer glowed. She felt drained and wanted desperately to just go home, but she nodded to the three judges and their wives. So they smiled and took the podium. Their appointed spokesperson tapped the microphone to see if it was still on and it was. Lights suddenly turned on. Media folk were nudged awake. But all the judges, their wives, and all the others kept nodding that they'd done not just a good thing, but an *excellent* thing.

The spokesman said, "I want to thank our dear Lady Stephanie for her infinite patience with us, and I do mean *infinite.*"

Even at home, everyone had kept their TV's on, and kept watch. As soon as they heard the crowd chanting, "Lady Stephanie, Our Lives for you, Our Lives for you." They looked at their clocks, *Three in the morning!* And woke everyone else up who couldn't make it. The spokesman continued, "We are blessed far more beyond what we are worthy, if worthy at all, by your presence, your husband, and your people." And the crowd cheered as if it were mid-day.

"We have decided to *put an end* to all Christian differences! No judge, no official, none in the clergy shall from here on require any form of worship, lead any form of worship or study that pronounces a factional difference! From henceforth, any differences practiced shall be *individually personal* as is the right of everyone's God-given freedom."

Stephanie began to have new tears and everyone immediately saw and understood the difference. Her glow was back! Golds, and warm reds, and blues. People were beginning to say to each other, "I think we've really got it this time. Look how she glows!" And the people began to chant, "Freedom,

Freedom, Freedom . . ." More than Stephanie could have ever hoped for, and the *faithwalker* had no idea this would happen, neither had she planned it to be so.

"Also, we are going to endeavor to aide, make accessible any help you need, or your people need, or others who have been baptized by you, or to those they baptized, *any* help they all need, and they are welcome *anytime* to our local podiums! We have found them to be people of impeccable characters. We have even asked some to be our judges but they have all declined!" More fervent cheering. "Lady Stephanie, please come to the podium and let us know if you approve, if you desire any changes or additions."

Stephanie sat in silence, not believing what she was witnessing. Rebecca, Lynnara, Mandy, and Carla, were all up front yelling for her to step up and speak. The whole crowd began chanting, "Speak, Lady Stephanie, we love you!"

She wiped the tears from her eyes and came to the podium, but then she walked around it to the edge of the stage, and spoke, and all could hear her clearly. "Wow," she waved her hand around about the stage. "So much unbelievable *stuff* has happened right up here. I mean, you got to meet my *demon* father. You got to see me *kill* my *demon* father. We had my dear husband Captain Joshua's funeral service up here. And then I married now *Captain* Vaughn up here. But I tell you straight from my heart, even all that does not compare to what you have done for yourselves just now!"

The crowd fell completely silent with tears running down. Her glow was all gone. This was just Stephanie. No Lady or other title to it. Not even her being a *faithwalker*. Just her. "How could I say such a thing? Because you've just made the crucial difference in every single one of your lives between each one of you and Almighty God and his Son, the Lord Jesus." She paused to let it settle in their hearts. "Now, full responsibility for your souls, *because of* your new freedom, rests squarely and fully on each individual's shoulders where it belongs. Where it has *always* been. My people, the dear Appendaho, who sacrificed all their lives for *me,* just so I could attain what you have witnessed," she wiped tears from her eyes, "Even they partake of your spiritual victory this hour. They have a saying. No one has a right to come between an individual and the Tree of Life. This day have you fulfilled that calling. Thank you so much for your love. Frankly, I have been in dire . . . need of it." And with a sob, she bowed her head, and began to walk away, but the spokesman took hold of her arm and brought her back to the stage front. Everyone got on one knee then waited. Even the viewers watching TV, when they saw it, even though they had no idea of the plan the people there had worked out, they all got down on one knee, too.

"Lady Stephanie," and he brushed a tear from his eyes, "We give our solemn oath that we will do all we can, even give up our mortal lives, to protect your unborn child!" And Stephanie collapsed to her knees weeping. *If only it were that simple.* When the people saw her reaction, they knew without any doubt they had surmised the correct reason for her grief. "Lady Stephanie, if you are not able to share with us your exact troubles, we understand."

Stephanie shook her head, and forced herself to stand up. "I'll use the podium for this so I can lean on it!" When the people heard *that,* they thought, *She has to lean on it?* And she walked to the podium. "I'm going to tell you the truth, and of many things you have never heard, nor experienced. You have so honored me. You *are* all my true friends, and everyone watching as well from their TV's. I can feel you." She dried her eyes and stood up straight.

She explained about how heaven worked, how the Ethereal worked, about Jargono, his wife Karen, and about why her unborn child is so special. Then she explained about the truce between Heaven and Hell and why this particular child violated it, how heaven hadn't even considered it until the objection was made, and *then* she explained the terrible consequences.

And then she wept, and said, "And now that you are so very dear, I don't see how I can put you all in danger." And she let out a howl as if a wounded animal was dying. And then she vanished!

The people were dumbfounded and all their hearts broke. There was no good solution to this. They had all just prayed for *that* child's safety and for Lady Stephanie. There was much discussion. The same groups formed again. And after each group made their decision, they sent their representatives. And after they had firm consensus, they all picked up and went to Lady Stephanie's quarters! Including all the media, trudging across the field, down a block, then around the corner.

Standing outside her building, people fit into every crack, corner, roof top, and chanted. "Come out, Lady Stephanie,

Come out to hear our decision. We are one!" And they kept repeating it.

Mandy and Carla, Lynnara and Rebecca went in but the door between their apartments was locked, but they all could sense she was alone inside. Mandy remembered how Stephany had pulled her out of the gutter in spite of the evil ways she had treated Stephanie. She pulled her long medium brown hair behind her, out of the way so when she saw Stephanie, she could fully face her with support. Carla, whom Vaugh rescued at Stephanie's direction, Mandy's sister, did the same with her dark brown hair. All wondered where Vaughn had gone but knew that he wasn't here because he had even more urgent matters.

Little Lynnara sighed, then put her hand on the doorknob, bowed her little head, then opened the door! She turned to Mandy and Carla, and said, "Just Rebecca and me, please!" And Rebecca tossed her straight long dark brown hair behind her and her dark eyes smiled up at them, very pleased with the privilege her best friend Lynnara just gave her over the adults, and they went through the door and relocked it! Mandy and Carla were quite surprised. Lynnara, her bouncy brown curls bouncing, poked her head back through the door. "'Cause Mommy can't talk to any adults. But she can still talk to us. I know!" And she relocked the door.

Stephanie was upon her bed praying but she knew Heaven had closed up against her. She could tell. No more visits from ancient ancestors. No more help. She was alone and she had no idea what to do. And Lynnara and Rebecca climbed up on each side of her, and hugging her tightly, they said together. "You're not alone Mommy. We're here." And they all wept together.

CHAPTER 8

The Faithwalkers Are Going to War

Marta stood under the Tree of Life when the students arrived but everyone could tell she wasn't her usual self. She simply started their lesson. "What did Adam see in Eve at that very *first* moment when she brought him the forbidden fruit?"

They had left last lesson with Marta *insisting* the children find an answer, but the children had a greater concern right now. They kept urging various older students to speak until Ralph finally took up the mantle. Maybe it was his red hair. "Teacher Marta. Well, we were all wondering. You seem bothered. Usually, you're so cheerful."

Five-year-old Carrie pushed her red bouncy hair from her eyes again, and blurted out. "You haven't told us 'bout Lady Stephanie in while."

And Sarah, being older, and allowed to follow things down there more closely, leveled her sharp green eyes into her teacher. "Marta, what's Lady Stephanie going to *do?* I don't understand."

Teacher Marta's lip started to quiver, and she quickly turned away from the class. Everyone knew she loved Lady Stephanie more than *anyone.* She still wore her hair Like Lady Stephanie and still had a blue and gold ribbon tied on her central braid.

Marta kept drying her eyes and waiting for her tears to stop, but when they wouldn't, she finally turned around, anyway. When all her students saw she still cried, they became upset. This was *Heaven. Are we supposed to cry up here?* Many thought.

Knowing how her students felt, Marta said, "I don't know what's going to happen to Lady Stephanie!"

And all the children gasped. They thought their teacher knew *everything.* And being *up here,* how could they *not* know everything.

Marta smiled a sad smile, and then taught them. "That's a common misbelief. One that actually got Lucifer and Adam and Eve into trouble. They thought because they were at the top, they knew everything. *That* was the last lie they told themselves to try to reassure themselves that their other misconceptions were going to work!" Marta sobbed deeply, then collected herself.

Ralph said. "It's Ok Teacher. We can go back to the lesson, or wait till tomorrow."

But Marta shook her head. "No. Actually, this will fit in nicely. As I told you before about being caught between right and right, that is the trap our dear Lady Stephanie finds herself in. Yes, and my own heart, too!"

The children all gasped, but then the older students

realized they felt it, too. They just hadn't given their feelings as much thought.

Marta continued. "But unlike what our first Father and Mother did when they were trapped, Lady Stephanie hasn't stepped outside of what's right to try to solve her terrible problems, and neither has King Vaughn."

Carolyne raised her hand and got the nod. "But that's so *hard.*" Six-years-old, in Heaven, and she began to rub her chest. "I feel the pain right here. And I'm not even down *there!*"

Ralph couldn't help wondering aloud. "What if it was *us?* I mean, if *we* were *them!*"

Marta found herself straightening with pride! She double checked herself because pride can be tricky, but then decided this kind was definitely appropriate. "Lady Stephanie is a *real faithwalker!* True *faithwalkers* walk in the very midst of pain and they don't let it force them to be evil."

But Carolyne repeated her question. "What are they going to *do?*"

Marta glowed. "I really don't know. We don't know. And they don't know. All begins to seem hopeless. And the Lord has been silent. But I think there is a much greater reason we are *all* entering into their pains, and why the Lord is silent."

The class all waited but no answer from their teacher came forth.

Marta finally said, "This is the pain that Adam felt when he first looked upon his beloved wife Eve!' The children all gasped. "So what was he looking at? What was the trap? And his solution?"

Grinchback tugged on his Master's arm, "What have they decided? There was too much glow to make it out. What are we going to do about all that glow? But what are we going to do about *Karen*? And what are we going to do about the truce? And . . ."

Highest Councilor ScrabaGag whirled on Grinchback and almost smacked him and sent him sailing into the wall the way his former Master GrrraGagag used to do, but the thought of acting like *him* stopped him. "Underling. Keep your wits about you. I told you, the masses of people are fickle. And their heroes can't escape this, so all that *glow* has a very short shelf life. But I believe you would agree, in spite of all that *glow,* the more pressing matter is definitely Karen. Unfortunately, we are powerless to help."

"But Master, we should be joining in the fight to help Jargono and Vaughn."

The Highest Councilor let out yet another demon sigh, but this time it was exemplified by a dullness everywhere and sluggish ripples. "Our *Father* has decided that to preserve the *balance,* what stays below must *remain* below. We cannot interfere." Then he peered into Grinchback's eye, and added, "That includes *any* help you might be thinking of giving to your *friend,* your other *Master!*" And the Highest Councilor squinted hard at Grinchback.

The underling let out the exact same sigh of his Master, but he also seemed to shrink a bit.

ↅ

Jargono and Vaughn paused, floating in the Ethereal Corridor over the first town, using the coordinates Trevor provided. Jargono asked him, "You said *Trevor* gave these to you?" Vaughn nodded and Jargono shook his head. "Never thought he was anything much, nor would ever be. Your wife, again?"

Vaughn smiled, "You are correct." Then Vaughn laughed and turned to Jargono. "I was going to kill him after discovering he had poisoned our food! I had even taken a mouthful, but Spot, you met my dog," And Jargono rubbed his wrist indicating he remembered, "He hit me so hard I spit it all out, then Spot tipped the whole pot into the fire and *that's* when I saw the gray smoke looking very evil and much alive. I threw Trevor up against a tree, and I was in mid swing when my wife leapt upon my arm!"

Vaughn waited for Jargono's reaction. He could see he was envisioning it all, and his eyes were wide, trying to imagine Vaughn and his wife in an actual fight! Vaughn continued, "Well, I was already in mid swing and poor Stephanie slammed into Trevor!" then Vaughn looked down, then away, which caused Jargono to nudge him.

"What happened next? Why'd you look down and away?"

Vaughn had never seen him this rivetted on a mere story. "Ahh, I, well, I . . ."

Jargono grabbed his arm and turned him to face him, "You *what?*"

Vaughn sighed, "I was *really* angry. You can understand that."

Jargono turned dark and glared at Vaughn.

"Alright, alright, no need to be threatening. I grabbed her by the front of her dress, and . . . Ok, OK, I threw her a good ways away and she landed kinda hard on the ground."

Jargono ran his fingers threw his hair and shook his head. "Was that wise?"

"Ahh, not really, but I was still so angry I went back to killing Trevor. I kinda heard Stephanie say, '*Vaughn,*' like that, with that *exact* tone, '*Vaughn. I said NO!*' The next thing I knew I was hurled a good ways away and landed hard."

"And that was it?"

"Ahh, no. I was still so angry. You know how stubborn I am. So I bounded up and started running back at Trevor, and I hear my wife's voice in my head saying calmly, 'Vaughn, when I say no, it's NO!" And I ran right into some invisible wall, and I knocked the wind and sense out of me. Then she proceeded to redeem Trevor!"

Jargono leaned back in utter amazement. After a pause, he said, "Maybe there *is* hope for Karen. If you think about it like a scale, Trevor was as far as you could be to the end of the nothing scale, and I think my wife is as far as a human being could possibly go to evil on the human scale."

Now it was Vaughn's time to reflect, and he simply nodded. Then Jargono looked hard at Vaughn, "I would *really* hate to have to kill you two, or even diminish you at all!"

Vaughn just shrugged, then began to inch closer to the demon town but Jargono grabbed him. "I wouldn't do that.

Their Ethereal sense is probably already pretty strong. We could have a whole army up here in no time!"

"You think they can already *travel?*"

"I do! I just sense it. Which will make everything that much more difficult."

"Can you block them? Stephanie said you blocked her powers. Can you block them *all?*"

Jargono rubbed his chin in deep concentration. "Perhaps . . . yes, I think so, but I would have to devote my entire power to it. Which means you and Stephanie would have to destroy them all on your own! I'm not sure you can do that."

Vaughn ran his hand through *his* hair. "Do we have a choice? And what if your wife shows up?"

"Then we'll all lose miserably. Let's see if we can figure out where she goes, and what other things she's cooked up."

Vaughn called the orb to him and brought up a map of the town but then zoomed out. "Anything strike you?"

But Jargono shook his head. "Nothing stands out that would allow her to hide the kinds of numbers and types of creatures you believe she has."

"Jargono, you remember the beginning of the entrance to the path to the Sacred cave?"

He nodded. "You could be standing practically against it and wouldn't see it. But how could that kind of trick be employed *here?*" And he waved his hand at the map.

That's a key word, here. "What if it's *not* here?" And Vaughn raised his eyebrows.

Jargono laughed. "Well, there's no way the Ethereal would let them do that downstairs, not even their *Father* would allow *that* . . ." Jargono suddenly had a realization. "He wouldn't allow it *downstairs* because with all that you think Karen has created, it could possibly be a threat to the Ethereal, plus, their *Father* is far from being an idiot, and you already hurt him badly by humiliating him, so he'd not take any more chances with special humans."

Vaughn knew Jargono was thinking way past him. "But if not downstairs, where else could the Father do anything, and on that scale?"

"You're quite good with the orb. I'm OK. Karen is the one with exceptional abilities here. But what you did to the Ethereal orb system I think surpasses even my wife. Can you refocus the orb on the Ethereal Corridor?"

"But Jargono, there's no way she could hide *that* undetected up here. All the Alpha would know for sure."

Jargono materialized an ordinary piece of paper then began doing a bit of origami. When he was done, he handed it to Vaughn. Vaughn turned it over and over. Its surfaces were twisted and turned so many times that it couldn't be told which was the true outer or inner surface. "You think she . . . folded the Corridor into the physical some way?"

"I don't just think it, I *know* it. Because *I* once entertained the thought with her and even explained how I might do it! Scan the Corridor for energy fluctuations."

It took a while to retool the orb, but when done, Vaughn hit the run program and right next to the town they were at was a long swath of tremendous energy. Jargono nodded with understanding, and said, "Unless you're up hear and happen to run right into it, you'd never know it was there. But like the entrance to the path to the Sacred Cave, if you don't find the *exact* entry point, you're just going to run into a wall! Now scan for any fluctuations just within the energy field." After Vaughn did that, Jargono pointed. "There's the door!"

Vaughn leaned back. "When I was at your palace, before I popped in on you, I went exploring." Jargono nodded as if saying, *Of course.* "Your section had zero safety devices as far as I could tell, but *her* section was filled with them. I didn't feel like wasting my time with that. Then I came to you. I don't think it would be easy or perhaps even possible to enter and go undetected."

"No wonder she's so cocky and arrogant. Can you retool the orb to scan inside?"

Vaughn attempted it but the orb kept rejecting the effort. "No."

Jargono thought a while. "What if we sent the orb directly in? Could it record what's inside then?"

Vaughn nodded, and said, "I wouldn't expect Karen's security to be set to detect inanimate objects. But one, how would it be navigated? And two, it could still be seen."

Jargono held out his hand and a small orb materialized. "Can you sync your orb there, to this one?"

Vaughn laughed, "No. But I can sync that little guy to this one. And I suppose I could navigate that little orb with this one. *But,* we're dealing with creatures, and creatures have extra sense about them. No matter that this guy is small, I think it wouldn't make a difference to them. They'd spot it the moment it entered their area."

Jargono sighed, then spoke a word, "Stealth." And the orb disappeared. Then he slowly waved his hand until it gently bumped into Vaughn's nose and he flinched! "*You* couldn't detect it. Reveal!" And the orb came back in sight right in front of Vaughn.

"Give me a moment." Vaughn did many manipulations with his orb, then took Jargono's and twisted sections of it in more ways than Jargono could keep up with, then hit a few of its buttons, then set it back to floating. Then Vaughn went to his orb again, hit a button and the orb disappeared.

Jargono was astounded. "How did you do that?" Just then Jargono flinched and Vaughn hit another control and the orb appeared right in front of *his* nose!

Jargono laughed, "Well done Vaughn, very well done!" He meant it and Vaughn knew it. "Let's send it in?" And Vaughn nodded. His finger whizzed within his orb and the stealth orb sped off. Halfway to its destination, it disappeared. Jargono watched over Vaughn's shoulder.

The orb went through the doorway and entered into a long tunnel. Vaughn hit *analyze* and the orb began sending back power readings. Vaughn looked to Jargono with raised eyebrows, so he peered at the numbers and shook his head.

"She's surpassed me, again! What she's done is . . . well, you see, the Ethereal Corridor also occupies the exact same place as all physical matter *besides* the Corridor we travel in up here."

Vaughn nodded in recognition. "Actually, Stephanie explained a bit of that when she described how she came and healed me just before I would have died."

Jargono looked shocked again, but nodded. "Well, what my lovely *wife* has done is to pull out all the Ethereal Corridor that occupies the physical surface area of the surroundings. Then she folded the whole damned thing creating that energy spike in the Corridor, and then she simply folded out an opening, which is the tunnel the orb is in now."

"But . . . it's still not *physical.* The creatures . . ."

"Are part Ethereal, part physical. All she needed to do was take a single Earth demon into her new realm. He enters because he's ethereal. But once up there, or *in there,* she uses the interrelation within the demon between its ethereal part and its physical part . . ."

"My *God!*" Vaughn couldn't help but interrupt. "And then once understanding that relationship, she uses it to imbue, or create the same relationship, the same *physicality* within her whole sequestered Ethereal Chamber."

Jargono's eyes about popped out. "There is *no way* you should have been able to understand *that!*" Vaughn just shrugged, and Jargono continued, "My lovely *wife* would then have all she needed to create her secrete army."

Vaughn's Master Orb started dinging and live imaging began to appear. "My God! Lord Jesus."

Jargono's face was a picture of fright!

ℰℐ

"You're not alone Mommy. We're here." And they all wept together feeling Stephanie's pains. Then Lynnara dried her little eyes and whispered into her third bestest Mommy's ear. "You can hear them calling you. Allll of them."

Her Mommy nodded.

Rebecca said, "You taught us good."

Lynnara said, "NO ONE has a right to come between *anyone* and the Tree of Life."

Rebecca said, "Or when they pray."

And Lynnara said, "Or what they want to *be.*" And she chirped out her last word.

Rebecca said, "And they want you to know because we all love you so much." And little Rebecca threw her arms wide. At that point they began tugging on Stephanie's arms. Little Lynnara's eyes began to blaze and Stephanie felt her power enter into her and uplift her. Eventually, Stephanie couldn't resist it, and she opened the door and Mandy and Carla flooded in and wrapped her in their arms.

Mandy pulled Stephanie around and held her cheeks between her hands. "We are *sisters.* If it wasn't for *you,* I would have *no* life at all, or *worse.*"

Carla took her next in the same way. "*We* are sisters, too. And what *you* suffer, we all swear to suffer, too!" Carla had been rescued from being a sex slave to a corrupt judge because Lady Stephanie had her secret service follow various people that eventually led to Carla's salvation!

Lynnara spoke up, "They're your *sisters* Mommy. That's *their* choice."

And Rebecca said to Mandy and Carla, "You can go now!" And they looked at her and wondered, but they listened to her, too.

Our will can rebel against many things, many things more powerful than us, that *can* conquer a *part* of us, yet, cannot keep us from rebelling, *cannot* in fact conquer the person inside the body. Even good-natured friends can't move a stubborn soul. But the love of an innocent, sweet, little child, without exerting any conquering power at all, physically so easily pushed away, yet, without appreciably exerting their will, can move any soul susceptible to true goodness.

And Stephanie came out of the building and stood before the people on the little stone patio, shocked to see their overflow *everywhere*. Little Lynnara tugged on her Mommy's dress and Stephanie knelt down. "They're *allll* here Mommy. And on the TV's too. Because we all decided together!" And she kissed her Mommy's cheek.

Stephanie sighed, not understanding, so she helplessly shrugged and looked up. The spokesman bowed low to her, and then everyone else did the same. "We love our newfound freedom. And our first official decision together as *one,* is that we would rather die *for your child,* than live without *that* child!" And he pointed to her tummy.

Before Stephanie could react, little Rebecca tugged on Stephanie's dress, and whispered, "I have something I want to say to *everyone*. Can I?" And when she said everyone, she threw out her hand.

Stephanie nodded.

The spokesman held the microphone to her and Rebecca came forward on the patio. "My Ranger Vaughn saved me when my Mommy blew up. Then he saved everyone else, my people. But, well, he was only supposed to save Lady Stephanie, and himself. So I asked him, while he was doin' like this . . ." She sat down on the stoop, put her head in her hands, and kept shakin' it.

The people smiled, saying, "That's Vaughn."

"So I asked him. I whispered in his ear like this." And she put her hands around her mouth. "But I can't whisper it to you now 'cause then you won't hear, so I'll just tell you. I asked him, Ranger, why you save me when you shoulda just save yourself? I didn't understand so I asked."

The people looked to each other, never hearing such a thing and not planning this at all.

"You know what Ranger Vaughn said?"

The corners of Lady Stephanie's mouth turned into a smile, and she knelt down to be at Rebecca's eye level, and said, "One little life, even the smallest, is worth everyone. 'Cause if one little life isn't that important, then no one is."

Rebecca said, "That's right." And she looked up at the spokesman and smiled a proud little smile and pushed the microphone back to him.

"Lady Stephanie, I don't understand how God works, but as it is written that out of the mouth of babes we shall learn, we all swear unto you now, that as little Rebecca here has indicated, that is *exactly* how we all feel now." And the crowd began to chant, "One Little Life, One Little Life, One . . ."

"And that means, dear Lady Stephanie, that when you choose between us or *that* child," and he pointed directly at her tummy again, "we all want you to choose your child. *Your* child is *our* child!"

And the crowd chanted at the top of their lungs, "Your child is our child. Your child is our child." And everyone at their TV sets chanted along, "Your child is our child!"

The spokesman went to speak again and everyone hushed. "It's still, of course, your decision, but we wanted to make sure you knew *ours!*" Then he leaned over and kissed the top of her head because she had sat down on the stoop to weep some more. "Let's leave our Queen in peace now." And everyone quietly disassembled.

But Stephanie suddenly stood up, her tummy looking like a ball of fire. She cleared her throat. "Alright." And the people stopped and came back. "A good Queen *cannot* ignore such a united will of the people. Alright. So let's prepare for war! A war like no other. A war right from legend with fire-breathing dragons and horrible monsters, and real demons. I want all the holy people across this country to do only two things. Baptize those who are truly ready to receive their new heart and new spirit with the Holy Ghost, and I want weapons made. *Holy* weapons, like out of Legend!"

And people started chanting, "Holy, Holy, Holy . . . awake United for Christ and be *Holy.*"

There was a rumbling in the Ethereal coming from the Father's room. Other Alpha began to whisper, "Well, he boxed himself in, all of us with his *stay below* edict."

King Mafferan looked over at his beloved wife who was still amazed at what she beheld in the golden vision. Then she turned to him with tears in her eyes. "We *forsook* them. The Ethereal wants to *destroy* them. Their Earthly enemies vastly *outnumber* and *overpower* them. And yet, they have come to be more noble than *everyone* up here!" And her eyes blazed with black and gold.

Mafferan bowed to his wife, knelt down, took her hand, and said, "My Queen."

Then she thought about her anger. "Everyone except our God. The Lord Jesus is ever beyond us. And yet," and she looked back into the golden vision, at all the people glowing with profound love and bravery, "He is always with us!" Then she looked at her husband. "Did you expect this?"

"No."

"Did you *foresee* it?"

"My beloved wife and always my Queen. I had absolutely no knowledge of *any* of this in any form."

Yinauqua strained her heart and mind but came out with no sense of the future. She looked into her husband's eyes and softly spoke, "The *faithwalkers* are going to war! Like in the Legend!"

As we look back in history and we consider the young Pharaohs who ruled the world, or Alexander the Great, and many other young people who performed extra-remarkable feats, we try to explain it away so that our own lack of accomplishment won't make us feel too uncomfortable. Well, they never lived long back then, so they had to grow up fast. That's why they married so early. Yet, *faithwalkers* never advertise themselves, and the ones who are good, or even holy, mostly go unnoticed in our recorded history.

CHAPTER 9

The Truth About Power

The class refused to leave! So Marta continued the lesson that had become so much more. "So what was Adam looking at? What was the trap? And his solution?"

Ralph said, "Eve had to have looked *way* different."

Carolyne whispered, "She died. *Inside.*"

Sarah said, "But she was still alive, sorta."

Marta said, "As we discovered in the lesson before last, Eve felt with all her heart she was doing the right thing because for the first time in her life she felt meaningful, and being meaningful *had to be* right. That *feeling* in her heart of being meaningful, that *was* a right kind of feeling *but* it was misplaced to feel that way about disobeying the Lord. Well, when Adam first looked at his wife and saw how she changed, he immediately looked into her more deeply than he ever did and he understood *exactly* what was going on inside of her. And yet, he couldn't help his first reaction which was what?"

Ralph was quick with the answer. "He backed away. He *knew* it was wrong. He could *see* she died."

Marta nodded, then asked, "In that split second when he backed away, what was Eve's reaction to it?"

Five-year-old Carrie said, "She got scared, 'cause she could see she did wrong."

But Elaina, being twelve, went much further. "She came to Adam all happy that she *finally* was showing him how much she loved him and he backed away from her. She was devastated. I'd want to run and hide."

Aaron, thirteen, shook his head in dismay. "My God! She would have been so vulnerable, feeling like she was betrayed by Adam, or something. Lucifer could have told her *anything* after that. All I can feel about this is Eve drowning in darkness!"

Marta nodded slowly, sadly. "And as soon as Adam, who loved her more than anything saw *that* reaction, what did he have to do?"

Ralph said, "He had to try to *immediately* reverse it."

Aaron said, "It wasn't wrong to try to save her from being *completely* lost! So he ate the forbidden fruit."

Marta raised her index finger. "You're right Aaron, *but* there's a whole lot more to what you just said that needs to be unpacked. What did you mean by she wasn't *completely* lost?"

Aaron hadn't thought about this, only that the picture of understanding was correct. Now he looked more closely. "She came to Adam with good intent. Yes, she had died. There was darkness in her, but she also had to be glowing with the love she felt for Adam, so she was still alive, in a way. Besides, I don't see that she actually turned completely away from the Lord like Lucifer did."

Ralph followed right up. "But I think she would have if Adam had kept backing away. Then she really would have been totally lost!"

Aaron's eyes widened. "Adam knew this!" And then he fell silent with realization. The whole class felt it and went silent, even though they didn't understand the feeling like Aaron did.

Marta said. "Aaron. It's time to take your step into manhood! Face the hard decision, accept the pain, and *walk* through it, just like King Vaughn and Lady Stephanie, down *there* walk!"

Aaron stood up from the grass and came forward and Marta smiled and indicated he should step into her place. He squared his shoulders, ran his hand through his dark brown hair, and spoke his heart. "Adam is terrified, more than when he first saw Eve. When he backed away and saw her begin to fall hopelessly into eternal damnation, he *had to* try and save her because she *still* had life in her. He *knew* it was wrong to eat the forbidden fruit, but it would have been *more* wrong to let his wife completely die like that! Caught between right and right. Just like you said, Teacher Marta." And he went to go back and sit down but Marta took his arm and held him in place.

"So he decided to completely disobey the Lord for his wife?"

With a tear in his eye, Aaron shook his head. "No. I think Adam decided to die with her, so they *both* had a chance to live!"

And Marta said, "That's our next lesson, dear class. Let's explore what Aaron just discovered. And let's pray this will *not* be the kind of solution our heroes down there will find!"

Jargono turned pale and he shrank before Vaughn's very eye. It was another new experience for him and he didn't know how to deal with it. It was the feeling of being overpowered, of doom for all his superior understanding and his visions of world rule. In another time and place, Vaughn would have welcomed, no, *rejoiced* over such a sight, but this time, coupled with what they viewed from Jargono's little stealth orb, Vaughn could only run his hand through his hair and shake his head, and wipe the water creeping into his eyes.

Vaughn looked deeply into Jargono. He put up no walls to defend his mind or heart, and Vaughn knew only a single, righteous course to approach. The question was, how could *he* strengthen Jargono! Vaughn turned back to the orb, not wanting to miss anything.

When the orb had first entered, their attention and focus was to a sky dotted as far as could be seen with red fire-breathing dragons. Every once in a while, reveling in their strength and power, they would crane their necks and raise their heads and spray fire through the air. They were enormous but obviously still quite young! Now the orb dropped much lower in the air to avoid running into them, although, every once in a while, one of the dragons would swoop down and pick up a cow from one of many pens that dotted the valleys.

And *then* both Jargono and Vaughn backed away from the orb, at first not understanding what their eyes were seeing. The hills, themselves, seemed to be . . . moving! Vaughn eased back to the blue orb and sent it even lower. It wasn't the hills. It was the trees! No! Wait! He sent the orb still lower. It wasn't the trees. It was what was climbing, *teeming,* all through them! Greenish, reddish massively muscular creatures with short triangular claws on their hands and feet, and they did have *hands,* climbed through the trees, chewing off branches, consuming frightened birds while astonished squirrels looked on from the very treetops, some even having the bravery to bark at these ungodly invaders. And the monsters were *fast.* Every time a bird finally decided to abandon its nest and young, before they could fly far enough, a monster's hand whipped out and plucked them from the air and shoved the whole bird in its mouth in one fluid, natural motion.

They were smooth skinned and their rippling musculature drew the eye's attention. Then one looked up from a treetop where it had just consumed the tree's top along with the squirrel in one giant gulp. At first, Vaughn was sure it sensed the orb, it *did* have large pointy ears. But what it was really doing was swallowing its massive bite, the bulge slowly moving down its throat. Then it opened its mouth wide and belched!

Their faces had green eyes, folds of tough hide, pointy teeth in front but massive molars further back. Yet, these faces were distinctly humanoid. Vaughn looked at Jargono. "Do you *know* what these are?"

Jargono shook his head. "I know what they're *not.* These *aren't* the Earth demons. I know what their life is, and it's not *that.* These only have, maybe, ten percent ethereal in them. The Earth demons are fifty-fifty.

Vaughn asked, "Have you ever studied the Dark Ages?"

Jargono laughed, "Knights in shining armor? With swords and arrows and spears?" He laughed harder. "Not very interesting."

"And castles," Vaughn said.

"Yes. I actually do like castles. I was even thinking of building one for myself." But Jargono knew Vaughn well. He wasn't making small-talk. "What's your point?"

"We were taught they had castles because of the wars they fought against other men. OK, I had thought. That makes sense, but I still always felt it was overkill, especially when all the enemy had to do was just surround them and cut them off from supplies. Castles for that kind of war never really struck me as the best strategy to invest all those resources in."

Jargono laughed again. "So they built them to protect against fairytales?"

"But that's just my *point!* They *wouldn't* have invested so much against a threat that wasn't *real!*"

And Vaughn, when he had said that last word, *real,* seeing Jargono was still vulnerable, grabbed Jargono's forehead and imparted to him the vision he had in the holy mountain! Vaugh did it so fast, Jargono didn't even have time to flinch, and the next thing he knew he was floating in a trance and seeing visions of a time long ago, with elaborate castles, fire-breathing dragons, and gargoyles climbing the walls. He saw the giant javelins bring down another dragon, and someone ran forward and doused a pile of the giant spears, that had just been dropped down, with some kind of glowing oil.

Archers leaned from parapets and every single arrow found a gargoyle and they fell from the walls dying in mid-air! Then Jargono was taken back in time and shown how the castles were built, their intricacies, and he realized Vaughn was right! These still standing relics upon which myths and legends were built, were *in fact,* vestiges of myth and legend that was real!

Jargono came out of his trance, realized Vaugh could have killed him at any time, even before he went into the trance, and he asked him, "Who *are* you?"

Vaughn shrugged. "The more important question is *what* am I? I've been a stranger in a strange land. But more important, now, is that I am your friend!" And Vaughn offered him his hand.

I've never had friends. Not a single one. Never needed them. But is this just out of need? "For now. It seems I'll have to abrogate our former agreement. There's no way we can bring all *this,*" he waved at the orb vision, "to a close any time soon, if *ever,* and *that* is predicated upon even surviving from minute to minute. We now have a formal truce *indefinitely* with a six-month withdrawal buffer where no hostilities can be brought for six months after the truce is ended."

Vaughn withdrew his hand! And *that* surprised Jargono. "You're *declining?*" He didn't mean to say it with *that* meaning. It was a meaning, saying, *How could you leave me in such a horrible position,* along with, *How could you be that stupid?*

"My friend. You are *better* than a *damned demon!* And one of *them* is my *friend!* That has proven to be the deciding factor in winning so far, and may, yet again, contribute to it. Would you like me to show you?" And Vaughn held out his hand to place on Jargono's head, again, but he instinctively backed away.

He stared at Vaughn, wondering. *His wife was using the same approach. I see that now. But she wasn't actually trying to deceive me. She was actually sincere with what she offered and it was something akin to* this! *She couldn't love me the way I wanted, though, because she loved him more, much more. But I had taken that for an insult. Now I see that was wrong.*

Jargono appraised Vaughn with a newfound respect, which was another new feeling. An *awkward* feeling. There seemed to be some kind of strength in *this* kind of respect that he had been quite unaware of, nor was he clear about exactly what this new strength was and how much benefit there is to it. "You said you made friends with a *demon?* That's *ridiculous.* They're *cannibals.*"

Vaughn held out his hand again. "Please. It will help you understand."

But Jargono declined by shaking his head. "I like to figure things out on my own, although I must say, the vision you gave me was the *only* way you could have persuaded me." And *that* made Jargono think, as well. Like it or not, he felt gratitude. He was able to put *that* label to *that* feeling. And *that* feeling of gratitude was similar to the strength he now felt from the new respect he had for Vaughn. That new respect was also close to the strength he had felt when he loved Stephanie, and when he married Karen!

Jargono let down his defensive posture and rubbed his face. "Is *now* really the time I should be absorbed by such distractions?"

Vaughn shrugged again. "We need all the strength we can get. Your power comes from your superior will!" Yes, Vaughn meant it, and Jargono *knew* it. "Stephanie's power comes from something very close to what you are just beginning to feel. My question to you is *this.* Had you *both* started out at the *same* time learning about your powers, *who* would be stronger, *who* would be superior, *you* or my wife?" Jargono was seven years older than Stephanie.

It was a *shocking* question but one Jargono knew Vaughn wouldn't have asked if he didn't think he could answer it. Jargono looked at Stephanie in a whole new light, how could she have managed for so long and under such terrible threat from him? All he had considered before was that he was vastly superior. But now Vaughn's question caused him to reassess. *I couldn't have tolerated even a tenth of what I did to her if that had been done to me!* And a new respect for Stephanie just flooded into him! And then he compared that to how Vaughn and him just reacted to the *same* orb visions. *He took all this vastly better than I did!* And for the first time, *ever,* Jargono felt someone to be *better* than him! That didn't mean he didn't think he could easily kill or defeat Vaughn any time he wanted, but *that* is a clearly different dimension.

He looked back at Vaughn and realized that Vaughn was calmly following all his thinking easily! *He understands me in these things better than I understand myself!* And that was yet another new experience, and along with *that* yet another new feeling.

Vaughn smiled what Stephanie would call his special smile. "In case you don't know what *that* is, it's humility!"

Jargono had never thought about it past declaring such a thing *foolish,* because he was always so superior to the rest of the Appendaho.

Vaughn cleared his throat. "You still haven't answered my question! You're trying to run from it!"

Jargono's eyes went wide. He didn't like the sound of *that.* Who would have been stronger, him or Stephanie? *Her powers have consistently surprised me. Every time I've encountered her, she is vastly stronger than what I expected. But* that's *only a single dimension. She's far more able to endure hardship than I am. So is Vaughn! I've never experienced real hardship!*

Vaughn grabbed Jargono's shoulder. "Now you're just beginning to understand. Normally, if these were *normal* times, I'd let this all rest right here and give you a week, a month to work it all out on your own." And Vaughn stopped right there.

Jargono nodded. "We may not even have the day."

Vaughn turned dark but controlled his power leakage as Jargono had warned him. "You see what I've learned from *you?* Most all of the battles I have fought and *won* have come from some of the new feelings you are now considering. All of those battles I was *always* vastly overpowered! You *need* that kind of strength added to you *now!*"

But Vaughn simply folded his hands across his chest, but at the word, *now,* when Jargono saw him move his arms, he thought Vaughn was going to grab his head, again, so Jargono had put up a defensive shield! Vaughn floated there in the Ethereal Corridor staring into Jargono's eyes. "This kind of thing you *need,* I can't give it to you! It's *your* choice, my friend, not mine."

And Vaughn turned away, looking back into the orb, "My God!" He reached out his hand and beckoned Jargono, who sensed even Vaughn was overwhelmed. There in the orb, a giant very black tail whipped out, grabbed a dragon out of the air, fire breathing and all, pulled it downward and *dropped it into his Great Eye!* There before them was the Father of the Ethereal with HrorrarrAggrang floating above Karen, who dressed sharply in a full length black dress, her golden hair shining against it, while she stood on a baren hill looking none too pleased.

The Father belched out some fire. "Perfectly delicious." Vaughn realized that technically this wasn't a truce violation because the fold in reality was still partly Ethereal.

Karen coldly spoke. "If you keep doing that, I'll never reach my goal."

HrorrarrAggrang snaked out his long dark tail to the next hill, gathered in a bunch of gargoyles from the trees, and dropped them all at once into his Great Eye. "I like their flavor, and there's no fire to get rid of. And what *exactly* is your goal? You have vast numbers right now, why not use them *now?*"

Karen smiled sweetly wondering how much longer she had to tolerate this *underling's* stupidity. "I already have a clear advantage, so what's the rush? I don't want just a clear advantage. I want it all to be over in a single day!" Both demons' eyes grew wide. "I estimate I need three dragons and twenty-five gargoyle for every large town that really have become full-fledged cities now. And I need one dragon and ten gargoyle for every midrange population center. And I need five gargoyles for every small town in what used to be the whole United States!"

Vaughn and Jargono looked at each other and Vaughn offered his hand again. "Friends?"

Jargono took it without hesitation. "I *choose* to be your friend, and all that belong to you!"

Vaughn merely shrugged, saying, "Well, that goes without saying!" But he didn't let Jargono's hand go, now that he was willingly open to him. A kind of bond began to form, at first around the edges. It was all of what Vaughn intended to do for Jargono, but not in mundane detail, but the *feelings* Vaughn brought to Jargono's defense! And Jargono couldn't fight it because it was strength adding to his, supporting him. And he'd *never* felt supported, *ever* before.

Still holding onto Jargono's hand, with *very* controlled power, Vaughn turned exceptionally dark as he looked into the orb's vision and imagined Jargono fighting them all and Vaughn defending him!

Jargono's eyes widened and the hint of a tear in each eye formed as he beheld in Vaughn's heart a strength and tenacity that was a wellspring of seemingly unlimited power, and power all dead set on defending *him! This is what friendship is!*

And Vaughn let go, and merely said, "Only a very small part of it!"

Then Jargono grabbed Vaughn's arm and wrenched him to look into the orb. The Father asked Karen, "When are you taking care of that infernal pest of a girl and her *child?* That was our deal. I help you create all this, and you rid us of *them.* You've already failed *numerous* times. "

But HrorrarrAggrang couldn't help himself, being overcome with all this newfound freedom. "You know, we don't have to end all this when Queen Karen accomplishes *her* goals. We could *restock!* And make all this an Alpha *retreat!* Can you imagine? We could sell entry!"

The Father didn't appreciate the interruption, but as usual, HrorrarrAggrang always provided him with delightful surprise. "Well, my *friend,* what exactly would they pay with, and how would you control entry?"

"They'll never find the doorway without us. We simply wrap our tail around them so they can't tell where they're going. As far as *payment,* we'll *barter* for them to vomit up something they consumed! Trust me Father, it will be well worth it to them! This place is Heav . . . errr, Hell for them!"

The Father roared in laughter, his ripples enlarging with spasmodic accelerations, his shimmering glowed red all over the place. HrorrarrAggrang said, "Father, I haven't seen you laugh that way in a *very* long time."

"What's not to laugh about? Our new Demon Karen friend here, has provided us with all *this*. Plus the *only* orb that will soon be left functioning. *And* can you imagine the combination of just those two events? In here, will be the *only* safe place Alpha will be able to consume because we'll make it a rule, they can't consume each other, at least in here. And, lastly, most deliciously, I feel that *girl* can't possibly escape Karen *this* time." And his Great Eye lowered over her but she waved it away!

"Don't try to bully me. There's no need," she said sweetly. "We'll just have to work out new compensation."

"For what," the Father asked.

"If you want to restock, that's fine by me, but you can't do that without me."

HrorrarrAggrang lowered over her and chimed in. "You're using your *husband's* power. None of what you have is *naturally* yours."

She smiled at him and tickled him under his sort-of chin. "And that matters *how?* It was his power originally but I've altered it so much it's become all mine. He knows *nothing* about creating new life forms! But if you want me to keep all this going . . . hmm, I'll have to think about what you'll pay me. Maybe a seat on the High Council? Hmm, maybe I can *consume* the Highest Councilor?" And her smile could have dripped honey, which sent both the other demons into fits of laughter imaging Scraback being consumed by *her.*

The Father said, "Yes, I think that would be justice, indeed. But what about the *girl?*"

Karen laughed uncontrollably. When she finally got her composure, she spoke. "From the first time I saw her with that *stupid* doggy look in her eyes, I *hated* her. Just something about her. Don't worry. I've picked out *ten* Earth demons that will *very* shortly come her way!"

HrorrarrAggrang said, "They're not mature yet, and Jargono will find out."

She waved her hand. "He loves me. And, actually, I love him, too. I can keep him busy, but we have to work out how he and I can safely join again. He can't find out what I've become. Not yet. As far as not being mature, they're plenty mature enough to kill her with that child. Actually, she never killed her father. It was that oil, whatever *that* was, that did it. But she has no more of it, and even if she had, there wouldn't be enough."

Jargono grabbed Vaughn again, "I know my wife. If she told them she was *going* to kill your wife, it's already begun!"

Vaughn looked at Jargono. "Start building castles. *Lots of them.*" And Vaughn vanished.

CHAPTER 10

Is There Faith beyond a Doubt

Marta determined to keep her composure for this lesson but that proved to be quite difficult, so, again, she just let her tears flow. When her students saw it, they did the same, though the boys tried hard not to be overcome.

Marta said, "We *must* continue with our lessons no matter how we grieve. Let this be the way we honor our heroes down there!" And they all smiled and nodded their heads in appreciation.

"Last lesson, Aaron left off by saying, 'Adam decided to die with her, so they *both* had a chance to live!' I find this to be a *remarkable* opinion. Can you give us any more, Aaron, that would prove it actually happened that way?"

Aaron came forward as before and stood where Teacher Marta had been. "Adam knew his wife would be lost if he rejected her. He knew nothing short of eating the forbidden fruit would keep her from feeling rejected. He wasn't eating the fruit to deny God, or to think he knew better. Maybe he wasn't sure what would happen to him if he disobeyed God. I don't think he really knew. But he *was* sure what would happen if he didn't. Eve's life was his life. But seeing she *still* had some kind of life, that she wasn't totally lost, I think he felt he would become like that, too. So he ate so she wouldn't be lost completely, and so they could be together."

Elaina wiped tears from her eyes. "I don't know what I'm crying more about. Adam's love, or Vaughn's! I mean, look at what he's about to do! But I think Adam had a sense that there was hope, because if he saw no hope, he wouldn't have sacrificed like he did. No, he *knew* there was hope for them both even though he knew they would die! Aaron is right. He died with Eve so they both could live!"

But Ralph also saw something more. "At the same time, we have to realize that we've taken all this time to discuss what happened, but it happened in like, well, seconds? Look how long it's taking us to think this all through! But all of it rushed through Adam in a mere second or two! *Plus* all those feelings he never had before. Being terrified, feeling pain that was overwhelming him. So I think it was like when we feel like we know something but then we can't explain it, or like we don't know it but we know it. So right *NOW,* Eve is standing there holding out the fruit and all Adam knows is a feeling he has to eat it, and to help him follow through, he says, well, she doesn't look dead, so I'll eat! After all, it *is* knowledge, and besides, we're in charge!"

And Elaina said, "Yea, that makes sense, and God, knowing Adam had forgotten his reasoning that got him there, only responded to Adam's last thought, the one he'd remember!"

Aaron said. "I agree. All of this had to happen just like this because we know all the things we just said about Adam and Eve and the situation are all true. So their thoughts and feelings had to follow their natural course in the short time they had."

Marta said to their surprise, "Adam found the *only* way possible to save us all!"

Stephanie took Carla, Mandy, Rebecca, and Lynnara, to a grassy hill just outside of town that she loved to visit. There was such cute wildlife there she knew the girls would all adore, and she felt she more than owed them for at least giving her back some hope, or at *least* a direction to go in. The worst thing for a *faithwalker* to be was *directionless.* In other words, without meaning. They all dressed in matching brown peasant dresses courtesy of the *faithwalker* to celebrate their loving sisterhood.

Little Lynnara froze cold, *shrieked,* and she threw out her hands wide. A solid golden barrier like a dome appeared around them and an instant later *unnatural* life forms crashed into the dome and bounced off but the protection collapsed as Lynnara fainted. Carla, Mandy, and Rebecca screamed, and Stephanie instantly created a power wave of crystal-clear golden light with solid gold and blue shards that burst out from around them in every direction.

It caught the Earth demons by surprise and cast them away but they immediately rebounded, their twisted half-human half-demon faces showed their anger and their craving. Stephanie knew they had been sent for her, specifically for her unborn child. Stephanie looked over at the girls. *They can't be here.* Lynnara stood up and straightened her new dress. Her eyes burned with golden fire. Stephanie waved her hand sending them all to the only place she knew was safe, but little Lynnara, to Stephanie's shock, remained. "I'm not leaving you Mommy! If you die, I die!" Those were the *same* words Stephanie had thought when she first saved Vaughn from the blackness that came out of a self-destructing human turning into a demon. It made Stephanie wonder how much other knowledge Lynnara had acquired when Stephanie had bonded with her in the Dead Forest so she would be able to save herself and protect the Seed to the Tree of Life.

Little Lynnara threw her arms open again and the same protection formed except this time she added blue to it like she saw her Mommy use. The demons bounced off again, their muscular arms and long clawed hands and feet flailing. The dome held, wavered, then collapsed. Lynnara picked herself back up from the ground, at the same time, Lady Stephanie took advantage of Lynnara's protection and put all of her power into the same ball of energy she had hit the Highest Councilor with, a crystal clear sharp ball of blue energy with golden energy restrained inside. It hit one of the demons and blew him to hell.

The other demons stopped and looked at each other then changed strategies. They slowly circled the two girls. Stephanie knew it would be useless to try that attack again. She remembered how her demon father was fast enough to dodge anything she threw at him. Lynnara's thoughts appeared in her Mommy's mind with the image of the cage that *Karen* had used to imprison the child. Stephanie nodded.

The demons all reached out their clawed hands at them and black, ragged streaks hurled forth. Stephanie recognized the Black Oil. She and Lynnara vanished and reappeared behind one demon and Lynnara quickly threw a Karen-type cage around the creature then Lady Stephanie hit the whole mess with another ball of energy blowing everything to hell. "Two down, eight more to go," Stephanie said, smiling at her daughter.

All the demons re-assessed again. Three of them disappeared, then reappeared behind Lynnara. The girls tried popping away but couldn't. Stephanie knew immediately that the other five were concentrating on keeping them where they were at. Lady Stephanie sent a wave of power at the demons to keep them from her daughter, but no sooner than they had appeared behind her, one of them disappeared and reappeared behind Stephanie. Caught in the middle of sending power to defend Lynnara, she was only able to mount minimal protection and the demon's claws ripped into her peasant dress and shredded it.

He got through Stephanie's protection and she went down with a scream. Little Lynnara became a total ball of energy and sent all her golden power into the demon and blew it apart! Stephanie stood up. "Lynnara, you have to *go. Please.*"

But the little girl refused. She resolutely stood her ground, saying, "*No.*"

Stephanie's back burned from something but she couldn't consider it now. The seven remaining Earth demons circled again. They shot their black oil again. Stephanie and Lynnara tried to pop away but only Lynnara succeeded. The Black Oil covered Lady Stephanie and she went down screaming. The demons rejoiced, knowing this would be easy. They didn't care about the little girl. They weren't sent for her.

Lynnara popped behind one, threw another cage around it, then holding out her little hands like she was grabbing something, she brought her hands together and the cage shank around the demon and sliced it into bits while it howled.

But the other demons converged on Lady Stephanie to rip her apart and eat the fragments while she was in her torments from the Black Oil. Their mouths drooled. This was their promised reward that would speed their maturity past their siblings. But when they were almost upon her, she rolled on her back and a huge fireball of red, blue and gold exploded around her. It totally incinerated two, blew another three away, but another one disappeared right before the demon got hit. And it reappeared just as the blast had left Stephanie while she was recovering and it slashed through her arms and the front of her dress. Little Lynnara screamed and sent all her power against it and drove it away.

But they were getting used to their energies!

Vaughn materialled between the demons and the girls. He was so black they could hardly see him. They all leapt at Vaugh. He spun and kicked three of them and drove them far away. The other one, he held by the throat! The demon tried his best to claw at him but couldn't penetrate anything but his ranger uniform. Vaughn ripped the demon apart with his bare hands! The other three looked on in amazement then focused back on Lady Stephanie and popped behind her.

Lynnara threw up another dome as her Mommy seemed to wobble. Vaughn held out his hand and a staff appeared in it, and he shouted at the girls. "Duck!" They hit the ground just as Vaughn's staff whirled above them.

The demons thought it funny and one caught the staff in his hand, but it immediately turned to a serpent and in one gulp, consumed the demon. The serpent seemed to smile then went after the last two demons who popped away.

Vaughn looked at the serpent, saying, "Guard," and it nodded!

The last two demons looked at each other, then at Stephanie as she collapsed. They knew she would die along with the child. They looked at Vaughn and Lynnara, whose eyes were now deep red. They looked at the Serpent standing guard. The demons sighed knowing they wouldn't get their meal and they disappeared.

Vaughn rematerialized by his wife. Lynnara was already there, and placed her little hands upon her Mommy to heal her, but she *shrieked*, and fell backwards! Pains tore through her little heart. "*Mommy!*" She hadn't been worried because she knew she could heal her third and best Mommy. But now, all she saw was death for her and little Michael.

Lady Stephanie rolled over, saw that Lynnara was safe, and then looked into Vaughn's eyes. Lying on her back she held up her bloody arms to Vaughn, she looked down at her ragged brown dress and the bleeding claw rakes all over her body. With knowing tears in her eyes, she cried, "Oh, Vaughn."

It was unthinkable to either of them. Lady Stephanie's tummy still glowed but now there were black spirits inside of her swirling inside the glow of the child and then out. Little Michael was fighting the attack! When Stephanie saw and felt this, she looked back up into Vaughn's eyes, "I'm so *sorry*," she gasped.

But Vaughn refused to accept the meaning. He looked up to Heaven and prayed, "Lord God from the beginning, who took my forefathers under his wing to make a great people to serve him. *Now,* this woman right here, through her devout service, *sacrifice*, and *love,* she has brought your people back again. Save her now! And our child."

But there was no answer! Stephanie knew this time there was nothing to save her. "Are you able to hold my hand?"

Vaughn fell to his knees and the gore from the battle fled off of him and he laid his staff down between them, and took her hand in both of his. He felt the terrible evil that was slowly, unavoidably overcoming his beloved and their child. The evil came to her hand to drive Vaughn away, but his righteous anger wouldn't allow it, so the evil, knowing that power couldn't stop it from finishing its work, left Vaughn alone.

Stephanie weakly held on. "I'm so sorry. More than *anything* I wanted to give *you* this son. And you have given me more joy than I ever deserved." Lynnara was on her little knees praying but no one seemed to listen.

King Mafferan had to grab onto his wife again. "You *can't* defy the Lord's decree. There is to be absolutely no interference. At least Lynnara has proven herself."

"But she *can't even come up!* Not from that kind of *death!*"

"We're sworn we can't interfere *down there!* But as soon as her soul hits the Ethereal, I'll be there to fight for her and she *will* come up here. I *swear it!*"

"Oh, Mafferan, it wasn't supposed to end like *this!*"

The Highest Councilor smiled but Grinchback was clearly disturbed. "What's the matter with you?"

"Master, how can I say this? It doesn't feel right. Just like last time when one of *them* had to actually save *us*. I just feel that if she *dies,* and they don't win, we will be on the wrong side of the Eye."

For the first time Highest Councilor ScrabaGag looked very deeply into the Eye of his underling, not in a threatening way, but his phrase about having a feeling had been too common of late. And there it was! The Highest Councilor couldn't believe it. "Grinchback, did you know you have the gift of prophecy?"

"Me? Oh I don't know Master."

Then the Highest Councilor considered how he might help. "If I open a portal directly above her, pull her inside, I can command even that type of Black Essence to leave her and even her child. I would have to save both or none at all."

Grinchback was amazed. "But what of the Father's decree?"

"That's the reason I haven't done it, Grinchback. I'm afraid no matter what we do now, we have lost, if your feelings are correct."

Vaughn held her hand to his lips. Little Lynnara came over and leaned on Vaughn. She *hated* that she couldn't hold her Mommy. "Is Mommy gonna die? And *Michael?*" She gasped a sob.

Vaughn was silent, still not believing *any* of this. Lynnara began to cry. "Why won't God hear my prayers? I don't understand."

And neither did Vaughn. The last time this happened and Stephanie was brought to life-ending grief, precisely because the reality she was in *didn't make sense,* she turned the Black River to stone. When she had died before, with the very Seed to the Tree of Life still around her neck, and this cursed evil all over her blocking even her ascension, Vaughn had prayed that *nothing* made sense, and that if she died like that, then *that* reality was essentially cursed forever. *Where was God?* And he was right! And the Seed to the Tree of Life knew it, and gave its own life to bring her back.

But what of now? The Tree of Life sprouted for them. It was safe now, for all the Earth. In time, little Lynnara would find her intended mate, and raise up children unto the Tree of Life. Kneeling beside her, Vaughn watched little unborn Michael fight for the good he had already become but that light grew dimmer, and he felt his beloved wife's heart breaking, and Little Lynnara breaking inside too . . . with her *still* waiting on him to answer her question, "Why won't God hear my prayers? I don't understand."

It still *doesn't make sense!* The experience Vaughn had when he had received the Holy Ghost came to him, and what the Lord Jesus had said to him, *I shall place in your hand the Staff of my Indignation, as well as the Staff of Life. Receive the Holy Ghost.* And then he remembered in his vision that *wasn't* recorded in the Holy Bible, that the very same staff brought the child back to life to his mother.

The Holy Ghost will teach us all *things, things past, things present, and things to come.* It didn't say only the things written in the Holy Bible. Vaughn looked over to Lynnara. "Do you *still* have faith in Almighty God, in his Son, the Lord Jesus?"

The question wasn't mocking. Her Daddy just wanted to know. She placed her little hand on her heart to check if it was really still there even though God was ignoring her. "I don't understand why God is ignoring me. He's not supposed to do that, and I was told He always hears me." She paused. "But I'm only a little girl and there's so much" she held out her arms, "I don't know. It doesn't feel right to just turn off the faith I still have in *here.*" And she tapped her chest.

Vaughn smiled and looked at his wife. "And you, my love, my *faithwalker.* Do you *still* have faith in the Lord God, even though He has brought you to *this?*"

Her eyes went so loving, so warm. "Oh dear Vaughn, once I wrongly doubted our Holy, True God. Even *twice* when Matthew had me. Now? I can't doubt what I *know* is Good. I can only doubt myself, that somehow, some way, I myself have brought this evil upon us, and . . ." she burst into tears. "I'm so sorry, and she clutched her tummy. I'm so *very* sorry little Michael."

"No, you *haven't* Mommy, I would know. You've been *good!*" And she threw herself upon her third Mommy, and even though the Black Essence tried to force her away, she held on against the increasing pain and pressure until Stephanie called to Vaughn and he lifted her off and set her down, bawling.

Vaughn knelt on his knees and picked up his Staff of Indignation, but also the Staff of Life, and he raised his voice to the Heavens and held up the Staff. "You Heavens, and all that *are* therein." And a mighty thunder went up from where he stood and rolled upward! "Behold what *Almighty* God has placed in *my* hand!" And the thunder roared again even more fiercely. "Not in any of *your* lame hands!"

He looked down at his wife who struggled to watch her beloved husband, amazed at what he was doing. "The Staff of the *Lord's* Indignation." And *again,* the same thundering roar, "But also the Lord's Staff of Life!" And this time the Staff glowed brilliantly and the stillest Peace emanated from it. "As the Lord God of my forefathers and of *me* is my witness, you shall *not* die, nor our child, in *spite* of everyone above and below and here on Earth or *anywhere* else."

And as Vaughn knelt before his wife, he placed the Staff upon her and her hands upon it, and stepped back.

The Staff of Life glowed brightly and the Black Essence howled, and the Staff tuned into a glowing serpent, and bit Lady Stephanie on the neck! The Black Essence fled to her feet but the Lord's Serpent sucked up all life into it, the life of Stephanie, the life of little Michael, *and* the Black Essence.

And the *faithwalker's* body lay without life, nor little Michael's life. And the Serpent released his hold on her neck but there were no wounds. Then it opened its mouth wide and a mighty wind came forth from it, and Lady Stephanie glowed while she still held onto the Serpent.

And Stephanie looked into the Serpent's eyes and knew the Spirit of Almighty God was within, but she also felt little Michael was *gone,* and the loss devastated her. "Please, I beg You, give me our child, or take my life back because I'm not worthy any longer, Oh Lord, who is always Good, no matter what!"

And the Serpent opened his mouth wide and a mighty, glowing wind came forth, entered into Lady Stephanie's nostrils, and her tummy glowed mightily. And the Serpent turned its head to peer into Vaughn's eyes, then became the Staff again!

Lady Stephanie kissed the Staff and hugged it, and little Lynnara did the same, and Vaughn picked up his wife in his strong arms. Stephanie looked down at Lynnara. "Hold onto Daddy, we have to take a trip to go get your sisters." She wrapped her arms around Vaughn's leg and they were about to disappear when a *very* unexpected visitor showed up!

CHAPTER 11
What Are the Odds

Revelation Chapter 11

And there was given me a reed like unto a rod: and the angel stood, saying, Rise, and measure the temple of God, and the altar, and them that worship therein.

2 But the court which is without the temple leave out, and measure it not; for it is given unto the Gentiles: and the holy city shall they tread under foot forty and two months.

3 And I will give power unto my two witnesses, and they shall prophesy a thousand two hundred and threescore days, clothed in sackcloth.

4 These are the two olive trees, and the two candlesticks standing before the God of the earth.

Queen Yinauqua stared into her husband's eyes. "I love Vaughn, so much! He's exceeded even you my beloved husband."

The Highest Councilor looked into Grinchback's Great Eye and slung his great tail over the underling's shoulder. "What do you feel now?"

Grinchback looked inside himself then up into his Master's Great Eye. "Hope."

Karen rejoiced at the two demon's report. She looked triumphantly at the Father and HrorrarrAggrang. "Well?"

Jargono felt an unknown pain cross his heart as he watched his wife in the orb. It wasn't just the strategic loss. There was an emptiness like he felt when Vaughn showed him about Karen, but this was even a different kind of loss, something even more profound but he couldn't figure that out. It was just a feeling. At the same time, his heart distinctly pained for Vaughn. What could be said to his new *friend?* He still hadn't got used to that feeling. He knew how others would act but he had always thought that kind of behavior to be whimsical, foolish, or weak. Not now. And with Stephanie's loss, he knew his own wife's fate was lost also, and he felt compelled to express his common grief to Vaughn.

As he materialized, he began to immediately, sincerely, say, "I'm so sorry for your . . ." And when he met their eyes and saw Lady Stephanie was still alive, he picked her right up out of Vaughn's arms, and twirled her around cheering! Then he set her down and reached over and hugged Vaughn, slapping him hard on the back, and he then even picked up little Lynnara and twirled her, too, and she promptly threw her little arms around his neck and kissed the nice man on the cheek!

Everyone was stunned, including Jargono, himself, as he gently set Lynnara down. "Ahh, didn't your husband tell you? We have an indefinite truce."

Vaughn smiled, and added, "With a six-month buffer after the truce ends before we can attack each other."

Jargono saw they were just about to travel so he begged their pardon and was about to leave when Stephanie called him back. "Jargono." She looked deeply into his eyes. "Thank you."

He was about to leave when he noticed something that he felt extraordinary. He looked at Stephanie's tummy and pointed to it with raised eyebrows and Stephanie merely raised hers in return. He looked at Vaughn, and Vaughn smiled broadly. Jargono straightened. Another new rush of feelings came to him. He hadn't really considered having children, what with planning his world rule and all.

He shook his head. Too many strange new feelings. "I watched as the demons returned and boasted to Karen of your demise. Karen was ecstatic. I thought they'd killed Lynnara, too. But now I understand what child they were talking about." Then Jargono became aware of the carnage all around. Demon filth littered the ground all over and he turned very dark. With a wave of his hand, it all instantly burst into hissing flames and then a bright light annihilated the vapors.

He leveled serious eyes into Stephanie now, deeply appraising her. She no longer kept him out and he finally learned what the Sacred Treasure *had been!* She shrugged her shoulders at him. He nodded. "Well done, *faithwalker!* Well done, *indeed!*" He then returned to his appraisal of her. He had never answered Vaughn's question.

Jargono turned to Vaughn. "The answer is definitely your wife!"

Stephanie looked over to her husband, questioningly, but he just smiled his special smile.

Jargono turned to her with a serious bow, then looked again into her eyes. "We have had battles. I understand you meant well, *very well.* Both of you have made me think and see many things differently, to *feel* differently. I confess I don't understand much of it, and my goals are still the same. But I'm willing to make the past to *be* past. Your husband now calls me his friend! And as you have just witnessed, this new feeling of friendship has brought me here."

Vaughn chuckled. "That's his way of saying he's *considering* being our friend, too, in light of all that's going on."

Jargono saw how Vaughn tried to make it less awkward for him and that amazed him, too. "May I?" he asked Stephanie, and she nodded. He looked into her again to see the battle she had just fought. Her feelings inundated him. Predominate over it all was her utter love for everyone else, especially her unborn child. Little Lynnara's powers shocked him, but he saw that same strength in her, too. Jargono shook his head when he felt Stephanie be hit the first time by the demon in her back. It was if he could feel that himself. And then many more attacks that tore into her. And the fierce struggle against the poison within her, as she *still* fought for everyone else until she collapsed and Vaughn showed up. He ended his query there.

Lady Stephanie bowed her head to him with the thought, *It is what it is.* "Aren't you curious to know how I survived?"

Jargono was hesitant. "It's enough that you *are* very much alive."

But Lynnara, as usual, had been watching *everything* very closely and she took Jargono's hand. He immediately felt her sweetness enter into him and it was a feeling so contrary to *anything* he had ever felt. He laughed to himself that it might even be some kind of great power, to which Lynnara just smiled into his eyes as if knowing his thoughts!

The last time Jargono had encountered a child with Stephanie, she had bit the same hand because he was inflicting pain on her mother. Now this child also made him think and experience new things. It was a bit too much. He patted Lynnara on the head and was about to leave, when he turned and said to Stephanie, "I'm sorry for all that I put you through!"

Lady Stephanie was as shocked as Vaughn and Jargono, himself, who had no idea at all he would say such a thing. He had always known his thoughts, if not all his feelings, but now he beheld himself in a very disarmed way. Those were *his* words that came out of his mouth.

Lynnara tugged on his tunic and Jargono looked down into knowing, understanding eyes that he couldn't seem to look away from. "Mr. Jar . . ." She couldn't remember how to pronounce it. "Well, anyway, that's just Life!"

He didn't pick up on the capital L, but the child's meaning hit its mark. Jargono sighed, and looked at Vaughn. "I really shouldn't even be asking this." Then he looked over toward Stephanie but couldn't look her in the eye.

Stephanie smiled as loving a smile as ever. "I'll do everything I can to save your wife!"

Jargono felt something strange, a pressure in his chest, a tear in his eye. His wife had just almost successfully murdered Stephanie. From what he saw when he entered the *faithwalker,* she *was* dead! All he could do was just nod and vanish.

Stephanie looked with deep love into her husband's eyes but before she could ask how he accomplished all this with King Jargono, Vaughn just said, "All I did was pick up where you left off back at the village!"

That was when Stephanie had honestly given to Jargono all the love she could muster in hopes of changing him! "I can't resist you any longer," she said, and wrapped her arms around him in a passionate kiss. Lynnara wrapped her arms around Vaughn's leg in a mighty hug and they all vanished to pick up her sisters.

When they popped in, Carla, Mandy, and Rebecca knelt at the Tree of Life whose golden vision just closed. They ran into each other's arms and Stephanie knew they had watched everything. Mandy said, "I can't *believe* this place. It's so beautiful. How did you *ever* find this in the middle of all *that?*" She waved her hand indicating everything outside of the holy mountain.

Little Lynnara had heard her Mommy and Daddy talking about this and her Mommy had explained to her what happened to the Seed to the Tree of Life and how Michael came to be but not like she saw in the underground. This was *love.* And Lynnara looked up at Mandy and said, "Mommy created all this." And she waved her little hand around. "Because God told her to."

Mandy and Carla looked at Stephanie who just shrugged and went and knelt down before the Tree of Life. It was now taller than she was and thriving. "What can I say before Thee?"

Rebecca and Lynnara went off together with Lynnara telling her best friend *everything* that happened. Vaughn came over to Mandy and Carla who both kissed him on the cheek. "I have to go see another *friend*. He needs my help, too." And he disappeared.

And reappeared in the Highest Councilor's room, whereupon ScrabaGag floated up to him and put his very black arm upon him, and said, "I respect you!"

Vaughn burst out in laughter, slapped the Highest Councilor on the torso a few times, leaving glowing hand prints, and said, "That means you *really* want to eat me."

Grinchback's eye smiled wider than ever and came over and wrapped his tail around Vaughn in a friendly embrace. "You *know* we were watching *everything.*"

Vaughn laughed again, saying, "You and every single Alpha *except* the Father and Horrrara-what's-his-tail!"

That brought huge laughter from the demons. Both Grinchback and His master kept on calling out, "What's-his-tail, What's-his-*tail.*"

But Vaughn turned deadly serious. "Shall we?" And the Highest Councilor waved his massive arm and they all materialized in the demons most secret room, whereupon Vaughn brought up all the surveillance from Jargono's stealth orb.

When he was done, Grinchback said he liked the idea of a demon resort. But the Highest Councilor said. "Well, at least we're all enjoying ourselves before we *all* end up on the wrong side of the Greatest Eye. I have to hand it to the Father. He wasn't just an old demon who was past his time."

But Vaughn smiled his special smile at them and Grinchback's brow went up. "Master, I have no idea what he's going to say, but I *think* we're really going to like it!"

Vaughn pulled up the image of the stealth orb. "I've held it in *this* very hand." And he placed it upon Grinchback's head and instantly everything about the little orb flooded him, so much so that it was almost like he'd consumed. He began to float sideways. The Highest Councilor gave Vaughn a questioning Eye but Vaughn just pointed to his underling who was righting himself. "Master, don't you understand what Vaughn just did for us?"

His Master squinted at him, and ScrabaGag said, "It wasn't me who embarrassingly floated sideways."

"Jargono's orb is connected to an actual orb *system* that *they* are running!" the Highest Councilor still didn't appreciate the details. "Master, *Karen* created the Father's orb from Jargono's and her own powers and technology."

He *still* didn't get it.

Grinchback looked at Vaughn, so he finished for his friend. "Karen would *never* pass up this opportunity!"

The Highest Councilor was clearly getting frustrated, so Vaughn said, "Don't act like such an *old* demon! The Father's orb is on Jargono and Karen's system!"

But Grinchback added, "But I'm sure Jargono is unaware of it, I'm sure she's hidden it from him, but I'm *also* sure there is no way she doesn't *still* control it!"

The Highest Councilor's colors lit up in red's and purples and browns. "And I have before me the two best orbists *anywhere!*"

To which Vaughn honestly and humbly replied, "Yes. I think we can take control of the Father's orb! And *even* lock Karen out."

"And even make her see what we want?"

Vaughn crossed his arms across his chest and stared at the Highest Councilor. "Who did you root for? And what were the odds?"

Grinchback spoke up, "Ninety-nine to one. Ahh, Master did change, but too late. Actually, I'm quite a rich Alpha now, having first priory at consumption for a whole Ethereal month!"

Still with his arms crossed, Vaughn turned powerfully dark but held that power within. Which impressed the demons and made them even more cautious. Then Vaughn asked the Highest Councilor, "Can you undo what you and the others have done to Karen?"

Grinchback turned to his Master with a questioning eye, but the Highest Councilor went deep into thought. "She won't be willing. She's too powerful, now, to force her."

"What if she was preoccupied?"

The Highest Councilor thought more deeply. "If you want to save her life for your . . . *friend,* our power must be withdrawn from her very slowly, otherwise she dies a horrible human death. I don't see how that would be possible."

"Can you do it from her tree?"

ScrabaGag shook his great bulbus head. "It has to be done directly because this kind of transformation could only have been done directly. But even if it *would be* done. She was lost to you from birth, before birth."

"I know about that,"

And the Highest Councilor looked over to Grinchback. "I see you've kept your other Master well informed." Grinchback wound his tail up around his head.

But Vaughn said, "I was into *everything* when I was *neutral*. You have no secrets any longer from me since that time!" Grinchback began to uncoil. "What you two need to figure out, is how to gain access to the Father's orb and then how best to use that, and when. I'll be far too busy with everything else."

Grinchback turned to Vaughn, "Master," he forgot himself that the Highest Councilor was right there. "I mean . . ."

But ScrabaGag patted his underling on the back with his tail. "It's fine, Grinchback. I know *I've* earned your utmost loyalty. Your devotion has been well proven. You've risked your tail more than once even against my ignorant wishes but for my best interest. As I said, earlier, I respect master Vaughn, also, and I'm not in the least bit insulted that you do, too!"

Grinchback bowed to his Master, "There has *never* been *any* Alpha like you Master."

And Vaughn nodded his agreement. "True."

The Highest Councilor then turned to Vaughn. "Even with Jargono as your ally for now, even with all the power you all can muster, you're still way overmatched for what Karen has created. The Father has forbidden us to interfere, but even if we could leverage what you've provided to us, we still couldn't destroy enough of what Karen has done if she releases it upon an open Earth. It's just too much and growing every day."

Vaughn said, "I know, but let's just take one step at a time."

To that, Grinchback and his Master acknowledged, and Vaughn vanished, leaving the orb behind, again.

Grinchback went over to the orb and quickly manipulated it, then frowned. "Master, the betting odds haven't even changed at all, in spite of their recent victory."

"Still ninety-nine to one Grinchback?"

"No Master. Ninety-eight to two."

His Master smiled. "Let's get to work, my faithful underling."

CHAPTER 12

Mirror Mirror
Inside All Men, Who's
the Fairest of Them All

5 And if any man will hurt them, fire proceedeth out of their mouth, and devoureth their enemies: and if any man will hurt them, he must in this manner be killed.

6 These have power to shut heaven, that it rain not in the days of their prophecy: and have power over waters to turn them to blood, and to smite the earth with all plagues, as often as they will.

7 And when they shall have finished their testimony, the beast that ascendeth out of the bottomless pit shall make war against them, and shall overcome them, and kill them.

Lady Stephanie rose early singing an Appendaho tune of thankfulness while moving about their apartment in her fluffy pink bathrobe. Vaughn woke from a peaceful sleep and silently listened. Little Lynnara came out of her little room, rubbed her eyes and sat on the couch listening silently, as well. Stephanie, then sat on her cushion in front of the large mirror at the primping area beside the bathroom door, and began brushing her hair. Vaughn watched her through the open doorway, her tune doing something indescribable to his heart, it was so searching, so mysterious. *I never knew she could sing like* that!

Jargono had told them late last night he and Karen would be castle building, today. His wife loved the idea of a more secure place. He left unsaid what he thought they should do. Stephanie turned to Lynnara, and said, "This time, you're going to listen to your third Mommy."

It was the way Stephanie came out from her tune and shifted into a very firm tone that gave Vaughn a second thought, and Lynnara nodded her head. Stephanie raised a single eyebrow at the child, and Lynnara harrumphed, saying, "OK Mommy, but I helped save you before."

"You did, no doubt about it. But this time, you're going to listen. Do you understand? It's dangerous to you and to all of us, if you, as a little child, thinks she always knows best. Don't you think?"

And Lynnara did think about it. "Yes, Mommy. It makes sense."

"I'm going to send you and your sisters back to the Tree of Life. From *there,* if the Tree permits you, you can watch, and pray, and do as the Tree guides you all." She looked at Vaughn then back over to Lynnara, eye to eye. "No *more,* and no *less.* Do you understand?"

"Yes Mommy."

Vaughn got up and showered then brushed his teeth then donned his brown ranger uniform, reached under the bed and pulled out his bow and quiver filled with arrows. He put on his vest. Lynnara's eyes went wide when she saw the weapon and felt the power within them. He turned to Stephanie, handed her an arrow, and said, "*Faithwalker*, I need a real lot of these."

She smiled. "You're a *faithwalker* now, too!"

"But nowhere near to your capacity."

"I can produce the arrows but not the blessing. It's a *warrior's* blessing. Not in my faithwalking department."

From the living room couch, they heard Lynnara, "Wooooooe!"

Then without even a wave of the hand, Lady Stephanie said, "Look in our bedroom, dearest."

Vaughn went in, and saw one side of the room stacked to the ceiling with the very same bows, quivers, and arrows but there was no power in them. "Now I need jugs of olive oil."

"Light or regular?" And Vaughn was surprised to hear her offer up the blessed Light Oil which he had thought she couldn't produce except from the Black Oil or the Light Oil he had to give her.

"I think the Light Oil is a very different kind of blessing. I think just regular."

Without even so much as a head nod, the bedroom floor filled with half-gallon jugs of oil stacked in crates. Lynnara squeezed up onto the cushion next to her Mommy to watch more closely. She took a little hair brush from the shelf under the mirror, the one her Mommy said was all hers, and she started brushing the tangles out of her curly bouncy brown hair just the way she saw Mommy do it.

Vaughn took his staff from the corner of the bedroom, then came to stand in the doorway and leaned on his staff, saying, "In my vision, the back room where this staff had been kept had just been sealed so the Muslims couldn't find it. That means they kept that room active until then. Why?"

Stephanie and Lynnara *loved* when Vaughn got like this, his *point-making* mode. Little Lynnara shrugged her shoulders while his wife only smiled.

"The only thing of note in that back room was this Staff." And he pushed it forward a bit then back against his shoulder and side of his head. "In the immediate larger connecting room were many jugs all stacked up, but there were no other indications that they made the oil there, nor was it a market. Everything else was weapons or weapon related. Why?" Again, the shrug and smile.

Vaughn took his staff, went over to the jugs of olive oil Stephanie had just created, then raised the Staff of Indignation, saying, "Gracious Lord God, the Lord Jesus who placed this tool into *my* hands to do your service. This *is* Your Indignation." And the Staff begin to glow mightily in blackness. "Put your Warriors Blessing upon all this oil!" And Vaughn extended the Staff and waved it over the crates of oil. The glowing blackness extended out from the Staff mingling around all the jugs and then disappeared within them. The girls only nodded and began helping each other with some very stubborn hair tangles.

"Vaughn," Stephanie said. "Last night I couldn't sleep, so I popped over to the Dead Forest to examine Karen's tree."

Vaughn's brow raised because he knew the dangers for Stephanie. The Dead Forest is where she had died. Every human being born into the world immediately gets a tree in the Dead Forest and it manifests that person's full personality through various tree appearances. The branches above are for the mind, the roots below are for the heart, the trunk is the soul that connects the two into one. But the demons control the Dead Forest and use the trees to influence people. A change to the tree makes a change in the person and vice versa. Through their orbs, they can focus on a tree and turn the tree into the vision of the person and vice versa with that, too. They find it easier to understand the depths of people by looking at their trees rather than their flesh bodies. So their attention is highly attuned to *their* Forest.

After Stephanie noted her husband's concern, she continued. "She's got her tree even more elaborately protected than before, but now that she's become an actual demon, she needed to mask that from her husband. So she took from Jargono's tree a tiny twig involving his perception of her and she *grafted it* onto her tree!"

Vaughn turned squarely around to face his wife and began leaning on his staff, again. "She could do that?"

"Apparently so. It's not at all obvious, and it's such a tiny piece. I had to search Jargono's tree very carefully to see from where it came. Apparently, he never noticed and he simply grew a new twig there, but I could still see the tiny scar. But to *me,* it was obvious on her tree because her tree is now so *black!*"

"I don't understand. The Jargono I know, now, would see that."

"No, because his little grafted twig onto her tree will capture his perception and only allow him to see what *he wants to see!* Otherwise, all the trouble she went through to do that doesn't make sense!"

"I'd hate to see what he would do if he could really see it, then."

"Well, that's the thing. I'm going to need his help to get to Karen's tree the way I need to without her knowing. To do *that,* he's going to have to face reality!"

"How does his tree appear now that he seems to be changing somewhat?"

Stephanie looked through the bedroom doorway in amazement. "Well, pretty much as we see him! He has a number of new buds on branches of understanding and their corresponding roots, some of which have sprouted but are *very* young. He even has a couple swollen buds of action across from the branches of understanding. And he has the expected additional glow in his trunk that's now feeding the new growth. So I would say the man is actually sincere. *But* the new growth is *very* fragile."

Vaughn shook his head. "And you think when you show him the truth of Karen' tree, it will kill all his progress."

"Vaughn, I spent hours delving into the depths of her tree. I forgot I wasn't even supposed to be down there that long. But I guess the demons decided they wanted no parts of messing with me. Anyway, I searched her whole tree. *Vaughn,* there's only a tiny portion of her trunk that dates all the way back to just before she was tainted in her mother's womb. It's a tiny portion of latent glow that was suppressed by the taint but refused to die. At first, I thought I'd just hack her tree down to *just* that part!"

Vaughn narrowed his eyes at his wife.

"I know, I know. I caught myself. Vaughn, that would leave her as a vegetable for a very long time, and *if* that little glow part could grow up, I really don't think Jargono would recognize her as anywhere near the person he loves."

"So she's hopeless."

Little Lynnara, without missing a brushstroke and concentrating on a tangle in her Mommy's hair, said, as a matter-of-factly, "No she's not!" And kept on brushing.

"Well, Lynnara is right, I hope. Since Karen grafted onto her tree, I even thought of grafting a part of my tree onto hers!"

To *that* both her husband and daughter reacted with surprise, then little Lynnara stopped brushing, took her Mommy's cheek and turned her to look into her eyes for a moment, then went back to the tangle, and said, "No, *that* won't work!"

Stephanie smiled, "You're right. My graft would be instantly rejected no matter how small."

"So it *is* hopeless."

Lynnara just shook her head and rolled her eyes. "Daddy's not listening!"

"Vaughn, in the beginning when God made Adam, then took Eve out of his midst, *by that* the Lord separated the true wives for all generations of men. In other words, Karen's tree *came from* Jargono's tree!"

Lynnara stopped brushing, and Vaughn's eyes went wide. "But which part would you take from Jargono?"

"He'll have to tell me that! I don't know, nor do I think I should choose for him."

Vaughn ran his hand through his hair. "We're going to have to explain all this to him, together, I think, but I don't know when he'd be ready to receive something like this, if ever!"

Little Lynnara vanished!

Jargono and Karen stood upon a large hill and he was in the process of explaining to Karen the kind of castle he envisioned. He created the foundation of it, then asked his wife what she thought. She'd point to different things, suggest changes and he made them. Then she'd change her mind and he'd change them again. Back and forth they went. She seemed to be really enjoying herself, proud she had a husband with such power, creativity, and artistic flair.

Little Lynnara whispered at Jargono from the Ethereal Corridor, "You have to go potty!"

Jargono shook his head, and Karen said, "You don't like my change?"

"Oh. No. No, it's just I don't want to pause doing this, but even for me . . ."

Karen laughed. "OK, let's both take a bathroom break. Meet back here in half an hour."

Jargono looked at her skeptically, so Karen revised. "OK, one hour." And Karen disappeared. Jargono popped up to the Corridor quite surprised to find little Lynnara there. She took his hand, saying, "Mommy and Daddy need to talk with you right now." And she popped him back over to her home!

Stephanie and Vaughn were right in the middle of discussing what happened to Lynnara, but Lynnara, still holding his hand, paused in the Corridor with Jargono, and whispered. "Close your eyes. I have to make sure their decent." So he closed his eyes, but he could hear what they were saying. Little Lynnara's sweetness was, again, invading him, but along with that was the amazing fact that she transported *him,* and that this was *obviously* a very spontaneous plan on the child's part! The next moment they were both standing in front of Stephanie and Vaughn!

Lynnara took her place back on the cushion and resumed her hair duty. Then she looked up, and said, "Well, you were *just* talking about it!" All three of the adults looked at her then at each other trying to discern the meaning of her word, *just!* Then Lynnara said in a sing-song voice, "Talking, talking, *talking* . . . so I just did it. See?"

Both Vaughn and Jargono ran their hands through their hair. Stephanie waved her hand and created an arm chair fit for a king. It reminded Jargono of when he had done the same for Stephanie, and he sat down.

Vaughn looked at him. "If I was going to approach something like this with any regular folk, I would take a very long time to set it up."

Lynnara sang again, "Talkin, talkin, *talking!*"

They all paused to stare at her while she kept untangling Stephanie's stubborn hair knot. "Mommy, I could fix this with my powers, but I don't want to. I think some things need to be just regular like."

Vaughn rethought his approach. "We're *men,* and we need to rise to the challenge."

Lynnara said, "That's better!"

And at that point, Stephanie burst out laughing really hard. "I'm sorry, but . . ." then she laughed some more. Lynnara just smiled.

Vaughn and Jargono looked at each other. Jargono felt something difficult was coming fast, but in light of the ladies and their reactions, it did something strange to him, but not a bad strange.

"Stephanie has examined your wife's tree *extensively.* She's found a way, a *possible* way to bring your wife back from destruction."

Now Jargono sat straight up, and he changed his chair into a normal wooden straight-back.

Stephanie looked into his eyes with love. "But I can't do it myself. I *have to have* your help."

Jargono was about to wave his hand to take them there, but Lynnara said, "Ooohh, there's more!"

They all looked at her, again!

Stephanie continued, "In order to be able to do all this, to disarm all the protection Karen has around her tree, you *need* to face reality, to see clearly!"

The implication that he *didn't,* startled him, but then he realized that his wife had been successfully hiding things, but *this* sounded ominous. He nodded for them to continue.

Stephanie explained how Karen grafted a part of his tree onto hers and why.

Jargono whispered, "What does she look like?"

At that point Vaughn leaned forward upon his staff, and said, "You *already* know!"

Stephanie looked at Vaughn amazed at how right he was. "He's right. Our trees are *reflections* of us. You *know* your wife."

Jargono shook his head, thought deeply for a bit, then he looked into their eyes. "And you want to help her, anyway? How?"

Lynnara answered his first meaning. "Because they love you!"

The weight of the child's remark struck them *all!* Jargono rubbed his face. Vaughn and Stephanie looked at each other in amazement, but when they looked at their feelings, they saw the love. Jargono was having a hard time with all this and little Lynnara climbed down and went to lean on him. "Mommy and Daddy are good people. You're good, too!"

Jargono sat with his elbow on his knee and his head propped up in his hand, leaning over, unable to look anyone in the eye.

Vaughn continued, "Time is short, my friend. We're *men.*"

Jargono took a deep breath, then looked Vaughn in the eye, and nodded.

Lynnara said, "Mommy wants to . . ." she couldn't remember the word, graft. But she remembered the meaning, "take a part of your tree and give it to your wife. But you have to decide." Then she looked at Vaughn, and said, "There! Easy!"

Easy! Just like that. But the idea intrigued Jargono and when the adults nodded in confirmation, he shook his head. "Amazing."

Vaughn said, "I'm going to be blunt. Your wife has *really* messed herself up. Stephanie thought of taking her tree all the way down to just the best part but . . . well, that wouldn't work. *But* you two were always meant for each other. In the order of Creation, *her* tree originally came for *yours.* "

Stephanie continued. "She's already proven your tree can be grafted onto hers. But I *can't* make that decision myself. *You* have to decide what part of yourself to give her! My hope is, that once this is done, if I prune her tree properly, it will encourage your part, which is *still* her because you two are *one,* to flourish and correct her."

Jargono was thinking he should be the one to prune her tree but Vaughn stepped in, "Jargono. I have trusted my wife many times with my life and I would do it again. *You* can't prune her tree. Do you understand?"

In a sing-song voice again, "Because you love her so much. Your hand would like shake, or something!"

Stephanie shook her head and motioned for the child to come and leave Jargono alone, but he said, "It's alright. She's fine!" Little Lynnara smiled a broad, *SEE-smile* back at her Mommy.

Vaughn said, "Jargono, Karen is a woman, Stephanie is a woman. Only a woman can understand how to do this right, but only *you* know which *part of you* she is supposed to have. There is a mirror inside every single man that contains the perfect reflection of their true wife, the place in him from where she was taken in Creation. You take from *that* part of your tree, she'll immediately make it her own, and that will *override* what the demons have destroyed!"

When he heard Vaugh mention the demons, he grew incredibly angry and the room shook. But Lynnara patted him on the head, saying, "It'll be OK Mr. Jar . . . It'll be OK. Mommy's good at fixing *everything.*" And she threw out her arms.

Jargono looked into the child's eyes that were blazing with innocent, loving golden light. And he kissed her on the forehead, whereupon Lynnara turned around, whispering, "He kissed me! Right here."

Jargono stood up and the chair disappeared. He rubbed Lynnara's head, saying, "Thank you for bringing me here and having such good sense. But *next time,* you check with Mommy and Daddy *first.*" Everyone noted his sternness and Jargono was gone.

CHAPTER 13

The Staff of Judgment

8 And their dead bodies shall lie in the street of the great city, which spiritually is called Sodom and Egypt, where also our Lord was crucified.

9 And they of the people and kindreds and tongues and nations shall see their dead bodies three days and a half, and shall not suffer their dead bodies to be put in graves.

10 And they that dwell upon the earth shall rejoice over them, and make merry, and shall send gifts one to another; because these two prophets tormented them that dwelt on the earth.

Yinauqua looked perplexed and asked her wise husband, who had also just backed away from the golden vision, "Should they be doing that? Messing with another individual's tree? Trading *parts?*"

There was no quick answer. Wise King Mafferan wanted to say, NO, but he couldn't, and he wondered why. It wasn't that he couldn't bring himself to say, NO, about them, it was something different. "I don't know!" After further thought, he said, "But that seems to be the general rule, now, concerning them! No one knows up here, nor down below!"

But Yinauqua saw his meaning and frowned. "The Lord knows. He *always* knows."

Mafferan paused to check himself, then nodded. "Sometimes, the wisest folk can be *too* wise for their own good! They get *too* caught up in themselves."

Yinauqua smiled, hugged him, and said, "That's why he made us *both* to be *one!*"

He hugged her close and kissed the top of her head, and nodded.

☙

The Highest Councilor had been studying his faithful underling for a very long time, as his tail had split into many parts, and his arm, too! And they *still* kept flying through the orb. At one point, Grinchback was so engrossed in concentration that he got some of his appendages all tangled up and he had to look over to his Master for help. Finally, he had to admit, "I think I need Master Vaughn. I found the connection Karen *indeed* kept to the Father's orb, but she's so encrypted it, I can't get in."

The Highest Councilor said, "Well, let's focus on the other half of this. The Father also said that soon his would be the *only* orb. How does he intend to do that?"

"Master there are only two ways to accomplish this in the short term. One would be to kill Master Vaughn, then apply for an end to the deal. That would bog down, and the Father could simply end all orb function in a rebellious, seemingly out of control rage. But that wouldn't actually destroy our ability but merely rule against it. That means I think he's going to trip Vaughn's failsafe and crash the whole system."

The Highest Councilor scratched his bulbous head with his tail. "But the way I understand it, Master Vaughn made that failsafe on an *individual* basis. If an Alpha messed with his program, only *that particular* orb would fail."

Grinchback took note that *his* Master called Vaughn a *Master!* "That is how I understand it, too. Which means, somehow, they have to affect *all* the orbs all at once. But HrorrarrAggrang possesses ancient orb knowledge we know nothing about. This might be easy for him. The only other way would be to mess with this orb right here, but I don't believe that will be an option because Master Vaughn simply won't let them have what has become *his* orb."

"Send to Master Vaughn that you need him."

Grinchback popped away and into the Ethereal Corridor. It was becoming increasingly difficult to have his arm reach through the orb into Vaughn's mind. Gladly, he found him and his wife in the Corridor as well, looking over an Earth Demon town,

Vaughn smiled, "Grinchback, my friend, I was just thinking about you!"

Stephanie still couldn't get used to Vaughn calling him friend, let alone *being* friend to this demon. It wasn't that long ago that Grinchback tried to eat her, Lynnara, and steal the Seed. When Grinchback saw her glaring at him, he bowed to her, "Lady Stephanie, when I saw your recent victory, I celebrated. You have made me quite rich!"

Vaughn laughed, "He bet on us to win!"

"You're a *male* demon, right?"

It was an odd question which Grinchback didn't know how to answer. Sexes between the Alpha were only mentioned in Legend. "I suppose so."

"*Men!*" was all Lady Stephanie said. "How's the handprint?"

"Oh, I wear it as a badge of honor! I'm thinking of making it into a new Alpha fashion statement.

Vaughn had to contain himself, and the look on his wife's face wasn't' helping.

Grinchback got to the point. "We need your help very badly. We're at an impasse, but I think you shouldn't proceed with your plans quite yet," he motioned down below, "because it's obvious to us the Father and Horrra-*what's-his-tail* plan on killing you, because they would have to, to ensure their plan isn't foiled."

That caught Stephanie's attention. "Vaughn?"

But he brushed it all away. "From as long as I can remember, practically, everyone's been trying to kill me. I'm *hard* to kill, and even harder now than before. Grinchback, are you hungry?"

That got his attention and Stephanie, too. "*Vaughn!* What are you doing? The last time you fed *him* it went *very* badly for us."

Grinchback's eye was already drooling but he wasn't aware that his friend had suffered on account of feeding him. But then he remembered Master Vaughn always keeps his word.

"Master Vaughn is a man of *integrity*, Lady Stephanie. I believe that is a major reason you love him so!"

To hear the demon call her husband a Master, and speak of integrity, well . . . "*Vaughn, what is going on around here?*"

"This time, my love, my Queen, you're going to love it." He looked at Grinchback, "You ready?"

Grinchback bounced up and down, nodding. Vaughn disappeared, grabbed an Earth demon that was roaming by himself in the nearby woods and disappeared then reappeared back up in the Corridor and before the Earth demon could react, Vaughn *shoved* him at Grinchback!

Though Grinchback was still an underling, head to tail he was a good bit larger than the Earth demon and he immediately wrapped him up in his tail. Shocked, Stephanie threw up a barrier to prevent the Earth demon from popping away or communicating to anyone down below, but Grinchback responded, "No need, Lady Stephanie, all that is automatically accomplished when I wrap them up."

The Earth demon didn't understand until Grinchback raised his bulbus head over him and began opening his Great Eye. The Earth demon tried to free his massive arms but couldn't. He couldn't use any of his powers, either. Grinchback's Great Eye dripped on him! But Vaughn held up a hand. "Earth demon, if I asked you some straight questions, would you tell me the truth?" It looked at Vaughn like he was crazy. Vaughn smiled, "That's OK, after he *consumes* you, *he'll* tell me everything you now!" And now the earth demon began to fret and struggle mightily, as fear overpowered him.

Grinchback looked over to a gawking Lady Stephanie, "I love my new Master Vaughn! He helps me *play* with my food!" And Grinchback slowly consumed the earth demon, semi-soul and body all in one! For a while, Grinchback floated in the Corridor looking quite drunk. This meal had a lot more power inside it than was expected, almost like consuming another Alpha, which experience for Grinchback was quite rare. When he was done digesting, he righted himself, and was noticeably darker and larger!

Vaughn looked at him in question, and Grinchback replied, as he looked over to Lady Stephanie. "They still think you're dead! He was *quite* surprised to see you up here. They don't know you killed *both* their sires. How many demon villages did you say there were?"

"Three?"

"Try *ten!*"

Stephanie shouted, "TEN?"

"Ten. I'll give you all the locations. May I?"

Vaughn nodded, then turned to Stephanie. "It's OK. It'll sting a bit."

Stephanie looked at him as if he was an *idiot,* seeing as how he knew Stephanie had been wrapped up in a demon's tail and almost eaten right after she had come and healed Vaughn. "I think I *know* that."

"Oh, yea, right"

Grinchback said, "You two are *very* funny!" He split his arm and put the tip of each on their heads. Not just the Earth demons' locations, but *all* of the Earth demon's knowledge fed into them! When it was done, Vaughn and Stephanie looked at each other and both said, "Oh God!"

Stephanie asked, "What are we going to do with all the women whom my *father* impregnated. They give birth *very* soon, so we have to act *now*!"

Vaughn didn't answer. He looked over at Grinchback, "You want a front row seat? Stick around! Might be some scraps!" Grinchback's eye began to drool again.

Stephanie shook her head, then bowed it, and a moment later, she said, "They can't escape."

Vaughn looked her in the eye and Grinchback, too. "No matter what you see, have faith!" Stephanie nodded and Grinchback thought upon the deeper meaning of the word. Vaughn vanished and reappeared in the middle of the town. Hey all you Earth *rejects*. You want to *play?!*"

They all perked up their big pointy ears not believing how lucky they were. That is, until Vaughn took the bow from around his shoulder and showed it to them. At *that,* they all laughed and began waving their arms for Vaughn to shoot them, knowing no earthly weapon could do much if any damage, especially a stupid bow and arrow.

Vaughn smiled knocked an arrow, took slow aim, and they laughed even harder. Then he shot, and then before any of them knew it, he'd shot *ten* and they all immediately fell over dead! When they saw *that,* they all rushed him.

Vaughn emptied his quiver down to the last arrow and Grinchback looked at Lady Stephanie, and said, "He's out of arrows." But she just pointed.

Vaughn reached out his hand and the arrows all returned back into his quiver and he emptied it again. Forty-eight dead demons and that hardly mattered. They swarmed Vaughn, and Stephanie lost sight of him under a huge and growing, living, no, *existing* mountain of squirming demon flesh, all trying to get a claw on their meal.

Grinchback looked concerned and peered over to Stephanie, who wasn't exactly calm, either. Grinchback asked, "Under these *particular* circumstances, uh, what does the word, faith, *mean?*"

Stephanie looked into his Great Eye and she was shocked to see genuine demon concern! And respect? "What is going on, here?"

"Very simple, my Lady, your husband has proven his worth to us and that we are stronger as friends than enemies! Without him, we would have long been on the wrong side of the Eye, but if we don't get his help *very* soon . . ."

Just then a big hunk of Earth demon flesh flew up into the Corridor. Stephanie *yelped,* but Grinchback's tail whipped out and dropped it quickly into his Eye! "Master keeps his word!" Then a badly wounded but *still* alive Earth demon appeared and Grinchback wrapped him up but ate him right away before he died.

The demon mound began to get smaller, until Vaughn stood up and they could visibly see what he was doing. The demons were clawing him, biting him, casting black oil on him, had ripped off *all* his clothing but not a drop of red blood could be seen. Instead, Vaughn physically tore then limb from limb! When the stragglers saw *that,* they began trying to pop away but couldn't. Then they just tried fleeing the old fashion way but ran right into an invisible wall which Stephanie began shrinking in diameter.

Vaughn bowed his head, and the Black Oil fled off of his body. He held his hands out to Stephanie indicating he was naked, but she said in his mind, *What if I like what I'm looking at!* He dropped his hands to his side looking helpless. He had no clue how to use his new powers to clothe himself. Stephanie chuckled and a brand-new ranger uniform appeared on him. That's pretty much *all* he wore. Ranger uniforms with lots of pockets.

Vaughn picked up his bow and quiver and finished off the last of the Earth demons that were trying to flee. He flicked his hand upward, and in the Ethereal Corridor it started to rain earth demon parts. Lady Stephanie, without thinking, covered her head with her arms, "My *hair!*"

But Grinchback said, "Not to worry, my Lady, I'll not let any touch you." And his tail split into may parts, grabbed every single scrap and forced them all directly down his Great Eye!

When Vaughn popped back up, Grinchback looked stuffed. Vaughn looked at the demon, then looked at Stephanie. They knew from the demon knowledge they'd acquired that the Earth demons had *not* done as they were told. They did *not* stay secret, but were terrorizing much of the country side and consuming quite a few. Which meant that instead of at the very minimum six months before maturity, it would be any week now!

Stephanie pointed down to the town, again, because people were starting to come out. Vaughn turned to Grinchback, "I'll come as soon as I can." And he and his wife went down to the village.

All the women, wearing raggedy brown dresses, were pregnant with demons and they fell down on their knees begging them to help. They *knew* who Lady Stephanie was, they had heard she was dead, but now seeing her, they had hope.

But Lady Stephanie was repulsed by them, because when she had entered their minds and hearts, she saw their utter vileness, the sexual worship they engaged in, thrived in. Stephanie knew she'd been no angel, but what was before her now in these so-called women made the worst of what she had *ever* done look like holiness.

She looked into Vaughn's eyes with scorn, but then a man came forward. It was *Trevor*, his light brown hair was all oily and matted and his blue eyes were dull, but it *was* Trevor with a pregnant woman on his arm. "First," he said to Lady Stephanie, "Can you *please* fix this?"

Lady Stephanie's eyes flashed hot red and the wound in his cheek that he had Vaughn replace to hide his identity instantly healed and the taint was gone. Not only that, his clothing was fresh common browns and his hair was clean for the first time in, well, he couldn't remember, and his blue eyes were now sharp. Trevor noticed how easily she performed it all. In the next moment Vaughn and he were in each other's arms slapping their backs. "You got my message," Trevor said.

"That I did, my friend. But there are *ten* towns now, not three."

Trevor nodded. "That doesn't surprise me. Well, let's heal these folks then do what needs to be done."

But Stephanie couldn't muster it. "Trevor," she looked at him with a helpless expression. "I can't."

The woman on his arm fell to the ground. "We had no choice. I even begged Trevor to impregnate me before the demon but he refused because if he did, they'd discover him. *Please.* Or just kill us all quickly, *please.*" And all the women begged for the same relief.

Then the woman who had been with Trevor, said, "We were brought up from birth with this secret religion. We were told if any of you found out, we would be tortured and put to a painful death. But Trevor told me, at the risk to his own life, the truth about *you, Lady Stephanie.*"

And she flattened herself to the ground, clawing at it, hoping to be swallowed up because *none* of what she had felt or did with the Earth demon could be forgiven. It was so far beyond any mercy at all.

But something she said struck Vaughn. He looked at his wife. "Do you remember the video they showed all of us in school of how they treated the secret Christians up North?"

Stephanie rubbed her face and then rubbed it again. The video was burned into every small child's conscience how even little children had been horribly tortured. And every student was told the same thing would happen to them if they even *thought* about the old ways. Stephanie remembered how she was in class when she blurted out questions that weren't deemed appropriate, how she worried about being sent away.

And now, here, before her, was the ultimate product of those very same evil tactics only employed to an unimaginable level. Stephanie turned away and gasped and sobbed. She still wasn't ready to help them, though. How could she? Their *demon* unborn children clung tightly to their mother's very souls.

Little Michael began to glow inside of her. He was trying to make his Mommy think about something, about how hard she fought to protect him, gave her life to protect him against the demons. But those women's curse was worse than *anything!* They would fight, they would *die,* just to be dissolved forever, if it was possible, just to be free of an *evil* pregnancy!

Stephanie turned to her husband. "Oh Vaughn, what do I do?"

What could be done? Vaughn held out his hand and the Staff appeared within it. As soon as it did, many of the women cringed while others wept. Vaughn turned to the women. "Form a line, a single line all the way down this street. This is the Staff of the Lord." And when he said it, it thundered. "The Staff of his Indignation, but also the Staff of Life. *We* cannot judge, but in this hour you shall all pass under this Staff, and *it* will judge you by the power of Almighty God, even the Lord Jesus."

And when he called the Lord's name, many shrunk back and others wailed. He turned to Trevor. "It's the best we can do."

An hour later, a *precious* hour that Vaughn knew he couldn't afford to waste, but knew it had to be given, he stood, Staff in hand, at the far end of the line. He extended it above the kneeling women and proceeded to walk down the whole line.

Immediately, many fled from under its presence and burst into flames. But the others, rolled over and cried in anguish and delivered prematurely, and they rolled away from the mess, and *it* burst into flames. The last woman was the one Trevor obviously fell in love with, and she passed the test and was delivered.

Then Lady Stephanie prayed over Trevor. "Lord Jesus, no one knows better than this young man of these things. Let *him* be your judge and your mercy to those that are delivered!"

And Trevor assented to the prayer. "I know you two have much to do. Give me the locations of all the other villages and I'll go there. I can travel like you! They've had me do it for so long, somehow, it's become innate in me."

And Vaughn and Stephanie popped back into the Corridor. She looked at Vaughn and said, "If Jargono were doing this, he would have just immediately burnt up the whole village. Done. That quick. But how do *we* have time for everything?"

"Stephanie, you could *never* be like that, and you know it, no matter the reason. We can only do what we can do, but do the *right thing.*"

And that was it. That's all Vaughn said. Stephanie was expecting more of a conversation, a point made or two, after a while. "So, you learning from Lynnara?"

"Talk, talk, *talk,*" he said impersonating her. "Shall we move to the next village?"

"Vaughn, I think we have to do them all in one day! Because if Karen finds out . . ."

"Agreed. It's going to be a *very* long night."

By midnight they had destroyed five and Grinchback was *definitely* larger and darker. When the Highest Councilor finally caught up with his underling in their secret room for a progress report, the Councilor stopped in mid float. He eyed his much-changed underling, and Grinchback immediately bowed and fessed up. Highest Councilor ScrabaGag's laughter continued for some time until he finally wiped his eye.

Grinchback said, "Their taste is exquisite, Master. Far more power than you would expect."

"Well, Grinchback, I'll tell you a secret. That was our goal all along! To turn the whole Earth into *that!* But turning it all into *that,* would allow us to go there directly since so much of the Ethereal would already be there, and who upstairs would object to us consuming a few Earth demons?"

Grinchback nodded with understanding. "But Jargono stood in our way, and we needed Master Vaughn to save our Eye. But now that Vaughn has made himself indispensable to us, we have to cancel that plan."

"Not only that, Grinchback. The Earth demons know they're our food. They'll do everything they can to cut us off. And Karen will, too, unless she's given more power here."

"So it's best if Stephanie's plan actually works."

"It is, just like you've always warned me, my very *faithful* underling."

Grinchback smiled at that. "Master, I've never ever consumed so much!"

"Well, it won't do you any good if your other Master doesn't come and help us. At the same time, if they fail to destroy them before they reproduce, we're all finished. They couldn't handle that swarm, let alone what Karen will be unleashing. If it wasn't for Vaughn needing to stay alive, they would have no way to separate us from the Earth, then the Earth demons, nor Karen would be any problem at all."

Grinchback shook his head *again.* "What your saying is that if Vaughn wasn't holding our orbs hostage, then your former Master GrrraGagag's Earth demon plan would be perfect. For him, as you say, being a prophet, himself, I feel he was *extremely* narrow sited. A prophet is only as good as being able to understand the whole picture!"

Now Highest Councilor ScrabaGag considered consuming his underling again, because he really began to sense something that was exceptional. "I don't understand. Why don't you explain it!"

Again, Grinchback was amazed. "Master, what moves you to act this way, in a way no Alpha has been before?" But then he thought about what Vaughn showed him of the Father and HrorrarrAggrang. "Correction, except for the Father and Horrra-*what's-his-tail?*"

The Highest Councilor still couldn't get over that they adopted Vaughn's *pet* name for the deceptive, ancient demon. "It just makes good sense, but really, it was *you* who brought me to appreciate it."

Grinchback gave his Master a new think-for-your-own-Eye-look! But his Master didn't understand. "You said GrrraGagag was a prophet but you *ate* him. You said you thought I was special, maybe a prophet, and I was indeed eaten, but I'm back and have encouraged you to set up a relationship with me but also with Vaughn that only that kind of thing happens with the Father in secret. Who is the more reliable demon? GrrraGagag or me?"

It truly was a think-for-your-own-Eye question with only one obvious answer. "You Grinchback."

"Then I tell you this. The Earth demon plan was wrong from the start, born out of irrational grandiosity! For as much as you told me it was all just an act your former Master put on, I think that *act* he put on, deep down came from the Eye sickness that his act was based upon! And the *reason* he has been able to hide certain things from you even though he's *inside of you,* is because he hides those things in the depth of his insanity where your reasoned, well-thought-out Eye does not want to go! No flattery, Master."

The Highest Councilor turned even newer colors representing the wealth of understanding he now gained. But he also realized for himself he would have *never* gained this understanding if he had consumed Grinchback. To say the least, it was Eye opening for understanding.

Grinchback's Great Eye smiled, knowing his Master's thoughts. "That is correct, Master! But to the question at hand, the rest of the answer is that the plan for the Earth demons does *not* take into account the larger picture. The glow is at *least* an equal balance to us. It would *never* have allowed the Earth demons to gain full control of the Earth. That great gap *there,"* and Grinchback had brought up a great gap early on in Forest history, "was, as Master Vaughn explained it, what he called the Great Flood where *their* Father destroyed the whole Earth except for a giant boat with *only* the specimens of life *He* desired. Did *our* Great *Father* foresee *that?"*

ScrabaGag wrapped his tail numerous times around his neck and rubbed the side of his huge bulbous head with his tail trip. "There has *never* been an underling like *you* Grinchback!"

Grinchback's eye smiled to each side of his head because he knew it was true. "Well, Master, it was *your* desire that created me! But here is the larger picture. Neither Vaughn, nor Lady Stephanie, not the folks *upstairs* want another Great Flood. They all want time to allow the glow to win souls before they're lost to us. But *we* don't want the Great Disaster either because it's such a waste of good food. Master, there is no record of how long it took the Alpha to consume all those departed souls from the Great Disaster."

"You're saying it's best for all involved to maintain an area of balance! Not to gain significant advantage! But *our* Father . . ."

"Deep down has the same Great Eye sickness as your former Master!"

For a long time, they hovered together, the dirty blue light casting unusual shadows of them across their secret ethereal room. *"Grinchback,* let's say we, err, wanted to do something, err, well, on a large energy scale but didn't want to get caught. How would we do that?"

"We need a lot of help."

"You said Mafferan helped Lady Stephanie turn our Black River to stone. You know that created a mining and refining industry for us?"

"Yes Master, to *both* points. In other words, Mafferan's action hurt us in one way, but also gave us whole new industries and extra value from that! He *understands* what we were just discussing! The balance!"

"Might we be able to somehow arrange a very quick meeting?"

"Master, Vaughn told me *their* Father ruled that none could interfere."

Just then, a very *holy* presence invaded their *secret* room. Mafferan smiled, and shook the Highest Councilor's tail tip with minimal smoking. "The edict from our Father above all was specially pertaining to the last event concerning the wanted but unwanted child. This is what we have to do, *now*!"

CHAPTER 14

The Tangled Web
We Weave

11 And after three days and a half the Spirit of life from God entered into them, and they stood upon their feet; and great fear fell upon them which saw them.

12 And they heard a great voice from heaven saying unto them, Come up hither. And they ascended up to heaven in a cloud; and their enemies beheld them.

And the children finally couldn't stand the suspense, so Sarah asked, "Teacher Marta, why have we been reading this Holy Scripture?"

Marta's eyes drifted upward. "I'm not sure! It's just a feeling! And I've always let my feelings guide me to teach you and it's always seemed to work out."

Aaron asked. "So why have your feelings led you to do this for us?"

"I don't know! But I think it has something to do with Lady Stephane and King Vaughn and all the terrible things that keep happening and the fact that NO ONE," she looked up and shouted her last two words, "seems to be helping them, at all!"

King Vaughn and Queen Stephanie had just finished destroying the sixth demon town and again delivering many women from their unwanted demon offspring. Their souls had a very long way to go but at least they had a chance. They were floating in the Ethereal Corridor over the seventh town and Stephanie was weeping from exhaustion. Her head hurt terribly from all her deep concentration and she couldn't seem to heal it at all, and little Michael was rebelling against his Mommy doing anything further. Everyone has limits, even a *faithwalker*. Vaughn wasn't far behind. Every fiber in every muscle felt weak and sore, and Stephanie couldn't heal that, either.

"Vaughn, it's five in the morning. It'll be light soon. I'm sure Karen and Jargono won't be castle building this morning because both of them have so many other responsibilities. Each knows if they try to hold the other there, it will look suspicious. With her concentration free to roam again, she'll focus her mind on the demon towns and know right away what we've done. And we're in no way able to fight her *now!* We've failed." And she broke into sobs because it was true, in a way.

Vaughn pulled her to him and hugged her close, and stroked her head. "Well, we did our best. It just wasn't meant to be. We need to go home and rest and then begin our own castle building all across the country! And we need to prioritize it as number one. The times have changed! That's all. But we're still *faithwalkers*. Even I have accepted that of myself, now. That little Lynnara, she's a handful, isn't she? You didn't know when you rescued her what we were in for, huh?"

Stephanie couldn't help but laugh but weakly. Just then an . . . Ethereal Quake shook them both *violently* and Vaughn held onto his wife tightly as she erected a protective blue, gold and red shield around them. Then a stronger quake but this time a huge very black portal opened over the demon town and the Earth demons were all pulled up into it! Then there was calm!

Vaughn asked Stephanie, "What was *that?*"

She started crying, then said, "Answer to prayers we had in our hearts but *didn't* really pray forward?"

Then the quakes hit again. Vaughn noticed that the town below experienced no tremors at all. This was *ethereal only!* And then the quakes hit again. And a while after that, *again.*

Vaughn and Stephanie looked down at the town where people were starting to come out into the streets. Stephanie looked at Vaughn. "I think we have enough left in us to finish this now, if all the rest of the towns look like this. And, *they do!*"

Listening to his wife, holding her in his arms, King Vaughn transported them down to the town to judge the women.

೧

When it was over, the Highest Councilor and Grinchback looked *much* larger and darker, and Mafferan was waving his hand around the orb and above his head trying to clear the ethereal smoke from all the Earth demons he had to incinerate because there were far too many to consume.

"These orbs need a smoke filter," Mafferan observed.

"That's not a bad idea," Grinchback proclaimed.

The Highest Councilor shook his dizzy head. "What a waste. I wish we could have just caged them."

Mafferan paused in his futile smoke dissipating efforts. "I should have thought of that. Grinchback, why didn't you tell me?"

The Highest Councilor bore his Great Eye down upon his overly stuffed underling, "Yes, *Grinchback,* why *didn't* you tell your Master?"

Shocked, afraid that consuming so much had addled his Master's Eye, Grinchback could only coil into a ball, pleading, "Sorry Master, *sorry . . .*"

But then both Mafferan and ScrabaGag broke out into hysterical laughter all pointing at Grinchback, then repeating, "Sorry Master,"

Grinchback slowly uncoiled. Watching *those* two sincerely laughing together but for their *own* reasons, but, indeed, *similar* reasons, was truly an Alpha historical site, but one that would never be recorded. He had accessed Vaughn's stealth program with Mafferan's help and programed all the orbs in a loop to record normal viewing *only,* but also with a rare, actually never in orb history, Ethereal Quake alert flashing in red! And all the next day all the orbs kept flashing it preventing any further orb use until the alert mysteriously departed!

Highest Councilor ScrabaGag, his arm dripping in black oil, extended it to Mafferan in friendship! "Job well done. I must say, it will be with great difficulty that I will proceed as normal with my Ethereal affairs and keep from laughing."

Mafferan shook his arm profusely with both his hands and the oil smoked. "Same to you, my *friend*. Same to you."

Grinchback decided to try. "What about what Karen has done. All that she's created is still far too much for the Earth and the balance we just temporarily protected!"

But Mafferan shook his head. "We got away with this, I *think*. But we certainly couldn't with anything else for quite a while. Highest Councilor?"

ScrabaGag agreed. "Besides, when she unleashes all *that*, it's going to every city and town, and then some. There's simply no way we, by ourselves, can deal with all that. And we are the *only* ones who would dare try. King Mafferan?"

"Agreed. The Earth has a small reprieve, then it's up to them! Times are changing."

Grinchback nodded deeply. "Yes, the *seasons* are definitely changing." And both Mafferan and his Master noted he changed their wording.

Mafferan staired deeply into Grinchback's Great Eye. "Well, I never thought it possible. Well, you two have a wonderful Ethereal day." And he made to leave but both demons called him back and both asked him.

"What didn't you think possible?"

Mafferan looked them both in their Great Eyes. "Among my people we have a saying, We never tell people these kinds of things that we see inside them. They must learn of it from the inside out! Good day!" And he vanished!

Both Alpha peered into the other's Great Eye wondering, because they knew Mafferan was serious, and they also knew that was the same kind of thing that was told to Lady Stephanie!

∾

"Where have you been?" asked Yinauqua in a tone that was not to be escaped, dodged, or fooled around with in any way.

King Mafferan opened his full heart and his mind wide and peered into his wife and she rushed inside him with abandon. After a bit, she whispered. "I shouldn't have asked!"

Mafferan smiled warmly. "Ahh, wisdom, even for us up here, sometimes comes a bit late!"

"You have spoken the truth, my husband. I'm sorry I put you through so much grief. Your secrets I will guard *forever*!"

∾

Everyone was assembled *again* in the Darkest Room. A low growling thunder startled all the Alpha who were packed in tail to tail. When the ominous noise startled them all, they bumped into each other which startled them even more, which caused a ruckus, and they bumped more into each other . . .

A booming voice with the feeling of a Great Eye descending upon them all froze them all in mid-startle. "QUIET."

Then the Father appeared on the Highest Stage. "Why is all I see in my orb a red *QUAKE ALERT*? For the *whole last day!* The last time we had an unheard-of quake, our Black River turned to *stone*. I want *ANSWERS.*" And his last word stung every single Alpha Lesser Eye.

Every Alpha stayed perfectly frozen in place, not wanting to attract the Father's attention, but Alpha Great Eyes darted around peering at each other, looking for someone to blame. Grinchback and his Master caught each other's Eye noting they both wanted to laugh but dare not. They and every other Alpha wanted to know what the Father meant by "Why is MY orb . . ." Everyone knew the Father had no orb, except for the Highest Councilor and Grinchback. Both thought it was the perfect touch to put the red QUAKE ALERT on the Father's orb, too, even though it wasn't on their orb system! *How's* that *for a tail in your eye?* They were quietly thinking. They also noticed that HrorrarrAggrang was nowhere to be seen, but that was no surprise.

"And *where's* my Earth Demons? Where is that *bitch?* I summoned her a whole day a . . ."

A silky sweet voice replied as Queen Karen faded so gently into the Darkest Room sporting a blue glow that lit everyone up! "*My* Earth demons are just fine. And *my* orig- errr, my plan is working just fine. If you could just bring yo- I mean, if someone could just bring an orb *here,* I'll show you. And by the way, that *bitch* with her *pooooor* unwanted child is *dead!*"

Everyone kept stone silent. Many had never met her, but she was an Alpha Legend and rumored to have more power than most any of them. So no one would dare tell her. Besides, *She thinks too much of herself. It's about time she got her comeuppance,* was the common thought.

The Father squinted over at the Highest Councilor. "Well, since this is *all* under you, go *fetch* your orb!"

And Queen Karen smiled sweetly, saying, "Yes, go *fetch!*" sounding like he was a mere Earth doggy. The Highest

Councilor and Grinchback vanished and reappeared by their main, large dirty blue orb. ScrabaGag waved his massive arm and one of his ethereal walls disappeared and he and Grinchback began pushing their orb to the Father's Darkest Room. But all the way there, though wisely silent, they knew.

Once back at the Father's, they kept saying, "Excuse me," as they muscled through the crowd to the Highest Stage where the Father liked to float. Since Karen was there and requested the orb, they placed it in front of her, bowing, and saying, "*My Queeeeen.*" Then they took their place again at the very back of the room where they could keep an Eye on everything.

Queen Karen brought up images of the first town but . . . "Wait, there's something wrong here." There were no Earth demons. She checked on the rest of the towns with the same result. At the tenth town she decided to look back in history, but while she waited for that to be gathered, she said, "They've probably all went on a little trip."

Grinchback rubbed his still very full belly, belched so everyone could hear, and said, "Yes. A little trip. That makes sense!" The Highest Councilor thwacked him hard on the back with his tail tip. But many other Alpha snickered in silence, thinking, *There's more to that fool underling than meets the Eye.*

In the dirty blue orb, there the Earth demons were, doing what they always do, and then . . . a red QUAKE ALERT, and then, a whole day goes by with a red QUAKE ALERT, and then, no Earth demons! She checked three other towns, but the next one she checked . . . "What is *he* doing *there?*" And all the Alpha watched what they already knew. There was

Vaughn slaughtering all their Earth companions but *no one* had told the Father.

"But . . ."

The Father, in a very low, controlled voice, which was never a good sign, began to call for the Highest Councilor so he could ask how he let all this happen, but he had already materialized next to Queen Karen, adjusted the orb focus to expand into the Ethereal Corridor, touched the dirty blue screen at a certain point, then enlarged that image portion. And there *she* was!

There was Lady Stephanie, head bowed, glowing, and casting a dome of power over the demon town. The Highest Councilor turned to Queen Karen, and bowed, saying, "*Oh GREAT QUEEN,* didn't you tell us all she was dead? And that her husband was *nowhere* to be found and that maybe he killed himself? Didn't she tell that to *all* of us?"

Every single Alpha in the Darkest Room, although they *hated* the Highest Councilor, as they were supposed to do, they all affirmed *passionately* his words. The Father's Great Eye lowered over Karen, but she paid him no mind. She was trying to figure something out in the orb. The timelines weren't quite right because the first six were destroyed in sequence, but the last four were . . .

The Father *hated* to be ignored and snatched her up with his great tail and held her over his Great Eye. But she *still* didn't react! "Tell me why I shouldn't just consume you right here and now. You are an *experiment!* An experiment I think gone horribly wrong."

She nodded over to the orb and all of the sudden images of fire-breathing dragons and gargoyles appeared! All *that* was supposed to be secret. The Father's voice appeared only in Karen's head. *Now why did you go and do* that? *You could have thought of something else to save your Eye.*

And her voice appeared in *his* head. *I don't like to be humiliated,* especially *in front of* them, indicating the Highest Councilor and his underling.

Everyone waited to see if she would be consumed, but also everyone was rivetted on the orb. Karen, still hanging over the Father's Great Eye, spoke sharply, this time. "After I rule the Earth with *them* in about two-weeks-time, I'm going to open an amusement park, and for a *fee,* all Alpha will be able to safely hunt game! So says this *experiment!*"

All Alpha eyes drooled. The Father had no choice but to put her back down. "Well, there are *some* secrets that are well worth waiting for." And at *that,* the Father bellowed, "*Solutions.*" And he was gone!

Karen went immediately back to the orb to pick up where she left off but the Highest Councilor turned it off and he and his underling began to push it back. "I'll have to see if I can find you an orb of your own somewhere, now that you're one of us. I think there might be an extra *training* orb in the nursery that we can spare. Or perhaps HrorrarrAggrang's orb is still around!"

But Karen shot back, "I have . . . err, things to do right now. That would be very nice."

CHAPTER 15

My Home is My Castle

Revelation Chapter 13

And I stood upon the sand of the sea, and saw a beast rise up out of the sea, having seven heads and ten horns, and upon his horns ten crowns, and upon his heads the name of blasphemy.

2 And the beast which I saw was like unto a leopard, and his feet were as the feet of a bear, and his mouth as the mouth of a lion: and the dragon gave him his power, and his seat, and great authority.

3 And I saw one of his heads as it were wounded to death; and his deadly wound was healed: and all the world wondered after the beast.

Carrie blurted out. "Dragon? Like the ones the demons just created?"

Marta's eyebrows raised. "The book of Revelation is sealed even from us, dear Carrie. But my feeling is that what we are now seeing is the beginning of . . . something."

At noon day they awoke, arm in arm, then heard the door between their apartments softly open then close, then the patter of two pairs of feet, someone climbing into the bed, and *then* two pairs of little eyes on each side of them, eagerly awaiting the story.

Rebecca whispered to Lynnara across the bed on Stephanie's side. "Ask her!"

Lynnara shook her head. "Ask him."

Vaughn and Stephanie rolled on their backs, saying, "Ask what?"

Both little girls rolled their eyes, and both said, "*What happened?*"

Vaughn answered. "There are no more Earth demons."

The girls jumped up and down on the bed then dove onto them with grunts all the way around. They climbed up over them till they were close to their eyes then said, "Tell us."

They had so very much to do, but Stephanie nodded to Vaughn. "Well, Lady Stephanie, here, put a big dome of power over each town, then I went down and asked the demons *very* politely if they wanted to play!"

"*Play!*" the girls both remarked.

"Yes. Play. But they weren't very friendly at all."

Lynnara couldn't believe it and in a knowing tone, said, "Daddy, they're demons. They don't play." But then thinking about her experience, she amended her instruction. "Well, they *play* with their *food.*"

"Well, anyway, that's *exactly* what they had in mind, so I slew a lot of them with my bow, and then . . ." he paused, having learned the fine arts of storytelling from his wife.

The girls jumped up and down on them, saying, "Then *what?*"

"I tore them apart with my bare hands!"

Two sets of little eyebrows went up, went down into a squint, then they said, "No you didn't."

But Mommy tweaked Lynnara's cheek, and said, "He most certainly did. I saw him do it!"

And with *that* in their minds and little hearts, they ran out of the bedroom, across to the other apartment hollering, "You're not going to believe *this!*"

After Vaughn and Stephanie had finished with the Earth demons, they had picked up the very sleepy Mandy and Carla from the Tree of Life, and the two children who had fallen asleep before it all happened.

Now, Carla locked the apartment door so Stephanie and Vaughn could have privacy to clean up. She turned to Mandy with a serious eye, but Mandy said, "Yea, yea, I know. There's a lot more trouble coming. What else is new?

"Actually, I was about to say, we'd better get cleaned up and eat, too, because you are *not* going to want to miss *this!*"

And the little girls' eyes went wide, asking "What?"

But all Carla would say was, "You'll see if you're ready."

So the little ones rushed into the bathroom to brush teeth, wash face, and get dressed.

"What Carla? What now?"

"Oh, the *worst* is yet to come. You really won't believe what you're going to see. But first, after we eat, and go out with our sister and brother, then you won't believe what you're going to see!"

Mandy sighed. "You know I hate it when you do that. And you're not going to tell me?"

Carla smiled. "This time I'm actually allowed to. But I won't! Get ready!"

On the other side of the apartment door, Lady Stephanie had pinned King Vaughn to the bed, saying, "We need just a bit more time together after all that happened."

"What did you have in mind? I'm yours to command."

Stephanie licked his nose then bounded off the bed, ran into the bathroom and locked the door.

Vaughn got up, tried, *again*, to do what he saw his wife do a hundred times, and ended up with his trousers on backwards and his shirt inside out, and no underwear. He decided it was best just to start over and do it the regular way. *Faithwalker*, he said to himself as he shook his head. Vaughn went to the little tiny guest bathroom and cleaned up then came back and called to his wife through her bathroom door so he wouldn't let any cold air in or any of the steam out, "I have something to do. You'll be great without me."

Vaughn popped away and reappeared over Jargono's new castle. Seeing only Jargono inside in the main common area, he popped in. "Quite magnificent."

Middle Ages artwork and tapestries hung in the great room with in kind furniture and a throne. Vaughn smiled, saying, "The throne is a nice touch. Let's go to the armory." And they popped over there.

It was filled with all kinds of the most modern weapons. Vaughn looked over at Jargono. "What would you say if I told you *none of these will work?*"

Jargono smiled, "You know I would say, prove it."

And to that, Vaughn said, "Let's go!"

And they reappeared where they were before in the Corridor. Vaughn waved his hand and the orb appeared and Jargono summoned his stealth orb and sent it in. While they waited, Vaughn tuned into the 'Father's' Darkest Room courtesy of Mafferan *infecting* the Father's new orb and he replayed what happened.

Jargono said, "Well, that explains her mood, said she needed a *very* long bath, but I knew she was going somewhere so I had her followed! Not by me because she would sense it, but by another of these with a new special tracking function that actually works no matter if you're down there or up here. It can transmute itself! But once it leaves our realm, other than location tracking, it doesn't give me any recordings, *yet.*"

Vaughn shook his head not even being able to imagine how he did it. "Today I tried to dress myself like I've seen Stephanie do a hundred times."

Jargono raised his eyebrows. "My trousers were backwards, my shirt inside out, and I had no underclothes."

Jargono put his finger to Vaughn's forehead just for a brief instant. "Don't give up. Try it again next time. So no more Earth demons?"

"I don't think so, unless your wife has hidden some more."

"She wouldn't be *this* upset if she had." He used Vaughn's orb to bring up his normal tracker orb watching his wife. "She's down in one of the towns hurling rotting Earth demon parts around, interrogating the women survivors, and cursing. I think she'll be occupied for quite a while but if she heads in our direction, I'll get a warning. What do you have in mind?"

"We're going to catch one and take it home! You're home. Ours isn't built yet. Wanna help?"

Jargono raised a single eyebrow. "This will be interesting. But you're right. I hadn't thought about it."

"Jargono, your wife knows your powers. She knows some of Stephanie's, too. You think she would create those to be susceptible to anything but her?"

It was still difficult for Jargono to think about his wife doing *anything* to really harm him, but Vaughn knew his thoughts, and said, "She thinks she's in control, but she's not. Have you thought about what Stephanie has proposed?"

With a deep sigh he confessed. "You know, for so long I was *sure* I was the *best,* the *brightest* human being alive. But *your* wife has consistently demonstrated a genius I never considered nor thought the quality even worthy. I was very wrong. And her solution is beyond *anything* I could have understood."

"Well, to be honest," Vaughn sighed. "I think Karen is also brilliant in a special way. Let's see if we can help her live up to it in a way that won't destroy her and everyone else."

"Agreed. I think I know the part of my tree that will work, but your wife will know after I show her whether I'm right, even though it's my choice. How do you want to play this?" And he nodded down below as orb surveillance began to come back.

"Agreed. And, by ear, my friend, by ear. That one, all alone by the creek."

The gargoyle was plucking fish from the water. None of the others seemed to have discovered that food source, yet."

Vaughn and Jargono entered through the doorway, which was more like an invisible Ethereal Tunnel, careful to avoid Karen's alarms, which actually weren't that many due to the utter secrecy and difficulty finding this place and the exact entrance. After they were inside, they popped over to the creek.

Vaughn spoke to it. "I like fishing, too."

But without hesitation, it leapt at Vaughn but was caught in a cage of blue and red energy that Jargono threw over it. It immediately tore it apart! He threw another cage this time with green energy mixed in. It took him longer. He tore the blue and red out and *ate* the green! Probably because it was green!

At that point, Vaughn turned very black with righteous anger against the abomination, but he controlled for any leakage as Jargono had taught him, and when the gargoyle lunged at him, Vaughn upper cut him on the jaw and knocked him out! Jargono was amazed to see that his own powers were useless and a simple punch to the jaw worked! When they saw the beast begin to come to already, Vaughn hit him again back into unconsciousness so they could carry him back through the tunnel. Once out they disappeared, and reappeared in a dungeon that had chains with wrist collars on it.

Vaughn chained the first wrist but the beast came to and Vaughn had to jump out of the way. The surge forward of the beast was so powerful, the links on the chain stretched a bit and the bolt in the massive stone wall made a sound and dust came out from around it! The beast looked *exactly* like the humanoid gargoyles on buildings except, in the flesh, it was reddish green with a thick hide that was taut across its massive musculature but a bit saggy in its fierce face. It's eyes were green, it's ears large and pointy, and its elongated hands and feet had short triangular claws. Yet, these were quite different in appearance from the Earth demons which seemed, well, more demonic!

"Wow," Vaughn said. "I don't think we have long to experiment." Vaughn took his ranger pistol from his side and unloaded it into the beast's head and torso. The bullets dented the tough hide a bit and fell to the floor. The gargoyle scratched his forehead, picked up a bullet and put it in his mouth then, not liking the taste, spit it out.

Vaughn held out his hand and a loaded rocket launcher appeared in it. He looked at Jargono, who began to wonder. Vaughn shot the beast dead center, while Jargono threw up a containment field. When the smoke cleared, the beast was brushing himself off and tasting the soot! Then it *smiled* at them! As if saying, "You have anything else before I kill you?"

Vaughn said, "Start with what you think has the least chance to work and then escalate."

Jargono nodded. He hit it with a standard red fireball. The beast had even inhaled some but simply blew the fire through his mouth! Next was a straight blue ball of energy that had *zero* effect. He tried laser, highly focused blue, red, and green energies. The green the beast treated like a water spout and tried to drink it!

"Are you able to do like Stephanie?"

"Of course." Jargono hurled a glowing golden ball of energy at the beast and it blew him back against the wall and shredded some of his flesh.

The beast was enraged and leapt at them. Jargono threw up an energy barrier but it went right through! The bolt in the wall came halfway out. Vaughn said, "Make it glow a *lot* more"

Jargono frowned. *That* was against his energy ethics, but he did it. This time the beast crashed into the wall and the wall shook. When the smoke cleared, a portion of its hide was completely gone and it oozed red and green blood. It's left land was blown off and lay in a corner, wriggling. Vaughn pointed to it.

Jargono experimented more on the loose appendage but *nothing* worked effectively. Vaugh put a drop of Light Oil in his palm and blew it at the hand. The drop floated in the air until Vaughn pointed directly at the hand and the drop fell on it. It smoked but *still* didn't disintegrate.

Concern began to harden Jargono's features like when he first saw what his wife had created. "What have you *done* Karen?" He said out loud.

"*Karen!*" the beast growled. When they looked at it in surprise, it laughed! But not only that, its hand had regrown! Now tired of the game, the beast grabbed the chain in both hands and ripped the bolt out of the wall and swung it at them!

Jargono disintegrated the chain and the beast laughed at him, waggling his freed arm mocking Jargono's stupidity! Vaughn slammed the cell door closed and the beast bounced off, but not before the thick iron bars bent from the impact. The gargoyle laughed then sprang with all fours and grabbed the bars and began slowly bending them open.

Jargono stepped way back, saying, "Well, it won't make a good pet." And that enraged the beast which meant that it understood what Jargono just said! Vaugh motioned down the hall and they popped there as the beast climbed out of the cell between the bent bars, then, with fangs bearing and drooling a green slime, it barreled down the hall at them.

Vaughn held out his hand, again, and his bow with a knocked arrow materialized. "I wouldn't if I were you!" And the beast stopped, looked at the weapon, laughed, and leapt the rest of the way, and Vaughn shot it just once. With a surprised look on its face, it dropped dead at their feet.

It wasn't the only thing with a look of surprise. "Armory," was all Vaugh said. When they got there, he said, "Useless." And Jargono, without even waving his hand, made it all vanish. Vaughn held out his hand again and the arrow that shot the beast with its blood still on it appeared. "Are you able to clean it?"

Jargon focused and intense silver beam he rarely used because it also glowed too much, but the blood turned to ash and Vaughn banged the arrow clean against the wall, then handed it to him.

At first touch, Jargono wanted to drop it right away, but he knew he had to hold on. "What power is in this?"

Vaughn pulled out the mediaeval flask and showed him! "Ancient power from the time of the vision I showed you." Then Vaughn held out his other hand and one of the jugs he'd blessed with his staff appeared. "You won't be able to make this Jargono. Sprinkle just a little on all your weapons." He handed it to him and it was hard for him to hold the jug so he set it down on a bench. "Can you make the arrows and the bow and quiver?"

This time Jargono did wave his hand and the armory filled with them. "Make sure you place those giant crossbows instead of your cannons and create these," Vaughn waved his hand and one of the javelins from the holy mountain appeared leaning up against the wall. Whenever you finish a castle, anoint all your weapons. When you run out of the oil, let me know." Then Vaughn vanished and reappeared with Stephanie at the grassy hillside with all the girls.

Stephanie's brow knit together. "Vaaauuuggghhnn, I thought we were going to build castles together. I didn't know you would be gone so long."

He kissed her long and deeply. Lynnara tugged on Mandy's and Carla's dresses. "I love when they do that! Kiss." And then she thought more about it. "Because they *love* each other."

Stephanie eased back from him. "You think that a kiss can make up for that?"

He gave her his special smile and she hit him in the chest. He asked, "Did you include the secret passages?"

"Yes, dear,"

"The secret armory?"

"Yes, dear. If you'd have *been* here you would have seen it all. Ahhh, I also made a few upgrades."

"Upgrades?" He asked with a concerned brow.

"Well, Joshua was always telling me about geothermal energy but that it wouldn't work here."

Vaughn didn't like the sound of this. "And?"

"Well, I put electricity in the castle, all through it, and real plumbing. You know those plans you put in my head really were from the Middle Ages. Also, I really *filled* ten of the floors with small apartments! They all have heavy oak doors reinforced with iron straps, so they fit with the castle's original style. Also, I created two more sister castles just like this one so we can fit everyone in safely! But it's *all* the heavy stone you showed me." And she purposefully made herself look proud, which made Vaughn even more suspicious.

Vaughn noticed she dodged his question. "*And?*"

"Well, we have refrigerators, freezers, between dry and canned and frozen goods we have enough food for the whole town I think for a year even if I'm not around to restock it!"

"Stephanie, what's the *source* of the electricity?"

"Well, geothermal!"

"How? You said Joshua said it wouldn't work here."

"Well," she paused then smiled shyly.

"Stephanie, it won't work here because the geology is all wrong. There are no thermals from lava or underground volcanic activity." There was an ever so slight rumble then shake under the ground. But *very* slight.

"There is now! But *only* under the castles, and I'm still refining it a bit!"

Vaughn became flustered but she grabbed him and gave *him* a passionate kiss. When she was done Vaughn had a dreamy look about him.

Lynnara tugged on her sisters' dresses again. "Daddy always gets that kind of dumb look after Mommy kisses him like that!"

When he came to himself, he commended his wife. "That's brilliant Stephanie."

"I had to pay a quick visit to this scientist Joshua told me about. He recognized me immediately and offered any help he could be. So I said I wanted to look into his mind. *Vaughn,* it was so complex! I never knew science could be so complex like *faithwalking!* In a way."

"Well, you've got your work cut out for you. A lot of castles to build in a short time. I should be going."

"Oh no you don't. Not yet." And she grabbed his arm and they disappeared. And reappeared in a large ornate bedroom with a huge mediaeval iron-framed bed fit for a King and Queen. Suddenly he was dressed just like a king and she a queen. "Oh dear!"

"What my Queen."

"I've never worn this many layers of undergarments!"

"Not a problem." Vaughn said as he swept her off her feet and gently laid her on the bed.

CHAPTER 16

Heartwood

4 And they worshipped the dragon which gave power unto the beast: and they worshipped the beast, saying, Who is like unto the beast? Who is able to make war with him?

5 And there was given unto him a mouth speaking great things and blasphemies; and power was given unto him to continue forty and two months.

6 And he opened his mouth in blasphemy against God, to blaspheme his name, and his tabernacle, and them that dwell in heaven.

All the children shuddered, but Aaron said, "Satan is really jealous of us. But the fury of his hatred is, I don't know."

Ralph said, "Intense. Completely feels out of control, and yet seems to follow a plan. He rages, but very carefully directs his destruction."

Little Carrie said, "I'm glad I'm up *here.* I'd be so scared down *there.*"

And many of the students nodded but didn't feel comfortable feeling that way. They knew they weren't supposed to fear evil, and they didn't, but still, it made them feel like they might . . . if they were down *there!*

Marta nodded slowly. "Maybe," all the children's ears perked up, "maybe that's why our King Vaughn and Lady Stephanie have suffered so very much."

Ralph said, "So they can get used to so much evil?"

But Marta shook her head. "No. So they can get used to the extra depths of goodness they'll need to fight it!"

The children never thought of Goodness quite like that, so Sarah asked, "Why would they have to get used to goodness?"

Marta began to shine with brilliance they'd never seen from their teacher before. Many of the students began to *Oooooh,* and *Ahhh,* but Marta was unaware. Revelation seemed to be coming to *her!*

"You all felt the *intensity* of the evil expressed in the Holy Scripture I just read. Remember how we figured out how Adam was so overcome with many, many thoughts and feelings all at once? Well, I think that intensity of evil we just felt is something like that along with an actual force of will that *pushes* it along."

As Marta described all this, the children shuddered again, but Sarah wanted a counter to it. "But what about what you said about goodness?"

Marta smiled, and it comforted them. "That is part of our next lesson! I want you all to meditate and imagine what such extra depths of goodness could be like!"

For the next ten days all three *faithwalkers* built castles. Vaughn had to restock blessed oil for Jargono many times.

All over the United for Christ they were amazed at what Lady Stephanie was doing for them. So was the military.

At first, they thought Captain Vaugh was kidding, though they liked the nostalgia of castles. But when he showed them the mysterious blue orb Lady Stephanie had told them about during her long confession right before they all pledged their lives to her, and Captain Vaughn showed them the recording of his and King Jargono's experiment with a real live gargoyle, they all went on bended knee shocked such evil wasn't a myth, or wasn't a myth any longer. From that time on, they all focused on military castle strategy and how to effectively function as a team there.

Standing atop a smaller hill gazing up at yet another geothermally powered castle, Lady Stephanie asked her beloved husband, "Vaughn, there are so many smaller towns that don't have protection yet. What are they going to do? I remember when I was in class what seems like ages ago and I asked why all the small towns have been ignored for the larger ones?"

"I've already given a military order to evacuate them all! Just like in feudal times, it was the same way. The small towns fled to the castles for protection. Jargono told me it would be any day now."

She wrapped her arms around him and leaned her head on his shoulder. She had been wearing nothing more than just brown peasant dresses and all the people kept saying, "She looks just like one of us." But many others kept saying, "She *is* just one of us. Her power doesn't make any difference to her. She hurts even *more* than us. We all saw it. Evils chase after *her* more than us. I wouldn't want to be her!" And others said, "Thank *God* she *is* who she is." And to that they all said, "Amen."

"I'm exhausted and there's still so much to do."

Vaughn turned pitch black and he reached out his hand and his Staff appeared within it. "Jargono says it's time."

"Now? Really. *Now?*"

Vaughn leveled his eyes into his wife's, with a special seriousness she hadn't seen before. He sounded so much like a full-grown man, but more than that. He sounded and felt like a King, but with the weight of the world on his shoulders, but, also, something more that Stephanie just couldn't place. "Yes, my love. It's *time*. And I want you to know something. You have no idea how happy I am that I was able to help *you* make little Michael. I feel like he's even *more* than both of us put together! And now, we've finally got what seemed like only a dream- the responsibility to supply real true goodness to so many people. But now, also something we felt but at the beginning we dare not consider it. We have the responsibility to *defend* them! Remember our conversation so long ago in the ice-cream parlor? How I said I felt our gifts were meant for so much more, and to *beat* the evil we were encountering?" And he placed his Staff up against Stephanie's growing belly and little Michael glowed brightly through her dress and the Staff glowed back!

Stephanie bowed her head and went to her knees right there upon the wild grass, and prayed. "Oh Lord Jesus, have mercy on us this day, as we all as a country face greater evils than the world has seen, for even in Medieval times, they had not the numbers of evil beasts we shall now see. Have mercy on us, as we have turned to you with all our hearts and souls as a *whole* country." She knelt back on her haunches and raised her hands high to heaven. "I don't have the power in me to do all this Lord. Help me. Give the agreed upon sign!"

Vaughn went down on one knee, planted his Staff firmly into the ground between them, and wrapped his arms around his wife as a great whirlwind came up from around them. It rose high into the sky and then dark clouds quickly spread out from there with mighty thunder and lightning. It quickly spread across the whole entire country and the people looked up into the sky and knew, and cried out to the Lord for mercy, and they all fled to the castles.

In Legends and myths, they claim it was wizards who fought such evils. Mere wizards could not have done so. They were *faithwalkers*. They just didn't laud themselves, and they let the people think about them what they may. And, yet, many died in service to the higher good. They died then, as they will die now, and in the future yet a little while longer. They know the true meaning of the word, *Sacrifice*.

When the whirlwind had ceased, Vaughn picked up his wife in his arms and carried her into the castle for all to see. Then he climbed up the winding stone stairs all the way to the top and into a parapet which had a missing teeth appearance on top, and King Vaughn set Queen Stephanie down to sit on a stone bench. King Vaughn first took out from his left vest pocket his bottle of Light Oil, Heavenly Oil that Mafferan had given him when Vaughn had been appointed as a *neutral* arbiter, back before Vaughn received the Holy Ghost. He poured a small bit into his left palm and placed his hand to his wife's right cheek and she was immediately strengthened and looked up into his eyes.

Why does he look like that? I've never seen him look like that. And he looks so very holy. Vaughn put back the bottle of Light Oil, still a third full, and he took out the flask from the holy mountain that he kept in his right vest pocket, and he put a bit of blessed oil in his right palm and placed his hand on his wife's left cheek and she burst with energy and *fight*. Then he kneeled before her on one knee and took both her hands in his. "If anything goes wrong, and there's *a lot* that can go wrong, I want you to take this, and open it, but *not* until things go wrong, *if* they ever will."

And he handed her an envelope and she started to cry because it reminded her of the last time he did this. And sure enough, he said, "*This* is now the secret to all my strength and *all* my love!" And for some reason, she fell on his neck with her arms wrapped around him and didn't want to let go. Little Michael kept moving in her womb.

And then they heard a roar like no other, and they stood up. In the distance in a clear mid-day sky, only small dots appeared at first, but they grew quickly larger. The dragons were coming.

People had been lined up all across the top of the castle, but Vaughn yelled at them, "Get *below. Now!*" And they'd never heard such a tone from him before, and they all scrambled to their assigned places and every single man, woman, and child had some kind of weapon in case the castle was somehow breached and they had to fight to the very last soul.

The military were ready, and Harris, up on one of the dragon killer cross bows up in a small tower above them, nodded down to Vaughn as he, also, manned a dragon killer next to Stephanie. Way below, the very ground seemed to be moving, and then the castle walls below seemed to move. It was the gargoyles and Vaughn hollered out, "ARCHERS."

Small windows opened up in the walls, placed in a triangular pattern, and archers leaned out and began to fire and gargoyles began to die. Stephanie said to Vaughn, "Why are there *so many?* I thought you said three dragons and twenty-five gargoyles."

"*We're* here, and Queen Karen wants to make sure this time."

Stephanie squared her shoulders, raised her hand, and dark roiling clouds appeared with massive lightning bolts striking several dragons which fell out of the sky, dead. The people, watching through tiny windows and the military at their posts, all cheered. But then the clouds disappeared. Lady Stephanie brought them back, but they disappeared again.

She shot from her hand a blazing, fiercely glowing golden fireball and it hit a dragon and blew it apart. She leaned over the parapet and shot many mini fireballs and many gargoyles blew apart. A huge dragon came down out of the sky and Lady Stephanie shot another fireball but halfway to its mark it fizzled, and the dragon swooped down and sprayed fire across the castle wall, but the archers were ready and slammed their heavy blessed window shutters tight. As soon as the dragon passed, they opened back up and resumed firing.

Stephanie had tried to shield them from the fire, too, but her power failed *again*. Then the dragon veered and came back. The dragon killers fired but the dragon paused in mid-air, twisted, and the javelins missed. Then the giant red dragon headed straight for Vaughn and Stephanie, and Vaughn called out, "Lord *Jesus*," and ducked, pulling his wife down with him and he pressed his body tightly against her, forcing her hard into the wall, with his Staff still in his other hand.

The fire went over them, hit a small tower behind them, and swirled around it and was gone. "How did you like that, *bitch?*" It was Karen.

"Vaughn, how does she *do* that? How does she just nullify my abilities like their *nothing?*"

"She's a demon now, so the Black Oil is in her veins. That's a bit different from the Ethereal demons. I think it makes her even stronger! But maybe not for much longer. I think it's time for you to go to her tree!"

"*NOW?*"

He looked deeply into her rich brown eyes. "I don't think she could ever be more distracted."

"But, but . . . we haven't even talked any more about this. We don't even know if it'll work. And Jargono . . ."

"Is already there waiting on you!"

"What if it's a trap? We don't know . . ."

"We *do know.* And you *know it!*" He looked deeply into the depths of her person and seemed to pull something up, just like he did that time in the window so long ago when he rescued a pitiful girl from herself and her gang.

"I have to try," she said.

"You have to do more than try."

Fire blazed in her eyes. "I have to *win.*"

"The best place, the *best* chance we have is with *you* and her tree."

"But it won't be enough. You said that the demon had to be, what? Sucked out of her? And that the Highest Councilor said that was next to impossible."

"Next to impossible still means there's hope. That's all we have. Now *go!*"

It was a Kingly order! First time ever and she knew it. It was regal, authoritative, and meant to be obeyed, and Lady Stephanie did the only thing she could do. She threw her arms around him, and in the middle of a deeply loving kiss, she disappeared.

Vaughn turned so black waves of energy vibrated out from him. Karen came by again but this time he didn't duck the fire but held out his Staff. The fire swirled all around him but not even smoke touched his garments. She came by again with the same attack, this time trying to dispel his power, but it was to no avail. "Not yet, Harris."

Vaughn manned his dragon killer, but he had leaned his Staff against the wall in front of him, and Karen could see it wasn't in his hand. The dragon breathed fire again, but the

Staff turned into a mighty serpent which opened its mouth and swallowed *all* the fire, then breathed it right back in her face. Shocked, Karen veered her steed. "Now, Harris, *NOW!*" And Harris fired straight at her. But at the same time, Vaughn fired his dragon killer directly below them. And that is *exactly* where Karen tried to steer because the fire was above her. Had Vaughn not fired at the exact same time, he would have missed.

But now the javelin struck the evil beast dead in its chest. It flapped its mighty wings bringing it up even to the parapet, and within its mighty expression, its piercing, intelligent, but very evil eyes stared right through Vaughn. And then the light went out of those eyes, and it began to fall. Karen, all dressed in black, jumped off the beast and with a saber in each hand, she came down swinging so fast her attacks were a blur.

Vaughn's Staff parried all her blows, but just barely. *Angry* wouldn't describe her. "You made me look like a *fool.*" And she swung low, and as Vaughn blocked with his Staff, she gracefully flipped into the air over his head and tried to chop it off. But instead of standing back up, which would be the natural reaction after blocking low, Vaughn ducked into a roll and easily moved away.

Karen stopped to adjust her black dress, which had a slit in each side almost all the way up to her hips, and she smiled sweetly. "That was just for openers. You didn't know I trained ever since I was a little girl. And since I've been Queen, my husband has gotten me the best trainers in the whole world, and *not* just in weapons. In all kinds of the art."

She threw her hand down and a blaze of smoke went up. Vaughn sensed her sabers and parried various strikes, but she kicked him in the solar plexus which took his breath away and drove him back against the wall. Harris fired an arrow at her from his station, but she merely twisted, and it missed, and she laughed. Her back had been to Harris.

She came at Vaughn again, threw something into the air but Vaughn leapt atop the parapet wall and avoided the cloud. Then he summersaulted over her but swung his Staff, not at her, but at the middle of one of her sabers, and knocked it out of her hand and over the wall. But Karen was also on the attack with something similar in mind, and she kicked him in the neck just as he landed. She followed him through his fall then spun herself and like a constricting snake, she somehow managed to wrap herself around the Staff, and holding onto it with both hands she hoisted both her knees against her chest then kicked out with such force into Vaughn's chest that she rent the Staff from his hand and she tossed it over the wall.

With fierce murder in her eyes, eyes that were demon black, she drug the point of her sword against the stone floor as she slowly walked toward Vaughn. "This is for the Father, and to destroy all the orbs once and for all."

Her attacks again were like a blur, but somehow, between ducking and dodging, Vaughn managed to catch the blade between his palms and he kicked her in the gut, took the saber and tossed it over the wall. He finally spoke. "You really are a dumb bitch, aren't you? That's all Gary's chief whore could *ever* have been!"

It was too much. She whirled in place in a way Vaughn had never seen, and turned into smoke! The smoke surrounded him, disoriented him, and then she wrapped a wire around his neck and pulled it tight with her legs wrapped around him from behind. He was going to slam her against the small tower but she brought him to the floor before he could do that. Harris was up in the little tower above them, unable to help, watching helplessly.

೦

As soon as Lady Stephanie had materialized at Karen's tree, Jargono stepped out from around it. "Thank you for coming. I don't deserve *any* of your kindness."

They were the exact right words to speak. Stephanie looked over at his tree, which was intermingled with Karen's, and she saw actual progress toward goodness in Jargono. Still, it was hard to believe, and harder to trust. He motioned her around the other side. "I've been disarming her defenses from here."

He reached in to remove another energy thread and Stephanie's eyes immediately glowed with fire and without even raising her hand, that would have been too late, she made an energy shield to protect Jargono's back. A black cutting beam had lashed out from a hidden trap and was blocked. Jargono backed out of the tunnel he had created and shook his head. "You just saved my life from my wife! I didn't see that."

And that wasn't a mere statement, he was wondering how he missed it. "Jargono, she's a *woman.* Most men can't follow everything a woman does. But have you actually taken a *really* close look at her tree?"

"That's your department."

"Not any more. *Open your EYES!*" And she smacked him so hard across the face it knocked him over! But it wasn't just a physical slap. It was a *faithwalker-to-faithwalker slap.* When he rebounded in anger, she maneuvered herself between him and Karen's tree and when he saw reality, he collapsed to his knees and howled in pain and wept.

Lady Stephanie knelt beside him and wrapped her loving arms around him. "I'm so sorry I had to do that." And she hugged him for dear life, the value of both their lives! And he felt it, he *knew* it, and slowly straightened, then looked deeply into her rich brown eyes.

He shook his head at what he saw. "I've never felt anything like what you just did, from the slap, which I needed, to what you just did. Thank you." He slowly stood up. "Those *demons* did this to her."

"So let's try and *beat them.*" She grabbed Jargono by the arm and whirled him around, then looked into his eyes again and said, "Let's *win.*"

He looked at her oddly then. "If you hadn't loved Vaughn the way you do, did I have a chance?"

She looked him in the eye, "No. Not with the way you *were.*"

He nodded. "I understand that now. But if I had been even the meager way I am now?"

"If I had *never* known Vaughn, then most definitely yes!"

He shook his head, knowing it was the straight, heartfelt truth. "Thank you."

They turned to Karen's tree, and together they got through the rest of her defenses. Then he showed Stephanie where he thought she needed to take the graft from his tree. It was a *very* thin section starting at the very base, going *deep* into the heartwood, taking part of the central root, then all the way up until the trunk began to branch but no further.

"I think you are *exactly* correct. That most central part of you is undoubtedly from where she originally came. It's fascinating to see, and it gives me hope. May I?" he nodded and she began the excision.

A bright, super concentrated beam of golden light cut into his tree and as soon as she began, Jargono made himself a comfort chair and sat. She didn't have time to look at him but she could feel him. This was like having surgery without anesthesia. It occurred to her she could probably just cut the whole tree down right there and then, and that would probably kill him! She remembered the last time she had him in such a vulnerable position but she couldn't do it then because she hoped he would change. Then he killed her in the Sacred Cave!

Stephanie had sworn to herself that if she *ever* got that chance again, she wouldn't fail it. *But do oaths to ourselves count? I don't think so. They have to be to God or someone else.* She knew she wasn't going to harm him, and he knew it, too, as he sat helpless.

She extracted the graft then waved her hand so that it would float and not touch the gray Dead Forest floor. She went over to Karen's tree to make the incision but Jargono called out, "Wait! It's not time yet. She'll feel it like I felt it, and be here in a flash."

Stephanie shook her head. There was obviously more going on here than she knew. She looked over to Jargono but he didn't look at her. She came over and lifted his chin and turned his head to her. "What's going on?"

ↂ

Vaughn couldn't get the wire from around his neck, he couldn't get his fingers anywhere close to being under it. He knew Stephanie had to be waiting on him now and if he didn't do something quickly, she would pop back here and all would be lost. With all Vaughn's might, he toughened his neck so that the wire could only cut into his skin, then he kicked his feet and legs over his head and he managed to break the hold her legs had on him and the wire slipped over his chin and he landed on his feet just behind Karen's head because she had been on the ground behind him. The flesh at Vaughn's chin bled profusely but he had greater things of concern that had to be done *now.*

The leverage he'd created also ripped the wire from her hands and cut them, as well. They bled back. She quickly tried to stand but Vaughn was behind her and wrapped her in his arms. One of her hands was free, though, and she smeared her Black Oil blood on his face expecting him to collapse like before, but Vaughn just laughed. "I'm immune to that pain now."

She struggled with all her might but couldn't break his hold. Vaughn chided her. "You're at *my* home now. I have a nice little cell all prepared just like you did for our *daughter,* you pathetic *gang whore!*"

That threw her into a fit again. There was *no way* she would let him lock her up. She tried popping into the Ethereal Corridor but Vaughn held onto her anyway. And there they were, together in the Ethereal, but in the Ethereal, Karen began to grow much stronger.

"Fool. You're in *my* home turf now."

But just then pain wracked both of them!

"Well, well, well. This is *long* overdue. And so *very* yummy." The Highest Councilor had wrapped them both up together in his very long tail.

"Yes, yes, Master. May I taste?"

The Highest Councilor's underling came up and ran his Great Eye over her and *tasted* Queen Karen. Of course, she screamed but far more from the utter insult than the true pain she felt.

⌘

Jargono lifted his head and just stared into Stephanie's eyes not answering her question. She tried penetrating him but couldn't which worried her. But then Jargono said, "Now, right now, and we only have about a minute or so . . . I think."

His tentativeness wasn't reassuring at all, neither was the fact he avoided her question and blocked her from his mind, but what could Stephanie do? She went over to Karen's tree and sliced into it carefully but as quickly as she could.

⌘

Karen screamed in real pain now and when the Highest Councilor saw it, he squeezed even stronger. She tried to morph into her demon form to look at him Great Eye to

Great Eye but he blocked her. "Oh no, no, my dearest. None of *that now.*"

Grinchback ran his Great Eye over her again and tasted and this time she felt the pain of it down so deep it touched her very soul, which she never really believed she had. She did now!

The Highest Councilor then turned to Vaughn. "And what do we have here? Consuming you both might even give me enough power to actually consume HrorrarrAggrang!" When Karen heard *that,* she began to worry in earnest. The Highest Councilor turned his attention back to her. "What *Queen?* Didn't you tell them you wanted to *eat me?*"

Now Karen was finally afraid, and that startled her because no matter what, she never cared if she died before. Well, except when Vaughn struck her with a knife but that caring was more out of a desire for revenge than for her actual life. She had always felt that if she ultimately died, well then, so what! But now, something was wrong, very wrong, she *did care!* And Grinchback laughed. "Master, it happens *every single time.* They care!"

"Yes, my faithful, wise underling who *told me* this would work! Caring so deeply about the life you're going to *lose* is part of *consumption.*"

But somehow, Karen came to her senses. "You can't eat me."

"Oh *Queen,* I most certainly can and *will.*"

"Because, if you *do,* then the Father will consume *you.* I'm the *only* one who can run the game preserve." She smiled, having gotten back her composure in spite of the odd terrible pain she felt. She never knew consumption would feel like *this!*

"Master. She's right! But we can still eat Vaughn," And Grinchback ran his eye over Vaughn tasting him, too. He couldn't help howling from the pain.

"Grinchback, we're friends!"

And he replied, "And I always told you what that meant, that you would be my *first* choice at consumption. But even Mafferan warned you. You should have listened. But anyway, it's Master who will consume you."

And the Highest Councilor tried to pry Vaughn loose from Karen but he wouldn't let go. Vaughn laughed. "Well, if I *have to* be eaten, you'll have to eat her, too!"

The Highest Councilor struggled mightily to separate them but Vaughn turned even blacker than the demon and held on! Then Karen said, "Go ahead, eat us both! Then spit me out!"

Grinchback was amazed. He hovered his Great Eye over her. "You would *consent* to being eaten just so Vaughn would be eaten?" Grinchback peered at his Master, saying, "The Father can't blame you if she fully agrees." Then Grinchback looked back at Karen. "Do you know what kind of torment you'll experience? Even *if* my Master agrees to *vomit* you out? I know what that is because he ate me once!"

"I don't care! I don't care at *all,* just as long as you consume *him!*" But then something inside of her told her that was a lie! That she *did* care. So she said, "Anyway, you'll bring me back. You *have to!*"

The Highest Councilor now asked, "You give yourself *freely* to me, just as you did when I slipped my vibrating tail inside of you and turned you into an *Alpha?*"

Grinchback scolded him, "Master, stop playing and *consume!*"

Karen just wanted it all over with already. Talk, talk, *talk.* "*Yes, just do it. Just like you did me before!*" And she made those eyes at him and he could feel her giving herself entirely to him! So Highest Councilor ScrabaGag opened his Great Eye and sucked them both in!

༄

Stephanie had completed the graft and sealed it in carefully. After she finished pruning, Karen's tree responded immediately to the familiarity of the graft and accepted it and it already began to grow. The bark covered over the incision like it had never been there. But just as Stephane and Jargono were finishing replacing all of Karen's defenses, Stephanie mumbled, "This still won't work." She turned to Jargono, "I'm sorry. I really am, but all that evil, all that *blackness* in her tree . . . it's just going to overpower even *your* graft."

But just as she said that, the blackness began to lessen! It was slow but noticeable, but at the same time Lady Stephanie screamed, grabbed her tummy and fell over. It wasn't the pain of contractions. It wasn't the pains of new life. Jargono sighed, lifted her up, and teleported back to his castle and laid her in a guest bed, and sat next to her. "I'm sorry Stephanie. I really am. We wanted it to be any other way, but it was the *only way* to beat my wife because of my terrible blindness."

She opened her eyes in utter fright. "What are you saying?" But he couldn't bear to speak it.

She reached up and grabbed his tunic and fire came up into her eyes. "You *owe me!*"

Little Michael had been throwing a fit, kicking, pushing, almost like he wanted to be born but it was only six months. With her still clutching at him, Jargono finally found the strength. "The only way this would work, the Highest Councilor said, was if Karen gave herself willingly back to him the same way she gave herself willing to be a demon. And the only way you could cut into her tree without her knowing, was if she was feeling such terrible pain that she never felt before so she wouldn't understand what you were doing."

Stephanie now turned black with vibrating power. Jargono knew this kind of power he couldn't counter very well. It was the same kind that Vaughn used to withstand him before. But he opened up himself wide to her. "I'm very sorry. I *really* am. The only way Vaughn could figure out how to get my wife to agree to something like that was . . ."

And he couldn't say it as he choked up! Stephanie grabbed his head and *yanked* it toward her and delved inside his mind . . . then howled in grief. "Noooo, nooo, nooooo, ohh nooo." But just then something glowed and burned in her pocket. It was the letter Vaughn had given her, and Jargono pulled it out for her.

"He told me about this. To make sure you read it now. Would you like me to read it for you?" She was bawling so hard all she could do was nod.

The envelope said,

From Whence my Strength Now Cometh
and my Love Forever.

My Beloved wife Queen Stephanie,

I am sorry I had to do it this way, but I know that
if we had discussed this, you would never have allowed
me to. I could never fight with you, my dearest. I
know you would not have let me, because if the situation were reversed, I would not have let you. We love
each other so much.

At hearing *those* words, Stephanie said, "Stop, I know
this, *Stop.*"

But Jargono said, "He said you would say that but I was
to continue, anyway. I'm sorry."

But Stephanie said through her tears and sobs, "But you
don't know what that is. *I* wrote that *knowing* I was going to
my death, when I faced you."

Jargono brushed her tear-matted hair from her eyes. "I
think that's the whole point. But you need to hear it now but
from *him!*"

But our love is so great because it is founded in
that Love which is greater. We must always honor that
Love first, if our love is to be forever real. You did not
fail me, my beloved, by doing what you did today with
Karen's tree. You honored me. You allowed Love to be
fulfilled in your heart and actions. Love for the Greater
Good which a *faithwalker* always serves.

We are called together unto a higher purpose. We can only hope to truly be together, if we fulfill that purpose to its fullest. Yes, my love, I knew beforehand. Let me repeat it now so you will understand.

Stephanie, all we can do is do goodness to the fullest that we can do. We are not assured of any outcome, my love, only that we have and are able to do our part. We cannot fail our part as long as we keep faith and do it. We may not achieve the outcome we wanted, but we have not failed if we do the part that we are able to do. Do you understand that, my dearest? More than ever, everyone is going to need your unfailing love. *Everyone.* Tell little Michael I will always live through his prayers.

Please say yes, my dearest, that you will *live* for us all with all the passion you can muster, please. I cannot bear to face what I must face, if you do not truly say yes. Let the Staff of Life pass over us in Peace.

Your beloved husband forever in Love,

King Vaughn

She pulled a pillow over her head and wailed until she was hoarse. "I can't. I just can't take it anymore. I can't . . . I just can't."

Jargono began to weep. Then he suddenly felt something *alive.* His wife had returned from the dead, and she *was* alive. He materialled a royal blue plush blanket with Appendaho gold embroidery at its edges for Lady Stephanie, locked and sealed the door and put a heavy protection around the whole room so nothing could get in, but Stephanie would be free to leave, and he vanished.

And reappeared where the Highest Councilor and Grinchback were. Karen was floating weakly, and she looked like her old self again when they first met, but with something even better, *more* her. Jargono scooped her up in his arms, looked at the demons, and then began to ask . . . but the Highest Councilor cut him off.

"A deal's a deal, Jargono. You know that."

Jargono narrowed his eyes at them and Grinchback could tell he was about to do something rather violent. "Your wife needs you *now*. This particular time is crucial for her. Don't make Vaughn's sacrifice for nothing!"

He looked at her and could feel the truth of it. He dematerialized and went to a whole different castle than where Lady Stephanie was at.

CHAPTER 17

Living Without You

7 And it was given unto him to make war with the saints, and to overcome them: and power was given him over all kindreds, and tongues, and nations.

8And all that dwell upon the earth shall worship him, whose names are not written in the book of life of the Lamb slain from the foundation of the world.

9 And if any man have an ear, let him hear.

This time Marta had no glow, no shine, she didn't even look like she belonged in heaven! More like down *there! What happened to her?* Many of the students wondered, but then the older students told the younger ones, who weren't allowed to watch, that King Vaughn had died horribly!

"Then why isn't he up here?" they asked.

But all the older children could do was just shake their heads. They couldn't tell the little ones *that.*

Marta suddenly picked her head up. Then she shook it. "The lesson I intended to teach, well, we'll try tomorrow! Today shall be a time of prayer as if we *were* down there. I think, *sometimes,* being up here we lose a certain empathy for them *down there.* And that *weakens* our prayers. Let us all pray as if we were down there in the very *midst* of it all! Search, muster, find all the goodness you can, and send it all down *there* in prayer! They need every bit of all of it!"

All the children knelt together and as they began to guide their prayers down below, they were immediately met with tremendous evil pushing back! They felt it and gasped. And then they tried again. And again. And again . . .

*T*his is how Vaughn felt when I died! Oh God. How did he bear it? And then she remembered. *He didn't very well. He was going to* kill *himself. Oh Vaughn.* At hearing herself call her beloved husband's name, she wailed again. It cut through her like a hot knife, but she knew the pain would never go away.

He was so ashamed when he'd admitted that he was going to kill himself. Then she thought about the letter, again. *He changed my letter, though.* You allowed Love to be fulfilled in your heart and actions. Love for the Greater Good which a *faithwalker* always serves. *Was he trying to tell me something more? Oh God, I can't think.*

The Greater Good. She wailed again. *What Greater Good? I mean, not against you God. I mean, what Greater Good could possibly be served by his* Sacrifice. *Why does that word always haunt my* LIFE?

We can only hope to truly be together, if we fulfill that purpose to its fullest. *I think this was a slight change, too. Be together. Oh, Father Abraham, you said we would* always be *together,* even in death! *Even in death. But Vaughn was a* faithwalker *when he wrote this, so able to see the bigger picture. But not like me. Not like me.*

She began to examine the other parts of her letter that he'd changed. *More than ever, everyone is going to need your unfailing love. Everyone.* Tell little Michael I will always live through his prayers.

What was he really *trying to tell me? With Vaughn, there's* always *a deeper point. Unfailing love?* She broke down, again. *It sure feels like failing.* But little Michael began to stir, and she now remembered what her husband had told her about their son, that he was so glad that he was able to help in giving her such a child, that little Michael was greater than both of them put together! She wailed again. *You KNEW! Even back then you* knew *what you were going to do.*

More than ever, everyone is going to need your unfailing love. *Everyone.* Tell little Michael I will always live through his prayers. *More than ever? After all we've been through? And why stress* EVERYONE? *Can't we ever just think about ourselves,* for once? *But aren't we* included *in everyone? Oh, Vaughn, what were you trying to tell me? Please.*

Tell little Michael I will always live through his prayers. *That's like our secret code, I'm* sure *he meant it like that. Live through his prayers. What does he mean?* Little Michael began glowing mightily and Stephanie put her hands to her belly. *Yes, Vaughn, you live right here, I know. But was that your whole meaning? Oh God, I can't feel you Vaughn, not at all, not anywhere. You're just gone. But that's what you felt when I died from the Black Oil. OH GOD.*

And the last line he changed. Please say yes, my dearest, that you will *live* for us all with all the passion you can muster, please. *He emphasized the word* live. *Why? And with all the passion I can muster? Now?*

She didn't want to think about *any* of this. She didn't want to think at all, nor feel, nor even exist. But she could feel little Michael and there was no way she was going to let him down like she let her husband down, because she *is* the *faithwalker.* The only true good one left. *But how could I have let him down? I'm supposed to see the* whole *picture. Was I not doing my part, my* whole *part? Or am I not doing it now? Oh God.*

Vaughn knew. The whole time, he knew. We had to take Karen down, both to keep Jargono from breaking bad at a time when we couldn't afford it, but also Karen would have overpowered us all.

Let the Staff of Life pass over us in Peace. *What Peace? Vaughn, what peace? I have no peace, now.* Lady Stephanie sat up, now noticing where she was at. She also saw the way Jargono protected her in this room. *Wow! He really didn't want any harm to come to me!* And Lady Stephanie left the room and materialized back in the Dead Forest by Karen's tree.

It *was* looking much better. So was Jargono's tree. The extensive pruning Stephanie also did to Karen's tree, wasn't enough to take her person away, but it weakened her so much that it allowed her tree to support the most vibrant part of her, *first.* That's the way life works after a trauma. And the graft had begun to flourish and then spread *its* strength through her whole tree.

Stephanie remembered how much evil this woman had done to her and to Vaughn, and yet, here Stephanie was, *rejoicing* over the goodness now growing in Karen's life. She sighed deeply. Just then fire came up in her eyes and she whirled around with fierce golden glow. Grinchback hovered a safe distance away slathered in Black Oil.

"I'm sorry for your loss."

She eyed him closely. *He must have been there. He's* always *with his Master. He* must have known the plan. The *faithwalker* waved her hand and *all* the Black Oil turned to dust and she grabbed him by the neck again, but he didn't resist nor howl! "Tell me what you know and if you *dare* lie to me, it will be the last thing you *ever do!*"

He bowed his head as best he could and ignored his smoking neck. "The only way Karen could be restored . . ."

She shook him and the Ethereal rumbled. "I know all about that. Jargono told me. I *made* him. Tell me something I *don't* know!"

"After Master stuck his tail in his eye and plucked Karen out, Jargono looked at my Master with such a deadly calm I knew he was about to do something very foolish against my Master, so I refocused him on his wife."

But why didn't . . . "But why didn't he *demand* that Vaughn be returned?" And then the bigger picture began to dawn on Lady Stephanie. Her hand went to her mouth. *Oh God. Vaughn let himself be eaten on purpose, but he* wouldn't have *just killed himself. Especially not after his oath to* never *do that again.* Then she realized, "*Why* did Vaughn trust you two?"

"Please Lady Stephanie. I know, right now you can end my miserable existence at any time. Please let go."

She looked at her hand doing major damage to the underling and she let him go, but he didn't back away at all. "Your husband and I are friends."

"*Friends?*" She spit the word out for the ridiculousness it was. "*And?*"

"My Master and I have been *friends?*"

She shook her head then tuned from deep gold to deep black, and whispered, "You're trying to tell me that my ever-so-wise husband did all this solely based on *demon* friendship?"

It doesn't make sense. Vaughn may have had faith in it to some degree, but he wouldn't have just relied on it. And he's not answering my question because he doesn't want to lie, which means, she grabbed him again, and he blurted out, "Jargono did threaten Master, Lady Stephanie."

"You told me that, already." And then it dawned on her again. *Jargono was Vaughn's backup plan. As soon as Karen was freed, he was there. That was planned. But then why didn't Jargono go through with it? Vaughn depended on friendship with* Jargono? Lady Stephanie turned even darker, if that was possible, and she whispered because she was holding back so much power, "*And?*"

Grinchback looked away, and said, "Master said a deal is a deal."

There was another Ethereal Quake. *Everything* shook except Lady Stephanie and Grinchback. "Jargono betrayed my husband." She was about to go find him but Grinchback wrapped his tail around her, not in a threatening way, but to just stop her from leaving. Just before she would have obliterated him, he let her go and bowed to her feet, "Please Mistress Stephanie, I beg you to *think* before you act!"

Think before I act. She looked back at Jargono's tree. *I don't see that kind of treachery there. He could be masking it. But I know his tree so well now.* She looked back at Grinchback, thinking. *Jargono is no fool either. Demon* friendship? She laughed at the thought of Jargono trusting anything like that. With her and Vaughn, *maybe,* but demons? Never. She realized, "Jargono needed a way to ensure the Highest Councilor would do for Karen what he really was supposed to do."

"Yes, Mistress Stephanie."

"And so he made the deal with your Master *not* to fight to free my husband!" It wasn't a question. "If your Master did what he was supposed to do for his wife."

"Yes, Lady Stephanie!"

She turned very, very dark again and another Ethereal Quake hit. She was leaving for sure this time but Grinchback dove on her. She carried him along into the Ethereal Corridor before Grinchback was able to halt her from going to Jargono. "Destroy me Mistress, but not before you *think! Please!*"

What is there to think about? Grinchback answered for her, "That *my* friend Vaughn would have also been wise enough to know all this would happen, too! He *knew* Jargono needed a safeguard."

He's right! But that means Jargono would have known Vaughn would know . . . They both discussed all this in depth, how to protect their interests. So Jargono's betrayal of Vaughn was planned! *But for what? Then what other* interests *were they protecting?*

She looked at Grinchback. "You can destroy me now, my Lady, it was an honor trying to consume you!"

She grabbed him and pulled him out of his bow and met him eye to eye and looked very deeply into him. But then, "I don't believe it!" she said with incredulity.

"Believe what, my Lady"

She shook her head but had to say it, because of what she saw. "My people have a saying that we never answer that kind of question referring to what's inside you. You must find the answer for yourself from the inside out!"

She let him go. *I just can't believe that Vaughn would sacrifice himself solely for Karen, ensure her safe return without getting something more for himself. He knows how important he is to the Greater Good.* "Was there even a greater interest they could be protecting, Grinchback?" She asked in a far less threatening tone.

Grinchback bunched up his tail and shrugged pathetically. "I don't know that, my Queen!" he hesitated, then spoke further. "My Master and I had talked all this through extensively beforehand. A lot of it actually was *my* plan!" When he saw her begin to darken, again, he quickly followed up. "Not like that. I trusted my Master. He *wasn't* supposed to retain your husband. I had explained thoroughly to him that it was actually in all our best interests that your husband should live. I believed he understood and agreed."

"You *trusted* another demon? A *Master* no less? And you thought you were *wiser* than him?"

Grinchback lowered his Great Eye. "Yes, my Lady. Because I saw *my* color changes and then Master had the *same*, and I thought I could see that he felt the same. I believed him."

Lady Stephanie looked at this poor underling and couldn't believe he was telling the truth, but, "You're telling the truth!"

He bowed low, "Yes, my Queen!"

There it was again. He meant the royal address to her! She shook her head. *What is going on here?* Then a thought came to her which Lady Stephanie quickly owned. "Grinchback, Vaughn told me you had been *consumed* by your Master."

"Yes, my Lady. After our encounter, when you and Mafferan, together, turned the Black River to stone!"

Stephanie was shocked and Grinchback noted it. *This must have been part of what Vaughn couldn't tell me! But I can't get sidetracked now.* "When you were inside your Master, were you able to hear everything on the outside?"

"Yes, my Queen!"

She narrowed her eye at him, "Were you able to perceive everything *inside* of him?"

At that question Grinchback paused and brought his tail tip up to his temple to rub it. "Master had said that GrrraGagag was able to withhold certain knowledge from him even though he was consumed."

"But were *you* privy to all of *your* Master's experience?"

"I would like to say, yes, certainly most of it, but then again, Master obviously planned to deceive me for a while, and I wasn't aware of it. What if his whole plan was merely to use Karen to consume your husband? That's pretty long-range. Then that means after he consumed me, he hid that."

Stephanie ran her hands through her hair, working out a tangle. "That's because he *knew* he would set you free later! He had to know that because you've been intricate in his current plans. But for those he doesn't expect to free, I believe they *are* privy to everything because that makes the consumption more pleasurable!"

Grinchback nodded with knowledge, "You are very correct on that." But before she got ready to depart, Grinchback had to say it. "My Master instructed me to . . .make you a deal. I'm sorry. He said he would be willing to consider a trade."

Stephanie's hand went to her tummy as the babe leapt in her womb. "*No Michael!* If I did *that* to set Daddy fee, it would be the end of us. He made that *very* clear to me in his letter, and even before! He was so glad he could give you to me, Michael! And Daddy said, Tell little Michael I will always live through his prayers. We haven't fought this hard to save our child's life just to trade him away, no matter who it's for! *NO! Don't* speak to me again of such evil! It's the kind we could never overcome if we did that!"

Grinchback wasn't sure how much Lady Stephanie was speaking to her unborn child, and how much was directly to him, if any, but it didn't matter. Her meaning was very clear. "I understand, My Queen. I truly hope you find peace." And Grinchback disappeared.

Peace. Let the Staff of Life pass over us in Peace. *And where is Vaughn's Staff? There are* too *many unanswered questions.*

Lady Stephanie popped back to the castle to where she had left her husband, but when she arrived, she let out a sob, because it was as if she could still feel Vaughn's presence there and every fiber of her body and soul cried out for him. Harris immediately sensed her and called down from up on the little tower. "King Vaughn disappeared a while ago and we haven't heard back."

She took a deep breath. Now was not the time. "I know. How goes the battle without *Queen Karen?"*

Harris shook his head. "Apparently, she has gargoyle generals! Not the mindless savages we mostly see. They ride the dragons and command just like she did, maybe better! Your castle idea is *brilliant.* We've been barely able to hold on, but we're holding. But if they get any reinforcements, I think we're doomed."

Oh GOD! I think that's it. Reinforcements! *Vaughn* had *to know that, too. So he wouldn't have just sacrificed himself for Karen, alone. But, without Karen, they can't make any more dragons and gargoyles, can they?* Then Lady Stephanie got a bad feeling in the pit of her stomach. *Oh God, the Highest* Councilor ate *Karen, so he would know exactly how she did it! We're in bigger trouble than ever.* But then she also realized, *But Vaughn would have known that, too! This just doesn't make sense. Why save Karen only for all of us to be destroyed anyway?*

Lady Stephanie also realized, though, what it meant that Karen was gone, for now. Her eyes blazed and the sky quickly darkened. Great roaring thunder once again heralded the return of the *faithwalker,* and everyone knew it and cheered while lightning lashed out and took out many of the remaining dragons. The rest moved off at a distance, awaiting orders. Then a tightly packed tornado arose and cleaned the castle walls of gargoyles then spewed them high into the air where repeated lightning savaged them. *If only it was all that easy. I'm only a single faithwalker.* "How is the rest of the country fairing? Have they reported in?"

Harris nodded. "They're under much lighter attack than we suffered. They're holding but can't say they're winning."

"Harris, you witnessed Vaughn's battle?"

"Yes, my Queen."

"Did you see what happened to his Staff?"

"Queen Karen threw it over the wall."

That's odd. He could have just called it right back into his hand. But maybe he couldn't in the heat of battle. But then again, I don't think his plan would have worked if he had held on to it. I just can't imagine a demon consuming that *Staff.*

Lady Stephanie went into the Ethereal Corridor parallel to their physical world and searched for the Staff from there. She found it at the castle base stuck standing up, wedged between two granite boulders and she immediately popped back to the physical world and she pulled it out. As soon as she touched it, the Staff recognized her and glowed. She stood on the stones hugging the Staff to her breast and to Michael. She put her head against it just like she'd seen her husband do so many times when he was thinking deeply.

Images of the battle Vaughn had with Karen flowed into her. And then when Karen disarmed him, *That isn't right! I don't believe that!* Without thinking, she was questioning the Staff, in a way like she questioned the Book of Wisdom. The Staff showed her how Vaughn *purposefully* let it go when Karen took hold! *The Book of Wisdom! There's no way he didn't consult it before all this.*

Lady Stephanie popped over to their new bedroom within the castle, leaned the staff in the corner, then pulled open the lowest heavy dresser drawer then lifted the bottom panel to pull out the hidden Book. She went right to the back page where the index was, the record of all questions asked to it, and she sat down on a plush bedroom chair with padded fancy wooden arms.

"Can a demon be your true friend?" She touched the question and the answer appeared.

"What do *you* think?"

"Can a demon operate for the Greater Good over its own self-interest?"

"If its own self-interest *is* the Greater Good! It also depends upon what the underling is made from?"

Stephanie voiced her thoughts, "What does *that* mean?"

The previous page began to flash underneath. When she turned it over, her answer was there! "Underlings are made from what their sire has consumed, and most, also from the Black Vapors."

Stephanie shook her head, not understanding what to do with the knowledge. She flipped back to the index. Vaughn's last question was, "Can Highest Councilor ScrabaGag be trusted."

Stephanie was shocked Vaughn asked the book such a specific question. She used to follow *everything* he did with the Book, but she'd been so busy for so long. She touched the question not expecting an answer, but there was! "ROFL" *"What does* that *mean?"* she said sarcastically. The page underneath began flashing. 'Rolling On the Floor Laughing."

So Vaughn really did *know.* Lady Stephanie turned to the first page to ask her question. "Can Vaughn be rescued?" She prayed for a good answer.

"That answer is within you!" Stephanie grew dark. "Even *you?* Why does everyone and every *thing* want our child destroyed?"

But the Book of Wisdom answered. "You missed my meaning, *Faithwalker.* How come? From conception, your child is a marriage between True Meaning from the Tree of Life and True Words handed down through the Blessing of Generations to your husband from the Lord's chosen people. There is no more wisdom able to be offered at this time."

Feeling woefully inadequate, Stephanie wept. *The answer is within me? Oh God, help. I don't know. I just don't know.* "True tears have touched the Book of Wisdom. Your friend Arlupo says to tell you, Then *that* is your choice!"

Stephanie closed the book gently and rubbed the tears from her eyes. She thought she should take advantage of Karen being gone by visiting all the towns and destroying the enemy while she could, but she couldn't. All she could do was sit there doing *nothing.*

Finally, she got up, put the book away, and disappeared.

CHAPTER 18

When Plans Come Together

10 He that leadeth into captivity shall go into captivity: he that killeth with the sword must be killed with the sword. Here is the patience and the faith of the saints.

11And I beheld another beast coming up out of the earth; and he had two horns like a lamb, and he spake as a dragon.

12 And he excercisezeth all the power of the first beast before him, and causeth the earth and them which dwell therein to worship the first beast, whose deadly wound was healed.

Before Marta had a chance to say anything, all the children began describing their experiences. "I was scared. "I felt so suffocated?" "I kept trying but something evil kept pushing back." "I didn't feel my prayers went *anywhere*." "It was overwhelming."

Marta nodded. "That's why we need more depth to the goodness in us!"

All the students looked on in shock because they all realized that last lesson wasn't just because their teacher was upset and asked them to pray. It was in fact part of their continuing lessons!

Marta sternly looked upon every child. They hadn't seen, nor felt *anything* like this before, but it wasn't scary. Yesterday was scary. Marta said, "Why does the evil affect you all that way?"

Answers again blurted out altogether. "I don't know." "They cut me off." "They squeezed me." "It was suffocating."

And Marta spoke sharply, cutting them off! *"Enough!"* The children's eyes went wide! They still weren't scared, but . . . "Only one of you answered my question. The others just kept repeating what you *let* evil do to you! I asked WHY?"

All the children just looked at each other, but Aaron finally spoke up. "Elaina, when she said she didn't know. Our lack of understanding."

Marta nodded. "That's one reason. There are others. Sometimes we can understand quite clearly but evil will *still* make you feel that way. Why?"

The students began to wonder how Marta could know such things. Many wondered how old she was, what her life was like *down there.* She had been so sweet, but now? She was so tough, hard, but it still wasn't bad. Elaina said, "If we don't understand what evil is throwing at us, we don't know what to throw back? But even if we do understand, if it pushed against us harder than we pushed back, we get pushed over?"

Marta knew all their thoughts and feelings. She had been there. She looked steely eyed at the children. "I was fourteen when I came up. I've been here fifty-five years now. Enough time to make me forget, in a way, from where I came, from what I went through. But it's all come back to me now as I watch Lady Stephanie and King Vaughn. The reason the Lord Jesus went *down there* and became one of us, was *not* to forget *anything.* It was to build strength and understanding against evil through actually experiencing it in the flesh, in mortality, feeling mortal pains and challenges, and *even* death so that His natural reaction against all that evil while in mortality added extra goodness to the Holy Spirit that hadn't been there before! That strength, that understanding, that love, and faith is there for all of us, we just have to go *get it!*" And Marta disappeared!

And she found Eve sitting at a reflecting pool with her toes in the peaceful water and Marta crossed her legs and sat next to her. Eve said, "Stick your toes in. It's refreshing."

"I *can't.* I'm too upset, and I don't want to feel anything different right now. I don't think I'm a very good teacher. I resign!"

Eve didn't look at her, but just kept swishing the water with her toes. "You're free up here to do whatever you want, Marta. But I've *never* in all my life seen a teacher as good as you! And if I could choose a teacher for *myself,* it would be you, *only* you!"

"All *your* life?" Marta whispered.

Eve turned to look her in the eye. "Yes! You can turn in your resignation, today. I'll take over until I find someone else." Eve began turning away, but then turned back to Marta, looking her in the eye, again. "You never know what affect you have *up here* on *down there!* The *only* prayers I've seen that I feel may make the difference *down there,* are coming from *your* classroom, even right now!" When Eve saw Marta wondering how that could possibly be, especially with all the great saints up here, Eve said, "Sometimes, it's not the greatest that makes the difference, but the smallest that evokes the Lord's greatest attention! You've watched closely how Lady Stephanie and her husband have been so very humble. They *need* the prayers from *exactly* a kindred spirit like you! And like what you are making *your* students become!"

"Like *me?*"

"Yes. *Exactly!*"

"I changed my mind. I'm *not* resigning."

"That is your choice. You are always free up here."

In between laughing fits, the Father asked the Highest Councilor, who floated quite comfortably in the Father's Darkest Room, "Tell me, *again.* You created your underling to be your *friend?*"

"Yes, Father!"

"And that actually worked?"

"Yes, Father."

"And he, in turn, thought *you* became *his* friend?"

"Yes Father."

"Because of some stupid *color changes?*"

"Well, his changes were real. But yes, Father. Because his changes were real, he believed mine were, also."

"And then you convinced Grinchback to be *friends* with Vaughn and he came to *trust* that friendship?"

"Not exactly, Father. *Vaughn* convinced my underling to be friends with *him*, but I made Grinchback to be able to accept it fully!"

"And because of *that,* your underling then convinced Vaughn that, since you and the underling were *friends,* that Vaughn could trust *you?*"

"Yes, Your Blackest Darkness, that is how human extended friendship works. It's very infectious."

After the Father had another prolonged, uncontrolled laughing fit, he then asked, "And Grinchback *actually* thought he was enlightening *you,* Highest Councilor?"

"Yes Father."

"And *even* outsmarting *ME?*"

"That is the way the error of youth often works, but I had to employ very unusual construction in making Grinchback in order to make him *that* stupid."

"You hear that HrorrarrAggrang? Now you see why I *love* Scraback that much?" HrorrarrAggrang, calmly floating right next to the Father gave a slight nod. The Father turned back to ScrabaGag. "And you're *sure* you got what you needed from that *bitch?*"

"Oh yes, Father. She turned out *exactly* as planned. Only *she* was able to figure out how to make the fold in the Ethereal work. But now I have *all* her knowledge."

"But she's still human. I thought you needed a human element to make the game preserve work. We need more reinforcements soon because the *faithwalker* no longer has Karen to abridge her powers."

"I now possess the human element from her that I need. We made that taint *perfectly* and I simply took it from her. But they'll never know I took it because of the graft from Jargono's tree they placed into her. They'll think the graft destroyed it."

The Father turned back to *his* underling. "Well, HrorrarrAggrang, that's how it's done. With *very* longest-range planning starting with consuming all of the *faithwalker's* ancestors! And Scraback, you even fooled Mafferan into helping you?"

"I knew he was watching and that when I showed I needed help, he would believe it!"

The Father, HrorrarrAggrang, and ScrabaGag all had a laughing fit together, wondering how they might use this over Mafferan. Invasion of the Ethereal. Intimidation of the Highest Councilor. Prohibited interference upon the Earth. The list was endless but now the threat to their most important plans was gone. So much was gained and *nothing* lost except some uncontrollable earth demons they no longer needed. The Father turned to the Highest Councilor and said, "OK, OK, you can eat the underling now."

But the Highest Councilor said, "I'd rather keep him around. He's still got time. I haven't laughed this much, *ever*. And don't worry, I think within a month we'll have excellent reinforcements. Karen took too long but I know how to speed it up. Then we'll overwhelm them, get rid of *Lady* Stephanie and her child, and we'll have total victory. I'm also working on counters to the *faithwalker's* powers. My new generals will all have it. I took the counter from Karen, too!"

"Highest Councilor, how does the good King Vaughn taste?"

His Great Eye smiled from one side of his bulbous head to the other. "Exquisite. Nothing like him, ever. He's perfect."

❧

Lady Stephanie joined Larson up in the little tower where he manned a dragon killer. The little towers, strategically interspersed throughout the castle area, were the highest points of the castle, but Stephanie was considering an even higher point. "Larson, when is your marriage?"

He bowed to Queen Stephanie. "After all this is over, I think."

"Don't wait, Larson. Carla is the best of women and she needs to be married to *you*. We should never find better reasons *not to do good* than to do it. Marrying Carla is good for you both. I need you to teach me how to fight!"

Larson ran his hand through his blond hair trying to hide his doubts. "Beggin' your pardon, my Lady, but . . ."

"There are no buts anymore!"

Larson stared into her face. There was *definitely* something different about her. "Yes, my Queen. When . . ."

"Now!"

This castle predominately housed all of Vaughn's people, and to them, Stephanie and Vaughn were King and Queen, the title given to them right before they crossed the border into the South. Back then, King Jargono had cut them off and demanded they bow to him, but in response they began to chant, Long Live King Vaughn! And Vaughn came through for them when he wounded Queen Karen and Jargono had to rush her to a hospital. When Stephanie appeared later, the people were shocked because all thought, including Vaughn, that she had died fighting the evil King. They chanted again, Long Live Queen Stephanie and King Vaughn and the titles stuck even after they managed to escape here. But not just the titles, the love they all had for them was unquestioned. Even many of the United for Christ common citizens began to think of them as a King and Queen.

So Larson called together the few other rangers there and they all gathered in the open courtyard, which occupied one third of the castle interior, and they began with hand to hand combat. But unlike most all people, showing her only once was enough! They assumed it was her *faithwalking* powers, but it wasn't exactly. It was love.

And then she had them set up fresh dummies on posts the military used for practice and she began to show them all her powers of blowing things up, shielding, *everything*. Then she asked them all, "How do I use all these to fight, to *really* fight and *win?*"

They all sighed, but then one by one, a ranger would say, "What if you do . . ." And sometimes another would say, "But if you add . . ." And after a while she began to do combinations of things she'd never done before. Offenses with simultaneous strong defense to protect her vulnerability when she attacked. Many different kinds of attacks with new combinations of energies. Keeping up a continuous defense because they told her, "My Lady, there's not a second in the day or night or in between that you're not a target, and they want you *dead*."

And all through the evening, and all through the night they trained her without their Queen even taking a break. And she was pregnant! Which is another thing that mystified them. She could move with the agility of the best of their warriors. They couldn't figure out how, but what they didn't know was that Lady Stephanie believed in physical fitness and routinely put herself through her own training program, and when she learned she was pregnant, she *increased* her training time. They all felt embarrassed when they finally had to excuse themselves but she just kept on practicing and working out her battle strategies.

It was almost dawn, but *everyone* in the castle was still awake, because everyone had heard about *Queen* Stephanie now becoming a warrior. It wasn't that she hadn't fought for them before, but they were all quite aware that with the best of intentions she made everything up as she went along. But now? Now, they crowded up on the castle walls, squeezed through all the windows until not a single eye was without view of this remarkable hero. But they also surmised the reason for the change because many of them were holy now, precisely because of Vaughn and Stephanie. Every one kept asking, "Can you even sense our King, *at all?*" And the answer was the same. And that's also why they kept watch over her. They loved them both so much it hurt. And when they realized Vaughn had to be dead, the pain was unthinkable except there was their Queen becoming a warrior, a *true* warrior, before their very eyes.

And the common thought also was, "She hasn't even told us, yet. She wanted to spare us." When Mandy, Carla, and the little girls found out, they wept sore, but Larson told them straight that they couldn't go to Lady Stephanie with their grief. "She has to bear this in her own way. If we show her we know, it'll crush her. Leave her be." So, they left her be.

Carla wept upon Larson's chest, and said, "You know? Vaughn saved both our lives, and at the risk of his own."

Larson wanted to ask Carla right there, but seeing Lady Stephanie still pouring her heart out to learn *everything* she could, he just couldn't bring himself to ask now, so he rejoined the other rangers to finish their Queen's combat lessons.

At dawn they all turned in to rest, but one hour of sleep was all the *faithwalker* would allow herself. She got up, took a quick shower, put on her holy dress that she hadn't worn in so long, and then manually fixed her hair into her three traditional Appendaho braids. *For what I'm going to do, this needs to be done with the utmost careful action, the most meaning possible.*

She popped herself over to another town that was being continually assaulted. But she didn't go to the castle. She was in the yard outside. When the gargoyles and the dragons saw her, they knew, now, what she was. Word had spread. The gargoyles stormed her, and she began to whirl, and slice with various energies, all rotating until she quickly found what worked.

Like Vaughn had, she now had a tremendous blackness that offered her much protection against their strikes, though the blunt force she still felt, but she had learned how to take a hit and move with it, rebound from it, and keep on fighting, no matter what. She didn't care about the bruises, though she set inside herself a low level of continuous healing. Onward she drove herself, spinning, kicking, powers she never used before coming from her hands, her feet, out of her chest, and it seemed little Michael was even casting bursts of energy, too, but predominately it looked as if he placed a protective glow around his Mother emanating from her belly and surrounding her.

The people of the castle began piling on the walls to watch. Tears were running down their eyes. Word had spread of her husband, their King's death. An hour later there were no more gargoyles and the dragons, with the generals aboard, swooped down for her.

All three breathed fire upon her at once, and for the longest time that's all they could see. But when the fire had cleared, Lady Stephanie was kneeling on one knee, with a staff in front of her, and her head against it. Then she raised the Staff and lightning came out from it and struck down a dragon.

The general gargoyle jumped off and ran at her. She cast several powers at it but they didn't work. It dove at her but just when it looked like she would be taken, she leapt upward, swung her Staff, and caved in the beast's head! Everyone started cheering. The other two dragons flew off, but Queen Stephanie disappeared, and reappeared in the distance on top of a dragon behind the general.

There was a huge golden fireball in the air that lit up the morning sky as if there was a second sun. Then they saw Lady Stephanie slowly float back to them surrounded by a glowing sphere. When she came to their inner courtyard the people thronged her and brought her food. She *had* to eat. And when they saw how tired she looked, they brought her to their best quarters and she laid down and fell immediately asleep. She slept with her husband's Staff in her arms as if it was Vaughn, himself.

Hours later, when she awoke, after freshening up, she disappeared then reappeared in the Ethereal Corridor at Jargono's castle. She found where Karen was and looked in on her as she slept. Stephanie shook her head. "She's not the same person, and yet, she is." She popped into the physical world beside her bed and Karen opened her eyes.

"Have you finally come to kill me?"

Stephanie had no glow about her, no hint of power, though now she always had hidden protection running. "No, Karen. I've come to forgive you!"

Karen's eyes widened in fright, not understanding. Stephanie brushed Karen's blond hair from her eyes, and said, "You have a wonderful husband! Willing to sacrifice everything for just little you! And you let yourself be deceived so badly you were about to destroy him with everything else, even though you do love him."

She broke down crying, and weakly turned away. "Why are you here? To torment me?"

"No. We're in a battle for all our lives, Karen. The Ethereal has *no* feelings for us at all. You were just a pawn they had absolutely no respect for. They crafted you from birth!" And Stephanie waved her Staff and images appeared over her bed of the demon GrrraGagag while he tainted Karen in the womb and laughed about it. Lady Stephanie cut the scene off in the middle of GrrraGagag's rejoicing.

"Don't you want to get some payback?"

Karen couldn't believe what she just saw, but it began to make sense to her in ways like never before, almost like she was beginning to feel like a person, or something. But now, even that feeling began to make sense. For the first time ever, she looked up into Stephanie's eyes. "I don't deserve any of your kindness, nor your forgiveness. I've been horrible to you. Worse than horrible. I still don't understand myself very well at all. But being inside that *demon,* it did something to me. I don't know. I began to value my life differently." And she looked away, wondering.

Then Karen looked back into Stephanie's eyes, and said, "This is going to sound very crazy, but even though I was inside that demon and suffering the eternal pain of horrible tormenting hell, I was happy! Because I began, for the first time, to realize what it felt like being a person! Isn't that crazy?"

Stephanie leaned over and kissed Karen's forehead, and there was healing in the kiss. Then she went to find Jargono, but she didn't have to go far. He had been just outside the door, listening. Dressed in his usual Appendaho brown tunic, tan shirt and pants, his humble appearance gave no hint to the raw power and ability he possessed with ease. In a way, they both matched because Stephanie had been wearing her brown peasant dresses for some time now.

In the wide castle hallway, Jargono couldn't take his eyes off of Lady Stephanie, but it wasn't her simple plain garment that caught his eye. He walked fully around her several times without saying a word. The look in his eye was admiration, and he said, "You're finally beginning to understand." There was a lot more meaning to his words than just the current situation. He popped them both into a sitting room of comfortable baroque chairs fit for royalty with plates of delicious looking food on gold tray tables before them. But Stephanie wasn't there to eat, nor to be honored.

She leaned forward and moved the table aside. "You were supposed to be Vaughn's backup plan in case this little demon friendship thing didn't work out."

Jargono studied her. He just heard her forgive his wife which he still couldn't wrap his mind around. She didn't have to do that. They had a very well-reasoned strategic agreement. But now the implications that came with her statement mostly led to very unpleasant directions. He looked her in the eye and opened himself honestly. "That is very true . . . on one level."

Staring into him deeply, her rich brown eyes matching his intensity as brothers and sisters are often able to do, she said, "I know. And you made a deal with the Highest Councilor that you wouldn't force him to give Vaughn back if he fixed up your wife properly."

Jargono nodded. "Vaughn said you would figure it out."

"What I don't understand is why. What are you two gaining by all this? There's *got to be* more."

Now he was surprised that she figured out it was both their plans. "You figured out we shared a common strategic interest."

She shot back, "You didn't agree to it because you were *friends?*"

Jargono sighed. "For such grave matters, friendship could not be the determining factor."

She stood up now, darkening, and he noticed her *faith-walking* posture had suddenly matured even beyond her years. She spoke with a controlled, level voice. "Before this is all over, *friendship* might be the *only* thing that's left that makes sense. Were you two worried about the enemy reinforcements?"

"There was that. It didn't make sense that the Alpha would allow my wife to have the sole governing power over that, although she believed it to be so."

Now Lady Stephanie saw this went much further than she had thought on. "Then what? Why keep me in the dark?"

Jargono folded his hands and leaned forward. "There's no reason to, now. Your husband and I had extremely deep conversations on all of our experiences, especially with the Alpha. Including how my wife and even how I was influenced by the demons before we were even born!"

That shocked Stephanie. She didn't know what to say and so just stared openly at Jargono.

He nodded that he understood her feelings. "Since that time, I've come to understand my tree in very different ways, and have come to understand you much better, too. But for the purposes of this discussion, we both realized that my wife and I were part of a much more long-ranged far-reaching plan. Even putting us together, Karen and I, was set up by the demons. They needed me to teach her my power for part of their plan.

Vaughn and I *even* began to believe that him sacrificing himself the way he did was also anticipated and part of their plan!"

"What?" she whispered, and she transformed the royal chair into a simple wooden chair and pulled it directly in front of Jargono. "Then why . . ."

"Because the Alpha really left us no choice. Remember, they're the ones with the Dead Forest. They're tree *experts*, and what that means is they understand our psychology, really everything about us, much better than we do, but when we're in direct contact with them, they try to make us think we're smarter than them!"

"But . . . you're saying they planned to taint both you and your wife, wait for you two to grow up, put you together, create the horrible bind Vaughn and I were in . . .wait, they would have had to know about us, too!"

"Not specifically about you two, but they expected the glow to have a response so they kept watch for likely suspects, and you two were their first pics!"

"So you're saying they all along *planned* for Vaughn to sacrifice himself?"

"That is what your husband felt *very* strongly. And they went to great levels to set it up, including the very odd way Grinchback was created."

"But then the question is *why?*"

Jargono ran both hands through his hair. "I didn't know. I *don't* know. But Vaughn feels he does."

Jargono got up and went to a small handcrafted mediaeval end table, pulled open a drawer, and removed a King James

Bible! Stephanie's eyes went wide. "Vaughn gave it to me. My first ever Bible of any kind." He opened it to the thirteenth chapter of revelations and handed it to her.

"*I've* not even read this far yet. I didn't know Vaughn had. He used to be so far behind."

She sat silently and read to herself and her eyes began to glow. When she was done, she closed the Bible and handed it back. "Why was Vaughn so interested in that chapter?"

"End game. He felt that was what the Alpha were playing for. He had many deep dealings in the Ethereal that he wasn't allowed to disclose, but one thing he *did* say was that we, on Earth, had our Christ, but the Ethereal was supposedly still owed theirs!"

"So Vaughn sacrificed himself to try to save Karen, to keep her from destroying *everything,* but he also *wanted* to be where he's at to try and learn their *end game?*"

"Correct."

"But . . . but . . ."

Jargono smiled warmly. "He said you would say that, at *least* twice. But I have to tell you. He was honest with me. For a long time, he felt that *I* fulfilled that chapter! Except that he also knows I *despise* the Alpha, and they used me for greater plans they had."

"In other words, you're dispensable!"

"We all are."

"But back to my question. Doesn't this imply that Vaughn has some way to escape with the knowledge? What *way?* How could he possibly do that?"

"He said you were the way, you and your child!" Jargono pointed to her and then her tummy.

"*NO!*" Stephanie darkened so much the castle shook and Jargono noted her power level was far greater than what he'd seen before and that most of it she was holding back.

He leveled angry eyes into hers and scolded her. "*Child faithwalker!* You missed our *meaning!*"

Her mouth dropped open as she thought back to the Book of Wisdom which said the same thing. "Then what?"

"That answer . . ."

She growled, "I know, *I know.* That answer is within me."

"Correct."

She never thought, nor imagined asking this, but she looked into Jargono's eyes. "Can you help me?"

"First things first. I saw much of the training you were doing. Vaughn asked me to keep an eye on you! Here's your next lesson. Wave you hand and create something"

Perplexed, she waved and created an arrow on the black couch up against the far wall.

"Now, wave it back and make it disappear."

And she did as instructed.

"Now, as fast as you can, do that over and over."

So she did and Jargono just sat there. After a while it began to feel pointless until he yelled, "*Stop,*" and her hand stopped but the arrow still appeared! "Now, quickly, focus on what you did in your mind to create the arrow."

She did and she saw herself in a whole different light. The fast process was now so clear! She knew she had already been doing a lot of things without hand gestures, but she didn't have the understanding she just received.

"Now, using what you just learned, what can you do that you never could do before?"

That was a question Stephanie felt could take a life time to answer. "I don't know."

They vanished and Jargono brought her out to one of his fields where there were gargoyles roaming. When the gargoyles saw them, they charged. Jargono vanished. Stephanie didn't feel like fighting right now. This was ridiculous, so she tried popping away, too, but something interfered. The gargoyles were closing in. She wasn't sure what or who was blocking her but she tried one more time before she knew she'd have to fight. But *this* time as she tried to pop away, her mind became keenly aware of her process, just like with Jargono's lesson. And when she saw it, she also saw *exactly* what and how the interference occurred and she simply shifted her focus to literally *faithwalk* around the obstacle and she popped away into the Ethereal. *This* was a *phenomenal* lesson.

The *faithwalker* couldn't believe it. How long would it have taken her to learn this, if ever? Jargono appeared beside her, smiling. "It has many applications in defense and offense. After a while it will become reflexive! Let's go back, now, and talk some more little sister!"

Back at the castle, Jargono made Stephanie sit at an immaculate dining table and eat. It was carved from an oval shape but it had many contours that kept the eye tracing its edges. The dark grains were mysterious in their flow. Jargono cleared his throat and said, "Stay well fed, stay well rested, and stay alert, *always.*" After they finished roast duck, assorted vegetables and fruit in some kind of awesome sauce, Jargono asked her, "Why does Vaughn feel part of the answer rests with your child?"

"Michael."

"You named him before he's born?"

"Named himself!"

Jargono leaned forward across the table with piercing eyes, again. "That's a lot of presence for an unborn child."

Stephanie smiled proudly. "Well, you would have to say that Vaughn has a lot of presence."

"How well can you *feel* your child?"

"Excellently, I guess. I mean, he's inside of me."

Jargono shook his head at her in dissatisfaction! "You take it all for granted, which means you're unaware of the nature of a lot that you feel. But other women don't realize what they're feeling *at all.* Until it's too late. They have abortions because they think that's easy. *After* their child is murdered, *then* they realize they're missing certain feelings and they have other new feelings they can't deal with. The child's life was *inside* of theirs. In *your* favorite language, you can say there is a person *inside* a person.

"The women who have abortions had taken for granted that the child's feelings that were intermixed with the mother's were just *her* feelings of being pregnant. In other words, *no* feelings from the actual child's *life,* just feelings of having a big belly, or hormonal changes, emotional swings etc. After the child is gone, they feel the great loss of *meaning.*"

Stephanie nodded. "When I had died, after you *killed* me," she raised an eyebrow at him but he just nodded, "I was up in the Corridor and the Seed to the Tree of Life said it was going to give its Life up to save mine."

Jargono's attention ramped up considerably. "Amazing."

"Well, I argued with it!"

"Not surprising!"

"Well, because I said it was far more important than I was, but it told me that if it didn't honor even just one single faithful good life, then all lives lost meaning. The Truth is one person at a time! I feel that way about Michael, no matter what upstairs or downstairs or whatever says about whatever. I'm following what the Tree of Life told me, *showed me by living example!*"

Jargono nodded vigorously. *This* was *exactly* the kind of understanding, the kind of connection they needed. "Now, focus on Michael and clear everything else from your heart and mind."

She closed her eyes and concentrated, giving Michael full range inside her.

"Now, look for the connection to his father, life to life! A lot of people think there's only a connection between Mother and child. That's a lie. In spirit there is both! The child's life is also in resonance with their father."

Stephanie never thought about it, but always felt this was so. Michael's sweetness flooded into her, his love for both of them. Stephanie shook her head. "I don't feel it. It's like what I felt after Vaughn died. Nothing. Gone."

Jargono's eyes drilled into Stephanie's almost making her want to look away. "That's a lie. No one is ever just *gone*. The child is shielding you!"

Tingles went over Stephanie's arms to think that little unborn Michael would do something like that. It brought tears to her eyes. Stephanie spoke softly to her child. "Michael, is what Uncle Jargono said true? Are you shielding me from feeling your Daddy through you?"

Stephanie felt it a little humorous to be talking to the child like this though she automatically talked to him all the time. The child shifted in her womb! Stephanie's eyebrows went up. "Michael, we're trying to help Daddy, I need to feel what you feel."

The next thing Stephanie knew, Jargono was picking her up off the floor, she could hardly breathe. Jargono sat her back on the dining chair, pulled another up in front of her, and took her by both arms and shook her! "Now, go back *again*, but this time look for your husband *beyond* the pain!

Still reeling, Stephanie barely got the words out. "I don't know if I can. You don't know. I was captured by a demon, wrapped up in his coil, but even *that* didn't compare to *this!*"

Jargono lifted her chin so their eyes met. "I am far better practiced than you. I have far more experience than you. I'm far more *ruthless*, but pound for *faithwalker* pound," he firmly squeezed both her arms again, "*you* are the *real* faithwalker! I couldn't have done *half* what you've already accomplished! Find a way to walk around the pain, through the pain, *laugh* at it. Whatever it takes. Now try *again!*"

He's so firm. I've never had anyone treat me like this, except, maybe, Arlupo's father, but this is even different. "Give me a moment, please."

He let her go and took his seat at the other end of the table, and she began to pray within, but then it became vocal. *Lord Jesus. All the strength* "I have is from the goodness you have made me out of. Is it right that evil should be able to beat me? Please, help me. You hung on a cross, were tortured, and mocked. You experienced actual *death*. You, oh Lord, walked in hell, amongst *all* the demons. Help me to walk now, *please.*"

Jargono watched her intently. To him it was the psychology of prayer that probably made a difference. True, there is psychology in everything conscious. But for sincere lovers of Goodness, and if you are a *faithwalker* who loves God with all their being, then the very presence of the Lord will come down to you with an answer.

A brilliant glow lit up around Lady Stephanie, but it wasn't of her power. Jargono saw it, felt it, and began to shake from it, though he wasn't afraid. Little Michael lit up with his own glowing reaction. And a voice, gentle, but firm. "You *are* My chosen *faithwalker,* and I have given you a doubly chosen child. The Lord blesses you to be able to walk where thou wilt and bear what thou must." And the presence departed, and Jargono was astonished because he heard the voice of the Lord!

After a bit, Stephanie looked back over to Jargono. "I'm ready. Please help me."

But Jargono was still wide-eyed. He *still* shook inside even though the Lord's presence was gone, and he looked at

Stephanie in utter honesty, and whispered, "After *that,* I'm not sure I'm any help at all!"

But Stephanie looked at him sincerely. "You're so wrong. You have no idea. All the blessing meant was that I *would* be blessed. The Lord didn't say how that would come. Come help me. Please, I need you!"

Jargono had so many new and different feelings. He'd never really felt needed like *this* before. He'd never been called uncle before. He'd never heard the voice of God before. He'd never felt this small before but that didn't matter so much right now. He came over to Stephanie, they set their chairs in front of each other again, and he took her arms again, and held her eyes with his. "Alright. Start again, but this time, when you get right up to the point where you would make contact, I want you to pull back, then go forward again, then back, until I tell you to stop!"

"Just like I did with the arrow?"

"Yes, except this time when you *do* connect, the demon might have defenses ensnaring you. That could be part of the pain you felt. But even as much suffering as I'm sure your husband is going through, he will have found a way for you, Stephanie. I've gotten to know him well enough to say he's one tough little bastard because his love is so very strong. I just feel it. I just know it. Find him, and let him bring you into his protection when you meet!"

Stephanie began wiping tears from her eyes because what he said broke her up inside. *That truly* is *Vaughn.* But then she remembered Vaughn's letter that she should pursue with all the passion she had for life. Jargono had just inspired that in her, so rather than fight it, she let it flow, and her tears poured down.

Back and forth she went. Little Michael not minding at all. She lost track of how many times and for how long until at the very beginning of another approach Jargono finally softly said, "Stop," but she didn't stop. Her *effort* stopped moving her forward, but she let herself go into full faith and forward she moved naturally like a sailboat caught up in a breeze.

Michael took her straight to Vaughn! The same fiery pain came as before but she accepted it and walked right on by, or through, it was hard to tell. And then Vaughn noticed her presence, wondered if he imagined it, and Lady Stephanie said, "What, do I have to smack you again?"

And he couldn't help but chuckle, remembering how she had smacked him into realizing she was real when she came in spirit a year ago to heal him and keep him from dying. Vaughn laughed even while in the pits of hell. His spirit reached out and drew her to his center and there was peace! "Bring me Peace, Queen Stephane. Bring me Peace." And then somehow, he hurled her away and she came back to herself!

Jargono felt when she returned even before she was fully physically cognizant. Not wanting to waste even an instant, he asked, "What happened?" Stephanie was in a daze and Jargono shook her, again. "Focus. Don't allow yourself to be overcome. Clear your mind and heart and focus and tell me what happened."

So Stephanie explained every detail, and Jargono asked her, "What does he *mean* faithwalker?"

"I don't know. How can I bring him peace? Oh God, I really don't know."

"When you *first* heard him say that, what was the very first thing that came into your mind?"

"How could I *possibly* bring him peace?"

"That's the first thing you *remember.* Because you cast away what you thought was unimportant. Close your eyes. Go back in your memory to when Vaughn drew you into his center. You said there was peace in his center but he was asking you to bring him peace. Go into his peace then come out. Walk through the pain again into his peace, then come out and do this over and over until I tell you to stop!"

And Stephanie did as Jargono instructed. Back and forth into and out of pain and peace, pain and peace, over and over again, but this time it wasn't that many repetitions and he whispered, "Stop." But this time she did stop, but when she heard Vaughn tell her to bring him peace, it wasn't with a small p, but a capital P, Bring him Peace, and his letter flashed in her mind, and *then* the thought questioning how she could bring him peace. This time Stephanie came out of the trance at will and told Jargono everything.

"What was it about the letter, Stephanie?"

"Well, I think the whole letter, really, because that was my feeling, but I think my feeling, now that I think about it, was that there was something *in* the letter." So Stephanie pulled the letter from her inner dress pocket and read it to herself again, and the last line jumped out at her. Let the Staff of Life pass over us in Peace.

"Do you understand?" Jargono asked, but Stephanie shook her head. "Vaughn used to call the staff into his hand, have you done that?"

"I actually think I have when I went out to fight the hoard of beasts. I remember the dragons breathed fire. The next thing I knew I was on one knee with Vaughn's staff in my hand. But it felt right so I didn't question it or give further thought. I've been carrying it with me ever since. I actually left it in the corner of your wife's room."

"Vaughn's life is on the line *right now! Call the Staff!*"

The way Jargono spoke it, it was a command of direct necessity, it's meaning sinking into her depths. Without even thinking her hand shot out and the Staff of Life appeared. Jargono felt the tremendous power in the instrument and it felt to him like the presence of God that came to Stephanie, earlier. He took her firmly by the arms, again, and squeezed. "Listen closely. Let the Staff of Life *pass over* us in Peace."

Stephanie's eyes finally lit with meaning. "Oh my God. Is that possible? *How* is that possible?" She thought a moment. "Wait. You want me to call the Staff, send it back, then . . ."

But he shook his head. "I don't think that's necessary any longer. You know how it feels to effortlessly walk, now! But because Vaughn is inside the demon, you'll have to ask little Michael to help you do this! He has the most direct connection to Vaughn, even more so than you! And the Staff brought you both back from death. Michael knows this. It will be easy for him!"

Then Jargono took the letter from Stephanie and read one of its lines. "Tell little Michael I will always live through his prayers. That's how you do it, Stephanie. You're above all else, a prayerful person. You're strongest there. You'll need that extra strength if you're to get by the demon's defenses with *this.*" And Jargono grabbed the Staff and shook it at her. Its power shook him to his core, though.

Stephanie nodded, bowed her head again and waited for the prayers to come but they didn't. Feeling hurt in her heart that she was doing something wrong, little Michael began to kick, and when Stephanie put her hand on her tummy, he began to glow. "I'm such a *stupid idiot.*" She bowed her head again, but this time, she spoke to her unborn child. "Let's pray together. We love Daddy so much." And Stephanie sobbed but didn't restrain herself.

"Lord Jesus, we come now before you to send this Staff into the pits of hell for Justice and Life sake to the man you ordained to have it . . ." And even though they were just getting started with the prayer, the Staff disappeared!

Jargono said, "Don't stop. Go with it. Guide it!"

"Because You, Lord, deemed him worthy to judge the nations . . ." And then the prayers completely took Lady Stephanie over as she went down onto her knees. It wasn't just the words, it was their far-reaching meaning in prophecy and Legend. Some part of Lady Stephanie knew she was praying deeply, but what the other part of her focused upon was what lay ahead.

There was a twisted tangle of sinew type webs barring her entrance this time, but before that there was the fire of pain.

In one hand Lady Stephanie held the Staff of Life, in her other arm she cradled a little child, and when she looked down into his eyes that blazed like the sun with love, the child called her, Mommy, and she called him, Michael, and then they turned and she walked into the fire.

Lady Stephanie held up the Staff in front of the sinew, little Michael held out one hand, then, together, she swung the Staff wide while Michael swung wide his little hand, and the sinew tore open and they walked through. Strange fanged beasts bounded forward, not like anything she'd ever beheld. Her arm clenched little Michael tighter and she pointed the head of the staff at the beasts and they fled.

On they walked and everything went gray then deep black. They couldn't see their hand in front of their face, but without effort the *faithwalker* began to glow and so did the child. A long endless hallway appeared that looked like it had no end. At *that* point the *faithwalker* said, "I've had *enough* of this! How about you, Michael?"

And he nodded. "Do it, Mommy!"

She raised the Staff up, then brought the foot straight down and it thundered.

The Highest Councilor began to look a bit sick and belched through his Great Eye. Bulges began moving and showing under his torso. "Master, are you alright?"

"I think we ate too much the other day, Grinchback. The Earth demons must not be as digestible as I thought."

When she brought the Staff down, again, the tunnel crumbled and she was in the midst of thousands of consumed souls and demons and creatures. In a cross, stern voice, the *faithwalker* said, "Look to, you *damned*, point the way to my *husband* and his *father* or I'll make you wish you were still here when I get done with you." And she blazed so brightly, they all howled and cowered, but pointed the way.

And there, chained by the wrists and ankles to a black wall was Vaughn. He smiled, then wiggled his chains. Lady Stephanie rested the Staff in little Michael's tiny hand then reached out and spread her fingers and golden beams hit all four chains but they refused to disintegrate. But she could see the process and she adjusted the energies with an inner sense of meaning she'd not been this aware of before, and silver mixed with deep red shot forth this time and entered the chains and they crumbled and Vaughn walked free.

Lady Stephanie and Michael smiled at him and she walked up and handed him the Staff, but when she saw his chin and felt all his other wounds, her eyes blazed and he instantly healed and then she came out of the trance. "WOW!" She looked up from the floor into Jargono's eyes who was hovering over her. "Did all that *really* happen?"

He smiled, "You tell me."

So she sat down and recounted it all.

Vaughn took his Staff and smiled. He stood up taller. Everyone else there, who'd previously delighted in chiding him and tormenting him, fled from his presence. He walked over to a pulsating bulge. "Hmm, this looks demonly important. Lord God of my Fathers, Abraham, Isaac, and Jacob . . ." When everyone inside heard *that,* they cringed and tried hiding underneath each other. "Deliver me from the belly of torment and death because I am *not* worthy of it." And Vaughn grabbed the head of the Staff and swung the foot down hard on the pulsating structure.

The Highest Councilor's Great Eye spasmed once, then he felt better, then all of the sudden it spasmed *again* and with violent force spewed Vaughn across the dark Ethereal room! He immediately came to a stand, the Staff of Indignation in hand, smiled, walked over to the orb, reached his arm in deep, and did . . . something!

"Have a very nice Ethereal Afternoon. Grinchback, my friend. He hasn't eaten you yet?" And Vaughn vanished!

The Highest Councilor was summoned to the very Darkest Room where the Father and a smirking HrorrarrAggrang were awaiting his presence. In a calm voice, which was never good, the Father pointed to his new orb. "What do you see, Scraback?"

He shrugged. "It needs to be turned on."

Then the Father roared. "It *is* on. But right up here in the corner in *fine print* from a special security program that came with the orb, it has an orb address of the last communication coming to it. Guess from where?" The Highest Councilor looked over to his underling about to blame him.

But Grinchback rushed forward, threw his tail across his Master, while saying, "Please Father, have *mercy* on my Master, he had too many Earth Demons to eat, because, well, they were going to destroy Vaughn before Master got a chance to eat him and Karen for your big plan, and, well, Master said the Earth demons didn't set well, and he vomited up *Vaughn,* and, and, *he* reached into Master's orb, and, and crashed your *secret* orb."

Everyone seemed frozen. The Father looked over to HrorrarrAggrang, and said, "Would you please have *mercy* on the Highest Councilor?"

"With pleasure, Father."

Grinchback fled to a little-known place for homeless Alphas.

CHAPTER 19

The Unforeseen

13 And he doeth great wonders, so that he maketh fire come down from heaven on the earth in the sight of men,

14 And deceiveth them that dwell on the earth by the means of those miracles which he had power to do in the sight of the beast; saying to them that dwell on the earth, that they should make an image to the beast, which had the wound by the sword, and did live

15 And he had power to give life unto the image of the beast, that the image of the beast should both speak, and cause that as many as would not worship the image of the beast should be killed.

All the students had arrived early. They all wanted to be there before Teacher Marta arrived, and when she materialized under the Tree of Life, they all ran up hugging her! "What's this for?" she beamed with rainbow colors.

Aaron, being one of the eldest, spoke up. "Because you challenged us like no other up here. We stayed together as a class long into the heavenly hours of dusk, and we kept *trying*.

Even little Carrie wouldn't leave us. When none of us could do what you asked by ourselves, we paired up! One prayed for Lady Stephanie and King Vaughn while the other prayed for the praying person!"

Elaina said, "Carrie may have been too young to pray directly against evil, but she's so powerful praying for me! Together, we reached King Vaughn! At first, it was *terrible* for me. It was like we all discussed. I was overwhelmed."

Carrie pushed in front of Elaina and Elaina put her hands on her little shoulders. Carrie said, "I could feel how hard it was for Elaina, so when she was on her knees," Carrie pulled her down, "I did like this." And she threw herself onto her back and hugged her tight. Then she lifted her little head to look up at Marta, and said, "And I hugged Elaina as *hard* as I could and prayed love for her. *All* my love!"

Elaina said, "And I felt it! It was a strength that filled me and all of the sudden the pain I was feeling, well, it like parted like the Red Sea! And I walked in the midst of that pain. And then all kind of confusing things began to happen, and feelings, but Carrie's love was *still* there, she wouldn't let go."

Carrie said, "The evil tried to push *me* away, I felt it hurting my heart, but I said, NO! And I kept loving."

Elaina said, "It seemed like all of the sudden all those confusing things and feelings that kept rushing me, well, they slowed *way* down. But really, I think I just got faster, and even though I didn't understand what they all were or trying to do, I was able to just ignore them, and walk right past until we found Vaughn, and then we prayed for him to have Peace!"

And then other pairs came up and told their experiences, how each came in contact with various evils that were attacking or hindering Lady Stephanie and King Vaughn, and each pair defeated that evil!

Marta went down on her knees weeping and the children all wondered why, until they heard their teacher pray. "Lord God Almighty, who holds His mysteries away from the mighty, even up *here*, and delivers to the least of His servants the treasure of the work of Your mercies. We all thank you for blessing us to be a meaningful part of Lady Stephanie and King Vaughn's lives for your Goodness sake. Grant to us that Your Understanding and strength grow in us that we can continue to be a meaningful help to them against all the evils yet to come!"

And all the children said, "Amen."

And Eve, standing behind all the children, said, "Amen. Well done, everyone, well done! Thank you for teaching this old woman!"

Vaughn materialized in the formal dining room where his wife and Jargono were sitting at a dark brown shiny oblong table with contoured edges. Stephanie had her head bowed and Jargono leaned his elbows on the table with his head in his hands. As soon as Vaughn entered, Stephanie's head popped up and she was about to rush to him, but Vaughn held up his hand for her to wait.

He went straight to Jargono, who asked, "Did you get what we need?"

"They think your orb is dead, but I only turned its screen so dark even they can't see anything. But we'll be able to see just fine."

Jargono waived his hand and the wall behind Stephanie became a giant screen. With Jargono's mental commands the screen went live of the Father's Darkest Room! Stephanie heard them talking and twisted around.

HrorrarrAggrang had the Highest Councilor wrapped up in his coil with a barbed tail stuck in ScrabaGag's neck. "You can't consume me. You *need* me."

The Father lowered his Great Eye over him as well. "Why would I need *you* any longer? *You* destroyed my Earth demons then put that horrid *Quake Alert* on *my* orb."

"What Grinchback said is true." The Highest Councilor tried twisting around to find him but he was gone. "They weren't controllable and would have destroyed our Sacred Plans. You *knew* all this Father. *I'm* the one who was able to collect the Six Earth Essences we needed."

Jargono and Stephanie stared at Vaughn. "What's he talking about?"

Vaughn turned dark. "You're not going to like it at all."

The Father's eye smirked, "*You* think this was all *your* doing?" And the Father and HrorrarrAggrang burst out laughing. "You know how you made Grinchback to be the perfect *fool?* Well, *that's* what you've been to usssss."

"But only I can interface with their lab system. Without me, our Anointed One won't mature properly."

HrorrarrAggrang consoled the Highest Councilor. "Don't worry. After I've consumed you, I'll be able to handle things just fine."

"No you won't, because once you consume me, your energies will be different than mine *even if* you try to copy them. And I also know how to resist you even *if* you consume me."

"Where is the *lab*?" The Father asked.

"Not telling you and you won't be able to pry that out of me, either. I'll show you the inside, but that will give absolutely no clue as to its location."

HrorrarrAggrang waved his mighty arm and his orb appeared.

Jargono quickly motioned his fingers in various ways at the screen, pulled up an orb list at the right side, then said, "We don't have *his* orb on our system, either!"

Vaughn waved his hand and his blue control orb appeared. He stuck his arm deep inside. "Visual contact established. Scanning HrorrarrAggrang's orb. It's ancient. Stealth calling for it to connect to the Father's orb . . . got it."

A new orb name appeared on Jargono's orb list. "I'll download it during their nightly maintenance."

"You'll have to let me go," the Highest Councilor said with a Great Eye smile, then he floated over to HrorrarrAggrang's orb and stuck in his tail in a way they couldn't see, and then the lab appeared within the slightly dusty blue orb

There was a large glass cylinder in the center of a white rectangular room. Computer systems and electric relays lined the walls. People inside were covered from head to toe in white, air tight suits indicating a strictly sterile environment. The Highest Councilor beamed with pride as he zoomed out a bit more to capture all the lab works. His tail pointed to the center of the room at the glass cylinder. "*That's* lovely Queen Karen's womb suspended in a feeding solution. Inside is her egg." Then he pointed to tubes running into a common junction. "This tube carries the genetic material from Jargono that *I* took from his lovely *Queen* during the act of her *conversion*. This tube's genetic material comes from our dear *Queen Stephanie* that the Black Essence under *my* guidance took from her when the Earth demons infected her. This tube comes from her cursed child when he, too, was infected. And, finally, this tube is from the good King Vaughn while I squeeeezed it out of him during consumption.

"Here is where *my* Ethereal Power enters into that same junction." He pointed to a thick black tube that also joined the junction which was like a glass ball pulsing with gray light and black swirls. "Our power is mixing the components together and once finished will be implanted in the womb and our Sacred One will be conceived." Then he followed the black tube that disappeared into a large black metallic box.

"That black box contains *my* Ethereal circuitry which guides the process. I have a secret interface to it and pay frequent, timely visits to make the proper adjustments. As I said, you *need* me, but you *don't* need *him* any longer!" And he pointed at HrorrarrAggrang.

The Father looked over to his companion. HrorrarrAggrang laughed, and said, "Who designed that *particular* Black

Essence you've been using? You only *thought* you had control of it, but it listens to *me*, and *my* energy signal. I *commanded* it to obey you for the time being. *Fool.* You think you're the only one to produce a faithful underling?"

The Highest Councilor's Great Eye grew wider as he looked back at the Father who had placed a proud tail over HrorrarrAggrang's shoulders. It was completely clear the Father favored him. The Father's Great Eye smiled. "Can't you see the resemblance?"

HrorrarrAggrang wrapped the Highest Councilor up again. "But now that you've *pathetically* thrown up Vaughn, he's going to tell everyone what he's witnessed through *you!*"

The Father explained further. "But before they can object to *anything,* I'll have already restored the *balance* by consuming *you!* As I said, you thought *you* were in charge of all this? *Fool.* I'm not called the *Endless Father* for nothing."

And they all watched in amazement as HrorrarrAggrang ate the Highest Councilor! "HrorrarrAggrang, find that fool underling of his and tell him we want him to take a message upstairs that the infraction to the balance on *our* side has been *dealt with.*"

HrorrarrAggrang belched. "Finally, we got rid of him. I'll take his underling under *my* wing. This will be a lot of fun."

Karen had been watching from the doorway and when she sneezed, they all turned around to greet her. "Jargono, he stole my womb? My egg?"

Jargono quietly seethed inside. Stephanie looked at Vaughn with tears, "He stole from me and Michael?"

Vaughn walked over to Jargono. "There's so much more besides what we witnessed." And Vaughn tilted his head down and Jargono placed his hand on it.

After a bit, Jargono shook his head. "So much more. But at least I think I know a way to get rid of their game preserve based on what you just shared with me. The problem is that now that HrorrarrAggrang has eaten Scraback, he'll know we know all the intricacies. But it's not that hard to figure out." Jargono paused, then took everyone into a level but deadly serious stare. "I'm afraid they're going to throw everything they have against us."

Karen mustered a small laugh. "They have to catch us first."

But Stephanie sighed. "I think they wouldn't mind just chasing us all over the country, or even the whole world and destroying everything in every place where we've been."

Jargono radiated blue and green and red powers, the first time anyone had ever seen him waste a drop of energy. "Like it or not, we have come to be Kings and Queens. Such matters must be dealt with by *us* first and foremost!"

Vaughn feigned surprise. "I thought you made fun of the Dark Ages! You know, Kings and Queens and knights in shining armor."

Jargono just shook his head, "We don't have much time. I'm going to need at least three days to prepare what's needed to destroy that Ethereal Fold. They're probably going to begin releasing more beasts within *two* days."

Vaughn whistled a low note. "They're coming here, *right here,* to destroy us all."

And Stephanie looked into the beyond, shaking her head. "Hundreds of dragons, and thousands of gargoyles. We'll be overrun."

Karen came over to her husband. "Let me do something worthwhile. I know I don't have a right to ask, but I'll ask anyway. Give me power so I can take revenge. They've ruined my whole life so much I don't even know what *life* it was!"

Jargono looked over to Lady Stephanie for the answer!

Stephanie walked over to Karen and took her hands and looked into her eyes. "You're too weak. You'll need at least a month before you could handle even normal life, let alone any power beyond."

But Karen squeezed Stephanie's hands, looked into her rich brown eyes which, for the first time she realized didn't seem like stupid doggy eyes. It made her pause, and she looked away, then looked into them again.

"What do you see, now?" Stephanie asked.

Karen tried hard to control herself. She still very much had that side of her, but in her weakened condition she just couldn't, and she burst out in a sob which she immediately clamped her hands over and hung her head. "What have I been?" She looked over to Jargono. "Somehow, I don't know how because of the shape I was in, but I've always loved you! But how could you have *possibly* loved me?"

Jargono smiled tenderly, "In spite of all the demons did to you, I don't know, I'm not really good with those kinds of words in the love department. I just loved you at first sight.

You had something special to me that no other woman had, not even Stephanie over there!"

Stephanie took her hands again. "What he's trying to say is that he looked past everything to the real you, and that's where his focus has been. That's *what* he loves. The *real* you."

Karen smiled demurely, "More like he was *blind* to everything else."

And Vaughn chimed in, "Well, that just means he's an *ordinary* man."

Fire came into Stephanie's eyes. It was hard to believe she now felt the way she did for this woman who had wrought so much evil against her. But now, in *this* season they now faced, looking back in the past didn't seem right at all, no matter how much vengeance she should have been feeling. "Karen," she called her name with meaning and Karen couldn't help looking into Lady Stephanie's eyes where they lingered for some time.

Lady Stephanie then bowed her head. "Lord who *only* is Judge. Look not on our terrible failures, which are many, but unto your infinite Goodness which desires only good for us. Make this woman *whole*, for the first time in her natural life!"

A swirling light mixture of golds, blues, and reds appeared over Karen's head then slowly engulfed her. Stephanie let go of her hands and stepped back, while Karen went to her knees and bowed to the floor. Something she had never, ever done, nor desired to do. Then she straightened up and spread out her arms as if trying to embrace the Light that was still swirling all around and through her.

When that Light finally ebbed away, she stood up, put her hands to her tummy, looked at Jargono, and her voice came out strong. "I'm whole! For the first time in my life, I don't know, I feel alive."

Jargono looked over to Stephanie. "Can she handle it?"

Stephanie nodded, and Jargono stood and put both his hands to each side of her head then leaned his forehead against hers. "Now we'll truly be one together, and *nothing* will separate us." Jargono glowed surprisingly golden, but within that glow were many tightly controlled colors of energy that swirled back and forth from him, through him, and through his Queen. They stood like that for a good while and Stephanie finally came over to Vaughn and wrapped her arms around him and wept on his shoulder. When she felt his strong arms wrap around her, she balled even harder as his comfort inundated her, which released all she had been holding in. She felt so very safe in his arms.

"You saved my life," Vaughn said. "Into the depths of Hell itself, you came for *me,* and saved my very soul. You *are* the true *faithwalker.*"

And Jargono and Karen both said, "Amen"

Jargono then told everyone to sit down and they sat back at the table. In the screen, he brought up an image of the castle as looking down from above. "I have little satellites all over. I can see most of the whole country, both yours and ours! I *have to* destroy the Ethereal Fold where they're creating their beasts. That means the rest of you are going to have to defend this castle by yourselves. If we last to the third day, then Vaughn and I are going to the game preserve to destroy it. I can't do that by myself. Which *means,* that you two are going to have to defend this place by yourselves! That's just the way it is."

Vaughn looked at the ladies. "We may be able to keep them out for a while. There's three of us and four walls. And there's Jargono's military. But chances are, if we make it past the third day when I have to leave, you *will* be overrun."

Jargono nodded. "Then you withdraw into the castle and you'll be fighting inside! If you can just hold on until we get back, we might be able to drive them out and bring a stalemate. But without their game preserve, they won't be able to reinforce anymore. Here's the floorplan with secret passages marked in red. Notice that the passages are designed to give you escape around a corner but then come up behind the enemy. So if you keep your wits together, you can lead the enemy to one part, come up behind them, cut them off, destroy them then duck back into the passages."

Both Stephanie and Karen's eyes were wide as the gaped at the screen studying the floor plans, committing to memory how they would fight, and imagining what it would be like being swarmed by evil beasts, while their world would keep shrinking inside the castle until . . . there was no more world.

❧

"So, this is it," King Mafferan spoke to Cloud Walker, who watched everything in his golden orb.

Cloud Walker frowned deeply. "They've managed to walk the fine line perfectly. They hold us at bay with their threat of making the Earth an open Alpha-Heavenly battleground, but they create beasts that are part of the Earth, part Ethereal and use them to invade. They used just enough Earth resource to argue there's no violation, and seeing that Karen helped bring the Ethereal Fold into existence along with those creatures, their legal standing is clear."

Mafferan tugged on his graying beard which, for some reason seemed grayer, though that's not supposed to happen in heaven. "It won't be long before *their* Christ is *born*. Then I'm not sure how long it will take for it to grow up. Judgement Day is coming fast. The world needs to be deeply ministered to but there's no time as long as these battles rage. And to think they made their Christ out of parts from all of *them*. That's a lot of power packed into one vessel."

Cloud Walker remembered his own mortal days and how he labored for souls when the Earth was yet quite young. "I think that's their plan. Just keep everyone bogged down with war and run out the time they have left until the Antichrist comes on the scene. Then, when all *that* power shows up, the whole unprepared world falls easily."

"Oh, *there* you are," Yinauqua said to her husband. She no longer wore her beautiful Appendaho garment, but a brown peasant dress just like Lady Stephanie. "Can you believe our daughter has swayed Jargono and Karen so much?"

Cloud Walker shrugged. "I don't think they had a choice. None of them do. The only chance they have is to fight as one."

Both Cloud Walker and Yinauqua stared at Mafferan. Yinauqua finally nudged him and he looked up from Cloud

Walker's orb. His wife said, "You're uncharacteristically silent. *Why.*"

Mafferan let out a very slow, controlled heavenly sigh. "Because they've been very crafty in how they put all this together. I will say this, though, the castles are an *excellent* idea. Without them, everything would have been quickly lost. But remember back in Noah's day? The Lord said the whole Earth was filled with violence and he wiped it clean. But I don't think the Alpha want to repeat that kind of catastrophe. Look what's happening in the towns that have fallen. They didn't eat nor slaughter them all, just took out the military. All the rest became their slaves. That's not good."

"You're saying their goal is to enslave and preserve enough humanity to keep the Lord from destroying everything?" Cloud asked.

"Yes. And with everyone held hostage, if our heroes do survive, they'll in effect be hostages, too."

Yinauqua grabbed hold of his arm and her eyes teared up. "But that's *exactly* what we went through." Pains wracked her heart remembering her humiliation and the dread darkness that never seemed to end.

Without thinking, Cloud Walker responded. "Except King Locula was *not* the Antichrist."

Mafferan held his wife closely to his breast as his eyes scorned Cloud Walker for unnecessarily bringing up the obvious. Yinauqua was already overwrought.

ↁ

Stephanie excused herself and popped away and found Carla, Mandy, and Lynnara in their new Castle apartment back in the United for Christ. Antique furniture, dishes, and artwork populated the rooms. "Vaughn is alive and with us."

Little Lynnara looked up at her Mommy. "I told them but they didn't *believe* me."

After the girls hugged each other, Stephanie asked Carla, "Where's Larson?"

"Manning one of the dragon killers. Last I checked, he'd killed two."

"I want to take you all back to the Tree of Life. You'll be safe there. But first I want you to talk to the holy people across this country and let me know how many are pregnant and where they're located. Tell them to pack their bags and be ready."

"Mommy, when can I see Daddy?"

Stephanie picked her up and hugged her again. "We're all very busy fighting the bad guys. I can't stay long."

After they said goodbye, Lady Stephanie popped up to Larsson. "How goes it?"

He shrugged, his blond hair waving in the wind. "It's actually kind of boring. They *had* left ten dragons here. I've got three, each one of our other city castles have gotten one each. The other five left us and decided to burn down the city, the military base, *everything,* except the castle which they frankly don't have the power or numbers to breach. But it's breaking everyone's hearts to see their homes, their city destroyed. And from what I've heard, it's the same everywhere else, except they've taken a few of the smaller castles and enslaved all who were left."

"Tell me the towns. And by the way, I'm running a special on performing weddings. My fee is free for the next day or so!"

Larson bowed his head to Lady Stephanie then took a piece of paper from his pocket and wrote them down then she disappeared. *Can't ignore the small towns. It shouldn't take me long to recapture them. Besides I need more battle experience.*

She materialized in the Corridor over one of the fallen castles. The general gargoyle relaxed in comfort in the main court. Down in the dungeons were many military prisoners. At the pantry-kitchen area food was being cooked, and then Stephanie gasped when one of the gargoyles opened an oven. There were human arms roasting. The gargoyle began basting!

When Lady Stephanie entered the physical kitchen, the gargoyle whirled around. The next moment Stephanie threw a golden cage around it. The gargoyle tried to rip the cage apart but every time he grabbed the structure it burned deep into its hands. As the cage shrunk, it diced the gargoyle into pieces which fell in front of the oven. Lady Stephanie incinerated the pile of gore along with the human meal.

She went down to the dungeons and freed the prisoners then gave them all bows with full quivers. "Take your castle back room by room. I'll take care of what's outside." They started to chant for her but she cut it off. "Let's win first," she said with a loving smile then vanished.

This time Lady Stephanie went to the center of the small town where the gargoyles were pillaging homes. When the two dragons saw her, they breathed their fire down to engulf her. Lady Stephanie created a shield midway between her and the dragons and the fire couldn't get through. Dark storm clouds came. But the dragons were wise to what was going to happen so they descended, their massive claws reaching for her.

The *faithwalker* hurled a giant chain with iron weights at each end. One of the diving dragons couldn't avoid the contraption and got caught by its neck. The weights quickly whipped around and took off the dragon's head!

The other dragon was almost upon her when she tried popping away but couldn't, but she remembered Jargono's lesson, saw *exactly* where she was being blocked and dematerialized just when she would have been grabbed. She reappeared sitting atop the dragon behind the general gargoyle, who whirled around, but Lady Stephanie cross reached and pulled two blessed long-daggers from her sides. When she uncrossed her arms, the gargoyles head came off.

The dragon turned his head around to see what was going on, and Stephanie said, "You are a magnificent beast. Wouldn't you rather be *friends?*" She began to pat his neck, and when its head got close to her, she reached up and scratched it behind the ears.

Then the dragon spoke! "You are the *faithwalker* we are supposed to kill, along with your cursed child."

I'm really talking to a real live dragon! "Minor

misunderstanding, I'm sure. You really like those dumb crea-tures riding on you?"

"No, it's insulting. But our masters order it and we know nothing else."

"Well, for now, let's get acquainted. Hi, I'm . . ."

"Your Queen Stephanie, whom we're to kill along with your cursed child."

Let me try something. "What's for breakfast?"

"You're Queen . . ."

Stephanie cut the dragon off, "Yea, yea, I got it." She materialized further up the beast's neck and placed her hands on each side of its massive head. *Let's see what's going in there.* But there wasn't much else in its mind except what it kept repeating. *How about your heart.* The first emotion was a dominant battle rage. *But what are you,* really?

Nothing! The beast was like an empty shell except for its directive. The *faithwalker* began to concentrate on what a noble dragon would be like. *First, I have to give it a sense of worth.* She bowed her head placing self-reflection into the giant beast's mind and heart. The dragon stopped flying in midair, and calked its head up in thought.

Next, let's put in a little love for dragon pride. The beast reared its head back, and spayed fire in the air as if celebrating something. And now, *You don't take* any *orders from* anyone *unless* you *want to! And* now, *become a thinking creature for yourself!*

The dragon landed on a grassy hill beside the town and turned its head around, again, "What have you done to me?"

Lady Stephanie smiled, dismounted, and stood face to face. "I've helped you reclaim *your life for yourself.* I've given you *freedom.* Now you have a *choice.* You can *try* to kill me, and keep hurting my people, *or,* maybe you might feel like doing something else."

The dragon lowered its head to look more closely at this tiny girl and she patted and rubbed its snout. He turned his head and she scratched it behind an ear and it rumbled. Just then dozens of gargoyles came rushing up the hill and a general kept shouting for the dragon to kill her. But Lady Stephanie said, "Other ear, please!" And the dragon turned his head and got scratched there, as well.

The first gargoyles reached the top of the hill and lunged at Stephanie. Blessed sabers appeared in her hands. "Excuse me, I'll be back in a moment." Lady Stephani leapt over the brigade and her blades took two heads off. Then she let them rush her again and gargoyle arms and feet began flying everywhere. When the general saw *that,* he jumped onto the dragon's back and ordered it to kill the girl.

But the dragon just sat there. "You *dumb beast,"* the gargoyle cursed. *"Do what you're told!"*

The dragon reached up with its foreleg and plucked the gargoyle off its back, held it over its gaping jaws and dropped it into its mouth. Stephanie came up, and asked, "How'd he taste."

"Needs a little salt." Then more gargoyles came rushing up and the dragon incinerated them.

Standing again before the dragon, Stephanie said, "Thank you."

"What is, *thank you?*"

She pulled its head closer and gave it a kiss on its snout. "It means you helped me and I love you for it. And love means I have a feeling for you that you're very special and when I see you it makes me *very* happy. It means, if it's in my power to help and protect you and your friends, I will. Friends means that we care for each other, help each other, that your life is as important to me as mine! I don't value mine less, but I value yours more than if we weren't friends."

Another dragon, even larger, came soaring overhead, not understanding. When he began to dive to attack them both, Lady Stephanie shot a brilliant blue ball of energy with a golden center at the beast, but just before it hit, the blue energy turned black, penetrated the beast's chest and blew a gaping hole in it and it fell down dead.

She turned to her dragon. "What's your name?" When she saw he didn't understand, she explained. "A name signifies who you are, and it should have *meaning,*" And when Lady Stephanie spoke that last word, it sunk into the dragon's heart with the *meaning* of goodness!" The dragon lifted its head and roared, then flapped its massive wings and took to the air.

Lady Stephanie popped back to the castle onto the top deck and shouted at the dragon killer operator. "Don't shoot. This one is a friend!" And Lady Stephanie popped away and mounted the dragon. "May I ride on you?"

Again, the dragon was surprised, but catching on quickly, said, "You may. What would you like to call me, my name?"

"How about Avenger? Do you like that? The name has a lot of *meaning!*" Again, Lady Stephanie let the power of the word for goodness sink deep into its dragon heart.

"I like that name." The dragon veered back to the castle, but seeing Lady Stephanie atop it, they held their fire.

The dragon circled the castle once, saw all the gargoyles climbing the walls, and then breathed fire all the way around and incinerated them all. The people atop the castle couldn't believe it and began to cheer. Lady Stephanie called back, "His *name* is Avenger." And they began to shout, "Lady Stephanie, Lady Stephanie and Avenger, Lady Stephanie and Avenger!"

"I have to go, now," she told Avenger. "You're free. Be careful, because most of my people don't know you're our friend and they'll try to kill you."

"But *these* people know me. I am *Avenger*. May I stay here Queen Stephanie?"

"You'll have to ask them. C'mon, I'll go with you, then I really have to go. Light down over there on top of that little tower."

So Avenger touched down and everyone gawked. Stephanie said, "He likes to be scratched behind the ears. And he has something to ask of you." The dragon looked back at her, but Stephanie said, "Go ahead. It's alright."

The dragon looked at all these tiny people, and asked, "May I stay here? May I help you?

Astounded, they all cheered, "Avenger, Avenger . . ." Then the word spread that Lady Stephanie had befriended a dragon that now protected them!

CHAPTER 20

True Beauty
that Conquers the Beast

16 And he causeth all, both small and great, rich and poor, free and bond, to receive a mark in their right hand, or in their foreheads.

17 And that no man might buy or sell, save he that had the mark, or the name of the beast, or the number of his name.

18 Here is wisdom. Let him that hath understanding count the number of the beast: for it is the number of a man: and his number is Six hundred threescore and six.

Marta stood before the class under the Tree of Life, and asked, "What are your feelings about what we just finished?"

Carolyn's hand went up first. "Why?" When Marta stared at her and her eyebrows then raised, Carolyn said, "Why is it happening?" And all the students, even the oldest began nodding their heads and their hands went down.

Marta sighed and held her hands behind her back and began to pace back and forth. "When I was three-years-old, which is as far back as I can remember even being up here, my earthly mother *rented* me out to, how shall I put it, to people who made movies of children doing adult things with other adults."

Aaron and Elaina's mouths dropped, a few seconds later, Sarah who was only eight, did the same thing. Carolyn didn't understand at all and asked Sarah, "What does she mean?"

None of the children knew how to answer her, so Marta said, "Our private areas are sacred doors of life but evil people use or force others to disgrace the meaning of our private parts. But like you, Carolyn, I didn't understand any of that. For years that's what my Mom did to me. I never knew my earthly father."

Sarah started to cry, and other children came to hug her. Aaron and Ralph turned very dark. And Elaina said, "I'm so sorry."

Marta continued. "When I was eight-years-old I was sitting in a hotel room while the adults there were drinking alcohol and doing mind altering drugs. I was glad they weren't paying attention to me this time. I looked into a drawer in an end table and found my first and only Bible. In the beginning God created . . . I was captivated. That very night, as the adults had passed out, I read all the way through Genesis to when Isaac took Rebecca to be his wife. I went into the bathroom and threw up, because for the first time in my life I understood what goodness was, is, what decency is, and that God *hated* evil.

"I took that Bible with me, and one week later I had read through to the Book of Leviticus. Then I paged through to the

Gospel of Saint John and I read all of that. Then my Mom came to rent me out again and I said, 'God is *very* angry with you. I can't do this this anymore.'

Sarah asked, "What did your mother do?"

"She beat me and dragged me to the hotel. There, the two women were paying for me to have sex with them."

Carolyn said, "Oh God. I understand now. I took a knife and stabbed the bad man. That's how I ended up *here!*" She said with a smile.

There was more silence from the students.

Marta said, "I told the women God was very angry with them, that he had burnt up Sodom and Gomorrah because of what they were doing. They were *very* angry and began to beat me and force me to do terrible things. When they were done, I told them that the Lord Jesus died for us to make us better than that and they mocked me and forced me again.

"When I was ten years old, I asked my Mom why she did these things to me? And she said this is what her Mom had her do, and hers before her."

Aaron said, "How did you . . . did you . . .

Marta said, "When I was thirteen years old, I became pregnant and my Mother was very angry because she said I would get her in trouble. She was going to force me to have an abortion. So I ran away and I went to a homeless shelter. When the people discovered I was pregnant, they sent me to a doctor and they went to court and they ruled I had to have an abortion to *protect me.*"

Aaron asked, "Is this one of the reasons . . ."

"Yes. This is one of the reasons I love Lady Stephanie so much. I understand *exactly* how she feels. So I ran away again, and I prayed to the God I had read in the Bible. I didn't pray for myself because I felt I was too terrible because of all that I had done, but I asked God to save my child.

"When it came to be time, when I was in labor, *then* I went to the hospital and had my child. But somehow, maybe when I was under amnestic, I don't know, they found out about my Mom and while I was nursing, she came into my room and after scolding me, began to talk about my new daughter and how I would have to train her like my Mom trained me.

"Something came over me. I got up, I put little Sherrie in her crib, told her I loved her and that I would protect her. My Mom had fallen asleep in a wooden chair and I walked up behind her and then I took a lamp with its cord and I wrapped it around her neck and I strangled her to death. While I was doing it, I felt good, and I told her, 'You shall *never* hurt my child, you will *not* do to her what you did to me. It all ends *here.* God has despised you, your mother, and *all of you to hell!'*"

Carrie whispered, "Then what happened?"

"My daughter was adopted to a loving Christian family, and I was executed for murder, and I told the people that killed me that it was OK, that God would forgive them because I deserved to die, but my daughter did not. But here I am! The point is that God waited through many evil generations for me! *That* is the reason why the whole world is turning so evil. God waits for the very last soul he will save no matter how evil the world will get! And now, look at the good the Lord Jesus just blessed us to do for Lady Stephanie and King Vaughn! And I feel that part of the reason I was able to feel so *very* strongly to help, was because of my life *down there!"*

Jargono asked again, "You did *what?"*

He had interrupted his bomb building when Stephanie popped into his workroom and told him the story. After that, he summoned everyone to the dining room for early dinner so they could hear her tell the tale.

The way Jargono asked the question had all eyes on Stephanie, with the common thought, *What did she do now?*

And after she was done explaining it all she sat back and began to eat roast beef with mashed potatoes. Vaughn said, "You made friends with a dragon?" Stephanie nodded and shoved another piece of meat in her mouth.

Jargono asked, "What possessed you to think you could do that?"

Karen spoke up, then. "Well, she befriended me, so what's a dragon?"

That brought uncontrolled laughter for some time, until Lady Stephanie answered, "You know, it's not like I planned it out. It just happened! Each decision I made came at the spur of the moment."

They all just shook their heads with Vaughn proclaiming, "God, I *love* this woman."

And everyone said, "Here, Here."

One of Jargono's generals with crew cut blond hair came rushing in. "They're coming. Satellite picked them up right when they materialized only about a hundred miles away. The sky and the ground are full of them!"

Jargono vanished. Vaughn brought up Jargono's wall screen and as soon as he did the warning alert flashed. He clicked on it and there was the enemy. Stephanie's hand went to her mouth, suddenly losing her appetite. Karen, however, just calmly kept eating.

Jargono had taught Vaughn all about his defense system. He had a while ago, mined the upper atmosphere and could command them to drop any time he wanted. Vaughn said, "Let's make this a little more difficult for them." On the screen he drew a line from the minefield to an intercept course somewhere along their travel path. When the suggested destination flashed, it meant the timing would work.

"After all that hits them, they'll proceed much more cautiously."

Queen Stephanie's eyes suddenly looked up with discovery. "My King," Vaughn winced and she giggled, repeating, "My *King,* why don't we do the same thing. If we're trying to buy time, we could slow them down, too."

But Karen asked. "Don't we need the protection of the castle? I don't know. You want to meet them out in the open?

"Karen's right, *but,* if we pop in behind them when they run into the minefield, I think that might work. Fifteen minutes. Is everything in order, General?"

The man, crew cut blond hair, middle age but stocky, saluted, then said, "Yes, King Vaughn." Vaughn sighed, but

Jargono had made it very clear they were to take his orders as if Jargono was giving them, himself.

Vaughn began rubbing the soft beginnings of a beard. "In my extensive vision of mediaeval times, castles always fought the same way. I have to believe our enemy knows this. General, we have many hidden tunnels that go out in all directions. Is it possible to put archer brigades into the tunnels and come up behind the enemy once they attack the castle?"

"It would make targeting much easier, actually, and their backs would be to us. But it's also very dangerous because if they find the tunnels, they have direct access inside."

"But if we had to, we could place explosives . . ."

"Already there, my King. The problem is that's our last resort. It was meant to be used if our detector warned us they found a tunnel. But by what you want to do, if we had to blow them, we'd strand our men and lose all the archers."

Vaughn looked over to his wife. "Stephanie, you've fought them much more that we have. If we buried a bunch of them alive, would that *kill* them?"

"I really don't think so. But if you mined the whole tunnel extensively with the right kind of power, the blast would tear them up and if any survived, they couldn't survive being buried, too, I don't think."

"Alright, I want those archer brigades, but when they attack, it will first be every other tunnel. They'll shoot their first volley. The enemy will turn around and you'll shoot your second string. Then they'll run at you and you should be able to get off one more volley before you have to beat it. Once in the tunnel you send arrows back at them, too. Come through the tunnel and let some of them through, too. Have archers posted to immediately take out those we let in. Then blow the tunnels. Then we'll wait a while and they'll think we used up all we had, and then we'll do it again."

The general saluted, but then asked, "May I speak candidly," and Vaughn nodded. "If we destroy all the tunnels, we'll have no escape if we need it."

Karen spoke up. "There's no place to escape to. This is our last stand."

The general saluted. "Yes, Queen Karen, King Vaughn. We'll get it done."

Vaughn looked at the girls. "Well, are you ready?" They just shrugged and they all disappeared.

When they materialized in midair behind the enemy they were shocked at actually seeing the enormity. Seeing it from satellite didn't do it justice. The whole sky was filled with dragons, the whole ground below with gargoyles. Far up ahead they heard the explosions from the satellites, but none of the enemy here paid it any mind probably because it was so far forward.

Vaughn shook his, "I was expecting them back here to be distracted, but they're not."

Karen said, "They will be." And she reached around as if hugging her shoulders and then violently threw her arms open. An invisible force traveled into the center of the rear file and drove the dragons from the center into their neighbors so hard that their neighbors felt they were being attacked and responded in kind. They began fighting amongst themselves and killing one another. The next line up turned, saw the battle and the general of that line commanded they all be destroyed. In short order, the dragons turned around, breathed fire, then went in with teeth and claws and quickly dispatched them all.

Lady Stephanie sent glowing birds past them and instinctively the dragons snapped at them, but when they were in their mouths the birds exploded, blowing their heads off. *That* got the attention of the next line, who alerted the line in front of them.

"OK Ladies, follow me." Vaughn dove through the air towards the ground and the girls followed and the dragons followed. As they breathed their fire, Vaughn ascended sharply, and each girl broke to their respective sides. The dragons ended up incinerating a lot of gargoyles, to which their gargoyle generals cursed them out.

Lady Stephanie projected into the dragons' minds and hearts, *That's no way to talk to a* DRAGON, *king of the sky!* The dragons shook their heads, knowing it was Lady Stephanie, but still, the *meaning* was there. Stephanie shouted at the gargoyle, "I can't *believe* these *beautiful* dragons let *scum* like you ride them and send them to their deaths just for *you!*"

Karen picked up on it. "No, the dragons are *dumb, slow, stupid* beasts of burden. "

Vaughn couldn't help laughing. Karen was good at this. The dragons from the rear file all stopped and looked at each other. When the gargoyle general dug his spurs into his dragon, the dragon picked him off his back and threw him to another dragon who promptly ate him, then said, "Needs salt!"

The dragons then began to return to their rank but Lady Stephanie had other plans. She popped onto the neck of the lead dragon. "Hi. I'm Lady Stephanie," and she scratched it behind the ears. "I couldn't help notice how you stuck up for yourself and your dragon friends."

Now all the dragons, some twenty-five, stopped and hovered around Lady Stephanie. There was no need to rush and kill her now, she was *right there.* And Stephanie asked her next question. "If I may ask you, oh Feared One, what made you do that? Stick up for yourself and your *dragon* brethren?" And when she said the word, *dragon,* she put *meaning* into the word, into their hearts, and they all straightened and cocked their heads back then looked at each other realizing they all had the same thoughts and feelings! They'd never considered any of this before in their lives, but then again, they hadn't lived that long, but it *felt* that way.

One of the dragons spoke up. "We are *dragons!*" And he said it with so much meaningful feeling that the others all sucked it up, too, and began to say in turn, "We are *Dragons.*"

Karen spoke next. "I *used to be* a Queen Alpha in the Ethereal. *I* made the Ethereal Range where you were born!" They all peered more closely at her then recognized it was true and they all bowed to her! But Karen said, "Please don't bow. I'm not an Alpha any more, because I learned they were just *using* me. They didn't care *anything* for me even though, like you, I deserved honor. In fact, they abused me. So now

I *fight them*. I *fight them* with all I have and to my last dying breath, *Will you join me?*"

Some of the dragons puffed up, others weren't so trusting. Vaughn came over then because the rest of the dragon force had moved on. "I'm King Vaughn." And all the dragons gave a head bow. They'd heard of him. He was number one on their target list even more so than his queen. "Aren't we supposed to live by *honor?* You are *dragons."* And there it was again, spoken by a very different human but with the same *meaning.*

And Vaughn asked, "What does being a *dragon* mean to you?" And somehow, he took them all into his intense stare, and if you know *anything* about dragons, it's the intensity of their *own* stare. And when they saw that not only did he look them in the eye, but his stare was even more intense than theirs, they bowed their heads to him again.

When Vaughn saw they were at a loss for words, he explained it. "You're at a loss for words, because your *other* masters never wanted you to know your *own meaning."* And there it was again, and some angry dragons breathed fire into the air. "Because your meaning is so much greater than theirs! *You* are royal knights of the sky with a full *heritage* of heroic deeds and defending the skies from evil!"

Then Lady Stephanie placed into them every noble dragon story she could remember and she made some up, as well. Then she said, "*That* is your dragon *meaning.* OK, it was an *honor* to talk with such noble guardians of the sky. We don't want to delay you any longer."

But the dragons looked at each other then back at Lady Stephanie, King Vaughn, and Queen Karen and bowed to them. The lead dragon said, "It would be an honor to serve you."

But Vaughn said, "In *my* kingdom, *no one* is more important than another *especially* us! We *value* the lives that we as royalty serve being Kings and Queens."

The dragons all shook their big heads, amazed at the enormous contrast between what they had been and what they now became. "We desire to join you. How can we aide in *our* common cause?"

Queen Karen spoke next. "Your forces will overpower us, kill, maim, and *eat* us, and enslave the others like they enslaved you." The dragons roared. "If you think you can, would you rejoin your forces and share your new knowledge with other dragons? Then you all will be *free.* Free to do what you want because you're *dragons!*"

"As you wish, Queen Karen. We are *free!*" And they departed to rejoin their forces.

Vaughn looked at the Ladies. "Well, with their force being that large, it probably won't make much of a difference at all. Unfortunately, we didn't even slow them down. Neither did the mines. Let's go back."

When they arrived back atop the castle, they could see the dragon force darkening the horizon. Vaughn said, "Maybe another fifteen minutes."

Lady Stephanie knelt down and propped herself up on a stone bench. "Lord Jesus, I know we shouldn't be, but we're scared. We're scared because we just don't see a way to win. We know we can die with honor fighting. But you've made us so alive, given us *so much* meaning. We grieve if all that goodness You've bestowed upon us would be wiped away from off Your Earth. If it's our time, let us pass while honoring fully your Goodness, honoring *what* You are, Holy Father. If it's *not* our time, grant us victory rather than slavery."

And even Karen said Amen. But not only here, but somehow, Lady Stephanie's prayers were picked up and broadcast throughout the whole castle, and everyone was saying *Amen.* Jargono had commanded his surveillance, which was masked and extensive, that if Lady Stephanie prayed, it should be broadcast to all, meaning all of both countries!

Vaughn hollered out. "We sent all the mines ahead, so they'll be nothing to hinder them coming in. As soon as any are in range, shoot. But try to make sure that when you shoot, if your target dodges, your weapons find another enemy behind."

All shouted, "Yes, King Vaughn."

Wave, after wave, after wave . . . they came. They paid no attention to their troops who died and fell out of the sky. They weren't in a hurry, either. This was inevitable. So much fire had hit the stone castle walls that the people who leaned on them between each attack began to notice the stone was crumbling! When Lady Stephanie saw *that,* she bowed her head and the whole castle glowed! It even gave pause to the attackers. The stone was restrengthened.

Vaughn called out to his wife. "I think it's time. Karen, distract as many of the generals you can."

Karen began getting into their heads with the most distracting and annoying thoughts and feelings anyone could imagine. *You're more handsome than the rest. You're the weakest of them all. He just* laughed *at you! Are you* sure *you're ready to die?* She was quite good at it. Lady Stephane spread her arms wide and raised her hands up and the sky all the way to the horizon became a living mass of roiling black and grey clouds. And the lightning shower was massive. Then it stopped, then it started. Every time they blocker her, she went around. Dragons started to fall from the sky, and then Lady Stephanie got hit. If it wasn't for the automatic protection she now ran, she'd be dead.

Gargoyles were pouring over the top of the parapet. There had been so many, they were able to swarm past the archers. The clouds dissolved. Lady Stephanie's long daggers were in her hands even before she hit the stone floor. When she hit, the gargoyle's head came off. But Vaughn had a backup plan, and archers atop the little towers above mowed down the gargoyles below, some of the arrows whizzing by the embattled heroes by a mere hair's breadth. There was no time to consider it further.

Vaughn called for his Staff and slammed its foot down on the floor. Angry thunder rolled forth and the remaining gargoyles who had breached the top were hurled back over the wall. Everyone took their defensive positions. Suddenly, the castle shook. Stephanie hadn't quite figured out how to perfectly balance the geothermal generator yet. But that gave her an idea.

She threw a glowing dome of protection around the top of the castle, hollered to stop shooting, and reached out her hands as if she was grabbing something massive, too heavy to lift. Then she plunged her hands downward. And then she brought them up high. The ground shook terribly. Everyone in their castle fell over, but the whole castle was also glowing again. This marked the largest feat the *faithwalker* had *ever* done! While she ran her continuous protection for herself, she was now holding a dome of protection over the top of the castle, as well as holding the whole structure together during the quake and the *eruption!* Yes, from the midst of the open court outside the castle, superheated lava, ash and smoke spued upwards. Many dragons were taken out in that initial burst. The superheated gas cloud slammed into the castle walls and whipped around them and engulfed the whole structure. Moments after that, the flames followed.

Many who saw it thought they had descended into Hell itself. Billowing flames swept over Lady Stephanie's dome of protection. And the *faithwalker* collapsed onto her back screaming, but extending her hands out desperately trying to hold it all together so none of it would get out of control. She had started it, but she had no idea the kind of life of its own a full volcanic eruption would have.

When she felt herself failing, she knew everyone would die from what she'd done and it dismayed her and guilt savaged her, *What have I done?* And Vaughn dove on her with his Staff mashed between them and he wrapped her up in his strong arms and squeezed tightly. "I love you."

And her hands grabbed onto the Staff and she screamed with her last bit of strength, *"Lord Jesus, help us."* And all felt her power ebbing, and many fell to their knees waiting for the end. But the shaking began to calm, and the fire and ash began to settle. The dome of protection failed, but Lady Stephanie, barely conscious put all her last strength into the castle's structure and it glowed brightly.

Vaughn leapt up and peered over the wall. Many dragons and dragon parts were strewn over the landscape. No living gargoyles were close at all. There was a wide bed of steaming, churning, glowing red-hot lava up against the castle, but Lady Stephanie, gripping the Staff so tightly her knuckles turned white, refused to pass out. If she did, the castle would fall. Weeping from the pain and exertion, she held on.

Vaughn lifted her up in his arms, "I've got you, Stephanie. I've got you. Just hold on. Hold on a little longer. Help her hold Lord God." Then he turned her so she could see and her eyes widened.

She whispered., "Oh dear God, what did I do?"

The enemy force was far from decimated, but they had to withdraw, and they decided to withdraw hundreds and hundreds of yards away from the blast site. Jargono popped up. He *had to* leave his work for *this.* He felt like his whole castle was going to fall! When he looked at the landscape, he whistled slowly and shook his head the same. Then his eyebrows went up and he looked at Stephanie clinging to the Staff, barely able to hold on. Vaughn looked into Jargono's eyes, "She's holding the castle together. She, well, she created a volcanic eruption, and well, I guess it got to be a little more than she could handle."

Jargono burst out laughing. He peered over the edge again. Popped over to the other side and saw the same thing, came back, and said to Stephanie, "Do you realize what you've done?"

"I'm sorry. I'm trying to hold on."

"No, no *Faithwalker*. You just bought us the time we need! Hold on." Jargono extended his hands outward and spun around. The lava that was up against the castle slowly stood up and moved about six feet away. Then the space filled with water and steam rose up. "Every good castle deserves a moat." He looked down then waved his hand again and crocodiles appeared. "Just for affect." Jargono came back over to Vaughn, who still cradled Stephanie in his arms and he kissed her forehead. You can let go now, sleep, rest, you've earned it. And he put his finger to her forehead and Stephanie fell deeply asleep.

He turned to Vaughn. "The dragons could still attack if they wanted to, but I'm sure after *that* power display, they're a bit reluctant. But even more than that, their strategy works when *both* the dragons and gargoyle attack together. That divides our defense and gives the chaos they need. They won't be able to do that for a while. You and your wife go to my private quarters. I won't be there for a long time. Get some *sleep*. You look like hell."

Karen came up to Jargono and he laughed when he saw her. "You were *brilliant*. You know I watched you while I was working."

She flattened her mouth. "How can you do both at the same time. Don't *worry* about me."

"I *always* worry about you. You give my life *meaning!*" He kissed her and was gone.

She stood amazed at what he said. He'd never said that about her or anyone before. She also noticed that the bored look he usually carried somewhere in his person was gone.

Through the rest of the day, every now and then, a lone gargoyle would creep up to the glowing, wide lava bed surrounding the castle and reach out a finger. Even before it got close to touching it, it howled and scampered away.

CHAPTER 21

When Heroes Fall

HrorrarrAggrang followed Lucifer into the Ethereal and once there they folded their wings. Lucifer pointed to all the crystal-clear blue orbs within a vast great hall, and said, "HrorrarrAggrang, all this will shortly be ours, and ours alone. These *holy* angels have a great weakness. Do you know it, my faithful offspring?"

"I think there are many. They're constrained. Not free at all."

"Yes, all that, but *worse* than that, they have no imagination. They have no idea the lengths you and I will go to *win*. Do you know how we'll win?"

HrorrarrAggrang shook his head and Lucifer knelt to his ear and whispered, "Everyone in our fold, *everyone,* except just you and I, we will sacrifice just to gain *one* of them! But once we gain one, we gain them all. Because we're willing to sacrifice so much, but they'll *never* sacrifice even the least of them, *that's* how we win. Our secret, together. Sure, they've said their Light will go down to Earth, but *our* Light will wait till theirs is *long* gone. But where theirs is so gentle and kind, *ours* will be forceful and *demand* worship. Who do you think the human animals will follow?"

HrorrarrAggrang laughed.

"I can already imagine so clearly the lineage of humans we will use. It'll take thousands of their soon to be years, but *we* will prevail. What's thousands to eternity? They could never imagine our cunning and the offensive lengths we are even now willing to go. That's why we'll win."

When Vaughn woke up in Jargono's luxurious bed, he had no idea how long he slept but he hadn't felt that rested in a very long time. Stephanie still slept peacefully in his arms, so he just leaned back to study her beautiful countenance. She looked so satisfied in her deep sleep. He wanted to savor every moment of it. He gently ran his hand over her head to cherish her preciousness.

In her deep slumber she could feel his earnest attention and she smiled. Someone knocked on the door, then stuck their head in, a man about in his fifties, a head full of very neatly trimmed black hair said, "Beggin' your pardon, my lord, I was sent to ask if you desired food?"

At *that* Stephanie's eyes popped open. "God, I'm starving!"

The man laughed. "I would expect so. Saving everyone's lives can take a lot out of you. That's why you slept for a whole day!"

Both of them had the common expression, "*A whole day?*"

The man knew they wanted to jump right out of bed so he excused himself.

Stephanie, indeed, went to jump out of bed but this time Vaughn pulled her back. "*Vaughn,* I have to check on everything."

"Not yet, you don't. Did you forget about Michael?"

"*Michael,* and her hands went to her belly. Oh God, I feel so ashamed. I haven't even had time to think."

"Well, he hasn't forgot about you. See?" Michael was glowing. "I just wanted you to take a moment and feel *your* life again. What I saw you do yesterday, I'm speechless." And Vaughn truly looked in awe of her, at a heart so large he couldn't fathom it. That's where all her faithwalking power came from, from the meaning in her young loving heart.

But Stephanie shook her head at herself. "I should have thought about it a bit more, I think. Oh God, you have no idea how close I was to failing." She shivered, and Vaughn squeezed her and kissed her.

"There was no time to think. Only to feel, and your feelings always lead you right, *faithwalker.*"

"Why is everyone calling me that lately?"

"It's got to do with your heart, Lady Stephanie, that is so obvious for all to see, and love."

When they finally got to the formal dining room, the butler asked, "Would you like breakfast, lunch, dinner, or all of the above? You missed all of them!"

Stephanie looked at Vaughn and he could tell she wanted to say all of them. "What time is it, anyway?"

"Eleven at night, my lord. You two have actually slept longer than a whole day, and we're all glad for it."

Vaughn looked at Stephanie, "Brunch?"

"That's a *great* idea."

"Brunch, it is."

While waiting, Vaughn pulled up the screen and inspected the battlefield. Another gargoyle went up to the lava, put his finger to it, smiled, if you could call that a smile, and then stepped on top. A moment later he started to sink, to scream, and when he tried to jump off, he ended up pressing himself down further and howled and became stuck. A soldier leaned over and put the creature out of its misery, then he called back to his comrades, "I couldn't stand the noise."

The enemy army had moved closer. The dragons soared high above, out of range. For all the damage Stephanie's geological re-arrangement did, the enemy didn't look that much different.

Eggs, crispy bacon, sausages, crumbly hunks of bread, butter, orange juice, fruit with some kind of special cream sauce, pancakes, French toast, and when all that was gone, Stephanie looked up and asked, "Is that it?"

The butler asked, "What else would you two like, my Lady." He wasn't talking about Vaughn.

Then Stephanie looked at all the empty plates scattered haphazardly around her. "Oh my, Vaughn, why didn't you say something? I'm gonna get *fat*."

The butler straightened his black vest and said, "When you're with child, my Lady, that usually happens. I have something extra special I'll bring you."

Her eyes went wide, her eyebrows raised up in eager anticipation and she patted her tummy. "*Extra* special Michael." He started kicking in delight.

The butler came back with a generous piece of some kind of layered cake which he set in front of Queen Stephanie. There were nuts crumbled on top of a creamy icing with various colors of filling between the layers. This butler seemed particularly pleased and proud to be serving her. Then he took a silver flask and began to drizzle something dark atop it. "Dark chocolate, my Queen, with just a hint of rum, but nothing to worry for the child. It's called tiramisu, a special kind, a luxury from a time gone by."

The eagerness in his wife's eyes made Vaughn chuckle. They became like bright stars. Vaughn had never seen his wife enjoy food so much. She carefully took her fork and sliced off a corner and delicately put it in her mouth and then her eyes lit up even more and rolled. "My GOD! Vaughn, come here."

Smiling, he got up and she forked off another corner, he bent down and she shoved it into his mouth. "Wow!"

"I'm sorry Sire, but *that* was the last piece.

Stephanie looked worried. She looked Vaughn in the eye, was about to sadly offer him half, when he said, "Give my half to Michael."

To which Lady Stephanie heartily agreed. "You're so *wise*, my King."

Motion in the screen caught the corner of Vaughn's eye. A dragon swooped lower then dropped something to the center of the castle. As it got closer, they recognized it as a gargoyle.

Someone shot it with an arrow and it was dead before it hit the ground.

Then all the dragons, who had disappeared for some time, took to flight. "Oh no," Stephanie said in mid-bite. "We have to go up, *now.*" But she doubled back to her dessert and shoved the rest of it into her mouth.

As she went down the hall, people tried to talk to Lady Stephanie but her cheeks were bulging and she kept having to point to them. "I see the baby is just fine," the women would say." Some of the men asked, "Are you OK?"

Atop the castle again, the sky darkened with dragons. Lady Stephanie commanded everyone. "Don't waste your arrows. I'll take care of it!"

The dragons dropped the gargoyles and when they were halfway down a giant glowing netting appeared that quickly fill up. Then she made it twirl and it became like cheese cloth when you wring the liquid out. It began to rain gargoyle blood as the netting drew tighter. When the remaining gargoyles held in the clutches of the dragons saw *that,* they began to struggle. She tossed the net with the refuse away from the castle and a new net appeared. All the rest of the dragons went back to their base. All the soldiers shook their heads and went back to their card games, books, conversations. Nothing to worry about.

All the rest of the night was routine. Every now and then a stupid gargoyle would come, jump up and down on the lava bed, get stuck, howl, get shot, and die. But at noonday, one jumped up and down and it held firm. It died right away though.

When Vaughn and Jargono came to the dining room carrying huge duffle bags, they kissed goodbye to their wives, then told them to have a nice time, they would be back in about twenty-four hours. The women shrugged, and thought, *This isn't nearly as bad as we thought it would be.*

All across the castle everyone had settled into a routine-shoot a few gargoyles, switch game partners, and alternate taking naps. So when Dragons, *all* the dragons came and filled the whole sky, but they stayed up high and kept breathing fire, everyone thought it was like fireworks, a testimony to their brilliant Lady Stephanie who successfully defended their lives, their castle, their future. It was indeed a spectacular sight, an odd sight until it started to rain. *Acid rain!* Dark, thick, sulfur smelling, that didn't burn right away so no one paid it mind until they were thoroughly wet. Even Lady Stephanie got soaked. *What an* idiot, *I am.* Though she immediately dispelled the drench and healed the soldiers, everyone had scrambled inside. By the time they came back out, the first man through the door had his face torn off and they ate it with all to see.

And there was such a rush of gargoyles through the open door they literally trampled to death the soldiers that were pushed over. Lady Stephanie was abashed. She had been on such a high. But also, the soldiers made sure to shuttle her right away to the back, so when they told her the enemy was inside the castle, it was too late. Finally, she came to herself. "You *know* the drill," she hollered out. Immediately the men calmed and worked together, each having their rehearsed task. That's one thing Jargono stressed with ultimate strictness—practice, practice, practice until you don't have to think about it. You just do it.

Assigned soldiers went into the secret tunnels. Archers were always behind the infantry. When the front line hollered, "NOW!," the archers immediately hollered, "DUCK," and the arrows flew right after the 'k' sound of the word. Bodies of Gargoyles piled up in the halls so that they encumbered others from advancing and they had to clear them away. But Lady Stephanie began to lose men, and she felt it. At one point *she* hollered, "DUCK," and by training, they all ducked, even though no one shouted, NOW. Black lightning they'd never seen before, nor Lady Stephanie for that matter, zig zagged over their heads, tore into the castle walls and obliterated all the goblins completely down the hall, then she hollered, "REGROUP."

No one faulted her for this catastrophe. But Stephanie faulted herself. *Who else? They keep pouring in. I* have to *put a stop to that.* She popped away into the Ethereal Corridor to assess the battleground. The whole top of the castle was covered in gargoyles, they were even climbing over each other three deep! *I can't get in! Oh GOD, I can't get in. What am I going to do? If all these just here enter the castle . . .* She went to observe the walls. They were covered in gargoyles waiting for room to climb on top.

Then a thought came to her, *Where's Karen? Oh God.* But as Lady Stephanie's sense ranged out, she couldn't find her, anywhere. *Oh God, Keep her safe, wherever she is.*

෴

Jargono and Vaughn stationed where they were last time in the Ethereal Corridor and Jargono sent the stealth orb back in. The Ethereal Fold was a lot less populated. That was no surprise, but they also noted a lot of young gargoyles and dragons, which meant, *They really don't need Karen anymore.* Jargono looked over to Vaughn. "We have to make this so convincing they'll *never* try anything like this again. You stay here and monitor, if you just talk at the orb, I'll hear you. I need *your* eyes right *here*. Do you understand?"

It was an odd question put in an odd way. No doubt it was an order, but there was deeper meaning Vaughn didn't have time to assess. "But if I go in, too, we can cut the time in half."

Jargono grabbed Vaughn by his ranger shirt and pulled him eye to eye. "I don't have time for this. You're *still* a boy! You can't set the charges the way only I understand. You've *never* seen anything like *this.*" And using his faithwalker powers the duffle bags hovered by him and they all disappeared.

"How am I going to see you if you're invisible" A message immediately popped up in the orb. INSTITUTING UNCOVER MODE

Vaughn watched as slowly, carefully. Jargono placed orb charges against the invisible Ethereal Fold's perimeter. *This is going to take a good while.* At times, a young dragon would come up almost nose to nose with Jargono but he just held still and the young beast moved on. But Vaughn had a bad feeling about it. "Jargono, I think they have some kind of sense about you." His reply was that everything has sense, more than they know what to do with.

They were in the Ethereal where time distorts, but the orb had a timer and when Vaughn checked it, sixteen hours had passed! He couldn't believe it, and it looked like Jargono was only two-thirds done based on where he was at. And then the Alpha showed up. Not near where Jargono was, but did that matter?

HrorrarrAggrang, and of all demons, Grinchback! It looked like the old demon was serious about keeping Grinchback around.

"Grinch, come over here." Grinchback didn't respond fast enough and HrorrarrAggrang's tail smacked him across the head. "When I call you, you come. You see all that refuse lying around? *There!*" And his tail pointed at a dragon pooping in the air and it fell to the ground with a splat. "We need to keep things clean around here. Your new job, is to bury all this!"

"Yes Master," was all Grinchback said.

"And if I find out you've *consumed* any of the life here, *I'll consume you.*"

"Yes, Master."

Just then, HrorrarrAggrang squinted and looked generally in Jargono's direction.

"HrorrarrAggrang just made you."

Jargono froze. Grinchback had begun digging with his tail and he swung it hard and accidently scooped up some gargoyle poop and flung it to his side.

HrorrarrAggrang bellowed, "What did you cast in my *Eye?*" It wasn't that it burned particularly. It wasn't disabling at all. But . . . the utter *insult.* To have his Sacred Great Eye *defiled.* HrorrarrAggrang lost all sense of composure. He grabbed Grinchback with his tail, turned him upside down and *drug* his great eye through piles and piles of crap, and then drug him some more.

Vaughn scrutinized his *friend.* And at one point, Vaughn could swear he saw Grinchback *wink* right at him! It was probably just the poop in his Great Eye. "HrorrarrAggrang is distracted by Grinchback. He's forgotten about you."

HrorrarrAggrang ordered Grinchback to apologize, but every time he did, he had just the slightest touch of rebellion which the ancient demon immediately picked up on and it enraged him further. "Grinch, I'm going to beat you and abuse you until," he grabbed him again and shoved his great eye into a fresh steaming pile of dragon poop, "I *beat* every last bit of rebellion out of you. When I get done with you, *no one,* no self-respecting Alpha will ever even *think* about consuming you."

"Yes, master." And there it was *again.* The way he said Master wasn't Master, it was master with a small m. And the abuse proceeded again only worse.

"I wish you could see this Jargono. If I didn't know better, I'd swear Grinchback was distracting HrorrarrAggrang on purpose! To protect *you!*"

HrorrarrAggrang was true to his word. He kept abusing Grinchback but Grinchback kept on finding tiny little ways to *innocently* be off on the respect HrorrarrAggrang knew he was due. And on and on it went. After a while Vaughn kept shaking his head at it, feeling quite angry for his friend. But the last charges Jargono set were close by to where the demons were carrying on because the Ethereal Fold was oval shaped so the curving wall brought Jargono close up on them.

As Jargono set the very last charge, another young dragon came nose to nose with him.

Vaughn shouted, "Get out of there, *now.*"

HrorrarrAggrang noticed the dragon right away and immediately lashed out with his tail right at Jargono, but he popped away to HrorrarrAggrang's other side. HrorrarrAggrang scanned the area but wasn't looking in the right direction. But then he called all the dragons to come to him.

"Jargono, *get out*," Vaughn urged.

"This is too good an opportunity. You saw what they're doing. I *have* to take this shot. Start the countdown, NOW!" Vaughn automatically hit the button even though he didn't want to. Was it Jargono's power that made him do it? Or was it just the way Jargono had trained them? Or was it fear to disobey him? Vaughn had a sinking feeling and decided to go in. Besides, he *owed* HrorrarrAggrang, too.

But Jargono knew his thoughts! "I owe him a lot more, and *this* is what you tell *my* wife. I had to honor you by trying to destroy that bastard Alpha. Then you might be able to find some peace."

Two minutes. The baby dragons had already found Jargono, but when HrorrarrAggrang cast a dark wave of his Ethereal Power, Jargono was already gone and right next to the demon's right side. HrorrarrAggrang immediately spun behind him and Jargono crossed his glowing arms then whipped them open and a bright golden cutting beam sliced through HrorrarrAggrang completely severing him into two halves.

But the ancient demon's lower half took its tail and pressed the top half back in place! "Fool. I'm *Alpha.* You *can't* destroy me. I'm the direct spawn of the Father *Himself.*" And his tail lashed out. Jargono tried to vanish but couldn't, so bright green beams shot from his chest and chopped his massive tail into six different pieces that hurled past Jargono.

Grinchback raced after one and consumed it! HrorrarrAggrang waved his massive arm and all the pieces came back, save one. When he put his tail back together, it didn't feel, nor look quite right. HrorrarrAggrang smoothed out the inconsistency.

Jargono laughed at the demon primping his tail, "You're a proud son of an Earth *Dog* aren't you?"

But HrorrarrAggrang refused to be baited. Grinchback studied everything more closely then began to ease away. HrorrarrAggrang shot black oil from his eye that came out faster than any substance like that should be able to do but Jargono sidestepped it, stuck his finger into the stream, then tasted it! He spit it out, saying, "Not aged well. I wouldn't pay *anything* for that dragon poop."

Grinchback had moved quite a bit away but when he heard *that*, he couldn't help but laugh hard. He looked up at Vaughn, *directly* up at him, winked, and then slowly moved away further.

"He *knows!* How can he know?"

HrorrarrAggrang rushed at Jargono. But he didn't even bother to pop away. Instead, he became a bright golden glow, which shocked HrorrarrAggrang, knowing Jargono *despised* such waist. And then an intense golden explosion blew all the dragons apart and sent HrorrarrAggrang up against the Ethereal Fold wall. And *that's* when his Great Eye noticed one of Jargono's devices. Jargono hurled five different kinds of intense energies at HrorrarrAggrang who, out of reflex if nothing more, curled into a great ball.

Everyone had wondered just how powerful Jargono really was. Vaughn shook his head, "I've never seen anything even close to this kind of power. Stephanie put little wounds into them. Jargono deals major damage."

Then with all his might, Jargono called the ancient demon away from the wall and his devices. Vaughn checked the timer. "Jargono, twenty seconds. Popp away. *Please!*"

"Can't do that my friend. He's blocked me. Besides, I have to be *here* for it all to work!"

Vaughn's mouth fell open and his heart opened up. Vaughn called his Staff to hand, but Grinchback put his tail on Vaughn's shoulder, saying, "You have to let him finish what he came to do!"

Vaughn stared into his Great Eye, had so many questions to ask, but went back to watching the orb with Grinchback, who put his tail across both Vaughn's shoulders. In a strange way, the pain was comforting. Or was it the pain that comforted?

Jargono had called HrorrarrAggrang to him, and begrudgingly, the old demon floated forward. "Look *me* in the Eye HrorrarrAggrang!" Jargono called his name just right.

"Five seconds," Vaughn whispered knowing that for some reason, he had to tell Jargono. "four, three, two, one . . ." At the count of one, Jargono wrapped his arms around the ancient demon and the ancient demon wrapped his tail around Jargono, and Jargono exploded at the same time all the devices went off.

Vaughn held out his Staff in front of him and kneeled down with Grinchback behind him. It seemed the Ethereal Quake and wind, when there is no wind in the Ethereal, lasted forever. When it was done, nothing was left!

Vaughn replayed the last seconds, then he divided the seconds into microsecond frames, but it was always the same. It wasn't just an explosion Jargono created. He, *himself,* was the bomb. Vaughn understood that if someone like that wanted maximal force, they would have to sacrifice their very life! *Sacrifice.* That word Vaughn's wife so hated and so honored so many times.

Vaughn couldn't believe Jargono actually died. Vaughn just floated there before his orb in stillness, not wanting to move forward to the next second. It was strange to feel so alone, like he suddenly mourned the loss of the dearly departed. Grinchback floated Eye to Eye and put his arm on Vaughn's shoulder. "Master Vaughn, I am *proud* to have served you! Your greatest challenges still lie ahead. Your wife, too. But you two shall *never* be apart any more, even in death." And Grinchback vanished!

One thing Vaughn was glad about. He could play this all back for Karen. What he didn't know, was that Karen had a small orb and watched everything. Earlier, Jargono had sat down with her and explained his *new* view of the world, that even though he had hoped to rule the world and bring perfect order, he had begun to suspect that he had been woefully lacking in full understanding, and *that* lacking was purposefully caused by the demons both in him and her. *But,* the one thing they had now, more valuable than anything they had before, is that they now began to possess the very thing the demons had stolen from them. *This* made their whole lives worthwhile and there were only *two* people in the whole world who were good enough, brave enough, forgiving enough, loving enough, and true, that took the time and effort and suffering to help them gain it, and under *no* circumstances could they let harm come to them. He would assure Vaughn's survival and Jargono charged his wife, under *no* circumstances do you let any harm come to Lady Stephanie. In Karen's heart she now understood what this all meant, and when she saw her husband, who thankfully, she now loved more than any day prior, when she saw him blow up and take that demon and the Ethereal Fold with him, she didn't cry, she held her head up for the first time in her life with dignity.

❧

Lady Stephanie froze, and it was the wrong time for inaction, but she just couldn't reconcile her recent momentous victory and even praise from Jargono with what so quickly developed now. *What can I do? There's too many.* And she began to hear prayers for her from inside the castle. She knew they were implementing their plans perfectly. She also knew they would be overrun regardless. *Where are you Vaughn? If ever I needed you, I need you now.*

Stephanie finally came out of her stupor, and was about to go back inside and help anyway she could when in the distance she saw hundreds more dragons coming. There were already many hundreds in the sky above. She shook her head. *I'm by myself. If I came back to the physical world here to try and destroy the dragons, the gargoyles would overrun me like they did before. Faithwalker? What faithwalker?*

She couldn't help the tears of failure clouding her eyes and her breaking heart. *She* was the one responsible for everyone, and that had *always* been true, even more so than Vaughn, because it's given to the *faithwalker* to save the people when they can't save themselves. She understood that about her life, her purpose, now, and she accepted it. She was born to live for everyone else, and if she happened to find happiness here for herself at the same time, well, that was nice, but not her reason for being. *That's why I'm here, to find a way for them when there's none.* But now she failed and rushing back into battle just to die with her people was no consolation. *But if they go down fighting, I'll go down fighting with them.*

She wiped the tears from her eyes but the incoming dragons caught her attention again. They weren't acting like the other dragons. These came into the area not in the crude horizontal lines when they first invaded. These came in via triangles like flocks of geese. But it looked very much like a military maneuver. *What are they here for? The gargoyles are in the castle already.*

And then the triangles spread out as if on cue and crashed into the other dragons and began taking them all out with a merciless efficiency! Even though the new arrivals were vastly outnumbered, their excellent battle skills were able to dispatch the many other dragons quite easily. Some groups, though, rather than fighting seemed to be talking together, and then, just as fast as the battle began, it was over, and all the rest of the dragons came together as one, and then spilt into more triangles. *What is going on?*

And then the dragons swooped down towards the castle. Waves of triangles descended and then spread out and the whole castle erupted in flames along with the other two sister castles in the distance. Stephanie's mouth fell open. When the flames disappeared, there were *no* gargoyles to be seen. And then the dragons spread out through the surrounding lands incinerating more of the enemy and their camps.

One dragon came to Stephanie's castle and a woman in golden hair and black dress jumped down and ran right at the entrance shooting red fireballs and blowing up gargoyles who were waiting for room to push further inside. That woman was screaming, "Stephanie, I'm *here*. I'm *here*."

With tears in her eyes, again, Stephanie materialized beside her. "So am I."

And Karen whirled around and threw her arms around Stephanie! "Oh thank God! When I saw the castle breached, I thought for sure you were dead, because I know you, you wouldn't have fled! C'mon, let's clean up this *filth*." All

Stephanie could do was hug Karen back. Her arrival meant so much more than Karen realized. *I'm not alone anymore.*

They both went in, side by side. When one attacked, the other defended. They rotated back and forth with all manner of energy blasts destroying the enemy. And then the hall went to the right and the left and they split. Lady Stephanie's black lightning wreaked havoc. That was the one energy the gargoyles couldn't seem to counter, that the *faithwalker* didn't have to walk it around to get through. Still, she didn't rely on her black lightning a lot because Jargono had taught her that the enemy can get used to *anything.*

But now they came to many rooms, and one by one they had to clear them all out, because gargoyles packed into them all. Still, they hadn't found any of their men, yet. *Oh God, maybe they already ate them all!* And then, after working their way down floor by floor, both Queen Karen and Queen Stephanie came into the great castle hall which was the throne room. There was only one floor below this one, the basement. *Where did everyone go? There were thousands of people here.* That was their common thought. All the people in the castle couldn't possibly all fit into the basement. But the girls had even more pressing matters at hand. A very large general gargoyle sat on the throne chewing on a human foot and rage boiled through both women who fired energies at him at the same time.

Karen shot a straight laser like green and yellow beam and Stephanie a golden fireball but the gargoyle disappeared and the throne was blown up. The rest of the gargoyles attacked them. Karen pulled out her blessed sabers that she carried crisscrossed on her back. Stephanie pulled her daggers from her hips but continued with various energies and she also increased her automatic defense.

No matter that she was pregnant, the *faithwalker* whirled, flipped, spun, but sometimes, from the sheer numbers of enemy, one or two got through and knocked her over. She felt their impact, the jarring, but that's also what the daggers were for because whoever got that close to her, the daggers did their work and then she would flip back to her feet. She fancied little Michael was doing combat moves inside her womb!

As it happened, the gargoyles began fighting more strategically, as if they had someone guiding them and the girls ended up being maneuvered into the center of the room under a great brass chandelier. Back-to-back, Karen and Stephanie fought for each other. More than once, Lady Stephanie sensed an imminent blow at Karen, which Stephanie blocked with a protective shield. More than once Lady Stephanie got knocked down and Queen Karen leapt over her to disembowel the attackers trying to take advantage, and then Stephanie would flip to her feet, standing where Karen had been.

And then, in the corner of Karen's eye, she saw a motion above. The large gargoyle from the throne had appeared hanging on the chandelier. Stephanie was battling three gargoyles who were nullifying all her energies, so she was kicking, spinning, and swiping with her daggers, but these gargoyles were trained fighters unlike all the rest they had seen. And then the gargoyle above her head, suddenly had a rare weapon in his hand, as gargoyles had no need of weapons, and he swung down with a sword to cleave Stephanie across the back.

It was so fast there was no time to think. Jargono had always taught his Queen that if you had to think in battle, you were dead. Karen lunged at Stephanie and pushed her into her attackers. Stephanie immediately reacted to the enemy contact and sliced the throat of the one to her left, stabbed the one to her right in the heart, and managed a deep red fireball cast from her heart to destroy the attacker directly in front of her. Then she whirled around to face who had pushed her from behind and Stephanie froze. A gray glowing sword had cleaved Karen between her neck and right shoulder.

Their eyes met, and Karen said to Stephanie, "Thank you." And she fell dead at her feet. Uncontrolled heartbreak and rage erupted all through Lady Stephanie and the castle shook. Gargoyles were diving at her but bouncing off some kind of black energy barrier. A rumble gathered intensity and Queen Stephanie cried out, "No *more!*" Black lightning erupted from all over her body and struck all over the room.

When Stephanie came to herself, she became aware of the gargoyle in the chandelier laughing at them. He jumped down twirling a longsword that glowed with a strange gray. Lady Stephanie's eyes turned black. She sheathed her daggers at her side and Karen's sabers floated up into her hands. The gargoyle laughed some more and kicked Karen's corpse at her but without any effort Stephanie deflected it away.

"Do you know who I am?" the gargoyle asked.

There was *meaning* to the question but instead of ignoring it, this time the *faithwalker* decided to pay better attention. She looked deeply into this creature then squinted. *What are you? This doesn't make sense.*

"I'm *you!*" He gave her an ugly fang-filled smile. "Well, the best part of you, *faithwalker!* There's going to be a lot more of you, too!" As the shock hit her, the creature swung his sord but with the other hand fired a green energy blast into her midsection.

Lady Stephanie wasn't going to be caught off guard again. She parried the sword, twisted and the blast missed, and with her other sword, she went to chop his ugly head off. But he ducked, rolled, and swung back with his sword. Stephanie's saber went low to block, then she flipped away to reassess. *Somehow, I know I can't let that sword touch me. I just know it.*

Karen's sabers were perfect in feel and balance. Then they started to glow golden and Lady Stephanie smiled back. The gargoyle lunged, his sword speeding in many directions and then a gray-glowing dagger suddenly appeared in his other hand as he pressed in closer. Stephanie spun away again, then flipped behind the evil beast, but before she landed, a gray blast hit her and knocked her across the floor. He vanished, then reappeared beside her then dove with both hands on his sword's hilt to drive it through Stephanie's heart.

Stephanie rolled away as the blade drove itself through the stone floor! He vanished again, reappeared behind her and swung down his sword with both hands again. Stephanie's sabers crossed behind her and over her head and the gray glowing sword was caught in the saber's intersection. The interaction of the opposing energies slamming into each other exploded and blew them apart and across the room.

When Stephanie rolled to her feet and whirled, the gargoyle already stood in front of her, swinging down! Lady Stephanie crossed her sabers again and the explosion drove them apart again. But for Stephanie, it drove her hard against the wall she was close to and the blunt force knocked the wind from her and she crumpled. *He knew that would happen. He planned it!*

But her recognition came too late. Laying in the crevice between the wall and the floor severely limited the *faithwalker,* and her enemy knew it. That was his plan. She realized, *He's thinking ten moves ahead of me!* His attack came swiftly. Somehow, she knew her defensive shield wouldn't hold up against his sword's energy, so she put all her power into a golden fireball, but it fizzled. She *walked* around the obstacle but it fizzled again! All in a split second, Lady Stephanie knew she had one more microsecond to try to *walk around* one more time. There was no other choice that could be done in a single microsecond. She *walked* again, it failed, *again,* and the faithwalker's heart sunk, knowing what the next microsecond would bring.

But it didn't happen! A staff whipped over her, smashing into her enemy and driving him away. Stephanie's eyes had tears in them because Vaughn had saved her again, but he also witnessed yet *another* of her failures. "What would I do without you?"

Vaughn smiled his special smile just as a gray energy blast hurtled at him, but he slammed the foot of his Staff down on the floor and everything shook, and the Staff's power deflected the bast which slammed into a distant wall and blew a hole in it! Vaughn looked over at his wife with question in his eyes.

Queen Stephanie stood up, and brushed herself off. "Vaughn, they've put *me* into it. He says they're going to make more!" Upon hearing *that*, Vaughn darkened. "It killed Karen!"

The gargoyle slowly walked up, assessing this new situation. Vaughn noted the grey glow to his sword as Vaughn strode back to the throne room's center. The gargoyle didn't even pay Stephanie any mind!

Vaughn's Staff vanished and wrist and ankle braces appeared on him. He had no weapon in his hand. The gargoyle's smirk disappeared after he studied him. "We'll be making more of *you* too." Vaughn slowly nodded. Then the gargoyle repeated his proud question. "Do you *know* who *I* am?

Vaughn just kept slowly circling him. "Not important."

The gargoyle rushed him and Vaughn effortlessly blocked all his strikes with his braces and they parted and reassessed. The gargoyle noted that when his sword struck Vaughn's braces, the clash didn't even make a sound, let alone any energy explosion! The gargoyle came in again with the same result but then the dagger appeared in his other hand but somehow Vaughn grabbed his wrist, twisted the dagger loose, then flipped away. As Vaughn rolled away on the floor the gargoyle pursued him. But Vaughn suddenly reversed his direction, blocked a downward sword swing, then scissored his legs and brought the gargoyle down and held him there! The beast tried to pop away but couldn't! But he wasn't that worried because Vaughn had no weapon. Actually, now he did because somehow Vaughn retrieved the beasts dagger.

But instead of using it, Vaughn whipped it at a wall and it buried itself into the stone to the hilt. The gargoyle squirmed free and stood up shaking his head at him. "You're foolish." And another dagger appeared in his hand. As Vaughn stood up, the gargoyle tried popping behind Vaughn but it didn't work so he looked over to the redhaired girl and she smiled a Karen sweet smile at him.

"You don't talk much, do you?" the gargoyle said.

Vaughn just circled him slowly, growing ever darker. The gargoyle tried hurling various energy blasts at Vaughn but they all fizzled. Then he leapt at Stephanie but Vaughn's Staff appeared in his hand, he vanished then reappeared between them and his Staff swung upwards slamming the beast against the ceiling, then he fell to the floor with a thud.

Slower to get up this time, he began looking for an escape. Vaughn hit the foot of his Staff on the floor again and it thundered, the floor shook, and the gargoyle went down. Vaughn looked over to his wife. "Would you like another try? He's too easy for me." When he saw that hesitant look in her eyes, Vaughn said, "I'm so glad for what you thought earlier!"

She realized Vaughn had been watching for a while before he saved her. "Oh, Vaughn, what thought, which thought?"

Vaugh repeated them. "*He knew that would happen. He planned it! He's thinking ten moves ahead of me!*" Then he looked into her eyes with that *same* look he had when long ago she had laid him in her bed because he had been beaten so badly by her gang. She had confessed her wretchedness to him but he had countered her shame with, "Understanding has now changed you from what you were." He was saying that now. Queen Stephanie's eyes melted. "I love you so much, King Vaughn." And she saw he no longer winced at the title.

Stephanie walked up with Karen's sabers in hand and Vaughn stepped back. The gargoyle kept eyeing him, though, but Vaughn said, "Oh, you'd better worry about her!" And he smiled an unsettling evil smile.

Stephanie looked over to Vaughn and held up the sabers. "These were Karen's."

Vaughn said, "That's a fitting death for this abomination."

Angered at totally being discounted, the gargoyle rushed Stephanie who disappeared, showed up to his left side when he was expecting her to be behind him and she spin kicked him in his back and sent him down.

Vaughn said to him, "You know she's just toying with you."

Stephanie gave the gargoyle another sweet Karen smile, and he rushed her. Vaughn said, "He doesn't look like he's enjoying himself, any more. What do you think the problem is?"

Stephanie held her left saber straight down by her side as she used the right one to parry all his attacks. Then he swung down hard and she crossed both sabers as before and the blast split them apart and knocked her across the floor. The gargoyle laughed, looked at Vaughn with a smirk, but Vaughn just smiled back.

The gargoyle vanished, popped right in front of Stephanie as she stood up, but he was already in mid swing, again, and she barely had time to cross her sabers. He knew as soon as his sword made contact, the blast would drive her against the wall again and then he would finish her quickly, and *then*, without his power being blocked, he could easily beat Vaughn.

But when his sword struck the sabers, no explosion occurred! He realized she had withdrawn their power as Stephanie used the momentum of his powerful downward stroke by stepping aside and guiding his sword down to the floor, but she continued to spin and both her sabers, now glowing brightly golden again, sliced him in the back and buttocks.

He rose awkwardly and Stephanie hit his sword with a sharp silver beam and the weapon exploded in his hand, blowing off his fingers and knocking him back down. She threw a glowing silver and green cage around him and tightened it so that his arms were pressed in at their sides. He tried to dispel the cage but the cage, itself, annulled his abilities. She lifted her hand slowly and the cage stood him up straight as she walked up to it eye to eye. "I'm me. You're not. *I'm a faithwalker.* You're *not.*" And she held up her hands parallel to each other but a couple feet apart. "Watch!" She slowly brought her hands together, and as she did, the cage tightened. The gargoyle began to howl . . . until it didn't, and pieces of him squeezed through the cage mesh.

Stephanie then turned to Vaughn and fell into his chest. "But we lost *everyone,*" and she began to bawl deeply. But just then, people began pouring into the throne room chanting, "Queen Stephanie, King Vaughn. Hail the *Faithwalker!*"

A short while later, the entire throne room was filled with adoring people, military and citizens alike. Lady Stephanie didn't understand so a general came forward and explained after he bowed to them. "Beggin' your pardon King Vaughn, but I had to alter our tunnel plans. It became obvious to me that we would be overrun and that no manner of attack from outside as we planned would make a difference. After conferring with the other officers, we all concurred that either *you* and Queen Stephanie were going to save us, or you weren't, but if you *did* succeed but lost all of us, you'd never forgive yourselves. So we evacuated the whole castle to the tunnels which had ample room."

All the officers came forward, then the general spoke again. "But we disobeyed orders and submit ourselves for punishment." And they all kneeled.

Vaughn stepped forward with staff in hand and gently tapped it repeatedly on the floor. "What should I do with you?" They all bowed their heads. "Stand up, all of you, and look me in the eye." And they all stood and Vaughn walked up close and went on down the line of them staring into their eyes. "You all made *exactly* the correct decisions. In these situations, to rob experienced officers of their abilities to assess the ground in real time and to then make decisions would be very foolish, indeed. I trust you all, and I commend you. The castle is ours again. Let's go out and reassess."

And they all saluted and left. Lady Stephanie levitated Queen Karen's body and clothed it in royal garments and cleaned her up so that she almost looked alive and they proceeded out to the people. "I think Jargono would at least appreciate this much."

But Vaughn hung his head. "In another life, I'm sure he does."

Stephanie couldn't believe it. How could Jargono be dead? Stephanie took Vaughn's arm, and said, "After we present her body and they take her, I'm going back home and I want you to come, too. We haven't seen Lynnara and the others for so long."

CHAPTER 22

Homecoming

Lucifer asked HrorrarrAggrang, "Do you know what I *am*"

HrorrarrAggrang spoke proudly. "You are my Father. And all wise."

"Yes, yes, but something even more. *I* am an *artist.* Actually, the very *first* artist. Now the Lord had *intended* me to use all *my* talent in praising Him, in explaining all about *His* Greatness so others could gain better understanding. But then where would that leave *me?* Right? What am *I?* Just a discarded wing feather? You have *no* idea all that I can do because I have access to the very depths of the Lord and also to *everyone* else, and *art,* my dear underling, is the mainstay of all effective communication. And *I* control it *all.* But not only that. Because the Lord made me an artist that was supposed to represent *His* deepest qualities, that means I can see into *everyone's* depths and understand *exactly* what's in there! Which *means* I know *exactly* how to persuade everyone to follow *me!* How do you like *that* Prince HrorrarrAggrang?"

Prince? Prince? "I like it very much, Father."

Vaugh and Stephanie spent three days away from *every-thing*. Stephanie finally took her husband up on the offer of a sunny beach with crystal blue water and beautifully colored fish. Jargono's and Karen's death affected them far more than they could ever have anticipated. And since the military situation across both countries had stabilized, they felt it would be wise to just back away and see where everyone and everything settled.

It did, however, come as a surprise that waiting for them upon their return home to the United for Christ, the North had officially requested them both to return back to Jargono's castle and specifically to his dining room, but it didn't seem right. Still, they didn't feel it wise nor proper to ignore it, so they took each other's hands and materialized to where they were directed.

When they sat at Jargono's fancy dining table, they could still feel his presence. Actually, the whole castle was permeated with his artistry, his celebration of life! Yet, they felt they no longer belonged, and had no desire to infringe upon his memory. For all the evils up north, the people here still had a right to work out their grief and their destiny without them interfering. Besides, this wasn't Vaughn nor Stephanie's country any more, and the old corrupt government was sure to reassert itself. Nothing had changed, though Vaughn supposed the alliance between Jargono and the United for Christ would hold.

The butler, the same neat black-haired man who woke them from their long sleep, walked in and bowed, saying,

"Queen Stephanie, King Vaughn, while you were even in the midst of battle, I had received prerecorded messages informing me that both Queen Karen and King Jargono had died. Not only that, they had undetectable orbs that constantly watched them both, and as soon as they died, the recordings of their deaths were broadcast. The country, now, is in deep mourning."

The butler walked over to the wall and brought up the large screen. He turned to them. "King Jargono knew he was going to die, and he made his last wishes very clearly known to me, as I have been his faithful supporter through everything. I was aware of the enmity between you two, between your people and him and Queen Karen. I was also aware from *very* early on of both of your characters and bravery and how the contact you had with my King and Queen began to bring out in them the goodness I had always seen!"

Vaughn and Stephanie looked at each other with tears. "We're very deeply sorry . . ."

"Please, don't burden yourselves. Your last moments together, all of us have seen it for ourselves. We saw how you grieved and avenged Queen Karen's death and how you honored them." The butler took out a white handkerchief and daubed his eyes then placed it back in his pocket. "These are King Jargono and Queen Karen's last wishes in regards to you both. These wishes have already been made known to the whole country."

The screen flicked on showing Jargono and Karen sitting on the couch together, hand in hand, in the sitting room, on a lavishly patterned couch. Jargono spoke. "Our dear Countrymen, and to the United for Christ, and to our dear friends King Vaughn, and his beloved wife Queen Stephanie, our last will and testament concerning you is as follows:

"It had been my hope to bring a perfect order to a world lacking it. But as we went about such business, we became aware of powers and forces far greater than even what we commanded so easily. We discovered that these powers had deceived even us, my dear people, and had put us at great odds against King Vaughn and his people, and Queen Stephanie and her people. From that point on we had determined to correct our errors as best as we could, and to join forces with them and the United for Christ, for if we as individuals, as families, as nations and countries are to have even a glimmer of hope to even survive, we *must* join together and fight for our common good.

"King Vaughn and Queen Stephanie had been aware of such deception long before we were. In spite of us being mortal enemies, in spite of the great harm we had done to them, they risked our considerable wrath to enlighten us, to tenderly care for us, and to *forgive* us. The time of our friendship together, as short as it may have been, was the richest time of our lives.

"We have already broadcast to our nation through many actual recordings so that the truth is unquestioned, how King Vaughn came to be King and how Queen Stephanie came to be Queen. It is clear to all that though they sought no glory, glory has rightfully found them.

"We are not ignorant of the rest of the world. My Queen and I have also traveled abroad extensively. So, when we say this to you, know that it is with knowledge, not mere opinion. There are no greater people in the whole world to rule us than King Vaugh and Queen Stephanie."

"Wait. Woe, hold on a minute." Stephanie said, wiping tears from her eyes. "Vaughn, what's he saying?"

"My Queen," the butler said with so much love and respect, "I beg you to finish listening." And the butler continued the recording.

"At this point, upon hearing my words, Queen Stephanie is probably asking what I'm saying. *Faithwalker,* it *is* your time. Vaughn, long ago you swore an oath to bring righteousness and justice to this country. *Now* is your time.

"Even before you have heard this, I ordered certain people in my government to be arrested and shot for treason. All of the former people who turned your lives into a living hell are *dead.* You have, to the best of my knowledge, no living enemies left here.

"I have also informed the United for Christ of your new positions, that is, if you accept. They are eagerly awaiting word from you. Now, my Queen would like to say a few words."

"As my husband has already shown many recordings of all our history that explains better than words what I could possibly say, I will only say this. Dear Queen Stephanie, I love you."

Stephanie bowed her head into her arms that were resting on the table, and she wept. Vaughn ran his fingers through his hair, then looked up at the butler.

The butler walked up close to the screen. "There is much I am required to show you, if you will, teach you. In this archive here," he selected a folder on the screen, "is everything pertaining to our government, its dealings internally and externally. But *here,* are the instructions on how to run all of the technology that has been left for you. Some of this your Queen will understand better than you because *she* is the *faithwalker.*"

Stephanie picked her head up. "I'm always being called *faithwalker* now."

The butler bowed to her and with level, fatherly eyes, he said, "That *is* what you are, but more than a word, it's meaning pertains to an *exceptional* character, a *fortified* will, and a *love* that is all-conquering. *You* and your husband together brought my King and Queen back from the edge of self-destruction. I know much more about you two than you could ever imagine, as Jargono had been watching you from a very young age! Remember, he had been walking the Dead Forest for a long time, so he was well aware of your potentials!

"They entrusted me with knowledge of everything, because as they looked into my deepest depths, they found me honorable. I *am* the same to you, *my* King, and *my* Queen."

Vaughn looked over to his overwhelmed wife. "Do you want to take a week to think it over?"

Fire suddenly lit within her eyes and she straightened. "I'm sixteen years old now and *pregnant.* I think it's time I stopped crying so much and acting like a baby. We accept to be your new King and Queen!"

The butler smiled, and looked over to Vaugh with an amused expression because his wife had already accepted for him. Vaughn gave his special smile to his Queen. "The God of my Forefathers *and* of me has heard our cry for this country from back when we were here suffering. There will be *many* changes coming."

"You are scheduled in one hour to make your announcements to the *world.* Of course, I took certain liberties in your best interests, knowing your answers would be to accept these positions! Let me *stress,* the whole world is now watching you. Some you will find to be *fair* allies. A few may even be excellent. But most will want to cut your *throats.* I'm here to see that *doesn't* happen." The butler bowed, then took them in a steely dark-eyed gaze. "One hour, and your whole lives change forever!"

Stephanie stood up and Vaughn took her in his arms. She sighed, then looking into his eyes said, "We really are King and Queen now! But I don't feel like a Queen and I know you don't feel like a King."

Vaughn kissed her deeply. "You are my Queen."

She kissed him back with equal passion. "You are my King."

When they went to the main bedroom, they found it bare! There was a note stuck on the wall.

Faithwalker. Let your world now reflect the Goodness that is you. J. & K.

Stephanie bowed her head and the room was filled with what she had seen two years ago in a catalogue detailing Victorian Age styles. It was a time of high moral character and propriety. Even the legs on the deep mahogany tables had little skirts on them!

Then they went in to shower and prepare for their speeches.

∽

They all held very still in the Darkest Room. There was a different mood never to be felt before. There had also been rumors. The Father made his appearance without thunder or any fanfare at all. Many Alpha started quaking.

The Father spoke calmly. "We have had . . . setbacks. What I divulge to you, today, has been top secret from ancient times."

Eyes kept darting around. *What does* any *of this* mean? Was the common thought. This was all so ... what was the word? New!

"I *had* . . . a very faithful underling."

Underling? Was the common thought.

"We were together since the time of the beginning. He was ancient like me. HrorrarrAggrang."

Now it begins to make sense. Another common thought.

"He had *consumed* that bumbling *idiot* the Highest Councilor."

Cheers were the common reaction.

"The Highest Councilor possessed within himself certain *abilities* and *knowledge* crucial to our glorious future. I was quite pleased that HrorrarrAggrang now possessed it. But someone, whom the Highest Councilor was *explicitly* in charge of, maliciously and traitorously . . . ahhh, well, you all have been feeling certain *odd* quakes of late. It turns out that Jargono caused them in a plot to destroy us. Many of you know we honored him highly but he turned against us. He destroyed our wonderful game preserve."

The Alpha couldn't help it. They looked for something, *anything* to take out their anger upon. They had all been drooling in anticipation of live wild game hunting. All of that heightened expectation turned to deep frustration which turned to unbridled anger and they began assaulting each other. Some even began to *consume* others, until the Father calmly asked for quiet. Everyone ignored him.

His massive tail lashed out and knocked ever single Alpha upside down and stopped others in mid *consumption,* allowing their meal to wiggle themselves out since the consumers were afraid to move. The Father calmly spoke. "I asked for quiet. You ignored me. The very next Alpha who ignores me won't ignore anyone else again. Is that understood?"

All the Alpha shouted their support, and the Father said very calmy, "Quiet."

And everyone instantly shut up. "In the process of destroying our game preserve, Jargono also *attempted* to actually remove from existence HrorrarrAggrang."

What does that mean? Was the common thought. *Out of existence? Even the one* above *won't do* that. *Is that even possible? Alpha are eternal.*

"Let me explain to you what has happened. HrorrarrAggrang not only possessed the knowledge and ability to make another game preserve, he *also* was in charge of *our* Christ!"

The Alpha constrained themselves. There were rumors and eager anticipation.

"What that means is that our Christ is in danger of, well, being put on ice, *literally put on ice.*" That was the first time the Father's tone broke his calmness. "But we can *still* save our Christ and our *Game Preserve!*"

All the Alpha held completely still. *Can it be true? Is there hope?* Were the common demon questions.

"As you know, we *Alpha* are eternal. What *that* means is that HrorrarrAggrang is scattered across the Ethereal Corridor in tiny little pieces! *Very* tiny pieces. But all we have to do is put him back together again."

All the Alpha couldn't fathom it. The Corridor was *dangerous.* A free *consumption* zone. Others were already drooling at finding all the scraps.

"Therefore, I, as your Supreme Father, decree that until HrorrarrAggrang is put back together, no Alpha may consume another Alpha in the Ethereal Corridor. I also decree that *no one* shall consume *anything* that was HrorrarrAggrang, up to and *including* all that he had consumed!" The Father's Eye suddenly seemed to grow massive, so massive his eye loomed over every single Alpha! And they suddenly felt its pull! "Do I make myself *very* clear?"

All the Alpha yelled at the top of their Ethereal being, "Yes Supreme Father." They just wanted the presence of his Greatest Eye to *leave.*

❧

Stephanie told Vaughn in no uncertain terms that he could *not* wear his usual ranger uniform to appear before the country as King, that most people don't even know the rangers exist. But when Vaughn asked her what he *should* wear, and she had tried a number of different looks, she became flummoxed and threw down her arms in frustration. Then there was a knock at the bedroom door.

In walked the butler. "I took the liberty of gaining clothing for you, Sire, and my Queen. These things can be, well, rather daunting, but have no fear, that's why you have a well-seasoned butler." He pulled in a rack on wheels with the clothing hanging upon it. Then he went to leave.

But Stephanie asked, "Ahh, all this time we never knew your name. Ahh, are we allowed?"

The butler smiled. "My Queen, you now rule *everything*. You are *allowed* anything. But everything and anything is not always wise nor expedient. That's why Jargono went through great lengths to find an excellent butler. I had to teach him quite a bit, if I may be so bold." And he went to leave.

"Hold on," Vaughn said with a smile. "Didn't catch your name, or is knowing it not wise or expedient?"

The butler turned and bowed. "My name is hardly consequential, but it might be efficient to know it." He bowed to them again. "James, Sire, my Queen. Fifteen minutes, although your predecessors made it a point to always be late. Personally, I don't recommend it, but your predecessors didn't always follow my suggestions." And he bowed again and left.

Stephanie and Vaughn appraised each other. Vaughn had a red velvet vest underneath a black suit, with diagonally striped blue and gold tie. Stephanie had a frilly white dress overlayed with black lace that hid her pregnancy, though her extreme physical fitness carried everything quite well. Vaughn looked at her with a hurt expression, but she said, "No! Absolutely not. No ranger uniform." He hung his head.

She walked over to him and acted like she was brushing lint away, even though James was quite careful. It made Vaughn smile with a dorky kind of grin. "What," she asked.

"Nothing. I just love your care. I remember when you used to do that kind of thing when we first started together." Then he offered her his arm and she took it.

James had selected the study for the address with King Vaughn standing at a small podium that didn't block his fit physique. Lady Stephanie sat in a chair off at the diagonal, still in view but not imposing.

James spoke into a microphone in his official butler tone. "Our fellow countrymen, and nations all over the world. It is with great honor I present to you our New King and Queen, King Vaughn and Lady Stephanie."

Vaughn held out his hand and Stephanie took it and stood. When the butler saw it, he was well pleased. *How did they attain such manners? They look natural.*

They turned together and bowed to the camera together, then Vaughn held her hand to steady her as she reseated. Walking up to the podium, he smiled broadly and began his speech. "First, I want to thank our butler for his excellent taste in clothing." Vaughn held out his arms. "I simply wanted to wear my ranger uniform!" People all around the world began to laugh. "My Queen said," he bowed to her, then imitated her voice, "No! Vaughn, under no circumstances can you wear that!"

The butler smiled, shaking his head at the same time. Queen Stephanie turned red. And all the viewers noticed every single detail.

Vaughn turned serious. "But there was a good reason why I wanted to wear it. For one thing, they have a code, we call it, Rangers Word, and that means, if you ever give your word, you have to keep it. Also, once a Ranger, you're a Ranger for life. I like that combination, especially for my new position, because it means I will always keep my word to you!"

People in his country sat up straighter. In the United for Christ, they just nodded knowingly, and with wide smiles. And people all over the world had mixed reactions, with most thinking, *Oh,* that *kind of king and queen.*

"There's another reason I wanted to wear it. Down at the border, where I was stationed, anyone who saw that uniform knew there was always someone inside it you could trust to help. I, personally, brought murderers, rapists, extortioners, *drug pushers,* to justice. I *personally* killed some of them in the line of duty. Which leads me to my next point. We're *tough* bastards!"

James turned red, shifted his stance a bit, but other than that, he kept his composure. The people in his country began nodding with approval. The United for Christ people laughed hard saying, "Don't we *know* it?" And the people from the rest of the world began to feel uneasy.

"My last comment just earned me a whole extra hour with my butler on proper Kingly language."

At this point, people were hollering to anyone in their homes who wasn't in front of the TV to hurry up and set down. They were all slowly inching to the edges of their seats, unconsciously wanting to be closer to the experience through the TV.

"I think that lays a pretty good foundation for the beginning of our rule. Keep my word, be helpful, enforce the law, and be hard, so that anyone who would ever dare think to mess with us would know to regret it *before* they started!"

His look was so piercing through the camera that women swooned and men cheered, saying, "*That's a King!*" Some thought Vaughn might even be better than the last one.

"What my dear friend King Jargono, may he rest in peace, explained to you all so well through all that he broadcast, is all true. We face unprecedented times. There are still dragons and gargoyles errantly ranging the continent. Now, believe it or not, but believe it, my dear wife and Queen, along with Queen Karen, who gave her life to protect Lady Stephanie . . ." Vaughn bowed his head and paused, took a deep breath, and then resumed. "Those ladies *converted* a number of dragons to our side! They really did. In fact, those allies came and rescued Queen Stephanie. If you meet them, you'll be able to tell the difference.

"My first *word* to you all is this. I'm going to rid us of all the rest of the evil beasts. Personally, and with help." All across the world people were cheering. "Just like your former King and Queen, I also serve notice. *Stop* the illegal, mind altering drugs, stop *pushing* them. If I catch you, I'll *kill you myself!* I'll be talking with all our law enforcement, which I will be increasing substantially. We are putting an end to self-degradation and destruction. To all of you, I say this. You are all *persons.* Act like it!

"To our young women, whom we *depend* on for the life blood of our country, meaning the next generation, stop *whoring* yourselves! This isn't a new law. It's about self-respect. And to the *men,* stop *using* our women and then throwing them away, they deserve better from you!"

Everyone sat dumbfounded. From Vaughn's little home town, many were saying, "I remember way back when he talked *exactly* like that. He *means* it."

And many young women had a tear come into their eyes. Many young men looked at their shoes and admitted, "He's right."

"Both my wife and I have fought real demons inside their realm! And we have been privy to how they study us. They have many ways to weaken us, and when we are weak, we can't stand against the evils they now throw at us like dragons and gargoyles and more, much more to come!"

Many were looking at each other, stunned. "More?" they all thought.

"Most of us now live in castles, and at first, when you saw it, you laughed and joked about knights in shining armor. But there's something else that needs to be said about these Mediaeval Times which we only know from fairytales and a meager history lesson. They had a strong code of moral and ethical behavior in large part based upon their understanding that God is Good, and he will give us goodness and forgiveness if we ask. But *also* much strength to fight evil.

"I'm not talking about this phony religion this country foisted upon us. From this moment forward, *that* religion is *banned!*"

Lady Stephanie stood up glowing in rainbow colors with tears running from her cheeks. She was clapping, the butler was shaking his head but smiling too. The people couldn't believe what they heard. They thought their religion was just taking off before all that evil hit. Many more rushed to their closets, pulled up their floor boards and brought out very old bibles.

"None of the ministers or whatever you call them, shall guide in religious *anything* anymore. From now on, they have *no* funding, period. And if I catch you disobeying this order, *I'll kill you on sight, myself!*"

There was dead silence across the world. The one common thought was, *He really means it. He's given his word.*

"The reason for my harshness? Well, there are many, but predominantly, the demons have returned us to medieval times, and we need to return in integrity to there, as well! *That's how* you ended up with all those gallant stories of heroes braving hardships and *winning.*"

People were wiping away tears. They began to feel as if a weight were lifting off of their hearts that they hadn't even realized was there. They sat a little straighter. Their eyes became a little sharper. And their hearts began to fill with feelings that seemed familiar but they couldn't remember from where.

"We very much need to win, dear people. Please, we need to win and I and my Queen cannot do it without you. Because, frankly, to us, winning *is* you living good lives!"

No one had ever heard such *meaning* before. The same kind of words, yes, but *not* the way King Vaughn *meant* them.

"And lastly, some of you may have noticed I don't look like I'm reading." Vaughn lifted up the paper on the pedestal showing it to be blank. "My butler put it there for effect. As you can see, it's blank. Neither I, nor my Queen, as you will shortly see, need a speech writer, we need not to be told what to be or do, except, of course, by our butler." And Vaughn smiled at him. "Lady Stephanie, I knew I had to save the best for last. Please come up and speak to your subjects."

And King Vaughn took her hand, led her to the podium and then took her seat. She held up the blank papers, laughed, and tossed them behind her. The butler shook his head again. "Thank you, my King," and everyone immediately saw the deep love she had for him. "You look at us and you see what you think are young faces, but I assure you that we've gone through enough suffering for ten lifetimes!"

Everyone immediately rivetted on her face that had turned so serious so quickly. There was steel in her eyes they hadn't expected, though they remembered her now when she spoke to the country before. It all came back to them like remembering a vivid dream. *That's Lady Stephanie!* As if just realizing who she was. Many shook their heads, asking themselves, *What's wrong with me?*

She came out from behind the little podium and stood in front of it. She looked over to the butler, and said, "I'm sorry Mr. Butler, who doesn't think his name is consequential. I do! I love him so. But this dress isn't me." And she brought her hands slowly down from head to toe. Her hair was back in its traditional Appendaho three braids with her gold and blue ribbon in the middle of the central braid. She pulled them behind her, held out her arms, and twirled once to show off her holy dress of royal blue with golden and red Appendaho embroidery. She had adjusted the size of it to hide her pregnancy.

People across the country began saying, "It *is* her! I remember now. So much has happened since then,"

"I'm a holy woman, now. That's not a brag, just a fact. But my King, over there," and she inclined her head toward Vaughn, "rescued me from a terrible life. I had been a druggy, a *slut,* a wretched soul. My father, you may now recall as the haze falls from your minds and hearts, ended up being a half-human half-demon. I think it might have been an improvement over what he used to be to me as a child when he was just human!"

The people's mouths dropped open. Jargono had shown them much of their lives already, but this was different. The people had pains in their hearts they'd never had before.

"One night, after a few days when I had decided to stop taking drugs, after I had started to feel like a *person* again, I went to a party where my so-called *boyfriend,* the head of a drug gang, ruled. And I do mean *ruled,* just like the corrupt government we had before your first King took over.

"I went there naively wondering how I would get them to stop taking drugs, too. I was fourteen years old and he had *indoctrinated* me when I was just thirteen. I thought they were my family, because I had none. Well, my Dad abandoned us after he'd destroyed me, and my Mom worked all the time. You know how that goes. We're going to try to make the economic situation better so we *can* be families again."

No one had any idea. *She's a holy woman now? What does that* mean? *How did she do that?*

"As my husband commanded about illegal drugs, I want to make it clear, also. There will be no more government spon-sored mind-altering drugs such as Angel Seed. My husband, my King said he would kill you. Pray I don't find you first!" And right before their very eyes, Lady Stephanie spread wide her arms and a flaming column of fire appeared. Then she vanished that, and said, "Or even better, perhaps I'll just feed you to a demon! Do you think I'm joking?"

Everyone watching shook their heads at the TV sets.

"We are not living in times any longer where we can tolerate such debauchery. And don't forget, I came from such a life! As I was saying, I went to the party not knowing they had already planned to gang rape me, to fill me full of drugs so I didn't know up from down, and then brutalize me, and even to make a movie of it!"

Everyone sat still, hardly able to move as they all studied this lovely young woman and tried to wrap their heads and hearts around all the evil that assaulted her.

"I tried to run when I finally realized that even my home would be better than where I was at. But the head of the gang caught me by the throat, looked into my eyes and commanded that I would do whatever he said, 'Do you understand?,'" she spoke it like Gary had while she shook her hand to indicate how he shook her by the throat.

People's hands went to their throats and they began squirming and fidgeting, and looking away, but they couldn't look away for long. They *had to* watch Lady Stephanie, their Queen.

"Needless to say, I was terrified. I did manage to get them to let me go to the bathroom." Lady Stephanie began to brush away tears from her eyes. "I'm sorry, I'm a bit surprised by my display." But no one else was. They were wiping away tears, too.

"It's been so long ago, and we've been through so much more, I thought I was over this." She took a moment longer. "Anyway, in that bathroom I fell onto a stinking, fowl floor and prayed my heart out . . . and then . . ." She paused.

And the people said, "And then?"

She turned to King Vaughn with tears streaming down, "He stuck his head through the crack in a *second* story window! What are you doing here? I dumbly asked. I guess I'm here to answer your prayers. Dear people, it's been that way ever since!"

And everyone started cheering for King Vaughn. The common thought and saying was, "Now *that's* a King!"

"Every day King Vaughn is the answer to my prayers!" And she turned to him and opened her arms and he rose and they held each other tightly, as Lady Stephanie wept with a range of colliding emotions. King Vaughn whispered in her ear and she nodded and came back.

"Now I have a saying I often employ." And she looked back at him again. "This is the face I saw in that window that saved my life and made me a person, again." She looked deeply into the camera, and said, "I'm afraid my story isn't as unique as you think." She started to glow with rainbow colors and with sparkling tears and all the people said, "That's *definitely* her!"

"I tell you all this to let you all know, I love you. I really do know your hardships, and I really do know you are *all* persons, in *spite* of how low you may have sunk! *Now* is the time to climb up. Now. Back in the South, in the United for Christ where we fled to escape the corrupt government here, we found another corrupt government. They tried to destroy us down there, as well."

All over the world, people kept looking at each other, shaking their heads. *She said there was more suffering.*

"At one point, they locked my secret husband up!" and she looked at Vaughn. "A corrupt judge wanted to force me to marry him, and when a noble Captain married me to protect me from him because Vaughn wasn't allowed to marry in that country, that judge blackmailed me at the threat of harm to Vaughn, our adopted daughter, and his, now my people. And he *forced* me into his bed!"

At this point, people began falling onto their knees, many didn't know why, but it felt right, and their hearts seemed to be saying something much more than their minds could understand. *Are we praying to the* real *God now?*

Then Lady Stephanie smiled. "But *my* King Vaughn, rescued me again! He rescued everyone." And the colors she radiated spoke of thankfulness and love and that is *exactly* what every single soul felt and thought all across the world! If ever there was a speech, that no speech writer could write, that could so engender people to a greater goodness and respect, it was this one from Lady Stephanie.

"I told you before, and I tell you again, I *am* a holy woman now. King Vaughn is a holy man! And we, by the Grace of the Lord Jesus have won the United for Christ over to true Goodness. They *will* be a help to us here! Back home in the South, where our daughter is, and our sisters, but we came up here to help King Jargono and Queen Karen fight, there are now many holy people. The Lord had guided us to open up the knowledge that leads to a better life, a new heart and new spirit. It is our deepest desire to bring such knowledge here to everyone. But understand that this is far different from the religion you experienced here. And what I speak of can only be real in *freedom,* and *no one* has a right to come between you and the Tree of Life which is the Lord Jesus."

Is that the name of God? I think I've heard it from somewhere. The people up north thought. The people around the world had mixed feelings.

"Soon, there will be holy people up here as well. You will see it, know it for yourselves! I say to you this day, your King and I have just won a great battle against the demons who have brought such destruction upon us, but the war we face does not appear to be in our favor! However, what we just accomplished, all by the Lord's blessings, will give us time. I believe it should be a decent amount of time, as we, and your King Jargono and Queen Karen offered themselves to give you. Please don't waist it. I love you all, and please, have a good night."

And she bowed and James came forward. "Ahh, I'm the butler, my name is *James*. At first, I cringed at, well, the breach of decorum. We never belabor people with our personal feelings and lives. But I have to say, and I think I speak for all, we have all been made quite a bit richer this night. There will be many more of these personal encounters with our new King and Queen. But they have much to do to get established. I beg your patience with them."

CHAPTER 23

New Life

Marta was dressed in a look-alike Lady Stephanie holy dress, and the class recognized it. The girls were excited, saying, "Where did you get that?"

Marta beamed all kinds of colors. All the students knew why, because *all* of Heaven had watched King Vaughn and Queen Stephanie give their speeches. Spontaneous parties broke out all through Heaven, and it wasn't even the Sabbath.

Marta said, "I have a *wonderful* surprise for you!"

The little children began standing and jumping up and down, while the older kids shook their heads at their jubilance and smiled broadly.

Marta held out her hand and a beautiful young woman appeared in a really beautiful light blue dress with gold embroidery around the neck and sleeves and hem. She was golden, too, with long straight black hair, and the same color eyes as Lady Stephanie. Marta said, "*This* is Arlupo, Lady Stephanie's best friend. She made this dress for me."

Arlupo bowed to the students, many of whom had their hands to their mouths in surprise. The older students thought they recognized her and they sat with reverence. She was like a Legend.

Arlupo smiled with so much love. "I find that I can't imagine a better place in Heaven to be than right here celebrating with *you.* Teacher Marta asked me here to celebrate, but as some of you might know, my greatest honor in celebration is to teach Goodness!"

An older child whispered to little Carolyn, and she blurted out, "You *taught* Queen *Stephanie?*"

Arlupo turned serious. "We taught each other. I had knowledge in my mind she needed, but Stephie had so much knowledge of goodness in her heart that I never knew before. And *that's* my little lesson for you all up here. Most people, whether down there or even up here, think that knowledge is mostly up here." And she pointed to her head. "But that's simply not true."

The students all thought, *She* did *teach Lady Stephanie!*

"The knowledge in our hearts is more than *just* feelings. It's feelings with a whole lot of *meaning.*" And when Arlupo said the word, *meaning,* all the children felt something greater than themselves enter straight into their hearts.

Arlupo smiled and continued. "That meaning is like a whole page of story to the mind when the mind is only stuck on a single word. The Lord's goodness is *here.*" She pointed to her heart then waved to Carolyn to come up, and Arlupo sat on the grass and took her into her arms and hugged her. Carolyn simply beamed.

Arlupo continued. "In order for us to make a real difference down *there,* our minds are vastly lacking! Even up here. And our hearts need to understand much deeper, so we can feel deeper, so we can receive even greater *meaning,* and *that,* dear children is from where we gain extra strength!"

They all sat spellbound. Even Marta!

"Your teacher, a couple of lessons ago, wanted you to consider how you might be able to confront evil that over-whelms you. I tell you, it is through your heart, *only* through your heart, which has the power to strengthen your minds. Let me ask you, which is faster, your heart or your mind? Which comes faster, a feeling or a thought?"

After reflecting on the question, Ralph and Elaina both stood up. Ralph said, "We think the heart, because it can pack so many of its thoughts all together into one little feeling but the mind in the same time frame, well, only has a single thought."

Elaina said, "But when we prayed for Lady Stephanie, it seemed like the evil invaded my heart, or tried to, but Carrie loved so strongly, and I felt . . ." And then realization hit Elaina, "Well, I was just going to say I felt her *feeling of love,* but it *just* occurred to me that I just now saw the actual *meaning* of her love and how it worked inside me. I mean, her little love wasn't little *at all.* Her love *supported,* actually went inside me and like said, 'Here, this here, and that there in you has *value!* Because it's good in this way! And it was like extra strength!" Marta looked into Arlupo's eyes to see if she was on the right track, but Arlupo just smiled.

Six months pregnant came and went. The 'Breach of Truce' notice delivered to Mafferan had clearly stated there would be consequences if the unborn child *violation* wasn't dealt with. Noah and Mafferan had talked before, but not that much. After all, there were a lot of folks up here, and with all the various projects that continually came forth, it didn't always leave time to reminisce. But the knock and the *wait* to answer struck Noah as interesting.

"Well, hello there, my son. Why the wait at my door? You aren't afraid I'm drunk again, are you?" Noah smoothed out his tan shirt and checked to see that nothing was disheveled. He preferred a shepherds look, which wasn't exactly tidy in the first place, though it had been quite a long time since he'd engaged in anything like that.

Mafferan shook his head. Under normal heavenly circumstances, he would have laughed. "Father, I just came by to chat."

That raised an eyebrow. It was widely known that Mafferan's 'chats' developed into some kind of trouble that snuck up and hit you in the head before you saw it coming. Noah knew Mafferan had long ago been assigned to oversee the *lineage*, probably because, of all the saints, his suffering fitted him to be the best overseer. "Come in my son. What brings your troubled brow to *my* door? The last I checked, everything had taken a quite unexpected, really fantastic turn for the *best* down there."

Mafferan walked in and slipped off his heavenly sandals, and Noah guided him to the living room which seemed rather plain by Heavenly standards. Instead of cushy chairs, there were plain, rather unfinished wooden benches and wooden tables. It almost reminded one of the inside of a boat! Noah waved his hand and a golden orb came to light. "I know you'll be using it."

"Yes, well . . ."

This is serious. We all know how he begins when there's real trouble. "That doesn't sound good."

"Yes, well, what was it *really* like for *you* in the years before the Great Flood?"

Noah appraised him. Mafferan seemed quite direct, which was unusual for this type of call, unless there was, yet, a much deeper, hidden point to come. "What was it like? Knowing the whole world would be destroyed? And try as I may, no one would listen? What was it like?"

"Yes. For *you. And* for the world. What was it *actually* like?"

Noah released a rare heavenly sigh. He didn't like these questions. He was *here* now, and for quite a while, relatively speaking. *Why look backwards?* Nevertheless, he couldn't just boot a son out the door. Noah suddenly felt like he wanted a brandy! *I haven't had that kind of feeling since, well, since I was mortal.* "Well, you know. The calm before the storm!"

"Well, that's a bit of an understatement." And Mafferan got up to leave!

That startled Noah. This kind of behavior didn't make sense at all. "Hold on a heavenly minute, ahh, I wasn't done answering. You have to understand. *Everyone* in the world except for my closest family had done so much evil they had absolutely no feeling of goodness in them for me to effectively connect to. I mean, the goodness was in the trunk of their trees, mind you, but it was effectively locked away so that it couldn't be reached. *I* could empathize with it. *I* could feel it, and yet, I couldn't touch it, or wake them up to save their lives. Even my wife and children were touch and go for a while!"

Mafferan hadn't known that part. That made things even more dire on Earth! "So, you lived a few six hundred years before the flood. But still, that's a long time to suffer so much evil."

"Oh, it wasn't always that way in my life, my son. But you'd have to be there to see how quickly things could change. But a few good people can remarkably affect tens of thousands just by their mere presence! Their presence wasn't just contained within them, but it automatically spread out quite a ways like when the sun rises on Earth. Look, it comes up in the East and as soon as it peeks over the horizon, its light and heat travel all the way across everything in its sight. Good people are kinda like *that.*

"When I was a young lad down there, a mere one-hundred years old, I'd take a path from our village to the next one. I had to cross into a great field. As soon as I would enter, I could tell what kind of shepherds were there that day. If they were good, I felt it immediately affect my feelings. Same if they were bad. Even though I could hardly see them when I first entered the valley! If they were good, I felt good. If they weren't so good, I had to concentrate to drive away what projected from them. But for persons not so attuned, they also were affected, *however,* the good washed through them like water though a bucket with holes. But when *evil* washed through them, it was more like molasses running through the bucket. You get my point?"

"Perfectly." Mafferan looked at the orb and it became a real time geographical map of North America. In the South there were bright little lights dotting every so often across the whole land. In the North there were two *very* bright lights and the beginning of the same bright little dots.

Mafferan let out a slow sigh as to not disturb Noah, but that disturbed him more. "What's troubling you, my son? Everything down there is exceptionally, *surprisingly* very good. They've turned it all around, for now."

"You said one-hundred years old?" Noah nodded and Mafferan looked at the orb again and it went dark. When it relit, the time stamp indicated Noah minus five-hundred preflood. There was only one land continent and all across it were very many not-so-bright lights and every-so-often there were brighter lights. Mafferan drilled his eyes into Noah's. "What happened, as *you* saw it?"

Noah turned away. *Why does he* always *have to ask* these *kinds of questions?* He looked back at Mafferan, and pointed at the orb. "Those not-so-bright-lights, you know why they're glowing at all?"

"Because they're just beginning to understand goodness." That's what the initial appearance seemed like from this zoomed out view.

"*No!* They *don't* understand *any* of it! But it's like I told you with the buckets. The brighter lights are holy people, or next-to, but the dimmer lights are those where the brighter light flows *through!* You understand?"

Mafferan sighed very slowly again and Noah shifted around twice this time but he couldn't seem to get comfortable. "*Out with it, son.*"

"But how did it go from *this,* to . . ." Mafferan waved his hand in disgust and the orb moved forward five-hundred years, "*this?*"

Noah ran his hand through his heavenly white hair. "When the brighter lights, which were far fewer, were taken away from the Earth, then everything turned very dark, *very fast.*"

♋

Jean couldn't believe when Stephanie popped in to the store's back dining room, and she was *pregnant, very* pregnant! It's not that she didn't know. She had heard about it, and from the TV she *looked* it, but to actually see for herself felt so different. But Stephanie was also dressed merely in a brown peasant dress, not some queenly attire! And her beautiful wavey red hair brushed to perfection flowed freely with no braids at all. It made Jean self-conscious about her own blond hair only put into a simple pony tail and her own peasant dress though it was tan and not brown. She quickly smoothed her dress and ran her hands over her head to make sure any fly-away hair was mashed down.

Puppy, who was now, far from a puppy, took two running leaps off the wooden floor and both paws landed into Stephanie's breast. She had braced herself for the impact and rubbed him all through his ears.

"Puppy, *sit.*" And Puppy sat. Little Lana, in her usual pink dress, looked like she grew a whole inch, and her light

410

brown hair was now midway down her back, and she ran into Stephanie, next. Stephanie couldn't help the tears as she kissed Lana's head. With the passing of Jargono there was no more threat to their lives and it showed dramatically in their abundant happiness.

Jean beckoned Stephanie to sit in her usual spot at the simple dining room table. Stephanie looked around and sighed because of the comforting familiarity of home. Even though the old fading cream-colored walls still needed painting, and the small holes in the walls were exactly the same as before, along with the table and wobbly chairs and uneven floor boards, Stephanie couldn't help the love she felt for this store. Originally, it was *her* store she bought with part of the fortune Arlupo had left her. But then she turned around and gave the whole store to Jean, along with enough money to ensure a year to get on her feet.

Jean saw Stephie deep in thought, and said to Lana, "You can't treat Stephanie like you used to. She's a real live *Queen,* now."

Stephanie frowned. "Well, as your *Queen,* I give you all your first order."

Lana was all ears as she climbed onto Stephanie's lap to look closely into her eyes.

In a very serious tone, Lady Stephanie said, "I order you all, *including* Puppy," the doggie barked thrice, "to treat me just the *same* as you always did!"

Lana had her little hands on Stephanie's cheeks and looked into her eyes, then after a bit, she kissed Stephanie on both sides. "I love you. We *all* do." And she threw out her little hands to emphasize the word, *all,* and Puppy agreed with two barks.

Then, a surprise. From the back room *Spot* came out sleepy-eyed, stretched his back legs, then bounded to Stephanie. "Oh, *Spot*." Now there were tears. She held him by the jowls, saying, "This is the hero doggie that saved all our lives so *many* times. I've missed you *so* much." Lady Stephanie didn't even try to avoid the face washing. "But how did you end up way up *here?*"

Spot barked *four* times and Little Lana grabbed Stephanie's cheeks again. "He said, since our countries are friends now, he had nothing to *do*! So he came to live with us."

Spot barked twice. Then he barked a long roof. Lana said, "He wants to know how Vaughn is." Spot barked twice, then another quick bark. "He said he heard Vaughn was a King."

Stephanie rubbed his ears, again. "Yes Spot. He's a real King, and he's doing quite well but he misses you."

Then Lady Stephanie hugged Lana again then set her down and turned to Jean. Stephanie patted her tummy and then looked into her eyes, and smiled. Jean beamed. "I'm so happy for you. God knows, if anyone deserves the blessings coming to them, it's you."

Lana was leaning on Stephanie and placed her hand on her tummy then kissed it and Stephanie's tummy glowed. Lana said, "Oh! Yip, I'm your *sister*."

"His name is Michael," Stephanie said. "He told me!"

But Lana turned the surprise around, saying, "I know. He told me, too!"

Jean went to the kitchen to prepare food and Lana set about showing all the different tricks she taught Puppy and Spot. Jean hollered from the kitchen. "You won't *believe* how well the store is doing now. We've grown quite wealthy. I hired a *tutor* to teach Lana because I *hate* the school. Are you going to change education? I think we need all *new* teachers because they haven't changed *at all*"

Stephanie suddenly grew dark, waved her hand, a small orb appeared, she sent her mental commands, then waved the orb gone. "All fixed!" she said. "Thank you so much for bringing that to our attention. We've had *so* much to do."

Jean brought Stephanie's favorite beef casserole loaded onto her plate with homemade bread and she was delighted. Even though she now ate like a Queen, eating food prepared with such special love wasn't to be compared to. It reminded Stephanie of her and Vaughn eating her real mother's beef stew the day after she died but had been left in the refrigerator. Jean's meal brought back sharply all the love and sacrifice they shared together, a good bit of it right here.

Then Stephanie gazed deeply at them. *Oh God, they're so happy. Maybe I shouldn't ask.* After a bit more consideration, she decided. *No, I don't have the right to disrupt their happy lives.*

Lana stared deeply into Stephanie. "Mommy, Stephie doesn't want to ask us!"

Stephanie frowned and shook her head. "You're not supposed to blurt out other people's private thoughts, Lana." She needed to understand this.

Lana had never been corrected like this from her big sister and she hung her head, not knowing what to say. But then she couldn't help it. "But you need us. We *have to* go!" And then she touched Stephanie's tummy, again. "Michael just invited us!"

Jean looked at Stephanie understanding very clearly. "Stephie. You may be Queen, and married to the *best* husband *ever*, but you *do* need us with you! You do!"

"But . . ."

"That's my girl." And Jean stood up and opened her arms and Stephanie rushed into them with a sniffle. Jean patted and rubbed her back and little Lana hugged her leg tightly. "Always a *but*, but it's *our* choice. That is if you want to invite us."

Stephanie's heart ached to do so. *Jean is right. I do need them, even little Lana and Puppy and Spot.* Spot barked and Stephanie snuck a peek at him over Jean's shoulder. *You too?* Spot barked again!

"*Queen* Stephanie, oh my, but deep inside, you *still* need a mother. I know we're not . . ."

Stephanie cut her off. "Don't say that. Even though my Mom started to come back to herself, you gave me *so much love and care*. You *are* my Mom." And Stephanie reached down and pinched Lana's cheek. "And we're *sisters*. Wait till you meet your *other* sisters. They have *stories* to tell!"

Lana started running around. "*Stories, stories* . . .and I'm a *Princess,* too."

Jean said, "Then it's settled." She backed up and touched Stephanie's tummy. "When?"

"Maybe another month. Michael hasn't told me!" And they laughed.

Lana said, "I helped Mommy 'dilver' *three* babies!"

"Hush Lana. Stephanie's a Queen, now."

But Queen Stephanie looked seriously to her. "I didn't know you knew how."

"When I was married before, well, before you know who, I helped out in a hospital and they taught me. Up here they don't have any hospital close by, and one of my customers got the call that his wife went into hard labor. So I rushed over with him . . ."

Lana blurted out, "I went with Mommy. I *had* to!"

"And that started everything. People began calling for me to help bring new life into the world. I actually love it."

"Actually, Jean. I really *do* need you both. Please sit. I have so much to explain."

And Lady Stephanie told them all they had gone through to protect little Michael while both Jean and Lana sat completely silent, wiping away their tears. "You died *again?*" Little Lana whispered. "And Michael?"

But Stephanie shook her head. "Not exactly, this time. We were about to die, but King Vaughn laid his special Staff the Lord God gave him across our body. To get rid of the poison, the Staff sucked us all in, then put me and Michael back. We were alive inside the Staff!"

Little Lana's eyes were wide. She couldn't imagine it. Then Stephanie explained about how they had stolen genetic material from her, about the gargoyle they made from her, and the antichrist to come.

Both Jean and Lana shook their heads. Lana whispered, "I told you, you needed us. Don't worry. I won't let anyone hurt little Michael!" The way she said it seemed remarkable.

"What about your store?"

Jean smiled. "Carrie, a girl I had to hire after you left. She's quite capable. I've been considering making her a full partner, fifty-fifty. Everything will be fine. I'll go call her."

Lana put her hands on Stephanie's tummy, again. "Don't worry little Michael. I won't let them hurt you!" Michael glowed in response, and it made Lana glow, so she squealed in delight, then whispered. "He said he loves me."

Stephanie felt suddenly tired and Jean told her that her old room was just as she left it. So she cleaned up, and went to bed. The same bed with the same lumps, far from uncomfortable, was very comforting. Stephanie felt like she could be a child again, though by the time Stephanie got with Jean, she had already been through so much. Still, to be lying there in her old bed seemed precious and she drifted off into peaceful sleep.

It didn't come all at once. It only started as a grayness in the sky, until it filled the *whole* sky, until it turned very dark, then *very* black, and then the *deepest* black. But the transition made it less shocking and the light within Stephanie had a greater light within it and the darkness couldn't approach.

Then pains Stephanie had never known went through her and the darkness inched closer. With every pain it inched closer, until Stephanie woke up screaming which brought

Lana and Jean, and Puppy and Spot bursting into her room. They all climbed onto the bed.

Stephanie was soaking wet and Jean brought her a towel. She didn't want to tell anyone but Lana said, "You *have to tell!*" And she kept persisting until Stephanie finally gave in.

After Stephanie described it all, Jean had her hand to her mouth in fret. "What does it *mean?*"

But Lana pushed Stephanie back down into her pillow. "You have to go back to sleep to finish!" Stephanie had tears in her eyes. She remembered when little Lana had bit Jargono, and other things she'd said that *always* came true, like when the Earth demons attacked her and shredded her dress. But Stephanie didn't want to go back to sleep, so Lana said, "Don't worry Mommy, *I'll* stay with her." And she ran out of the room. When she came back, she was washed up and in her pink jammies, and she climbed into bed next to Stephanie.

"I don't know, Lana. Not this time." *I can't have her around a dream like* that.

But Lana started to cry. "Then you won't sleep."

Jean said, "She'll sleep sometime. It was just a bad dream."

But Lana scolded her mother! "It's *not!* It's *not* just a bad dream. It's what *is!*"

She wouldn't move! She grabbed hold of Stephanie by the tummy and Michael glowed, again, and Lana held on as tight as she could and kept crying until Stephanie said, "OK. I just don't like you around bad dreams."

But little Lana said, "Oh, it's nothing now. I used to be *scared*. But not anymore!"

Jean was surprised. "Lana, how long have you been having bad dreams?"

Lana laughed! "Oh, that started right before that bad man came. I have them *almost* every night!" Then she crawled up to Stephanie's head and began to pat it. "It's OK Stephie. We're *sisters!* I'm here for you!"

Amazed, Jean kissed them both on their foreheads, turned out the light, and left. But she left the door open.

Stephanie slept well into the night a peaceful refreshing sleep. Lana had kept stroking her head and Stephanie couldn't resist. But just before dawn, instead of the sun rising, the Blackness came and blotted out all light. Stephanie then looked upon the Earth as if far away and the whole globe was covered with that same Blackness. "The truce is broken, the Earth is *ours*." Then Stephanie was in hard labor, and every pain brought the darkness closer. Ever blacker hands reached out to catch the child when it came forth. Stephanie struggled to wake but she couldn't.

Somewhere, a little girl's voice said, "It's OK, it's OK, finish the dream!"

Suddenly King Vaughn stood with his Staff planted between the black hands and their emerging son, but as long as the Staff was there, she couldn't give birth, and she *had to* give birth *now!* Stephanie awoke with a fright and grabbed for Michael, but she wasn't giving birth. No signs at all of labor. She eased back into the pillow and Lana, who apparently had been awake, ran and got her Mommy and they sat down to hear the rest of the dream.

All Jean could say was, "The Ethereal you said has been so quiet. It's like the calm before the storm."

Stephanie looked into the eyes of little Lana, now only a six-year-old child. Lana sighed. She tried a lot of times not to tell bad news, but she never could help it. She held little Michael and cried, then she blurted out, "It *means,* you can't have little Michael *here.*"

Stephanie didn't like the meaning she picked out of the word, *here.* "I'll have Michael at the palace, Lana."

But she picked up her head and screamed! "*No.* It can't be *here.*" And she threw her arms out wide.

Jean asked, "You mean in this country?"

Lana tried to understand what a country was. She remembered Teacher showed her a round ball called a globe and that countries were all over it. Lana looked up. "No. The globe!"

Stephanie began to ball from the crushing weight of Lana's words. She was going to bring expectant holy mothers to the palace. Oh, it would be such a joyous palace, she had thought. *But now what do I do? Is it just* my *child? I can't let them risk coming, now.*

"Don't cry, Stephie," Lana said, patting her head.

Vaughn showed up in the doorway, his ring was glowing brightly. It seemed like a long time ago when that last happened. "Hey, sprout!" It was Stephie's pet name for little Lana.

"King *Vaughn!*" and she bounded off the bed into his arms and he picked her up.

Lana said, "Stephie, he'll know what to do. Don't cry. He *always* knows."

Vaughn sat down on the bed about to pat Stephanie's head but got hit in the side and knocked over by . . . "*SPOT!* How . . ." Then Puppy hit, a seemingly full gown golden lab.

Lana said, "He ran out of work so he came here. We're *all* gonna come *there*. Except . . ." She started to cry.

"Hey Sprout, would you hold something very special for me?" She picked up her head and nodded. Vaughn reached out his hand and his Staff appeared.

Her eyes went wide. "That's *it!* That's *it*. From your dream." And Lana began pulling her sister to roll over, until she did.

"I can't," Stephanie said, and turned back over. "I just can't."

Vaughn ran his hand down her head and petted it. He looked at Jean and she motioned for everyone to leave to the little dining room. After Jean told him everything with Sprout interjecting, Vaughn sat there holding his peace. He had given Lana his Staff to play with, but all she kept doing was balancing it on its foot and reaching up as high as she could and running her hands back down.

Vaughn said, "It could be a trick sent by the demons. They can do that."

But Lana simply said, "No." And Vaughn squinted at her. He wanted to brush off what she said, but he couldn't.

"I'll be *back.*"

Vaughn stood on the rainbow walkway where he had stood before when God Himself came and spoke to him. No one was there, now, not a heavenly soul. He called his Staff to him and it came even up there!

"Well, since there's no door to knock on," he raised the Staff up and slammed its foot back down and great thunder roared out from that place. When no one answered, he raised his Staff again, but Mafferan appeared beside him.

"No need. We *all* heard you the first time. Gave us all quite a *start!* Haven't had that much ruckus up her in, ahh, well, an *extremely* long time."

Vaughn described Stephanie's dream and Lana's interpretation and Mafferan said, "The child is correct." That was it!

"And you don't see a problem with *that?*"

"I see a lot of problems."

Vaughn sighed and leaned on his Staff. "I swore an holy oath *that* child would be born and be well. My forefathers came and blessed Stephanie and our *children.* What do you have to say about *that?*"

"You are correct!"

"Don't you see a little conflict there?"

"No, I see a lot of conflict, but we've all been told by the Lord God, Himself, not to interfere. You shouldn't even be up here, asking!"

Vaughn grew dark, and waives of black power began floating from him. Way in the distance he could hear crashes and wondered about it. Mafferan gave him his answer, "If you don't tone it down a bit, someone's going to come and throw you out. You're wrecking things!"

"God *never* told me *I* shouldn't be here! Nor that *I* couldn't *ask.*" He raised his Staff again, and slammed it down harder with his last word! Mafferan fell over! Heavenly abodes shook apart! And another man appeared whom looked familiar but Vaughn had never met.

"I've got it from here, Mafferan. It's a *family* matter!"

Mafferan shook his head. "Oh, I'm not leaving for this one! I think we all should wager!" And a golden orb appeared and Mafferan did something within it, then shook his head.

The man turned to Vaughn. "I've often heard you call my name, so here I am. I'm your forefather, Jacob!"

Vaughn eyed him. *This one is crafty, maybe even more so than Mafferan.*

"True, my boy!" Mafferan said, and they both glared at him, but he shrugged.

Vaughn repeated to Jacob the same things he told Mafferan *except,* to Jacob, he said, "*Your* father blessed us!"

Jacob simply said, "Correct."

And Vaughn slammed down his Staff *again,* even harder. Between that and the waves of black energy that were tearing more heavenly things up further away, many saints began to appear in bleachers they created just bit up the walkway from where they were at! There even seemed to be bowls of heavenly olives being passed around!

Vaughn shook his head. "This may seem amusing to you folks, since you're all way up *here,*" and Vaughn slammed it down extra hard. The bleachers were torn apart, the bowls of olives spilled out and dropped *somewhere.* "But I think it's not so funny down there, *especially* since it involves *your* future up *here!*" And he went to slam the Staff, yet again, but Jacob caught hold of it!

"My boy, you just can't go around up here acting like that."

Vaughn narrowed his eyes at him! "*Who* gave me this Staff?"

The saints had rebuilt the stands sturdier than before. They all looked at each other. No one seemed to know! Jacob said, "We *heard* you found it."

Vaughn shook his head. "The Lord God in Heaven," and Heaven shook when he said it, "and on Earth, even the Lord Jesus who is yet to return, gave to *me* this Staff to wield as I see fit!"

Jacob shook his head with fatherly correction. "There's a bit of misunderstanding there. As the *Lord* sees fit." But Heaven didn't shake when he said it. "You read where Moses used that very same Staff when he *shouldn't* have, and he was punished for it."

Vaughn narrowed his eyes at Jacob again. "That was because the Lord had *told* him how to bring forth the water from the rock the second time and it *wasn't* with the Staff. As of now, the Lord hasn't told me how to do *anything* with it. He's left it up to *me.*" And he raised the Staff again and Jacob caught it again. Everyone in the bleachers, which had now grown extensively, began to whisper to each other.

Vaughn pointed down below. "Right now, my *wife,* my *Queen,* is in mortal grief because we're going to be attacked from *below,* and you all sit up *here,*" and he yanked his Staff from Jacob's hand, and he shouldered Jacob out of the way, and slammed yet even harder! The bleachers fell apart again and olives rolled everywhere, "*doing nothing, offering nothing.*"

Jacob became serious. "We all told you, we're not allowed to interfere by the Lord's command. Do think you can *bully* us? Slam that Staff one more time, and I'll have to take it from you!"

Vaughn took them all in his stare, and asked them all. They all felt it pierce their heavenly souls. "What were the *exact* words the Lord spoke? Did He say no interreference at *all,* or just down there?" Vaughn raised his Staff again but didn't slam it down. He held it up, waiting.

Everyone looked at each other. They all thought the Lord meant nowhere, everywhere, but no one could seem to recall the Lord's *exact* words. Sometimes it was like that. Anyway, "What's the *difference?*" Jacob asked, obviously getting irritated at this impertinent *mortal boy.*

And Vaughn glared into his forefather's eyes, and said, "Because I'm . . . up . . . *here.*" And he slammed the Staff down, yet *again,* and everything fell apart again but *this time* they couldn't seem to rebuild, nor produce more olives! Father Jacob grabbed the Staff, and Mafferan said, "The boy has a point!"

But it was too late. Jacob, with his considerable strength, he wasn't called *Israel* for nothing, jerked hard upon the Staff, but instead of trying to match him strength for strength, Vaughn had determined he had a better chance going wit for wit. When Jacob tugged, Vaughn went with it, hitting his head right into Jacob and knocking him over!

"Sorry, you tugged me right into you!"

Jacob stood up, shaking his head. He had a heavenly welt forming on his forehead! He felt it, and said, "That's odd."

Jacob walked up, grabbed the Staff and twisted it sharply to rend it from Vaughn.

But the *boy* cartwheeled with the twist but his knee accidently hit Jacob in the head again, knocking him over, again. "Sorry, you're *really* strong." The heavenly host began to laugh, which only made Jacob more determined. He had a reputation to protect! He grabbed the Staff, twisted it sideways a half twist, and while he fell backwards, he shot his feet out, and tossed Vaughn over his head. "Have a nice trip back to Earth!"

Except Vaughn never let go! He held on, fell over the edge of the walkway, his feet hit its underside, and he sprung back faster than he went over! He zipped back over Jacob's head who also refused to let the Staff go, and Vaughn came to a stand where he had been right before Jacob tossed him. But Vaughn immediately went into the same move Jacob did, except Vaughn also twisted his body which tore the Staff from Jacob's hand. Vaughn's forefather fell over, and for some reason, he couldn't pop back!

Everyone suddenly realized the seriousness of this! Mafferan said, "My boy, we're not allowed to interfere down *there!* And he's lost his privilege already because he's heading down *there!*"

But Vaughn said, "Well, it's a *long* way down! What happens when he *lands?*"

Everyone shrugged. No one ever disobeyed. No one ever expected to be *tossed over!* Mafferan spoke with seriousness. "Nothing Good."

Vaughn caught his meaning and popped away and caught Father Jacob in free fall. "Are you going to bless my soul?"

"What are you talking about? You've already been thoroughly blessed. Please, take me back. I'm not supposed to be down *here!*"

"Think about how you felt when you wrestled that holy angel when *you* were just a man like me, well, a little older, a little *rusty.* Weren't you trying to save *your* wives and children? *How* hard were you determined to *fight?*" The answer had just come to Vaughn as he spoke the question!

Jacob and Vaughn fell through Earthly sky clouds and he could see the Earth coming up fast. Vaughn said, "Don't worry, I won't let you crash to Earth. I'll pop us down there safely. I'm tired of you *do-nothing* folks up *there.* I think you need to be down *here!*"

But landing safely wasn't the point, and Vaughn knew it. Jacob cried out, "What do you want?"

"The *same* thing you wanted!"

"Alright! Take me back. I can't do anything down *here.*"

"Give me your *word,* upon the name of the Lord!"

"As the Lord Jesus is witness to all, I will bless you with what you need to save your wife and child!" And Vaughn brought him back to the walkway. Jacob turned to him and now wore a glistening white robe. He held a glowing hand out over Vaughn's head. "The answer is now within you're understanding!" And Jacob vanished!

Everyone in the haphazardly patched together bleachers tried to determine who won the bet. Arguing began to break out, until Mafferan waved his hand and sent them all packing, so to speak. He turned to Vaughn. "It's really like it's always been with you and Stephanie. The answer is within you. And for this one, it's within *all* of you!" And he vanished, too.

Vaugh popped back to his wife who rolled over immediately. Jean and Lana and the dogs came running in, too, but it was the way they all looked at Vaughn. "What?"

Stephanie sat up in the bed and touched him, "Wow! Where have you been?"

Vaughn shrugged. "Just wrestling someone."

Little Lana said, "You're glowing all over, we can hardly *see* you."

But Spot had no trouble finding and licking his face and the glow subsided. After Vaughn told the story, the dogs kept dancing around. Everyone else sat on the bed dumbfounded, and Stephanie stood up and looked him in the eye. "You went all the way into *Heaven* for me? To challenge *everyone* up *there*, for me?"

"I've already went into hell for you, so I figured that was the next logical place!"

Stephanie threw her arms around him and hugged as tightly as she could and kissed his neck. She didn't say anything, because, *There are no words to express appreciation for such love! I am so blessed.*

Vaughn said. "We still don't know, though, what to do, only that there *is* an answer."

Lana asked, "Is that hope?"

And everyone said, "Yes, that's hope."

CHAPTER 24

Pro Life, Nothing Else

Arlupo let Carolyn go back to the other children but then she walked up close to the front of them. "What is the battle between good and evil, really?"

All the students looked at each other. There were so many different ways to answer the question.

Arlupo caught them all in her loving gaze. "Why are there so many different ways to answer?"

Sarah said, "Because you could mean . . ."

"I could mean?" Arlupo asked.

Sarah thought for a moment. "Because, to me, the battle between good and evil could mean a lot of different things." And the all the rest of the students nodded.

But this time, in response to Sarah's answer, Arlupo raised her eyebrows then squinted an eye at them all, indicating they should think about what they had just said, and Arlupo asked, again, "What is the battle between good and evil, really?"

Aaron hit his hand to his forehead. "Ahh, a little dense up here. We just answered the question without even realizing it. The battle between good and evil is between *meaning,* a lot of different meaning! The meaning of goodness and all the twisted, corrupted meanings evil challenges us with. Even the force evil uses comes from their meaning, just like the *faithwalker's* abilities that she uses comes from the meaning of Goodness allowing her to walk *everywhere*! The *faithwalker* walks by *meaning* with meaning!"

All the children instantly knew this was *exactly* correct.

Arlupo nodded so slowly, as if recalling something - the first time she had discussed with Stephie what a faithwalker is. Arlupo said, "All of us, at *all* times have meaning in our hearts. When our minds don't understand that treasure, that's what good meaning is, our treasure, then at the least, it goes unappreciated. At worst, we lose it! We lose it either by confusing ourselves, or evil so easily steals it a way, or twists it, because our mind and heart are not *one!* In order for our mind and heart to be *one,* we *must* have our mind to understand our heart and our heart to understand our mind, and in goodness they need to agree. *That* is the *only* way we can love the Lord our God with *all* our hearts, minds, souls, and strength! That's your last lesson, my dear children, for this season. May God bless you all, and give you *your* part to be against the evil to come!"

Vaughn sat alone into the wee hours of the night on a plush flowery printed Victorian style couch with three lobes to its back and a sort of crown worked into the dark wood over the middle section. He sat at the very end, not under the crown. Stephanie had gone through the whole castle and redecorated, otherwise the memory of Jargono and Karen would have been a constant pain in their hearts.

After a week of officially being King and Queen, the feeling had just come to Vaughn that this is, indeed, his home now, so he removed his brown ranger shirt to lounge in just his black tee and he simply tossed his uniform to the other end of the couch. After all, he *is* the King now, and he can do what he wants. Even so, he usually kept himself quite neat until he went to bed, that's the way his old farmer friend had lived, may he rest in peace, and Vaughn had decided he loved the meaning of the lifestyle. And in a way, it kept their friendship alive in his heart, a way to honor the sacrifice the old man made to try to keep Glen from catching Vaughn and killing him. But tonight something seemed to change in Vaughn as he tried to rub the frustration from his face and keep from falling asleep. *The answer is within me, in all of us. Then* where *in me?* Vaughn sighed. All the oaths, all the blessings in the world, in *every* world didn't matter if he didn't or couldn't find them and put them into action.

Spot came out of their bedroom where he kept watch over Lady Stephanie. He stretched his back legs, then went into the adjoining study and put his head on Vaughn's lap. He always knew when his master needed to pat his head and rub his ears. "Nowhere on Earth, Spot. *Nowhere.* That's the meaning. Little Michael can't be born *anywhere* on Earth. Then I thought about the Ethereal but that's *ridiculous.* He can't be born in Heaven, either."

Vaughn waved his hand and the blue orb appeared. He remembered hearing stories of the Bermuda Triangle so he pulled up the reported area, zoomed in, but all there was, was ocean, except for some odd currents converging.

Mafferan popped in, looked at the crown in the center of the couch, then sat next to Vaughn on the couch's edge, trying not to own the honor. "Up late? And out of uniform?"

Vaughn ignored his latter comment. "Would you sleep if *your* child was in danger like mine is?" It wasn't exactly a nice reply.

But Mafferan met his angry stare and answered him seriously. "No. No, I wouldn't. Unfortunately, there's another problem."

But Vaughn looked *him* square in the eye. "No, there's not! There's *no other problem* until I solve *mine*."

Mafferan nodded. "Alright. I understand. He's still missing a part here and there, anyway." And Mafferan began to fade away but Vaughn leaned over and grabbed him, which normally he shouldn't have been able to do.

"You mean HrorrarrAggrang? Already?"

Mafferan looked into his eyes with sadness. "I know you can't seem to catch a break, or if you do, it's not a very long one, but yes. Their Father ordered every single Alpha to scour the Ethereal Corridor for even the tiniest of scraps of HrorrarrAggrang, and let me tell you, most of them were tiny indeed. Jargono knew what he was doing when he did what he did. Anything short of that, we wouldn't be having this conversation now because the timeline to world doom would have been much advanced!"

"You said he's still missing parts?"

Mafferan laughed. "Well, the Father ordered that if he caught *anyone* consuming even the smallest piece of Hrorrar-rAggrang, he'd consume them, even if just any piece of those he'd consumed. He was to be put back together *exactly* as he was, which is possible because he's Ethereal. All those tiny little parts are actually Alpha-alive. But somehow, as hard as they scoured the area, there still seemed to be a bit missing. But the point is, there's enough of HrorrarrAggrang back together again that they took their *project* off of literal *ice,* and it's growing again. That much I got from *your* spy program!" And Mafferan leaned his head toward the orb.

Vaughn shook his head. "I should have been following all that closely, myself. Thanks for eavesdropping. And you have no clue where this *antichrist* is being grown, nor how long to maturity?"

Mafferan shook his head. "He's somewhere in there . . . somewhere." And the orb turned into a giant globe which Mafferan expended to fill almost the whole room, floating just a few inches free from the floor. "My expectation is that *somewhere* in or on this globe is an *extremely* tiny but *extremely* black dot! But I doubt you'll find it because I'm sure they've masked it. But what else can you do?" And Mafferan disappeared.

Vaughn held out his hand and his Holy King James Bible appeared. He reviewed the Book of Daniel and Revelations and any other spot which came close to insinuating the devil's offspring, but nothing really indicated where on Earth he should look.

He waved his hand and the giant globe began to slowly rotate, but it wasn't long before he stopped. *This is ridiculous. My eyes can't do this.* He left his study and went into the adjoining dining room, which of course was also now Victorian. The dining table was a medium brown rectangular walnut, with a heavy ornately carved central base and subtle contours to its edges which were also carved with a modest edging. The goal seemed to be to glorify the wood grain which it accomplished quite well. The matching chairs had deep flowery printed cushions at the seat and back and the wooden arms had a beautiful curve to them that ended in a swirl. Vaughn sat at the end closest to the screen, waved his hand, and it turned on.

James came over, which surprised Vaughn that he was still up. "Have you slept at all, Sire?" Vaughn just shook his head. "May I be of assistance in *any* way?"

Vaughn pulled up an image of the globe on the screen and made the image spin slowly. "I have to search the entire Earth for a teeny tiny extremely black dot of evil that is most likely camouflaged. Got any suggestions?"

James walked over beside him. "As a matter of fact, Sire, I do! I'm not just a butler. Jargono never would have hired just a butler. I helped him build *this!* The whole orb-computer interface along with Jargono's own powers that he inserted. What you need to run are these programs right here." He took a laser pointer off of a small knickknack table and pointed it at several different buttons and folders. "Now, Sire, you must do the rest. It would be too cumbersome for me with this little physical tool."

And James instructed him which further files to open, drag together, and what parameters to load. "Now hit search, and wait, Sire! All energy anomalies, whether physical, spiritual, Ethereal, or anything along that spectrum that is out of the ordinary will show up. Even subtle differences that are often still there if something has been cloaked."

So Vaughn pulled up another fancy dining room chair and propped his feet up! James' eyebrows went up but he bowed, and in a certain tone that indicated Vaughn wasn't quite acting with, shall we say proper royal decorum, he said, "As you *wish*, King Vaughn." As he went to leave, he noted to himself that the former king would never have done such a thing, especially on furniture like *that!*

Vaughn cleared his throat, and said, "James," and the butler stopped in the doorway, then turned.

"Yes, Sire. Is there something else?"

And Vaughn yawned then said, "I feel like you're an exceptional part of our team now. We're fighting evil that is far greater than *anything* in all our imaginations. And I *really* appreciate your sense of manners and propriety. It's just right now, I just have to do it like this!"

James immediately realized his King knew *exactly* what he'd been thinking and was about to apologize, but Vaughn cut him off. "No need to apologize nor watch how you think. I *need* you to be *you*. That's where your value is, in being *you.*"

James smiled, stood up straighter, and said, "I shall do *exactly* as you command, Sire."

Right after that, Vaugh fell asleep with his chin into his chest, waiting for the alarm to signal the computer program was done searching.

When Stephanie finally awoke, Vaughn wasn't in bed. After washing, throwing on a brown peasant dress, she went groggily into the study without much paying attention and almost ran into a giant orb globe of the Earth! "Woe!" Then she realized her tummy protruded too much to squeeze around, but also the *faithwalker* had no idea how to put the orb back to normal. So she popped into the dining room for breakfast.

James was already there waiting for her order but Stephanie walked over to Vaughn and bent down so she could look up into his face. He was covered in a royal-red fluffy blanket. She whispered, "How long has he been this way?"

James smiled. "I covered him ninety minutes ago, but I assume he went fast asleep right after I left. So, two hours."

Stephanie reached out her hand, but James said, "I wouldn't, me Lady. If you do that, he'll wake for certain!"

Stephanie wasn't used to a butler, but she found it amusing. "James, I was just going to pop him over to the bedroom." But then the look he gave her, a sort of hurt expression, made her think. "You knew?"

He nodded slightly. "Yes, my Queen. You have a very particular look when you get ready to perform such functions!"

"I do?"

And James nodded. "But I really couldn't describe it."

Just then they heard little Lynnara. "Woe! Wow!" She had come out of her bedroom into the study and she, too, almost ran into the thing. She bounded into the dining room in pink with blue poke-a-dot jammies, her brown curls all bouncing, and began to holler, "Mommy, there's . . ."

But Stephanie and James both put fingers to their mouths and shushed her, where upon she clamped both little hands to her mouth then walked over to Vaughn. Putting her hands gently on his knee she twisted around to look up into his face. Then she whispered, "Daddy's asleep."

James was there a second later and hoisted her up in his arm with her little head even with his. He whispered, "And what would the little Princess like to eat this morning?"

She smiled, then whispered back with big eyes, "Can I have a pancake with lots of that maple stuff?"

James set her down in a chair. "As you wish, little Princess."

Lynnara whispered to Stephanie who had sat down next to her husband. "Mommy, he keeps calling me little Princess."

Just then an alarm sounded and Vaughn immediately jerked his head up and opened his eyes. He went to move but that didn't go so well, so it took him a bit to get his legs down and to stretch out the kinks. Stephanie pulled her chair closer. "Whacha doin'?"

And then Lynnara was on his other side. "Yea, whacha doin'?"

Vaugh pointed to the flashing red program. "Apparently, James helped Jargono construct all this!" Stephanie was shocked. "He's much more than a butler. He helped set this program to detect any energy variations that might clue us in on our new enemy. Mafferan popped in and told me the Alpha's more or less put back together."

Vaughn split the screen and accessed the Father's orb that the Alpha thought wasn't working, but all Vaughn did was turn it deep black. And there was HrorrarrAggrang again, sort of! His tail seemed ragged and choppy. His Great Eye was more vertical than horizontal, and his great arm seemed, well, stubby. But his awareness seemed all there as he used his orb to guide . . . Vaughn split that half of the screen into top and bottom halves and brought up the view of HrorrarrAggrang's orb.

There, in the large glass cylinder was what looked to be a full-grown infant with gray glow and blackness continually flowing in and out of it. Stephanie took Vaughn's hand and squeezed. Her tummy, for the first time ever, radiated a blackness, and the infant on screen suddenly opened deep black eyes and appeared to stare right at them!

That half of the screen suddenly went dark then flashed a warning: INTRUDER ENERGY ALERT PROGRAMED SAFTEY TERMINATION

Stephanie had goosebumps. Lynnara was silent and climbed into Vaughn's lap and hugged him tightly, and Vaughn put his arms around them both and turned exceedingly black and gold. "It's alright." He held out his hand and his Staff appeared. He pointed it at the screen and a silvery energy went from the Staff into the system. "It just needed a little upgrade! That energy will be distributed where it's needed by the program already in place. Nothing to fear anymore."

But Stephanie said, "Was there something to fear?"

And Lynnara said, "Is there Daddy? Is there?"

James came in with their breakfast. Three crispy Sunnyside eggs, toast, beef fry for Vaughn, poached eggs and toast for his Queen, and a large pancake with maple stuff for their Princess.

Vaughn waved his hand and his plate came up to where he was at, even though James had set it at his usual seat at the other end of the table. Stephanie and Lynnara both moved chairs to sit right up against him. Vaughn shoved an egg into his mouth, wiped it with a piece of toast, then waved his hand and the whole screen was filled with the Earth energy program. There was only a single energy fluctuation, but it wasn't black. Vaughn zoomed in until his wife said, "That's the Middle East." And as Vaughn zoomed in more, all their mouths opened as the whole dining room filled with bright light!

Vaughn adjusted the filters as best as he could, but the brightness was still so bright they couldn't make out any detail. Vaughn sent a telepathic message to James, the first time he'd ever done that, and James came in, surprised, saying, "Sire?"

Without even thinking what he'd done, Vaughn said, "Are you able to tone this down any more so we can see?"

"This isn't the evil you were looking for Sire. It's far to the other side of the spectrum."

"How far?" Stephanie asked.

James manipulated some controls then said, "So far that I can't get a reading!" And he made some more adjustments to at least reduce the glare.

And Stephanie pointed. "Vaughn . . . that's our mountain! I had no idea!"

Vaughn stood up and walked straight over to the screen and put his hand upon it, deep in thought. "The answer was *always* inside of us. Jacob just blessed us to have what was already there! Or maybe, he added something a little extra." He turned to Stephanie. "The Holy Mountain as it now is, where did it come from?"

"Well, from God." But Vaughn kept looking at her for more answer. "Well, from God through us. Through both our prayers." And then tears flooded Lady Stephanie's eyes, as she repeated what she recognized to be their secret code. "Through our prayers."

"And *where* are our prayers?"

"Inside of us! Oh, Vaughn. But it's still on Earth. You think . . ." But Vaughn vanished!

And reappeared at *the* Holy Mountain before the Tree of Life with his Staff in hand. Before the Tree of Life, which had now grown broader but not appreciably taller, he raised his Staff, and spoke. "As the Lord God of Abraham, Isaac, and Jacob, and of *me* has given me this Staff to judge the world by, I ask that by the power imbued in it, place your extra protection upon this holy mountain so that *no one* can enter here except those from Earth that we shall admit or invite. NO ONE else except also those from above we invite, except their powers shall be *stripped* when they arrive!"

The Staff burst into silvery glow that radiated to the perimeter and was absorbed. The Tree of Life glowed in acceptance of Vaughn's prayer and he planted the foot of his staff into the soft ground and fell on his knees before the Tree. "Lord Jesus, whose Tree this is, you *alone* are given the seven seals to unloose and no angel nor man nor *anyone* but your Father is privy to it. So *is* this Staff of Your Indignation and Your Life. No one *anywhere* can come against the power you have imbued within it. Heretofore have I *never* asked you for a sign, nor a wonder, but I ask it now. Give me a sign I am correct!"

The Tree of Life turned into a vision of itself within the Sacred Cave and then it vanished! And reappeared on the side of a mountain in the ancient land that became Israel, and the tree glowed. and a man came to kneel before it as God spoke to him. And the man's hair turned white, and the ordinary staff in his hand, the Lord God turned into the Staff of God that Vaughn now had. And the man stood up and Vaughn knew him to be Moses.

The vision turned into the same brightness that outshined the sun and the Lord spake unto Vaughn, "Ho, young man who hath sought the good Wisdom of the Ancient, who hath not regarded anyone nor anything more than the Lord," and at the mention of the *Lord*, it thundered greatly and all the people down in the valleys shook with fright, "I have seen how thou and thy wife have been afflicted sore beyond your means, and yet thou holdest faith in Me without fail. I have set an open door before thee and Lady Stephanie, whom is thy wife, thine only wife, given to thee by Me. The Staff of Life and of Mine Indignation, which I had given to Moses, give I to thee, and thou shalt judge the nations. Whomsoever thou hast mercy upon, shall I have mercy upon, and whomsoever thou judgeth, I shall judge, for I have placed Mine excellent Spirit in thee, and thou shalt not depart from it." And the brilliant glow departed from the Tree and it became as usual.

And Vaughn, having been held to stand upright during the vision, not by his own strength, now fell on his face before the Tree of Life. "Who am I, *what* am I to hear such words, to see such sights, and I am but a mortal *boy*?"

And the Lord spoke again through the Tree. "Have I not chosen you? When your forefathers had settled in the land and had a *man,* an *evil* man for their King, I raised up a *boy* in his stead to be King over them, and he did after Mine heart. Whomsoever I raise up shall stand, and whomsoever I bring down, shall not stand, whether they *be* a boy or a man. Now, return unto thy wife and do what is in thine heart, for I am with thee."

And Vaughn looked up from the ground into the Tree of Life which had become a vision again, and saw, indeed, a boy stand before a quaking army of full grown men, and a giant chased them. And the boy took a mere stone and sling, and spoke, "By the Lord God of my Fathers, Abraham, Isaac, and Jacob, thou shalt drive away the armies of Israel *no more!*" And he brought down the giant and took the giant's sword and chopped off his head.

And Vaugh stood up, took hold of the Staff of God, and returned to the very bedroom from where he had left, and when he returned, little Lynnara said, "Ohhhhhh . . ."

And Stephanie said, "Oh Vaughn!" And she went down to the bedroom floor on her knees to worship God.

"What's wrong? I'm sorry I was gone so long."

Lynnara called for Spot who came rushing in and knew what to do. He put his paws on his master's chest and began licking him in the face, and the tremendous glow around him subsided. Lady Stephanie sat back on her haunches and took hold of his other hand with pleading eyes, waiting to hear what Vaughn would tell her. Little Lynnara jumped onto their bed so she could be higher up closer to their level.

With Staff in hand, Vaughn explained everything he saw and heard, then said to his wife, "Bring all those here to our castle whom you were going to bring. Go now and gather them! Take Lynnara as your witness to all the things I just told you. Our house shall be full of *joy*! I have to return to prepare the place for them!"

Stephanie stood up gazing deeply into her husband. *He has a new presence about him. A certain authority.* But it wasn't anything oppressive to Lady Stephanie. In fact, it was comforting. So she donned her holy dress, her traditional braids and dressed little Lynnara in a miniature version, who when she saw *that,* she hugged herself, and they departed.

Once again Vaughn returned to the Tree of Life, but this time he walked away and held his Staff up high again. "Lord God, the Light through whom all Freedom is, through whom God the Father created all things for there is none better, of old you had promised this mountain would again be filled with joy, I ask you now to prepare it to receive your people!"

And Vaughn closed his eyes, held up his Staff, and a thick cloud descended. Then Vaughn pointed his Staff in front of him, and slowly turned full circle. And while the cloud yet hung over the mountain, Vaughn departed and went down into the valley below!

And when the people saw him, not with any glow, or seeming power, but just an ordinary staff in his hand, and that he was a *Jew*, for they recognized *those* people on sight, they took up stones to cast at him, and others grabbed their farm tools and they rushed him. And Vaughn took the Staff of God and slammed its foot into the ground, and the ground shook so no one could stand. And Vaughn said, "The Lord God of my fathers, Abraham, Isaac, and of Jacob, and of *me* has returned to this holy mountain to fulfill prophecy and to keep His word that he spoke to his people in Ancient times. Now, the Lord Jesus Christ, whom is the Lord of Lords, and King of Kings, saith unto thee, Put away your perpetual hatred which you have used against my people to destroy them from off the face of this Earth. Lest I return with all the judgments and more that I wrought against your forefathers. For I say this, saith the Lord God, whose breath is in us all, I will have *Peace* in my holy mountain and its surroundings." And Vaughn vanished!

And he went to each valley surrounding *the* Holy Mountain with the same message and the same result. And then he returned home to the main throne room and it was filled with people! And Vaughn leaned his staff against the throne which Jargono had made for himself but which Vaughn had rebuilt for him and Stephanie. And Lady Stephanie, his Queen, took his hand then they turned to everyone. "Vaughn, all these are holy women with child, with their husbands"

"How many?" Vaughn asked, surprised to see the giant room filled.

Queen Stephanie stood straighter, then gave a slight bow to her King. "One hundred and forty-four women with child, and one hundred and forty-four husbands, all holy, having been either baptized in the water by me or other holy people, and having received their new hearts and spirits from the Holy Ghost either under the water or sometime after."

And they all gave bows, to which Vaughn waved it all off. "We bow to our Lord, only. Welcome to our palace. But you won't be here for long! You are all chosen through us by the Lord to fulfill prophecy because the Lord shall keep his word to my forefathers."

And Vaughn looked over the souls, and *many* were from the very people, his people, the Jews, whom he had rescued from the North over a year ago. But there were also others, who had managed to escape at a later time, who Spot, having stayed behind, had led across. And there were still others of the people of the United for Christ whom, when they heard Lady Stephanie describe how to receive the Holy Ghost and a new heart and new spirt, they, too, hearkened with all their hearts, all their minds, and all their souls. Now, they were all one family.

And Vaughn took the Staff of God in his hand and leaned it forward. "The lord Jesus bless you with peace. Please, James. Our wonderful butler, he shall accommodate you."

And King Vaughn waved for them all to follow James, who would find rooms for them all, and comfort. Jean, in her simple tan peasant dress, stood yet in the hall, and when Lana, who was in a matching dress, was finally able to, she rushed into Vaughn who picked her up and twirled her around. "Sprout! You're *sprouting!*"

"No I'm not." And she put her little hand to Vaughn's cheek.

But Lady Stephanie tickled her, and said, "Oh yes, sprouting, sprouting, *sprouting!*" It was the pet name Stephanie had given her from what seemed a very long time ago. Stephanie took Lana in her arms and hugged her and her deep gray eyes peered intensely into her sister. Jean came up to Vaughn and threw her arms around him.

Jean couldn't help but have tears, being in their castle and being overwhelmed by everything. "I didn't have time to tell you before. I still remember when I tried to slam the door in your face! What would I have done without you? You're my *son!* That's what you all are to me. My son and daughter."

Then Jean turned to Stephanie. "I'm ready!" Too which Vaughn raised his eyebrows.

Little Lana said, "We're getn' bap . . . bap . . . we're goin' under the water to say Hi to God!"

Vaugh couldn't believe it. "You, too? Sprout? You *sure?*"

Stephie put her down and she became very serious and her little eyes scolded Vaughn. "Lady Stephanie *said,* No one has a right to get between us and God. So *I* said, That's good 'cause I gotta go talk with him down there!"

Vaughn squatted down. "Forgive me! You are *absolutely* right, and we'll do whatever you need us to do to help."

Lana threw her arms around his neck and kissed his cheek then held his face in her little hands and stared into his eyes. After a bit, she said, "Stephanie said the demons attacked her and tore her dress up just like I saw they would. She was bleeding and really bad. She said you saved her."

"The Lord gave me the power to do that."

Lana pointed to the Staff leaning against the throne. "I saw that, too." Then she began to glow as she looked into his eyes. "You and Stephanie are both gonna be killed, you know. But that's not for a while. But they should have left you *alone!*"

Little Lynnara came up and put her arm around Lana, "We're sisters now, too. Yea, they should have left you alone. But they won't. They can't help it!" Then she turned to Lana and said, "I saved my Mommy's life."

Little Rebecca came up on the other side of Lana and threw her arm around her, too. "I saved Lynnara's life. But it wasn't easy. It hurt *real* bad."

Lana took them both in her little arms. "I told Vaughn about Stephanie when my Mom wouldn't. But before *that*, I *bit* the bad man's hand who hurt my Mommy and Stephie!" The other two girls were *shocked!* Their little eyebrows went up, their little hands to their faces. This had to be the greatest story *ever.* And they ran over to the throne, all three climbed in, and they swapped stories and formed an unbreakable bond together as the Holy Spirit interwove their souls with unchallengeable love and respect.

In the evening when everyone had been settled, after Jean and Lana were baptized, who immediately both received the Holy Ghost right under the water, Stephanie came back to the castle and found Vaughn sitting like before, his feet propped up on a dining chair, his chin tucked down to his chest, just in his black tee shirt again, and some search program running on screen.

She waved her hand and her holy dress disappeared for the brown peasant's dress she wore ever since their escape to the South. Then she pulled up a chair and laid her head on his shoulder.

Vaughn woke up and threw his arm around her. Stephanie said, "Apparently, we're both going to be killed, but not for a while!"

Vaughn laughed. "Ahh, I see Sprout did her duty." Stephanie nodded against his shoulder. "Well, the blessing did say we would *never* be apart any longer, even in *death*. So I'm OK with that!"

"Oh Vaughn, are you *ever* going to stop making me cry?"

"I hope not, as long as they're tears like that!"

"Jean is going to deliver our child. Do you *really* think it'll be OK?"

Vaughn took both her hands and stood up. "With the help of the Lord, I've prepared a giving birth gift for you, my only love." And they vanished right into the thick cloud that was still over the holy mountain. Vaughn called his Staff to him and raised it, and the mist was blown away by a gentle wind.

Stephanie started balling at the initial sight which she recognized, and buried her head in his chest. Vaughn said, "I also invited a guest." And Stephanie felt a soft hand on her shoulder and she immediately knew who it was and spun around into each other's arms.

Arlupo petted Stephanie's head. Then she straightened her best friend, and spun her slowly around to look at all their surroundings. Arlupo said, "Your husband did a fair job, didn't he?"

Stephanie's hands were to her mouth. Over the Tree of Life now stood the sacred Lodge that had been burned down at the Appendaho village. In fact, many of the buildings and structures and even the animals were *here!* The mountain had flattened and spread out even more and Stephanie could smell flowering fruit trees and could see them in the distance. And then the rest of her people materialized.

Vaughn took Stephanie by the arm and turned her to him. "They can stay as long as you want. But *you'll* have to send them back! *No one* from *anywhere* can come here without we invite them, and *only* those from Earth we choose can live here! *And* none of those we invite to *visit* from above have *any power at all!* I'm not risking *anything* when it comes to *you,* our *child,* or those you've chosen to dwell here!"

And Vaughn held up his Staff and the whole perimeter glowed with a new silver so Queen Stephanie could be reassured! She shook her head. "This is why you glowed so much when you returned. God did *all* this through you."

"Not only that. *This* Staff comes *directly* from God. No middleman, so to speak. And *that* means that what's wrought with it, *no one* has the power to undo! *No one!* You will all be safe here."

"But Vaughn, the Alpha will . . ."

"Won't be able to see *anything!* I checked! Once you're here, they can't see you. Or *anything* that's here."

"But Vaughn, they'll still know. They'll invade . . ."

"Who was the truce between?"

Arlupo smiled and took Stephie's cheeks in her hands and went nose to nose! "Between Heaven and the Ethereal. Heaven didn't break *anything!* This is all through you two! As you both were told soooo many times," and Arlupo chuckled, "the answer is *within* you!"

Vaughn explained further. "Even little Michael *doesn't* break their damned truce, because he wasn't sent directly down from Heaven as our Lord came, but Jesus decided to make him through us, *only* through us based on all *we* had searched for directly from the Lord. In other words, *we* asked for Michael! And *we* prepared ourselves so he could be made from us the way he is made! Now if they *do* want to contest, I'll go down there and defend us myself! But they don't want me anywhere near their orbs anymore."

Stephanie's hand went to her forehead, "How stupid could we have been?"

But Vaughn also added, "And technically, this holy mountain isn't *exactly* of this Earth. But it's not Heaven, either!"

Arlupo took Stephanie by the arm, and smiled at Vaughn. "So very nice to have finally met you. I'll have to tell you the story about when Stephie went through the Tree of Life vision to save you. I thought she'd *died* when she disappeared! And when she came *back* . . . her holy dress was shredded, she was bruised, bleeding from her nose and ears, and covered in her vomit!"

Vaughn's eyes went wide, his brow wrinkled all the way to the top of his forehead as he peered at his wife. Stephanie shrugged, "Ahhhh, yea. I might have left out a few details."

Arlupo winked at him, and Vaughn kissed her on the forehead. "But Stephanie *did* tell me about *you* and how you saved her. You're even more beautiful than she described! Thank you so much."

Arlupo just gave him a little bow, saying, "King Vaughn, we all do our part. That's all we can do. Nothing so great about that," she said with a smile so sweet Vaughn could taste it in his mouth, and smell its nectar!

Stephanie said, "I think . . . she put her hand to her tummy. It was glowing very brightly. I think tomorrow morning we need everyone here."

Vaughn bowed to his Queen and disappeared.

The next morning James had roused everyone at four-thirty sharp, and had everyone fed by six-thirty sharp! And assembled in the great throne room at seven sharp. Lady Stephanie and Vaughn stood in front of the throne and she asked them, "Are you all ready?"

They all assented together, and Lady Stephanie spread her arms wide, looked over to Vaughn, and he smacked the foot of his Staff to the floor and they all disappeared . . . and reappeared on the holy mountain. Vaughn said, "No corruption is able to enter here. The people *down there* are unable to pass the protection though they tried. You can visit them, if you like, but they can't come here, not even their little children. When I went down to talk with them earlier, they tried to kill me on sight! The same thing happened in every single valley,"

Stephanie turned dark when she heard it. "Let me give you all a tour!" And off they went.

Something kept ringing in Vaughn's ear. He kept wiggling his finger in it to no avail, until finally, a great rock dropped out of the sky, hit the dome of protection, and rolled on down! At *that* point Vaughn realized the sense of humor, and that the ringing was like a doorbell! "You're invited, King Mafferan!"

And he popped beside Vaughn and threw his arm over his shoulder and they strolled, talking in low voices until Vaughn said, "You want me to invite *who?*"

Mafferan said, "It will be the best surprise for your wife *ever,* even better than what you did right here, now!"

Vaughn's eyes were wide with more than just doubt. "I'm really not sure he could even get past the protection."

"Look, the poor Alpha is about to be consumed. When HrorrarrAggrang finally got around to wondering what happened to him, he discovered he went straight to *you!* The poor Alpha has no home. But also . . ." And Mafferan paused.

But Vaughn wasn't going to play this game, so he just waited, but Mafferan was being stubborn so Vaughn finally said, "OK, *what?*"

"Even if Grinchback isn't consumed, he just doesn't have long to live!"

"OK. Why? He's Alpha."

"Because of the way the Highest Councilor *made* him. More specifically, *what* he only made him out of! It was the *only* way for him to produce the kind of Alpha he needed to befriend you!"

"But he tried to *consume* my wife and daughter."

Mafferan waved that off. "Only because *what* he had been made from hadn't settled in quite yet. Very shortly, Grinchback will simply self-destruct! He was made to be *Alpha unstable!* He wants to be here with *you,* his friend! But also, HrorrarrAggrang in no way wants to lose what Grinchback is made from. Way too much time and effort and planning went into all that from start to finish!"

Vaughn shook his head. "Alright! I'll try. But I'd better ask Stephanie first."

But Mafferan grabbed his arm. "Don't do that! You'll spoil the surprise!"

Vaughn squinted at him. "You want *me,* to invite a *demon* into our sanctuary that I went through *great lengths* to protect against *all* corruption? And you *don't* want me to ask my *wife?*"

"That's correct!"

"You seem to be enjoying this. Are you going to stand *exactly* between me and my wife when I do this?"

"No, oh no, no, no. I would be a distraction. This is actually *all* about your wife. It doesn't really concern you!"

Vaughn rubbed his face, ran his fingers through his hair, rubbed his ring and waited. Moments later, a very concerned Stephanie popped beside him, blazing, ready for a fight, saying, "I *knew* all this was too good to be . . . where's the danger?"

Vaughn shook his head. Mafferan was *gone!* He'd wandered off somewhere! "OK. I'm sorry. I needed to get you here quickly because Mafferan just told me . . ."

"He was just here?"

"Yes, but he said he didn't want to be a distraction."

Stephanie narrowed her eyes at Vaughn because he'd just scared her almost to *death,* so she decided to bypass her husband's lengthy explanations. Then her eyes went wide and she said, "*What? You want to invite a* demon HERE?"

Vaughn stepped back a bit. Scratched the side of his head and then that *stupid* ringing was in his ear again, and he knew it was Mafferan telling him to bring Grinchback before it was too late. Sighing, Vaughn looked at his *very* pregnant wife, and said, "I have to play this by ear!" He raised his Staff and called out, "Grinchback, my friend, you're invited!"

And to *everyone's* surprise - because when they saw Lady Stephanie disappear so abruptly, they knew there was trouble, so they came back- now floating before everyone was the *demon* Stephanie's *husband* invited to the *birth* of their *child,* the child that everyone, almost, wanted to destroy!

Stephane grew dark, and looking at her husband, her power building rather quickly, she said, "Have you lost your *mind?*"

But Grinchback spoke, "I don't have long, Mistress. Mafferan explained it all to me. So I understand why I feel this way. Still, it seems I *do* possess *something* that is me, *Grinchback*, I suppose. And I just wanted to say, it was an honor working with . . ." and Grinchback never got to finish his thought . . . or was it even *his* thought? From the top of his bulbous head, splitting right through the middle of his Great Eye, he spilt open!

And a woman floated out and set two feet on the holy ground . . . and Stephane was about to faint but Jean held her up. "Stephanie," the woman said, and opened her arms wide!

And Stephanie squealed in pain through her tears, but joy, also, as she ran into the woman's arms, crying, "Mother!"

After that, another woman came forth, then another, and another, and another, until, save but a few, the whole of Queen Stephanie's matriarchal lineage stood around her, and Lady Stephanie understood who they all were. But one stood way at the back of all who surrounded her, and Stephanie eased herself through all the hands and hugs and kisses, to which she also offered generously, to stand before a woman of middle Earth age, with red and graying hair who looked *very* much like Stephanie did.

And Lady Stephanie, now dressed in her holy Appendaho dress, reached back and pulled her middle braid around and took off the ribbon, and said, "Mother Yana, I believe this is yours!"

And she took the ribbon, tied it in her own braid, and they embraced with special compassion. *This* was the woman, of all her other ancestors, who was responsible for this very day because long ago she left the Appendaho, broke a truce, and married a stranger!

And Yana spoke. "At the moment of me being consumed, I saw this *very* day! And for all this time I had hope, and I waited on you, my daughter, to save us all! If it wasn't for you," and she looked over to Vaughn, "and your *very precious* husband, we would have been damned forever."

And she went over to Vaughn and hugged him. "You are *exactly* as I foresaw you!" Then she turned to Stephanie, and said, "*Now*, it's time, and we shall celebrate before the Lord has us to move on. We've all sincerely repented and will now be at peace!"

Stephanie had a dumb look on her face. "Time for what?"

But then the first contraction hit her and Jean held her up. "C'mon daughter. Let's get you situated." And off to the birthing house they went with little Lana right behind!

Three hours! The same amount of time they say the Lord hung on the cross. Three miserable hours of screams which tore through Vaughn like he was being cut in two. But every time he went to go inside, little Lana came out first and barred the door! "It's OK *King* Vaughn, she would say with a tease, "This is for *women only!*" And then she'd go back inside and slam the door!

For Stephanie's part, the pains truly were labor pains, but *not* just the physical sensation. Because the *meaning* of those pains carried *all* of King Vaughn's and Queen Stephanie's suffering and prayers to protect this day! And every pain brought with it a companion prayer of thanksgiving with that recognition of the *true* labor for this child. Every pain that hit her was welcomed!

After three agonizing hours later, the door finally opened, and Jean came out. Vaughn rushed up, "What's *wrong?*"

She smiled, "Why do you think there's something wrong?"

With a dumb look on *his* face, he said, "Ahh, the baby hasn't cried. I heard no *cry?*"

Jean laughed at him and pinched his cheek with a twinkle in her eye. "Don't be silly. *Especially* this child, he doesn't need to cry. Why are you *still* standing there?"

And Vaughn shook his head and rushed in. There, all wrapped up, cleaned up, in a blue baby blanky, was little Michael at Stephanie's breast. Little Lana was watching closely as the child nursed. The child was glowing a soft gold.

Vaughn sat down next to them and was speechless. His mouth was open but no sound came out. Finally, it hit him, all he'd done for *this* child, and tears ran down his cheeks. Lady Stephanie smiled a very broad smile. Pulled Michael from her breast and turned him around to see his father. "Michael, this is your father, King Vaughn, who saved our lives so many times. And *those* on his face are true tears."

And Stephanie held out his little hand to touch them. Little Michael squealed, and Vaugh finally found his voice. "My son!" and he took him into his arms and walked out of the birthing house. With his little head supported by Daddy's hand, Vaughn slowly turned full circle, saying, "These, my son, are *your* people. This is *your* home. And *you,* by the Lord God Jesus, have been born holy!"

Michael made gurgling noises and little puffs of a squeal of joy, and then belched up some milk all over Daddy.

Stephanie laughed, and Jean said, "You have to burp the baby right after they eat, or *that* happens." Jean came and took the child and a glowing ring appeared on Jean's finger.

Lady Stephanie said, "You are also the mother to our child! When you need me, rub the ring just once. If you need my husband, rub it twice. If you need us both, then thrice. I will be back every four hours at first, and as needed, to nurse little Michael."

Then Stephanie turned dark! And turned to her King. "*Our* child is no more important than any other child in our country. As he is a living part of us and has been since conception, so it *is* for everyone's children and *their* parents. From this day forward, King Vaughn, there will be *absolutely* no more abortions in our *wretched* country. Do you *hear* me?"

Vaughn bowed low to his Queen. "Let's go tell them!" And they vanished.

At six in the evening Queen Stephanie and King Vaughn appeared before their country with no name from their palace study, a surprisingly large room with a heavy oak desk with animal clawed feet, and matching dragons facing each other across its back. Built-in glass bookcases framed in cherry wood lined every single wall.

Sitting behind the desk, in, of all things, his brown ranger uniform with many pockets, Vaughn went first. "Our fellow countrymen," he pulled his knife from his side holder and placed it on the desk in front of him, "As you can see, I snuck past James." And he stood up to show off his garments. "Weapons included." And he placed his ranger pistol next to the knife. "As a Ranger, I have to tell you, I'm *sick* of this country with no name *crap!* A Ranger, with all the dignity of that occupation, needs a country with a dignified name. I think we all do, including your King and Queen. From henceforth, we are the Northern United. But I don't take this second part of our new name lightly." He paused to give the people time to kick it around a bit.

The people repeated the new name to themselves a few times, some said it out loud, and a few liked it so much they shouted it at their TV's, *NORTHERN UNITED*. The people from the United for Christ couldn't help noticing the word, United, in the new name. With Captain Vaughn and Lady Stephanie now as King and Queen of the Northern, it wasn't beyond many of their imaginations that the two countries could become the Northern United for Christ! After all, it's North America. But people around the world groaned. They didn't want such unity.

King Vaughn continued. "You may not know this, but I've traveled quite a lot through our country. I was born and raised here in a very small town, but I am aware of many competing factions nationwide, and I will be calling many representatives from all the various groups to the palace, and we're going to figure out what needs to be done *better* than the crap we have now that's left over from before King Jargono. I know many of you will try to play me. I advise you, *don't.*" He pushed his weapons forward a bit. "Rangers like straight talk, have little patience for anything else. In these troubled times, Kings have no patience for *anything* other than the *best* from everyone.

That means their best efforts to bring prosperity and unity to all. What *that* means is that I'm no longer going to *pay* anyone to cooperate, to not make trouble, or for some debt you think the government owes you.

"Now look at me closely," Vaughn zoomed the camera in. "I don't care if you feel cheated, or you don't like this. If you want to *try* to make trouble. Go ahead! Do you understand? From now on, we are a *new* country, and I don't owe anyone, anything for past grievances. No one does. But goodness and love for each other are *very* inspiring. It motivates everyone to do their best, to forgive, and get on with *new* life. But Justice takes a very dim view of people trying to extort something for *nothing*." And Vaughn radiated blackness that the viewers could swear they felt through the TV.

"But I would also like to commend everyone, because faced with our imminent destruction, all differences disappeared and we came together as we should have. My Queen and I will personally be going across the country very shortly to rid us of the evil beasts still present.

"I am also in the process of creating royal knight brigades. Men of integrity who feel they're able to face great evil, and they'll be trained quickly and armed with blessed weapons and sent out to hunt the beasts down. Every town no matter how small must have what they need to effectively protect themselves."

Many people were nodding, noting his implied threat, which *no one* doubted, but also his stern demeanor gave them confidence he could actually fulfill his promises. All across the world plans began to be made to assassinate the new King and Queen precisely because they believed how effective they would be.

King Vaughn smiled. "I will also be expanding our Ranger services across the whole country, not just at the border, but I will also be *slightly* altering the qualifying test to become a Ranger. You don't have to *kill* anyone any more. Just beat them to within an inch of their lives or so!" Vaughn paused, to give the rangers across the country a good laugh. "Seriously, come up with a better test! I know it needs to carry with it the seriousness of the life and death struggle, but we can't be *wasting* all those who die. We just can't, especially after losing so much already. And now, my wife, my Queen has something *very* important to tell you."

Lady Stephanie came forward in her slimmed down holy dress shining rainbow colors. She stepped out to the middle of the study and her hands indicated her tummy, then she waived, and in the air, a beautiful picture of little Michael appeared. "Prince Michael is safely hidden away and thriving and no harm is able to come to him."

People all over the United for Christ began cheering, and chanting, "Lady Stephanie, Lady Stephanie, our lives for you, our lives for you and your child!"

Lady Stephanie spread her arms out. "Thank you all for your well-wishes, especially those in the United for Christ who steadfastly supported me and pledged their very lives to defend Michael and me. People of the Northern United, you probably don't know this, but down South, when they found out the terrible trouble I was in, the terrible danger because the demons threatened to invade Earth if the child was born, all the United for Christ came together and tracked me down in my apartment where I was weeping, and they chanted, 'Lady Stephanie, our lives for you. Our lives for you and your unborn child!' Stephanie brushed away tears. "They were all willing to die for me and Prince Michael. I want to say to them. You gave me the strength and the love I so desperately needed to make it to this day." And when the other countries heard *that,* they put out a very large bounty to kill the King and Queen and Prince, because it already seemed that the North and South were united.

And then Lady Stephanie became very dark. "Now that I've delivered my beautiful son, Prince Michael, and he's perfectly safe, I've set my heart on making major improvements for everyone. As I've discussed with our King," and she turned around and smiled at King Vaughn, "our economy can do much better. From this point on, government regulation will be controlled at the local levels with the main concern of how a new business will prosper your area. Local officials will be responsible to address complaints, and there will be officials over them. I am asking that any reports of corruption be brought directly to *me!* I'll solve it quickly, *personally."* And Lady Stephanie burst out in flames all around! She held her hands out warmly. "I hope everyone understands. By the way, no longer will the smallest towns be *ignored!* If you add them all up, their contribution is quite meaningful and significant, not to mention simply that their lives matter just as much as the larger populated areas."

Lady Stephanie crossed her hands behind her. "And now, on a more personal level. My life here when I was younger was *hell.* And I witnessed *all* the young women around me debase themselves every day and the young men hardly identifiable as *men* except for something swinging below their belt line!" She paused to let her bluntness sink in.

"You all are now privy, courtesy of King Jargono, and *some* of what we've already told you, to the life that I and my husband have lived. That is what *integrity* looks like. Now, I'm not, nor should I even consider policing your bedroom habits or wherever else you decide to *do it,* but I'm telling you, as sure as I held my newborn beloved son in my arms, as sure as I nursed him at my breast, as sure as I fought to the *death* many times to protect him so he could be born alive and healthy, there shall be no more abortion in this land! *None.* Just like the Earth demons I fought against, *abortion* is also an *unnatural disaster!*"

"Because my child is no more special than yours, in that each child comes directly from and *is* the very life of their parents. If you can't respect *that,* then what can you respect? Those performing abortions except to save the life of the mother, shall be put to death! Women caught having abortions, if their child can be spared, shall be adopted out and raised with integrity, if I have to run the orphanages myself! And that mother? Shall be put to death! What right do you have to live after you have *utterly* desecrated being a woman, the *meaning* thereof, *knowing* you, yourself were born into this world through your mother? I will fight to protect *your* unborn children just like I fought to protect mine!"

Lady Stephanie's voice then became overly sweet and she threw her hands to her face. "Oh, she's sooo cruel, our new Queen. Where is her *mercy?*" And then Queen Stephanie turned *very dark,* and replied in a hard voice, as she put her hands behind her again. "*Mercy?* I see you have a lot of feelings for you *own* life, but how about the feelings your unborn child has while being *betrayed* by his *mother* or her *mother?* Mercy? Every single pregnant mother *feels* the life of her child inside. And it feels like her *very own life!* You know why? Because it *is!* That's what being a mother is all about. *Your* life inside you, grows another *life* inside your life. And you *feel* it. You *know* it. And I don't care how much you lie to yourselves because it hurts too much to see the *truth!*

"So where is *your* mercy? You have committed suicide! Or as close to it as you can get. The Lord God does *not* forgive suicide, the intentional killing of yourself to end your life for no other reason than just ending your life for selfish reasons. We *cannot* tolerate any longer in this country, the Northern *United,* the worst division against ourselves possible. We *need* strong, loving, vibrant, courageous women of *integrity* to raise our boys to be decent, courageous, loving, and strong *men,* and to raise our girls to be the backbone of our society they are *meant* to be."

Then her voice became overly sweet, again. "But it's *my* life to do with as *I* see fit. Right?" Lady Stephanie leaned forward and squinted her eyes. Everyone watching TV felt she was peering into their depths, dissecting their very souls! "The most basic principle of Life, with a capital L, as in God, is that

Life gives to another life. But *all* life has the ability to bring forth life. You *don't* have a right to violate *that!* Not once that new life is started. Don't you understand that when you violate that most fundamental characteristic of life, you have stepped completely outside the very Essence of Reality, outside of *all* Goodness, with a capital G? Then what are you left with?"

And then Stephanie put her hands on her hips, and brought again that sickeningly sweet voice. "Ohhh, is that *all we are*, just a baby machine?" And then a *very hard* voice, again, as she leaned forward. "You *stupid* and painfully *selfish* women think that being the *future* of our society is just '*all we are, just a baby machine*'? And that's *nothing?* Or close to *nothing?* Death is too easy for you! God will give your *final* judgment!"

When King Vaughn heard *all that* from his Queen, he was, in fact, a bit surprised. But seeing her so passionate, having just given birth to their wonderful son, he felt it wise to hold his peace, for now. These feminine issues are quite delicate and a broad brush wouldn't seem to be sufficient. Further discussion, at least, did seem in order. But *definitely* not today, not after they spent the last nine months fighting for the life of their child. Many people felt similarly. Many nodded in perfect agreement, but other women suddenly felt cheated.

Lady Stephanie crossed her hands behind her back and now appeared without any power or glow. "Right now, I'm a mother for the first time for my own child, but I adopted a little girl a year ago whom I saved from a cruel death. Upon adopting little Lynnara, that changed my whole life because from then on I always asked how will what I do affect her. And now that Michael is born, and in an even more fragile condition being an infant, I am also keenly aware that we raise our children from the very ground on up. *That's* what being a mother *means.* The key word there is *raise.* As in nurture, teach, protect.

"But it starts even before birth. None of you know this about me, but I'll tell you now. The demons below sought to corrupt my child *before* he was born. They wanted to *taint* him and turn him into a monster. One little scratch from the creatures we fought, a drop of evil blood, and other things. That was their *preferred* result. And in fact, when I was battling the Earth-demons, they tore my flesh all up and I and my child were doomed!"

Lady Stephany paused to let it sink in. Everyone went dead silent trying to even imagine it. And then Lady Stephanie waved her hand and a hologram replayed what happened to her. Women started weeping when they saw how hard she and little Lynnara fought, how the love between them drove them to fight, and how bloodied Lady Stephanie became, and when she collapsed and little Lynnara raced over to her then screamed when she couldn't heal her, their hearts collapsed. Everyone felt their intense love.

Then Stephanie said, "That's what it means to be a mother. And here is what it means to be a real man." The hologram continued with what Vaughn had done and prayed and how God answered his prayers and how she asked God for her son back or take her life back. Many people, even up north went to their knees realizing for the first time how real God really is, and wondering what times they were in. People all over the world began to rethink the way they saw these western countries now, and some felt that assassination became all the more crucial.

Stephanie brushed tears from her eyes and continued. "There he was again, my dear beloved King Vaughn, to save my life and my soul again."

Vaughn stepped forward and wrapped his arm around her shoulders and said, "I can't let my dear Queen give me all that credit, because she just recently went into the very depths of hell to save me! She walked through the very fires of hell, amongst many evil beasts and demons just to save little me." And Vaughn waved his hand and amazingly what Stephanie experienced as she came to save Vaughn played before them. Stephanie had no idea how Vaughn did it because her experience lived, she thought, only within the depths of her prayers. Now, everyone in both countries had their eyes opened and were on their knees. People across the world began to call up their religious leaders *demanding* they explain what they just saw. They all thought hell wasn't real.

Lady Stephanie resumed. "So I want to warn women. Be careful what you put in your bodies when you're pregnant. Pregnancy is a sacred time for you. You carry within you an *innocent, guiltless* life within your not so innocent, not so guiltless life. You carry within you that which is greater than you! The Lord God will not hold you guiltless if you defile your child, *ruin* your child before they are even born! Do you understand? Queen Karen had been ruined before she was born by her mother taking the mind-altering drug we just banned! I went through extraordinary means to save her, literally a life and death struggle to save her, and then she turned around and saved me! So, let me repeat. *Abortion* is an *unnatural disaster* and so is allowing your child to be tainted in the womb when you put the wrong things into your body."

Lady Stephanie paused for a bit so everyone could catch their breath, and many finally began to ease back thinking she was done. Many hoped in their hearts they could finally retreat back into the safety of their routines and put all this, well, somewhere, maybe not behind them, but beside them to attend to later. King Vaughn had sat back down, so they began to feel safer.

But Lady Stephanie wasn't done, no, not at all! "And then there are those wonderful *supposed to be* men. Did you know my Earthly father *abandoned* me when I was seven years old? In a country like *this?* In a way, that was like a death sentence to me, and I almost *did* die because I had *no* decent fatherly guidance growing up and mother had to work all the time so I pretty much raised *myself.* You think under those circumstances a child can *raise herself?*" The castle trembled, as dark waves of power rumbled outward, they even seemed to rumble through the TV sets. Women were cheering *this* part of the Queen's message but the men tried to excuse themselves to the bathroom, or for a snack, but the women commanded them to *sit!*

But Lady Stephanie wasn't done with the men, no, not at all. "When you *so called* men have that little, tiny mind below your belt settle on a woman, that *other* mind on top of your shoulders says, *Hmm, she might get pregnant.* Or, *I don't care if she gets pregnant, it's on her.* Either way, you *know* pregnancy *shouts* at you. How about I pray a little prayer for you? You *know* the Lord answers *my* prayers. Lord God, as they care about their possible child, so, too, care about them! As they *ignore* their children, *ignore* them. Would you like that? That means absolutely *no* mercy for you. You get a little cut, it doesn't heal, it gets larger. You get a little pain, no relief, it gets *worse.* Sounds like Hell, doesn't it?

"And then, some years later you happen by and the mother of your child, whom you've *never* seen, or *hardly* seen, and she comes to you, and says, 'Oh, see your child?' hoping beyond hope you'll *be* a man, and you, being the *stupid dumb beast* that just happens to walk on two legs, you say, 'Oh, the child has my eyes.' *Stupid dumb beast,* that child has a lot more than *your eyes!* While you may not have carried that child in your womb, you're still connected from the very start through the *spirit* of life. That child, *your* child, resonates with *your* life through that spiritual connection. If the child does wrong, that wrong falls on *you!* In spirit. Granted, men can be a bit more dull in understanding what they feel, but it's there.

"So how about this, you wonderful *stupid dumb beasts* on two legs. From now on, *every* woman who is not married and pregnant is required to take a paternity test! And *then,*" Queen Stephanie smiled a *very* sweet smile, "*Whoever* that woman says is the father, *must* take a paternity test. If you *don't,* we'll assume the child is *yours.* And from henceforth, all fathers will be *required* to support their child as determined by the *mother* and the court. You don't get a say in how much! And if you can't pay? Wellll, don't worry, we still do have State Work Farms. Am I making myself *very* clear? And, OH!" She did a little eye role, her finger went to her cheek with a dumb expression. "*No* excuses will be accepted like, 'She *tricked* me.' 'She said she couldn't get pregnant.' 'I thought I was sterile.' Should I *really* have to *force* you to be real men?"

Lady Stephanie continued. "Now, for those women who wonder how they'll care for the child, you'll have options. You can come to a government home we'll set up, have your child, and then adopt him out to a loving, *responsible* home. Or, if you can care for the child yourself, you should do so. What you *shouldn't* do, is rid yourself of an *inconvenience.*

"Now, with this in mind, it would do you very well to use some forethought. And what would do you even better, would be to realize there's a *person* inside your body that needs to be respected, loved and cared for *at least* as much as the body in which that person lives. When you have your *sex* and then walk away from the person inside that body, you have effectively valued their body over the person inside. There is no greater insult."

Many people began to squirm. People out in social settings watching her speech together, snuck glances at each other then cast their eyes down, then glanced again. They began to see something different.

"Now that I *am* your Queen, I can't help but love you all and I want you to be happy. That's why I've spoken these things straight to you. Without goodness in you, what do you have? And when you find the goodness in you that makes your person be *what* it is, then how can you *not* love and respect each other?" And she paused to let everyone search it out.

And automatically people began feeling goodness in them that they never paid attention to before. And many wondered, *How come I never noticed this in me before? But it's familiar.*

"The former ways of this country before King Jargono were hard, cruel, heartless ways. I remember a government official coming right to my door, and threatening me, telling me that *love* was dangerous! He did! He really did, because I had already loved your King, and King Vaughn was telling everyone else they were *persons!* The government official actually asked me, 'What's this *person* thing?' She paused again but without comment.

"That *horrible* atheistic government left you so emptied out. Well, I'm telling you, it's safe to *love* again! After we rid you of the evil beasts, you'll be able to safely rebuild your towns. The castles will always be there for you for safety. But we want you to make lives for yourselves, create *value* through your talents and hard work and *keep* most of what you earn. We will be greatly lowering all your taxes!"

People began saying to themselves, *It's safe to love, again.* They realized how much of that had been interfered with from their evil government. They had made everyone feel that it wasn't safe to value anything or anyone too much. *It's safe to love, again!* Having just seen the tremendous love between

Lady Stephanie and King Vaughn and Lynnara, those feelings still very much alive in them, they now began to feel they, too, should have such intensity in their *own* lives.

"And lastly, I will be visiting you all! I'm able to travel easily. And I'll help." She looked over to King Vaughn and he came back to the front of the stage and wrapped his arm around her shoulders, again.

"I couldn't ask for a better wife, friend, and Queen. I warn you now, great evil *is* coming to the world, but we have time to strengthen. That time is *now.* Shortly, we will begin sharing insights with you about goodness, and the Greater Goodness that is God. You've heard us speak of these things before. But now we'll be able to share with you *without* evil cutting us off." And with that, King Vaugh and Lady Stephanie bowed to their people and the broadcast ended."

James came forward, tugged on his black vest to make sure it was perfect, then bowed to them. "I have to say, you two make my heart so very full, and you make my job quite easy! That was magnificent."

Then James cleared his throat, looked around rather uncomfortably, until Lady Stephanie said, "Out with it, James, you're *family* to us!"

"Well, my Lady, I'm not sure how appropriate it is."

Stephanie squinted at him, and folded her arms, waiting. Vaughn cleared his throat. "Ahh, that means she wants an answer and to stop thinking that way!"

James stood up straighter. "Pardon me, my King, but I am closely aware of most, if not *all* of your nuances and meanings, gestures and such. I was quite aware! It's just that it's, well, very personal."

Lady Stephanie said, "I'm sorry, James, but I can't answer you if you're silent."

"Well, that is true." He straightened his black suit and vest, again, then said, "I have heard both of you talk at length on spiritual matters and I confess to being moved, actually quite moved. I feel I would like to talk, at some point, more personally so that I might avail myself to be, well . . ."

King Vaughn said, "You want to be baptized! Whenever you feel ready James."

Stephanie started glowing. "James, when we deal with people in such things, we're no longer a King or Queen or *anything* of note. We stand before God just as naked as anyone else. Please feel free to avail yourself of us in such matters, and when you do, we are all without titles."

"That's just it, me Lady. I am *always* your butler. There is no time off."

And Vaughn said, "Unless we order it. Consider yourself so ordered in such matters."

"Thank you Sire. But tonight is late, so perhaps at a more convenient time for you."

Just them Vaughn's search program alarmed, and James materialized the screen in the study. There was an anomaly located deep in China, and *very* deep in the Earth. James said, "How did you ever locate this so deep?"

"I integrated certain orb functions I understood quite well that dealt with unmasking. I simply kept peeling layers of the Earth back!" Vaughn walked up close to the screen. There, deep inside China, in the midst of a rugged mountain range, hundreds of feet below the Earth, was a single, pulsing, black dot.

James couldn't believe it. "China Sire. Nothing has been heard of them since over one-hundred years ago when the Great Religious War wiped them out. The last report recorded indicated the terrorists had spread the virus so broadly that the Chinese were dyeing literally by the *billions*. Even King Jargono, who traveled extensively on the international level, said there was no sign of life there."

Vaughn magnified the area and the blackness seemed to fill the room, actually suck out any light, and then the program was killed by an alert: WARNING WARNING WARNING HARMFUL ENERGY INAVISION. SHUTTING DOWN ALL SYSTEMS NOW

And all of the computer systems shut down! Vaughn brought his Staff into his hand immediately and pointed it at the screen. Silver energy went in, and seconds later everything rebooted, but the program King Vaughn used had been destroyed!

Stephanie shivered and took Vaughn's hand. "I think we need to pray harder."

Vaughn said, "I think everyone does!"

She looked deeply into his eyes. "We're not getting in there, are we?"

"No, my Queen. I don't think we need to rush our deaths, do you?"

The *faithwalker* squeezed his hand even tighter, and all of her *faithwalking* sense answered, "No." Just then an alarm went off in Stephanie's mind. "I'll be back. It's time to nurse our son." And she vanished.

Vaughn turned to James. "I think I'll go watch." And he vanished.

James ran his hand through his hair and shook his head, wondering, *What would possess* those *two to talk about their deaths like* that?

www.TheFaithwalkerSeries.com

www.ingramcontent.com/pod-product-compliance
Lightning Source LLC
Chambersburg PA
CBHW020538120726
47903CB00001B/32